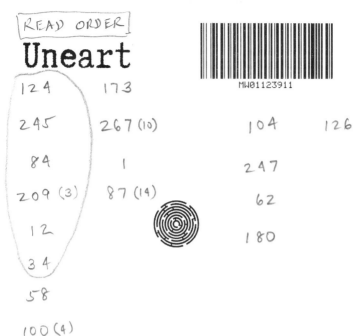

[SMALL PRINT]

READ ORDER

Uneart

124   173

245   267 (10)   104   126

84   1   247

209 (3)   87 (14)   62

12   180

34

58

100 (4)

Stories collected and edited by
Jessica Augustsson

Published by JayHenge Publishing KB

Published by JayHenge Publishing KB

ISBN: 1546501959

ISBN-13: 978-1546501954

Cover Illustration by Maximillian Kennedy
maxkennedy24.tumblr.com

Cover Design by Jessica Augustsson

What is Detective Fiction?

The biblical cross-examination of the two elderly lechers by Daniel to save the life of an innocent; Oedipus's discovery of the truth about origins by questioning witnesses; Scheherazade's story of a dead young woman hidden in a chest and a vizier ordered to find the murderer within three days or forfeit his life; Yuan and Ming dynasty tales of local magistrates who are involved with many cases simultaneously; Edgar Allan Poe's C. August Dupine who solves the mystery of the death of two women living in the Rue Morgue, a fictional street in Paris. Detective fiction has been around for ages, and has taken many forms, all in the pursuit of solving a puzzle, answering a question that has eluded others. In this anthology, more than a dozen creative authors have sent their mystery-solving sleuths to other worlds, both fantastical and futuristic. I hope you enjoy reading these stories as much as I enjoyed collecting and editing them.

Snuff
by
G.H. Finn

"What does it matter to ya?
When you got a job to do
You gotta do it well.
You gotta give the other fellow hell...

...Say live and let die"
by Paul & Linda McCartney

There's a new drug in town.

Or an old one, depending on how you look at it.

They call it Snuff.

If meth doesn't cut it... If you're numb to smack... If cocaine isn't all it's cracked up to be... If you've injected your eyeballs so often you can see out of the needle holes...

If you've tried everything else on offer, and you still can't get no satisfaction...

That's when you go looking for Snuff.

But pray you don't find it.

And that it doesn't find you.

I'd been looking for a particular snuff dealer for months. Not some teenager with a BMX bike and a jacket full of packets, spending all night peddling to pay for his own fix. I was looking for someone a lot higher up the food chain. I was in search of a top predator. And I had a line on him at last.

I was undercover, of course. My name doesn't matter. Neither does my appearance. I was faking both. I'm used to being a shadow hiding amidst darker shadows. The ID in my pocket said I was currently working for the US DEA. I kept very quiet about my real department. But no one asked too many questions. Officially, I'd been seconded for "special duties". They just figured I was CIA or MI5 or Interpol or Homeland Security or some other kind of spook.

Stopping the spread of snuff was my main concern. But it was tough. No one was even sure where it originally came from. There were plenty of theories. Haiti was a popular guess. Some thought Cairo. But others said New Orleans. Iceland was a distinct possibility. In other words, no one had any idea at all.

The guys in forensics had analysed small amounts of snuff seized during busts. It hadn't helped much. There seemed to be no one single recipe for making the foul dark powder.

The mixture varied considerably between samples, but the same *type* of ingredients kept turning up over and over again.

Ground human bone. Cremation ashes. Sawdust from a coffin. Dried blood. Graveyard dirt. Goofer dust. The desiccated residue of an Egyptian mummy. Iron filings shaved from coffin nails. Finely shredded shroud. Marble scraped from a gravestone. Hair and fingernail clippings from a corpse. Seed from a hanged man. Soot from a woman burned as a witch. Flayed skin. Dandruff from the dead.

While the specifics changed from batch to batch, the common factor was that snuff always contained some sort of powdered cadaver. The product was unlikely ever to get the approval of the FDA. Technically snuff wasn't *exactly* illegal. But conventional legality wasn't what was worrying my department. We always have our eyes on a bigger picture.

I'd picked up my suspect's trail in New York. I followed him from a boarded-up Santería supplies shop he owned down a dead-end alley in Harlem. The dealer was a fairly average looking black guy. He did seem unusually thin, and he kept his eyes hidden behind expensive designer sunglasses, but you'd probably have passed him on the street without a second glance. I knew he was wealthy but it hadn't helped his fashion sense. He was wearing red tracksuit bottoms, green sneakers and a yellow tee-shirt bearing a dayglo logo which read "High On Life".

He'd gone straight to the airport and flown to London.

On the plane, he'd changed into a classic tailored suit. After calling in at a private member's club in Westminster—the kind exclusively reserved for blue-blooded aristocrats, government ministers, and the sons of families with the oldest of "old money"— he'd taken a taxi. First to one of the capital's most infamous occult emporiums, near the British Museum, then to the edge of Brixton. Here he visited a very discrete Voodou store. Not the kind frequented by respectable worshippers. I nearly lost him when he left via a back door. But I'm very good at my job and I picked up his trail before he'd gone three blocks.

I was relieved when he eventually checked into a hotel. Once he'd gone up to his room I flashed some British "Special Branch" ID to the manager and he briefly panicked before he gave me the next room. Twenty minutes later, after launching a micro-drone into the air-conditioning ducts and doing some swift fiddling with spectral surveillance equipment, I was sitting in a very comfortable armchair, wearing headphones and watching a live video-feed from the suspect's suite.

An hour and a half went bye with no action. Then came a knock at his door. He answered it, letting in a tall, bald, moustachioed, Anglo-Mongolian man in his late fifties, flanked by a couple of huge lumps of walking muscle in Mandarin-collared suits who I assumed to be his "minders". These bodyguards took up position on either side of the door. One held a briefcase. Both had bulges under their jackets.

On my laptop, I watched and heard the whole conversation.

"Good evening Mr... um... I forget what name you're using at the moment?" said the bald, well-dressed far-eastender. He spoke in a gruff cockney accent.

"I'm registered as Sam Saturday," replied my suspect, "And I gather you are calling yourself Moriarty Manchu. But who cares? Any names will do. In our line of work identities are disposable. Shall we get on with it? You have the money?"

Moriarty Manchu gestured to the thug with the briefcase. "It's all there. I'm surprised you didn't ask for more." His eyes narrowed as he added both menacingly and suspiciously, "*If* this stuff is really as good as you say it is."

The man calling himself Sam Saturday shrugged. "It's not all about the money. I want enough. But I don't need more than that. Selling *snuff* brings me other rewards. But you can charge your customers whatever you want. Just as long as you are distributing it, you can make yourself as rich as you like."

"I intend to," said the Londoner. "But I'm not a fool. And I don't trust a man who isn't greedy."

Sam Saturday raised his eyebrows. "Whoever said I wasn't greedy?" he replied, as he opened a suitcase that must have been delivered to the room before he checked in. I watched as he pulled out a large transparent plastic bag filled with small packets of powder. They were dark and might have contained soot or dust or ashes. But I knew they were filled with *snuff*.

Manchu was still suspicious. "You won't object if I have the product tested before I pay you." He stated this in a gruff snarl of a voice. It clearly wasn't meant to be a question.

"Go right ahead," came the reply. Saturday sprawled languidly on his bed as the Londoner nodded to one of his silent henchman, who opened the hotel room door. A girl walked in. Tottering on high heels. I guessed she was in her late twenties. But she dressed like a teenager. It was hard to tell her real age under her heavy make-up. She was a Goth. Her skin was deathly pale, but that was the most colourful thing about her. Her spiky hair was black. So were her nails. And her eye-shadow. And her knee-high boots. She was dressed in enough black clothing that she could have disguised herself as a portable funeral.

"Hello, my dear," said Saturday as the girl came and sat next to him. "I see you've had s*nuff* before. How do you like it? A pinch on the back of the hand and a quick snort up the nose?"

She shook her head, and in a dull, monotone answered, "I prefer to drink it. Mixed with absinthe."

"Quite so," said Saturday. He went to his suitcase and produced a cut-crystal glass and an ornate, slotted spoon onto which he sprinkled the contents of one of the little packets of dark powder. Then he pulled a hip-flask from his pocket and – carefully – poured a generous measure of a thick and sticky green liquor over the *snuff*. The aniseed and wormwood scented absinthe slowly dripped through the snuff and into the glass. Saturday watched until the absinthe had dissolved all the drug and the glass was full of a murky, foetid-looking brownish-green liquid, then he handed it to the girl with a casual, "bon appétit". I'd seen swamp-water that looked more appealing. The Goth girl took the proffered glass, sniffed it, sipped it, then knocked it back, downing the drink in one.

I felt my jaw tense as I watched. *Shit*. I didn't like this. I should have stopped it. But I needed to be sure... The girl looked young... She would probably be all right... At least, that's what I told myself. Knowing it was a lie.

As I watched, electronically eavesdropping, I saw the girl fall back on the bed. She didn't move. She could have been dead. Saturday seemed unperturbed. Moriarty Manchu was anxious, eager, sweating with excitement.

"What do you know? What do you feel? Who are you?" he breathlessly asked the prostrate Goth.

She answered. I adjusted the volume on my headphones. Her voice was very different. To start with, it was male.

It was the voice of a man who'd lived, and died, in the nineteen-thirties. But I'm not about to tell you his name, or where he came from. He answered their questions. He told them what he did. And how he was caught. And why he was sentenced to death. He gleefully explained how he felt when he committed his crimes. And what it was like when they strapped him into the chair and threw the switch. I don't know how Sam Saturday got hold of whatever part of his body was in the *snuff*. But, back in the day, it wasn't uncommon for the prison guards to sell "souvenirs" after executions, so I can probably guess. The voice said other things too. But I will never repeat them. They were dark things. I had heard them before. Many times. Words not meant for the living. Some things should only be known by the dead.

"Satisfied?" asked Saturday, eventually, once the Goth girl had stopped talking. She was sitting up again now, stiffly, looking like death warmed up. Which I suppose she was.

"Yes," said Manchu. "But how does it work? I mean, how *exactly*?"

"You don't need to know that. And you wouldn't want to. It's not a hallucination, or past life regression, if that's what you are wondering. The experiences a person has while under the influence of *snuff* are real. They consume a little *specially prepared* extract from one of the dear departed, and, for a short time, they become that person. Mind and body and spirit, all joined together. You could call it a form of possession, I suppose. There's no hit like it. The kick is unique. For a while, just for a while, you really are someone else. You have all their thoughts and memories. You remember their joys and their sadnesses, know their victories and their defeats, feel their lusts and their jealousies. You *know* what it was like when they lived their life, because you lived it too. If they murdered someone in the nineteenth century, feeling a lover choke to death between the fingers of their hands, then you too committed that crime. If they fucked their way across a continent, taking a thousand lovers before succumbing to raging syphilis, all those memories, all those *sensations,* are also *yours.* I guarantee you, there is no other drug like it. With *snuff*, once is never enough. Nothing else will do. Life is the ultimate high. Experience is everything. Especially if it is someone else's."

"What's the catch?" asked Moriarty Manchu.

"Catch?" repeated Saturday.

"Yes," said the Londoner, "There's always more to pay, and I don't mean the cash you hand over for the product. What's the real catch?"

Everyone looked at the girl. If you could call her a girl. She appeared a lot older now. Taking *snuff* had put years on the way she looked, despite the make-up.

Saturday shrugged. "The candle that burns twice as bright lasts half as long..." he answered, "Snuff does take a toll. But isn't that true of all addictions? Every pleasure costs you treasure. Every vice has a price."

I decided I'd heard and seen enough. My worst suspicions were confirmed. This laptop had windows, but not the kind made by Microsoft. I had apps that opened portals, doorways and peepholes through the veil and into the worlds beyond.

But I didn't really need them.

I'd seen with my own eyes what Saturday was up to.

I waited until Manchu, his pair of goons, and the still swooning Goth girl had left. I'd already made a call. They'd be picked up as they tried to leave the hotel. They weren't my concern. They never had been. My target was always the one calling himself Sam Saturday.

I knocked politely on the door to his hotel room. Then I listened carefully. When I heard him get close to the door, I kicked it open with all the force I could manage. As I'd hoped, the door hit him in the face and I was into the hotel room before he knew what was happening. "You're under arrest," I shouted, "DEA."

I saw Saturday begin to pull a gun from the pocket of his jacket and I laughed at him, taking a sharpened Yew-wood wand from inside my jacket, "Not *that* DEA," I said, "The *other* one. I'm not interested in your mundane crimes. I'm with the Death Enforcement Agency.

The DEA...D.

I'm an undercover officer of the Necropolitan Police Force."

"Oh, fuck." said Saturday. "Necropolice? What do you want? I'm not breaking any laws."

I arched an eyebrow. "OK," he admitted, "Maybe I'm bending a few minor local rules and regulations enough that they might be in danger of buckling under the strain, but since when did that ever interest you guys? You don't care about human legalities."

"That's right," I said, covering him with my wand, "But we do care about the more important ones. And you've been breaking the laws of nature."

Saturday swallowed and tried to pull himself together. "I don't know what you mean," he muttered.

I stuck the wand under his chin. "How old are you?"

He squirmed under my gaze, trying to get as far away from the yew-wood as he could.

"I know what you've been doing," I told him. "Maybe you think I don't. You certainly *hope* I don't. Perhaps you imagine you can con me into believing you're just pedaling some appealing and appalling poison to people who should know better.

"But I *do* know what you're really up to.

"I have the Sight.

"And I have Seen."

"Shit," said Saturday. "What are you? Seventh son of a seventh son?"

"Worse," I replied. "I'm a lot rarer. It's your unlucky day. I'm the thirteenth bastard of a thirteenth bastard."

Saturday seemed to wilt the moment he heard that. He knew he wouldn't be able to hide anything from me. Just to rub it in, I told him what I knew. What I'd already seen.

"When it comes to snuff, you're a major player. The main supplier. You sell your wares, your 'product', and people buy your evil little powders. They give you their money. And *they* think that's what you get out of the deal.

"But they don't understand how the *snuff* trade really works, do they? They think *they* are the *users*. They take your *snuff* and get high by snorting and sniffing and glugging down the powdered corpses of others. But they don't know...

"They aren't the *users*. They aren't your *real* clients. They're just being used. *They* are your real *product*. Your real customers are the dead."

Saturday whimpered as he tried to crawl away from me and over to the bed. I kept talking.

"I've had you under surveillance. I've got it all recorded. Enough evidence to put before either the High Courts of the Holy, or the Law Lords of the lowest pits of Hades. And you can imagine what *they're* like. The damned place is full to the brimstone with lawyers. Neither Heaven nor Hell will look kindly on what you've been doing."

Saturday backed away from me. He knew he couldn't get past me. But he kept glancing at his suitcase.

"I saw what really goes on," I continued. "The silly little human takes a hit of *snuff* and they think they are using the dead as a drug. But you aren't just selling the powdered dead to the living. You're selling little shots of life to ghosts. That's the thing about sympathetic magic. It's all about connections. And connections go in both directions. A human takes *snuff* and becomes linked to a ghost, via what's left of the ghost's mortal remains. They share the departed spirit's memories, emotions and experiences. *But* what does the ghost get out of it? *They* get to know what it feels like to be alive again. The ghost gets to inhabit a human body, even if just for a short while. It has the chance to feel new emotions. To sample fresh memories. To taste life. You said it yourself. Life really is the ultimate high."

"And there's the rub. Because while the human user is under the influence of *snuff*, the ghost is using the human, siphoning off their vital energy, literally draining away their life. Every time they take snuff, they waste little slivers of their time on earth. They lose their lives, a drop at a time. Maybe it's a week. Or a month. Or a year. But every time, they get weaker. And the ghost gets stronger."

Saturday had backed away as far as the bed. He looked like he was waiting to try to catch me off guard.

"And *that* is where you come in," I said. "You're the middle man. The dealer. You want your cut. Not just cash. No, you want your share of life. Stolen life. What do you make the ghosts give you? Five minutes out of every hour of life they leach away from the living? Ten percent of the life they steal? Twenty percent?"

Saturday sat still but his eyes kept darting to the bag of snuff in his suitcase.

I stared at him and he flinched. "I asked you before and you didn't answer. Just how old are you? How long have you put off your own death by ingesting the lives of your customers? How long have you avoided being judged by the powers of the afterlife? How long have you been preying on both the living and the dead? Prolonging your existence through the suffering of addicts? Months? Years? Centuries?"

I looked him in the eye. I felt no pity. "It's not just the humans who are hooked," I said. "All ghosts are addicts. That's why they are ghosts. If they could let go and move on they wouldn't be here. But they can't. They won't let go. They're addicted to life. They may think they are sticking around because of unfinished business. A need for revenge. Or atonement. Or to watch over their loved ones. Or to be remembered. Or forgiven. But that's not true. Not really. It's *life* they are here for. They just can't give it up…"

Saturday had propped himself upright on the bed, trying to look casual while doing his best to seem like a broken man. On anyone else it might have worked. But I see things others don't. He was just biding his time. When he thought my attention had slipped, he took his chance. He lunged toward his suitcase and grabbed the plastic bag filled with tiny packets of *snuff*. He wildly ripped the bag open and hurled it at me, covering me in the dust of the dead.

I felt the spirits swarm and swirl in a cloud around me. I felt their hunger, their lust for life. For my life.

Saturday laughed, urging the ghosts on.

"That's it. Go on. Drain him! Suck his life away! Take it. Take it all."

The ashes of the hungry ghosts covered me. I felt their spirits in the snuff. Franticly trying to drain away my life.

"There's only one problem," I explained to Saturday. "I already told you, I'm D.E.A.D Literally. It's been a long time since I was alive."

Sam Saturday stared at me. And at the uncontrollable horde of ghosts in the dust, tearing at each other in their desperate frustration once they realized I had no life to steal. They had all been driven mad by their craving. Their insatiable hunger. Their desire. Their need. The hungry ghosts had entered an otherworldly feeding frenzy.

He could see it coming. He knew he couldn't stop them. Not all of them. Not that many all at once. The dead quickly realized that there was only one living thing in the room. Saturday screamed and tried to run. But before he took two steps he was engulfed in a whirlwind of snuff. A swirling black cloud of dead dust.

I smiled, satisfied. I'd need to vacuum up the remains of the ghosts before I left. Typical unclean spirits. But this was another case closed.

I looked around the room grimly. I've stayed clean for the past two hundred and twenty-seven years. Ever since I began this job. Taking one night at a time.

But I know I'll always be addicted.

All ghosts are addicts. All of us.

G. H. Finn keeps his real identity secret, possibly in the forlorn hope of one day being mistaken for a superhero.

Having written non-fiction for many years, G. H. Finn decided to start submitting short-stories to publishers in 2015 and was flabbergasted when the first story he'd ever submitted was selected. Since then he has had a wide range of fiction published and especially enjoys mixing genres in his work, including mystery, horror, steampunk, dark comedy, detective, supernatural, speculative, folkloric, Cthulhu mythos, sci-fi, spy-fi, crime and urban fantasy.

The Card
by
Damon L. Wakes

"The assassin is through here."

Alfonso followed the husband through to the drawing room, squeezing through the door close to the frame to avoid disturbing what was slumped behind it. Gruesome though it was, the sight of the body did not disgust him. It did, however, leave him somewhat disappointed. As the most famous private eye in London Superior, his cases were usually extraordinary. There had been the tailor found locked in his workshop, killed by a single needle through the heart. Then there was the priceless Foucard, burned to ashes in the space of time it took the gallery curator to turn around. Crime for Alfonso was not just a job: it was a passion. He was a connoisseur, and the wreck that lay on the carpet before him was peasant's fare.

Naturally, he could see why he had been hired. The first reason—as always—was that the family was exceedingly wealthy. They chose an investigator with much the same care as they chose a chaise longue, and the shabby blue suit of a police detective was bound to clash with the decor. The second, more practical reason was that the police lacked the unorthodox connections necessary to identify this particular corpse. Most police detectives knew little of the secret languages of the city's gangs and cartels and would be unable to interpret the myriad of little clues that to Alfonso were as clear as the expensive print on the house's wallpaper. Their piles and piles of criminal records may actually have given them a better chance than Alfonso when it came to matching a name to the face, but that blast from the pneumatic blunderbuss had evened the odds completely. Looking at the toes of the "assassin's" boots, Alfonso could already guess how the events of the evening had played out. Nevertheless, he began his interview.

"Mrs. Rugworth, could you tell me exactly what happened

here?"

"I thought I'd explained all that over the voicewire," Mr. Rugworth snapped.

"You told me your wife had encountered the assassin in the kitchen. You then refused to let me speak to her."

"Well? You can imagine how distressing that would be."

"Oh, Ernest!" cried Mrs. Rugworth, "I'd feel far better if I only knew that something was being done about this." She turned to Alfonso. "I went into the kitchen to pour a drink and he was there, waiting. It was all I could do to fetch the gun."

"Have you any idea how he got in?"

"No! The door was bolted all evening."

"He couldn't have climbed in a window?"

"We're on the fiftieth floor!" interrupted Mr. Rugworth.

"Of course," said Alfonso, eyeing the emergency ladder through the drawing room window. "How silly of me."

It was becoming apparent to Alfonso that his clients didn't know anything. It was apparent in this particular case and, indeed, in general.

"I'd like a few minutes to inspect the body," he said, kneeling down before the mangled face. "You may wish to leave."

Mrs. Rugworth took the hint, but her husband remained, arms folded. "I'd very much like to supervise your work." His tone suggested that he would not be persuaded otherwise.

"Very well." Alfonso took his favourite tool from his bag. It was a big one: a motorised saw blade mounted beside a large filing wheel. Pulling the cord to start the miniature kerosene engine, he engaged the gears and began to lower it towards the cavity in the face. Before it had a chance to connect, he checked behind him. Mr. Rugworth was gone and the door was closed. He waited a moment before switching off the engine and setting the tool down to cool. It had originally been intended for fitting monorail tracks, but seemed better suited to situations such as these. Unbuttoning the body's jacket, he began his real work.

The toes of its boots, he had already noted, were well worn. Not only that, but they were worn in a manner consistent with persistent contact with ladder rungs: not only had this man come through the window, he had been through other windows before. He smoked opium—the smell alone made that abundantly clear—and he was a gambler. A gambler and a cheat, going by the bundle of aces and kings stuffed in his pocket. When Alfonso found the empty wallet in the breast pocket, he saw his chance to grab some free money.

"Mr. and Mrs. Rugworth," he called through the door. "I believe I have the solution to your mystery."

Like the tailor and his dodgy electromagnetic sewing machine, and like Jaque "le clown" Foucard's self-destructing painting, the solution was unbelievably simple. Taking advantage of the upper classes' false sense of security, tucked away in their sky-scraping towers, this no-name thief climbed through windows to fund his habits.

"I say," Mr. Rugworth stared at the body. "It doesn't look like you've done anything here!"

Alfonso rolled his eyes dramatically. "A good detective," he explained, "always leaves the scene as he found it. However..." he retrieved one of the cards from the man's pocket: the Ace of Spades. "Do you know the significance of this?"

"A spade?" Mr. Rugworth took a step back. "Isn't that...the calling card of the Gravediggers' Gang?"

"I'm afraid it is."

"Good Lord!"

"You are right to be concerned: these people will try to strike again. However, there is some good news: they're only in this for the money. I simply have to find out who hired them."

"Oh!" exclaimed Mrs. Rugworth. "Oh, please do! I shan't be able to feel safe until then."

"Don't fret, my lady." Alfonso smiled and clasped her hand. "You need fear nothing while I am in your employ. Now..." he turned to Mr. Rugworth. "There is the small matter of payment?"

Alfonso began his long walk down the stairs, the bag of coins satisfyingly heavy in his coat pocket. It was a curious fact that often the least interesting cases were the most rewarding.

Damon L. Wakes was born in 1991 and began to write a few years later. He holds an MA in Creative and Critical Writing from the University of Winchester, and a BA in English Literature from the University of Reading. He always aims to write well-structured narratives formed of tight prose.

Jack Monahan, P.I. (Deceased)
by
R.J. Howell

Name's Jack Monahan, gumshoe. Yeah, you read the card right. I'm deceased but still kicking. Been dead for a good eighty years, not that you care. Nice "Federal Detainment Unit" you got here. Very clean. White. Adds so much personality to Chicago. And Chicago's such a nice little moon too.

Okay, okay. I get it. Interrogation. Fine. Pull up a chair. Might as well make yourself comfortable.

It started in my office.

My HQ is a reliable little ship, and at the time, was parked on the Springfield Space Station. Used to be a garbage disposal unit in a previous life. Not much for the eyes to feast on—looks like rhombus with wings and landing legs, held together by rust and my undying love—but it's my tin-can space baby. Got a pilot's cockpit (I use it as my office), a short hallway leading to the airlock (my secretary's desk is in there), and living quarters under the wings, and all the walls painted a dull teal (I haven't gotten around to changing it yet). It gets me where I need to go. There's the occasional FTL engine hiccup that leaves me sticking my digital thumb out the window in hopes that some passing transport can give me a tow, but for the most part, she's the best. I call her *Serena*.

There is the smell though. No matter how much bleach I pour on those flooring plates, I just can't get rid of that lingering stench of garbage. I've taken to sticking up those little ship air fresheners that smell like pine trees all over the place.

Anyway, there I sat in the pilot's chair, fiddling with the seating controls. Outside the view window, stars glittered on the field of black. The only lights on in my office were the floodlights that framed the window, casting a soft yellow-white glare over the navigational controls on the dash. A stack of blank invoices hid the guidance system's screen. I unbuttoned my cufflinks, rolled my sleeves up, cracked my knuckles, and lifted my fountain pen from its place wedged between the console's plating.

I hesitated, my hand poised over the first page.

Something's missing from this picture.

Ah, right. I needed a drink, bad. Without looking away from the papers on my desk, I fumbled the handle of the metal drawer on the front of the console. It banged open and I pulled out a pharmacy issue bottle of O-Neg.

Oh, didn't I mention? Vampire. Yeah, that heartbreaking she-wolf Maeve not only tore my heart out when she dumped me, she tore a great honkin' hole in my jugular and left me for dead. Didn't quite make it to the autopsy slab thanks to some ancestral blood-curse that had me sprouting fangs and avoiding direct sunlight for the rest of my unnatural life.

I unscrewed the cap and took a swig. The sweet taste of salt and copper slid over my tongue and down my throat right to the shriveled excuse in my gut for a stomach. Already I felt stronger, more alert, and ready to attack that stack of paperwork.

The high-pitched jingle of the access pad on the door behind me rang. It had originally been the boring *bee-doop* default before I changed it to an electronic rendition of the jazzy opening bars of *Broken Blue Sky*, but the polytonic tone doesn't do Joe Braxton's sax any justice.

I put down the bottle and made it look like I'd been reading papers this whole time. "Come in."

The door opened behind me and Gloria, sweet little Gloria from Cleveland with her four-inch pumps clicking on the flooring plates, walked in. "Jack, I've got a ping from Alan Walker and—"

She screamed that bloodcurdling scream that only petite waifs can manage. I twisted in my seat, my hand going for my Pulse Revolver. She raised a hand and pointed a single finger at the navigation console.

"Jack! Is that what I think it is?"

I looked between her finger and my makeshift desk. "I know it's a shock, but I am filling out my invoices. I took your complaint letter to heart."

"No, not the paperwork. The bottle!"

Okay. Not what I was expecting, but I can roll with that. "What's wrong with it?"

"Dammit, Jack! You swore off the blood, remember? The more you drink that stuff, the more scared I get that I'm going to start looking like a t-bone steak to you!"

"Gloria, sweetheart, you already look like a t-bone steak."

"That doesn't make me feel better!"

I wanted to say, "You're my employee, not my mother," but I figured she'd just yell at me more. Or take my bottle. So I screwed the cap back on and dropped it in my desk drawer. "Better?"

"For now."

I waved my hand holding the fountain pen at her. "What did Walker want?"

"Oh, his wife's run off with that red-headed Schwarzenegger again. He wants you to track her down and tell her she either comes home, or he cuts off her access to his credit chips."

Walker paid well. Damn well. I could power my ship for a week and eat for two on what he could afford. And yet, I couldn't quite manage to muster a thrilled-to-the-core reaction to this prospect. Most of the time, life as a self-employed gumshoe lacks the drama the old Vids promised.

But I like eating. And I like my ship flying.

And, yeah, Gloria likes having a paycheck. As much as I wish she'd do her job for free, the union would have me crucified if I short-changed her.

"Give him a ping back. Tell him I'll take the job, I'll need the first thirty percent wired to my account as a deposit, and have him send me a list of her last credit transactions and any information he might have on her whereabouts."

I'd turned back around in my chair and hunched over my desk, scribbling down my personal information in the "Biller" boxes.

"Got it."

Click, click, click. Silence. "Jack?"

"Hmm?"

"Jack, I really think you should turn around."

Grumbling, I did so. "What is it—?"

This time, the Pulse Revolver did come out of my holster. I knelt with one knee on my seat, using the back of the chair as both cover and a brace for my gun.

Maeve stood in the doorway of my office/pilot's cockpit, clad in a slinky red silk dress with matching heels. Her long hair, the exact same shade as the singularity of a black hole, spilled down her shoulders and framed her rather voluptuous breasts. She held Gloria against her, one arm wrapped around my secretary's throat, the other around her waist.

My mouth went dry.

"Jack, put down the gun. I want a civilized conversation, not a firefight." Maeve fixed me with an incredulous look. The hand that'd held Gloria's waist now rested on Maeve's hip. "And a Pulse Revolver? Really, Jack. You're a vampire. You have teeth."

Why was it the first response that came to mind was, "And you have a push-up bra?"

I lowered the Pulse Revolver a few inches so that it pointed at her midsection rather than her head. "Maeve, let her go."

"If I let her go, you'll shoot me." She held up a finger to silence my protest. "And don't even try to promise me you won't. You're a no-good lying rascal, Jack. I wouldn't trust you any farther than I could throw you."

I wasn't going to point out the flaw in that statement. Maeve had proven before she could throw me with little difficulty, no matter my two hundred pounds and boxy frame.

She seemed to notice where my train of thought was going and frowned. "You know what I mean."

"Fine. What do you want?"

"Though it pains me to admit it, I need to hire a private detective, and you're all I have left now."

"Hire me?" A baffled smile crossed my lips and I almost laughed. "Hire *me*? Maeve, you murdered me! You left me to bleed out in that abandoned transport on some Godforsaken moon. I've been planning how to kill you for eighty years."

Maeve shook her head, the arm around Gloria's neck loosening. "Too late for that, Jack. That's why I want to hire you. I want you to find my murderer."

Okay, at this point, I'll admit, not only was I sputtering, my gun had slid from being pointed at her gut to Gloria's feet. I was also kneeling a bit too high in the chair to use it as a proper shield. "Uh. Maeve. You're already dead. You're a vampire."

She rolled her eyes. "How very observant of you. Yes, I know, I'm dead but someone's done something and now I'm dying again. For good, this time. I need you to find out who. I'll pay you handsomely for it."

Those were the magic words. An interesting case, a real stumper of a mystery, and a really big payday. How could I pass that up?

I raised my hands, holding my Pulse Revolver away from my body. "All right. You've got me. I'll put away my piece and you let my secretary go."

Maeve flung Gloria away from her. Gloria stumbled and fell with a squawked curse. I holstered my revolver as Gloria picked herself up from the floor, grumbling.

"All right, Jack. Let's do business."

Maeve took a seat on the navigation console, crossing her long and gorgeous pale legs, and I settled back into my seat.

"Start at the beginning."

Maeve gave me a dark look. "Really? I would never have thought of giving you the whole story—"

"Okay, okay. Just tell me."

"I was making my way through Avondale on Chicago, tasting the local cuisine, hitting all the hot tourist spots—" In other words, she was making herself fat on the blood of hapless civilians. "—when I was set upon by four thugs. I manage to kill one of them—snapped his neck clean in two—but was overpowered. One of them stuck this in my neck."

At "this," she reached down the front of her dress and pulled from her cleavage a clear bubble about three inches across with a long plastic bit jutting from one end. I did my best not to stare.

I failed miserably.

She held the thing out to me. I took it and turned it around a few times between my fingers. "Okay, I give up. What is it?"

"I'm not sure. It's some sort of syringe. Here." She pulled the plastic from the end, revealing a thin steel needle. "They pumped me full of some sort of drug and ever since...Jack, I can't eat. Every time I drink, a few minutes later, I vomit it back up again."

"Is that such a bad thing?"

Damn. Sometimes, Gloria needed to practice that old adage "Silence is Golden."

Maeve rolled her head around and glared at Gloria. "Yes, it's a bad thing. I'm starving, girl, and I don't want to die. Jack," she said, turning to look at me, "find out who did this to me and how to fix it. I'm only a hundred and forty-eight—"

"Only?"

Maeve shot Gloria a glare. "Yes, *only*. Like I said, I'm not ready to die." She turned back to me, lower lip thrust out in a pout, eyes pleading. If I didn't know she could cry crocodile tears on demand, the look might've worked. Now, though, it just made me want to tell her to go to hell.

"Before I passed out, I heard one of them say a name. Bobby Sims."

I groaned.

Maeve gave me a puzzled look. "Do you know what this means?"

"Unfortunately." I swept the papers from the navigation console and dumped them on the floor. "Gloria? Man the engine. Maeve, go take a seat somewhere and strap yourself in."

Gloria: "Where are we going?"

Maeve: "Why?"

I turned to Gloria first. "Bronzeville, Chicago." To Maeve I said, "Because we're going to have a bit of turbulence getting off this space station."

Gloria's heels clicked away as she hurried to the engine room. Maeve frowned. "Jack, please tell me this lump of metal has thrust dampeners."

I grinned and flipped the switches for the take-off sequence to engage. "They were sacrificed."

"Sacrificed? What for?"

"Did you see those snazzy floodlights on the wings? The ones pointing at my name on the sides?"

Maeve gaped at me. "You didn't."

"Oh, I most certainly did." Gloria's ping of "Ready!" showed up on my screen. I clipped my seatbelt and eased the steering wheel back into my lap. I switched off the docking mechanism and pulled the boxy radio down from its clip on the ceiling of the cockpit. "I'd hang onto something if I were you. Gloria criticizes my takeoffs as needlessly reckless." I clicked the radio on. "Springfield? This is *Serena*. Requesting docking release."

I released the button and waited. After a moment, the docking technician's voice crackled over the speaker. "This is Springfield, you're cleared for takeoff." With a click and a hum, the docking clamps on my ship released and *Serena* floated free in the vacuum. "Have a nice day, *Serena*."

"Thanks, Springfield."

With that, I slammed my hand down on the thruster handle. The thrusters on the wings roared to life and the ship's body vibrated with the force. About ten minutes out, I activated the FTL engine and we shot off towards Chicago with a silent bang. As they say in the old Vids, I floored it and we were off, rattling and shaking the whole way.

On Chicago, there's a man named Tigo. Tigo and I, we've had occasion to meet before. In both cases, we shot each other. First time, he got me right in the chest. Had I been human, I wouldn't be talking to you now. Second time, I got him in the leg.

Needless to say, I was a little worried how this meeting might end.

Tigo's ship was parked round the bad part of town in Bronzeville, a small grungy city not too far from Bridgeport. His ship matched the city: small and grungy. From what my untrained eye could deduce, it'd been a military barracks transport before someone hacked off the top level, replaced it with an Ion Canon, and painted the whole thing black (though now it was more black, red, and grey with rust and peeling paint). Oh, and secured giant spikes to the four thrusters sticking out of the sides.

A real eyesore.

I'd considered my options at that point. I could've gone in all stealthy-like to catch Tigo with his drawers down. Or I could've blown something up out here and lured his boys outside, then run like blazes (trust me, nothing runs faster than a vampire sure he's about to be shot).

Yet, none of those options felt right to me. In the end, I dragged my M52 Automatic Pulse Rifle out from its hiding place under the pilot's console. Weighs about fifteen pounds and feels like I'm lugging a mini-canon around at my hip but damn is it a flashy piece of work. If you've got one of those on, most sane folk leave you be. I call her "Old Bess."

I strapped Bess to my chest as I stepped out of my office. Maeve stared at me.

"Good God, Jack, what is that thing?"

"This?" I hefted it, sliding the cocking mechanism down the barrel. "It's an Automatic Pulse Rifle."

"What do you plan to do with it?"

I pulled on my tan suit jacket over Bess's straps and untangled my tie from the central buckle. "Get some answers."

And with that, I strode out of my ship into the last rays of twilight and right up to Tigo's. Getting past the pair of guards at his open docking hatch was easy. One good wave of Bess at their faces and the docking hatch was not only open but abandoned, the sound of the guards' feet pattering on the concrete in the distance.

I entered Tigo's less-than-humble abode and followed the hallways until I arrived at his command center. He'd remodeled this room too. The standard sprawling map table in the center had been ripped out, replaced by four poker tables on a dark red carpet. At least ten of Tigo's boys lounged around the room, some sitting at the tables, drinking and gaming, others standing on the suspended walkway that wrapped around the room.

Tigo lounged in the captain's chair behind the poker table farthest from the door, a tumbler of whiskey in one hand, cards in the other. He's a short, dumpy little man, prone to wearing Hawaiian tourist shirts and brown dress slacks. Broad red face, little brown eyes, and mousy hair. Like his ship, a bit of an eyesore.

"Jack! What a—oh, er, um, right." He stared at Bess and I fancied a look of panic in his piggy eyes. He lowered his cards but kept the drink. "You mean business."

"Damn right I do, Tigo. I'm looking for Bobby Sims."

"Bobby? Haven't seen him." Tigo took a sip of whiskey, eyes averted.

"Come on, Tigo. Don't lie to me."

Out of the corner of my eye, I noticed one of Tigo's men—a bruno dressed in a dark green suit that matched the tables—inching closer, his hand on his Pulse sidearm.

I swung Bess around to point at his face. Bess made that slight, high-pitched whine of her power coils heating up for a fifty-round Pulse shot.

What I hoped they wouldn't figure was that I hadn't had the batteries to power Bess for almost twenty years. Making that noise was about all she did.

Thankfully, the man didn't seem in the mood to tempt fate or my trigger finger and backed down, hands spread and far from his gun. I turned back to Tigo and hefted Bess. "Start talking or I start carving holes in your ship, in your men, and most of all, in you."

Tigo held up his hands, one still occupied with holding his whiskey. "All right, all right! No need to be hasty. I'm willing to cooperate. Bobby's over in Avondale. He has a ship there, the *Albatross*. Ask the docking committee to run a search. He's registered. You got a death-wish, Jack. That guy's a real piece of work."

"You let me worry about him."

There was a soft clicking behind me, growing louder with each passing nanosecond. I turned and found Maeve standing in the doorway of Tigo's command center. Before I could speak, the whine of a charging Pulse weapon filled the air followed by—

Bzzz-zat.

And my back exploded in a fiery mushroom of agony.

Tigo shot me.

Again.

I probably screamed, I'm not sure. Instinct kicked in and I ran, praying that my undead feet would carry me faster than a second pulse shot. I grabbed hold of Maeve's hand as I passed, towing her along behind me.

"Jack—?"

I didn't answer.

"Jack, you're bleeding. And kind of burnt."

Really? Why, I would never have noticed. "Yeah," I managed between gasps. "I know."

Remember when I said nothing runs faster than a vampire scared of being shot? Yeah, well, I take that back. Nothing runs faster than a vampire who *has* been shot. We made it back to my ship in record time.

"Close it, close it! Gloria, get the engine running! Tigo's got an Ion Canon!" I tossed Bess down on the flooring plates, the polymer casing of the rifle slamming into the metal with a resounding bang.

"Since when does Tigo have an Ion Canon?" came Gloria's shout from the engine room below. Maeve smashed the buttons on the docking hatch control panel.

"Since now!"

The doors groaned shut behind us, cutting off the sound of Tigo's men firing at my ship with Pulse weapons and the deep bass hum of the Ion Canon heating up. I stumbled down the hallway to the pilot's cockpit, my wounded back screaming it didn't want me using my legs and my legs screaming that if I didn't sit down *right now*, my knees were going to give out.

I collapsed in the pilot's chair, disengaged the landing gear, and started the takeoff sequence. The high-pitched pinging of the Pulse shots ricocheting off the hull of the ship punctuated the roar of the engine and the shriek of the thrusters firing. We shot off the ground at a good 235 MPH just as that damn Ion Canon went off, tearing a crater in the concrete where my ship had been sitting.

Only through a liberal application of sheer dumb luck and pain-induced adrenaline did I manage to avoid getting blown out of the sky or plowing my poor ship into a skyscraper or some other poor bastard waiting in a landing lane. We ducked, weaved, and twisted our way through Bronzeville. A few minutes later, we broke through the city's outer crust, headed toward Avondale.

I leaned back in the pilot's chair, shaking. It was a miracle we got out of there without me killing us. How I flew with my hands practically vibrating is beyond me.

Around that point, the adrenaline high started wearing off and the pain came back full force. I entered into a whole world of misery, waiting for my supernatural healing powers to kick in and patch me up.

I found Bobby's ship in Avondale, just where Tigo said it would be. I didn't find Bobby. With a bit of convincing with the quiet help of Bess, I got Bobby's location from the locals. The man liked to hang around Pickits's Alley, playing backroom poker. Apparently, if I hung around the Alley long enough, I'd run into Bobby when he took his smoke break.

So that's how I ended up squatting in a dank little hole, wedged between a steel dumpster and a moldering biodegradable refrigeration box at 11:00PM Galaxy Standard Time (making it about two in the morning Avondale time on Chicago). Contrary to popular belief regarding vampire invulnerability, I was miserable. Not only was I freezing and my clothes and hair dripping wet but, like the rest of the alley, I stank of rotting vegetation and urine.

The alley itself was formed by three massive hundred-story concrete buildings, each sandwiched against the next to form a dead-end little pocket of refuse. Steel doors lined the walls around me and, across from my hiding place, a black metal staircase rose to the second floor of its skyscraper. A seedy-looking fellow stood near the mouth of the alley in an oversized duffle coat. I was pretty sure

I was getting mugged when I stepped out of there.

My preoccupation with that man almost cost me my head when Bobby stepped outside, saw me, panicked and pulled his own Pulse Revolver from its holster. The box beside me exploded in a shower of burning rotten synthetic cardboard. I ducked behind the dumpster, pulling my revolver from my belt. "Bobby Sims! I just want to talk, I swear."

"What ye swear don't mean nuffin' to me, dick."

I wasn't sure if he was referring to my occupation or my personality.

He fired again and his Pulse shot glanced off the top of the dumpster, the blast dissipating with a burnt sulfur smell. I hunkered down and peered around the corner, the muzzle of my revolver going first. I squeezed off a shot, the Pulse sending a shudder of recoil through my arm. Bobby responded in kind and I pulled back. His Pulse shot left a streak of black along the concrete.

"Let's be reasonable about this, Bobby! I've just got a few questions, that's all."

"And ye can ask them questions when yer dead!"

Oh, really? That'd be a laugh. Then again, I was already dead, so wasn't I fulfilling his threat already by asking him questions?

I smacked myself in the head with the palm of my free hand. "Focus," I muttered.

Bobby got off another shot. The stench of used Pulse shots filled the air with its acidic burning that had my nostril hairs perked at attention.

I peeked around the dumpster. Bobby stood in front of a rusted door set into one of the brick buildings and under a single orange solar light, making him a somewhat purplish shadow. And he'd have remained a shadow if I were human. As I ducked back, I closed my eyes, forcing my night vision to activate while keeping my ears peeled for any sound of Bobby approaching or calling in reinforcements.

Smarts were clearly not Bobby's area of expertise though, as he did neither. When I opened my eyes, the alley had lit up with a brilliant clarity that let me count the brass buttons on the coat of the sleazy brigand at the mouth of the alley, over forty feet away from where I crouched. I looked around the dumpster again and winced as that solar light sought to blind me.

Bobby was a big man, built like a fleshy juggernaut, head bald as an egg and a face that looked to have met the broadside of a moving transport. He wore an ill-fitting black suit with the buttons of his white shirt straining to contain his girth. Beside him was a great big stack of boxes that didn't look all too steady.

I took aim, careful to keep my revolver as tucked away behind the dumpster as I could. I did the math in my head. If I hit that one box, the one that stuck out slightly to his left, and knocked it out, the four on top would topple right over.

Taking a deep breath, I sighted down the barrel of my revolver and squeezed the trigger. The Pulse shot flew from the end of the gun, lighting the alley with a pale blue haze for a split second before the box exploded, and the four on top went flying.

They sailed down in a cardboard rain on Bobby's head. He swore and shot one of the boxes.

Ah, the wonders of Pulse physics. Sometimes, you shoot things and they fly away from you as though kicked. Other times, you shoot things and nothing happens. Still others, they explode. And then, once in a while, you shoot something and it goes up in a pillar of flaming glory.

Which is exactly what happened to poor Bobby. The box fell towards him, engulfed in fire. He yelped and dodged, his Pulse sidearm slipping from his grip and skittering across the concrete. I took my chance and approached him, my Pulse Revolver trained on his chest. I heard the pattering of feet as the lurking mugger ran off behind me.

"Okay, Bob. You move, I blow you to Hell, got it?"

He nodded with a grunt.

"Now, I've got a few little questions for you."

Bobby spat a wad of spittle on the concrete beside his head. "Ask, li'le vampy."

"Some of your boys attacked a woman a little while ago, a vampire with long dark hair and—" Oh, how to say this? Bluntly. "—a really big pair of melons. She would've been munching her way through the lower levels of Avondale."

"I remember 'er. Killed one of me men, she did. Snapped his neck clean in two."

"Yeah, that's her. Your men gave her some kind of needle injection and they said your name. I'm willing to bet they weren't doing this job on the side, right?"

He didn't answer, but the shifty look on his face was good

enough.

"Where did you get the needle from? Answer me straight and I'll leave here peacefully, okay?"

Bobby looked to be thinking it over. After a good twenty or so seconds, he spat again. "Lazarus."

I put on my best I-am-not-amused look. "And who's Lazarus?"

"Some bigwig science-man. Works in the Avondale Research Facility, up on Lawrence. He offered us ten grand a pop if we stuck his li'le needles in vampy necks. I got meself a boy who's good at spotting walking corpses. Got hawk eyes, he has. He points 'em out, my boys stick 'em with needles, we gets paid, and Lazarus gives us more needles. Don't know why, don't know what they do, and really don't care."

"Thanks for your cooperation, Bobby Sims. Don't get up."

He grinned at me. "Ye like stakes, dick?"

I frowned. "What?"

There was shouting behind me and I turned to find the mugger had gone and found himself a whole pack of thugs, armed with everything from thirty-years outdated Pulse side arms to boards with nails in the end. I groaned, fired all six of my Pulse rounds, holstered my gun, and ran for the fire escape ladder like the slavering hordes of Hell were after me.

Which they were, in a way.

Round this point, I asked myself, why was it that I'd spent so much of this case running away from things? Mostly, men with big guns?

I swore never to take another job from Maeve ever again.

I lurked outside the windows of the Avondale Research Facility. Inside were lines of white tables covered in all sorts of complicated-looking lab equipment and clear bottles. A man, thin and bony with a mane of bushy white-blond hair and a white lab coat, paced the lines, touching that, moving this, and lifting bottles to the fluorescent lights set into the ceiling.

Lazarus.

Why did he look like the stereotypical mad scientist? Did he consciously cultivate it as a fashion statement?

Standing outside in the cold wasn't going to answer these

questions so I set about picking which of the windows would be the best to break in through. I settled on the one on the far left, right above a filing cabinet and some sort of potted plant with small spiky leaves and large purple flowers.

I knelt on the lawn and pulled my electric glass cutter from my pocket. It's a snazzy little thing I picked up at a flea market on Las Vegas a few years ago. 'Bout four inches long and steel plated, it slices right through glass like it was paper. I activated the glass cutter and waited for it to warm up, keeping one eye on Lazarus.

The glass cutter pinged and a minute later, Lazarus walked out of sight. Stood to reason the man would walk back in right at the moment I got that window open, so I rushed with cutting the me-sized jagged circle in the glass. Eyes peeled for Lazarus's reemergence, I flipped the glass cutter around and pressed the rubber suction cup to it, hitting the vacuum button. The glass cutter buzzed and I pulled the circle of glass from the rest of the window.

No sign of Lazarus. I slipped through the window accompanied by the sound of shredding fabric as my clothing caught on the jutting edges. Great. Another suit ruined. My wardrobe budget's pretty thin at the best of times.

I landed as softly as I could on the cabinet then dropped to the white-tiled floor. I picked my way through the lab, searching for Lazarus or a handy glass vial with the words "THE CURE" written on it. What greeted me were lines of unlabeled bottles, beakers, and tubes, some high-tech-looking machinery, copper and rubber tubes, wires, and large plastic boxes with little lights blinking on them.

Something jabbed me from behind right under the ribs. Pain lanced through my left kidney and knocked the wind from me. I stumbled forward, hand on my back, my knees feeling like they'd traded my cartilage for jelly.

"You, sir, are trespassing. Unfortunately for you, I do not believe in calling law enforcement. Make peace with your gods."

I twisted, still unable to straighten with the cramping pain of my stricken kidney. Which makes little sense since, dammit, I haven't had to use a kidney for eighty years. They shouldn't hurt when some freak gives 'em a good jab.

Speaking of freaks, Lazarus the Jabber stood behind me, hands raised for more finger-stabbing, knees bent in a martial arts combat stance of some sort. He bared his fangs at me and hissed.

Curses spilled from between my clenched teeth. Just what I

needed. Another vampire. This damn galaxy was getting pretty crowded with the undead.

My hand slid toward my Pulse Revolver. It might not kill him, but six rounds through him would hurt like hell. "Yeah, well *unfortunately* I don't intend to die today."

I pulled the revolver out, my vampire speed kicking in and making my hand move as a rapid blur. I managed one shot before Lazarus jabbed my wrist with a short, sharp strike of his fingertips. Pain shot through my wrist and my hand went limp, my Pulse Revolver slipping from my fingers. Even twitching them sent tingles of agony up my arm.

I sidestepped his next strike and wrapped my arm around his neck. Next thing I knew, I was free-falling through the air. I slammed into the tile floor, gasping like a dying fish.

"One of us, I see. Well, no matter." Lazarus chuckled. "You will be dead quite soon, I assure you. Or..."

He looked thoughtful. I struggled to my feet, my twitching right hand tucked against my side.

"Or perhaps I will gift you with the cure. Yes, yes—how tall are you? Oh, five-foot-ten, maybe eleven, I'd say. Weight? Hmm...fourteen stone, I would guess. You'd do, you'd do quite well."

What the hell was a stone? And why did I have fourteen of them? And just how old was this guy? He sounded ancient enough to be from *the* original Earth. "For?"

Lazarus grinned and didn't answer. Figures.

He launched himself at me and I took a swing at his head. He dodged (vampire speed works both ways, sadly) and grabbed me around the shoulders, twisting my upper body to the left. I struggled, beating at him with my good fist and getting a good stab or two in with my right elbow. Didn't faze him a bit.

Three rapid jabs and I couldn't feel my legs anymore. Another and I couldn't feel anything below my navel. While I was somewhat grateful it didn't hurt like my kidney had, I was mostly scared out of my wits.

I don't get scared very often nowadays, not when a man can shoot me in the head with a Pulse Rifle and I get back up again five minutes later. After eighty years of being a super-powered corpse, not feeling your legs is more than a little panic inducing.

It was all I could do not to blubber.

And throughout it, Lazarus just kept smiling that patient, suffering smile, like my pain was somehow *my* fault and he was going to fix it for me.

Lazarus walked away only to return a moment later with one of those bubble needles in his hands. "This, my dear child, is the cure. I have worked so many, many long years to create it. I've had so many failures, bad strains, and dead ends, but now, now I think I might have it. We will be freed, child. Freed! Free to walk in the sun, to eat food like the rest of the mortals, to live. Think of it. Freedom."

He whispered the last, his eyes unfocused and staring at a point over my head. I tried to push myself up, but my right hand didn't want to cooperate and I flopped face-first on the tiles. Lazarus looked down at me.

"Now child, your cure awwa*iihkkkkk*."

It sounded just like that too. One minute, he was talking, no problem. The next, the tip of a wooden spear shot through his sternum, splattering me with blood. He stared down at the stake, gouts of blood spilling from his open mouth. His face turned ashen, his cheeks sunken, his eyes a glazed grey.

He toppled to the side, stake still in his chest. Maeve smacked her hands together as though to say "job well done."

"Sorry about this, Jack, but I had to."

"You...used...me."

Maeve rolled her eyes, her expression one of barely contained sarcasm. "Yes, Jack, I used you. What did you expect? I had to find the antidote for this freak's cure and the only way to do that was to find him, and the only way to find him was to use you."

She turned from me to root through the vials on the table behind her. After a few minutes and a second table, she held a single vial aloft, a wide smile splitting her face. She uncorked it, downed the whole thing, then smacked her lips. "Now, Jack, I have a job to finish."

My lips felt numb and my brain, sluggish. "What job?"

But she was gone. I pulled myself forward with my good hand, my joints shrieking with the pressure.

Click. Click. Click.

Again with those heels. Maeve returned, a sort of bulky steel box gripped in her hands. She placed the box down on the surface of the closest table and poked at what sounded like a control pad judging by the beeping. Maeve stepped back and looked down at me. "I can't let this cure happen. It would ruin us. It has to go. I'm sorry it turned out this way, Jack. I really did love you once."

Thankfully, my lips didn't want to cooperate, otherwise, I would've said something quite rude to the traitorous backstabbing she-wolf.

She pressed one final button before stepping away towards the door. "You've got three minutes, Jack. I suggest you run."

And all she left behind was the flutter of papers in her wake. Oh, yeah, and a great big bomb scheduled to go off in three minutes.

I really hated myself right then. Okay, I admit, I hated her too, but that was a given.

I don't remember much of it, but somehow, I managed to drag myself by my fingertips to that filing cabinet. I know I screamed a lot—howled really—and shouted a great deal I'm glad no one else could hear. The tips of my fingers leaked blood by the time I got my hand around the filing cabinet's handle.

Though it hurt like blazes, I dragged myself to my numb feet and pulled myself on top of the cabinet using my elbows. I knocked that plant off in the process and the ceramic pot smashed on the floor.

I think I ran out of minutes then, because the next thing I remember, I was on my back, my ears ringing so bad my eyes watered, and my body felt alternately like it had been stuck on ice and set on fire. And I still couldn't feel my feet.

Then standing over me were four or five men with M58 Rifles pointed at my face and wearing clear-visored helmets and navy blue body armor. I'm pretty sure they spoke to me but I couldn't hear a word and my lip-reading has gotten a bit rusty over the years. I did catch, "You are under arrest for arson," especially after that one helpful officer wrote it down on a little piece of paper for me.

The rest of it you know. Arrested, processed, allowed to heal, stuck in a cell, and now here.

So that's it?

We're done?

Hey, officer? If we're done, can I go home?

Officer?

Well, damn.

R. J. Howell is a writer, an artist, and a library circulation clerk. She holds a BA in Fiction Writing from Columbia College Chicago. Her art has been published in L. Ron Hubbard Presents Writers of the Future Vol. 28. This is her first fiction publication.

The Finder
by
Ariel Ptak

Florence looked at the photo on her desk. She set her fingers on a corner of it. She pushed it back towards the hopeful woman seated across from her.

"I'm sorry, but I don't do people," she said.

"But why not?"

"Because people aren't possessions. They're harder for me and my…resources…to track down," Florence replied bluntly.

"Can't you make an exception? Try, just this once? Please, he's my fiancé, he's been missing for days now…"

Florence sighed, glancing back down at the photo which the woman had not taken back. It depicted a smiling man - narrow, with a sharp nose and bright eyes. He wasn't particularly handsome in Florence's estimation, but perhaps there was something about him which made him shine in this woman's regard.

"This is the sort of thing that the police take care of, or ordinary detectives if it comes to that."

"I went to the police. They said not to expect much. My friends all say you're the best at finding lost things. I'll do anything. Please."

Lost *things*, Florence thinks. Possessions. Money, even. Not people. But the woman looks so sad and desperate and still clinging to hope despite all the best efforts of the world, and Florence wavers.

Love, friends, family - these are other kinds of wealth, aren't they? Could it be worth an attempt at least?

The ermine on top of her filing cabinet shook the fur across his shoulders and squeaked.

Perhaps.

She reached across the desk and took the photo back.

"I can't make any promises, but if you can give me a list of what he was wearing when he was last seen, as well as anything he might have had with him - a wallet, jewelry, anything…then all right, I'll try."

In the end it was the ring he still carried that called out to her. It wasn't an expensive ring, but there was a value in it greater than its material price. She followed it to a hotel one town over, to the attached bar, to a man in a broad-brimmed hat and smoked glasses and an expression as lost as anything she's ever seen.

Florence sat down on the stool next to him and placed two items beside his half-empty glass: her business card and his picture. He took a moment to realize the significance of these, to look at her in a mixture of shame, panic, and confusion.

"Your fiancé is worried," Florence said.

"Oh. Is she?"

"You didn't leave any word. She was afraid something terrible might have happened to you."

"Oh. I didn't…think…"

He wavered and turned back to stare at his drink. It was only early afternoon; Florence wondered how long he had been in here and how much he might have had so far.

"I'm going to be a terrible husband," he blurted out. "I can't give her…I can barely hold a job. She'd be happier with someone else. What was I thinking?"

Florence tapped her card, calling his attention to the print describing her services.

"I don't find people," she said bluntly, "only things. She knew this and she begged me to search for you anyhow. I'm not sure she sees her happiness the same way you do, but then, I don't know her myself. Still, it seems to me the best thing you could do is call, or write, or just go back home and talk to her face to face. In fact, I'd appreciate it if you did. I have had a very good success rate and I'd like to keep that if possible."

Florence stood, leaving the card and picture both beside his drink.

"I'll arrange for her to be at Borgenson's Café at noon tomorrow, just down the street from my office. You have the address there. Whether you come or not is your choice. Good day."

She wouldn't be changing the focus of her business, she decided as she left. Things were far easier to just pick up and return to the people who had lost them. People always had to decide where they wanted to be for themselves.

Still, perhaps this one time might prove to have been worth it.

Ariel is an artist and writer with a deep love for the legendary and fantastic. She has been previously published in Spellbound and Prairie Winds literary journals. More of her work can be found on Wattpad (wattpad.com/user/arptak).

The Tale of the Wendigo
by
C.W. Blackwell

Boston 1880

1. A Place of Ice and Bones

The priest stood at the center of a frozen lake; a pale being with a black frock that drifted at his feet and a collar that blended with the glare. Everything in that washed-out place was bleached with an aching cold that burned his eyes and froze the tears as they watered through his dark lashes. A line of trees blurred along the shore—a grey and curious feature that hung onto the horizon like some phantasmal strand curling out of the void. A figure appeared from that blanched direction, strange and singular—a darkness that interrupted the light. Soon the figure was upon him, a thin and monstrous thing of mostly bones and horns and a cavern of teeth that bit and chewed at the wind as if hunger was now the only edict in that vast and empty plane.

The thing grasped him by the shoulders, and shook.

"*Nolan,*" it said. But its voice sounded polite, almost annoyed.

Nolan blinked his eyes, and the world slowly returned. A pint of whiskey lay flat over his desk and had filled his trousers with booze. He turned to the voice, and his eyes now focused on a large man in elegant attire.

"Father Nolan, you've missed noon mass for…" The man counted on his fingers. "For the seventh time now, is it?"

Nolan sat straight on the stool and brushed his black hair over his scalp. He couldn't tell if he had pissed himself or if it was just the spilt whiskey that felt cold upon his thighs.

"Reckon I was scheduled for midnight mass, monsignor," said Nolan, his eyes small and bloodshot.

"Reckon you'd be wrong seven times in a row," said the monsignor. He scuttled behind the priest and fished a black-laced stocking from the bed in the corner of the room. "How did this get here," he said, raising a thick brow.

Nolan regarded the stocking with mild interest as it draped over the monsignor's finger like a dead serpent.

"Well," said Nolan, "I'd surmise that it once contained a leg. A leg that walked into this very room and laid itself on the bed."

The monsignor grinned, but it was a mix of amusement and admonishment. "This leg, was it attached to a body or just a ghostly thing that bounded into the room unannounced?"

Nolan tried to stand, but the whiskey was still boiling in his veins. Instead, he folded on the stool, and squinted at the bed.

"It was a woman," he said, as his eyes rolled back and then recentered. "Taller than most, with curly red hair. Her name started with an 's'."

"So you remember?"

"No," said Nolan. "Not a thing. There's a mark on the window, an impression of a forehead pressed against the glass. Must have been a hundred-eighty centimeters if even a King's inch." He bobbed his head as if losing consciousness for a moment and then returned to the world and narrowed his eyes. "There's a strand of hair on the pillow, red and wavy as a dead leaf in November."

"But you recall her name?"

Nolan pursed his lips and a smile spread across his face as if remembering something secret.

"Aye. But I'm not sure how. Reckon she must have whispered it into to my ear when I helped her through the window. Wait. Susanna, it was."

"Michael Nolan," said the monsignor. His voice had now lost every trace of amusement. "I've defrocked clergy for lesser transgressions. Truth is, I intended it this very morning."

"Bless you for your change of heart," said Nolan. He was now pulling off his trousers and fishing a dry pair from a pile in the corner of the room.

"My heart is unchanged," he said. "But I may still have use for you. There's a man in the hall, and his predicament is serious."

"Out there, waiting this entire time? How rude of us."

"He's a railroad man, and a friend of my family."

"Please, show him in."

"Goodness no," he said. He had been dangling the stocking from his finger the entire time, and only now let it fall to the floor. "Meet me in the rectory in ten minutes." The monsignor hucked a twisted ginger root onto the desk. "Eat this while you steady yourself. You smell like a damned brothel on payday."

Nolan lifted his nose as if smelling the space around him, then nodded in agreement.

The railroad man looked as if he were constructed of twenty-dollar bills, and his shirt was white enough to attract moths on a moonless night. He turned and regarded Nolan with a hopeful smile as he entered the rectory.

"Father Nolan," said the man, "Your reputation precedes you."

It took a moment for Nolan to determine that the comment was not sarcastic. He then bowed to the man, and settled on an empty chair beside the monsignor.

"This is Mr. Cooke," said the monsignor. "He is a friend of mine, and a man of great concern for the development of our territories."

"I see," said Nolan. There was a file on the table between them, and from it could be seen the glossy edges of photographic paper. "And which territories are most concerning to you, Mr. Cooke?"

"The undeveloped north of Wisconsin," said Cooke. "We are building a railway there, and well…" Cooke looked at the monsignor and then back to Nolan. "There's been a recent atrocity. Several passengers were pulled off the train last month and brutally murdered."

"Terrible news," said Nolan. "I'm surprised I haven't heard of it."

"I'm not entirely proud of it," said Cooke, "but I've had the information suppressed, business being what it is. The law knows, of course, but their investigation was cursory and inconclusive."

"Only the one occurrence?" asked Nolan.

"I'm afraid not. When the track was laid last year, we lost three men under similar circumstances. All brutally killed in the same manner." Cooke flicked his finger at the file on the table. "This last time, there was a photographer on the train, a government man. I paid him good money for his slides and his discretion."

"May I?" said Nolan.

Cooke nodded quickly. "Please do. Monsignor has told me of your intellectual abilities. I am a rich man, but this is beyond my ability to solve with money alone."

Nolan lifted the file and unfolded it over his lap. A sepia photograph slid from the papers, and he tilted it to the lamplight. The print showed a carnage unlike anything he had seen. The corpses of four men and two women lay torn and sunken in the snow with a coach car looming in the background. The ice was dark and mottled and entrails of the dead filled every corner of the photograph. A young man lay with his lungs spread over his coat like the wings of some strange bird. Nolan studied it and the others in the stack with his eyes narrowed in concentration as the other men watched as if they could somehow glean some truth from the muscles of his face. He folded the file and closed his eyes for a long moment.

"I'll not want to visit this place," said Nolan, finally. "Not in a thousand years."

Cooke looked to the monsignor, who rose and gestured at Nolan politely.

"I'll speak to him, Mr. Cooke. We do want to help. I'm sure Father Nolan is stricken by this tragedy as much as the rest of us."

Nolan only sat blinking, as if trying to cleanse the images from his bloodshot eyes.

"Yes," said Cooke. "Please discuss it. Of course I will pay your expenses. I just want to resolve this issue once and for all."

The monsignor walked Cooke to the door and they exchanged words briefly, and then he returned to where Nolan sat.

"Now that we're alone, I must tell you something," said the monsignor.

Nolan was slouching in the chair as though he might sleep. He peeked an eye open and said simply. "No."

"No?" Said the monsignor. "I'll be concise. Either get on the next boat to Dublin, or help Mr. Cooke on his investigation."

Nolan nodded slowly, rubbing his hands together as he ruminated on the monsignor's words. "Is there not a third option?"

The monsignor scowled.

"I could defrock you now and you can marry that blonde woman Susanna. Make an honest man of yourself. I'll marry you here in the chapel this weekend."

Nolan smiled into his hands, thinking of his nuptials and every decade that preceded it until he was dead. He also thought of Dublin, but only for a moment.

"I'll go, then," said Nolan. "But I'll need a new coat and boots. Plenty of spending money."

2. The Banshees of the Northern Plains

The train sped through featureless plains with only an aching whiteness that filled the windows, as if this part of the world was the very edge of creation and yet to be constructed. Nolan was half-awake when the train attendant approached with a cart, crowded with refreshments.

"Coffee, Father?" said the young man.

Nolan nodded. "Thank you. Leave room for cream, please. I'll add it myself."

"Very well," said the man. He poured from a tin carafe and handed the priest a cup and a small dram of cream.

When the attendant moved on, Nolan drank the cream in one shot and then lifted a bottle of whiskey from inside his coat and poured it atop the coffee to the very rim. He sipped the drink slowly, admiring both the quality of the brew and the steadiness of the tracks beneath him. He lifted a small dagger from inside his coat and thumbed at the blade, and then studied his reflection in the steel. The glare from the window made his eyes look grey like his father's eyes had looked the last time he saw him.

When the attendant passed a second time, he refilled Nolan's coffee, but the priest waved off the cream.

"Tell me, young man, what is the conductor's name?"

"Daniel Grady," said the man, as if it had been waiting there on his tongue.

"Has he worked this line long?"

"Since I've been workin' on it," he said. "Would you like to meet him?"

"Aye, I reckon I would. Perhaps once we stop at the Black River station?"

"I'll pass the message."

"Thank you." Nolan took a sip of coffee and smiled. "One more question. What do you know of the murders occurring there three weeks back?"

The man's face washed out and he stared into his cart a long while as if he could somehow find the answers there.

"Only heard rumors of it is all. I was in St. Paul when it happened, visiting my ma."

"I see. Lucky for you then."

"Yes, lucky. I'd tell you about it if I could, but nobody's sayin' much. Grady is the one to see."

"I reckoned so. Please tell him I'd like to speak."

"Yes, Father," he said, and then paused. "I can tell you there's a part of it that nobody wants to mention—only someone in your position might understand." He walked the cart back along the aisle, his eyes cold and hard as if he heard tell of some terrible thing that was born in the world and could only now hear it cry.

When the train slowed at the Black River stop, Nolan stood on the gunmetal steps of the coach as the land stilled and the boiler spit a furious whiteness at the sky. He held a single bag in his hand, black and checked with grey. He looked to the front of the train, and a man was now disembarking from the engine with a tight cap and heavy mustache that could likely be ascertained from the moon itself.

"Mr. Grady," called Nolan, as he stepped into the snow.

Grady walked to him with a smile that produced a dimple in his chin, dark and strange like the calyx of some otherworldly fruit.

"Hello, Father," he said. "Welcome to Black River station. How was your trip?"

"Like riding on a cloud," he said. "I imagine the closest I'll come to it this side of death."

The men exchanged handshakes and introduced themselves accordingly.

"I suppose you know I've been sent by Mr. Cooke?" said Nolan.

Grady shook his head. "Jay Cooke? No, I hadn't heard."

"It makes us associates in some way. Could you be so kind as to show me where it happened?"

"Where it happened?" Grady had a look about him like he was waiting for some password.

"Where those poor people were dismantled and strewn over the station. I have the photographs if you'd like to see them."

The man was now leaning backward as if wanting to retreat. He looked the priest over then glanced into his hands. "It was there," he said finally, pointing. "Just along the road."

They walked to that place, and Nolan stood atop the white earth without looking at it, as if the answers were instead carried in the sound of the wind and the stirring of the dark trees.

"Tell me, then," he said.

Grady exhaled, and his breath whipsawed into the air and disappeared. He reached for his coat pocket and began to build a cigarette, but a gust blew the fibers from the paper and they spread evenly over the snow beneath him. He let the paper fall to the ground, and spoke.

"I was over there," he said, pointing to the western side of the tracks. "Relieving myself in the grove of firs when it started."

Nolan raised a hand in the air.

"Not that part," said Nolan. "I've read your statement many times."

The man looked confused, and somehow worried.

"I want to know about the strange occurrence, the part only someone in my position might understand."

The man nodded, then rubbed his face with his hands.

"My grandparents were from Ireland, you know. But I haven't been to mass in months."

"I haven't been a while myself. No fault in it, really."

"You want to know about the shrieking, then."

"Yes, that." said Nolan.

"Well, when I was there in that spot I heard a crying out. A shriek of a woman like she was in some kind of trouble."

"But it didn't come from the train."

"No," said Grady. "It was in the wind, in the trees. Then there were more, many more. The shrieking came from every direction, loud and frightening like some kind of swarm was coming from somewhere I couldn't get a bead on." Grady was staring at the firs with his hand shaking against his coat. "You ever hear the sound of a dozen women shrieking and yelling and cussing loud as all hell in the wind all around you?"

Nolan looked to the sky thoughtfully.

"Not quite that many at once," he admitted.

"Well, I saw one of them, just whirlin' through the trees with hair red and fiery. A ghost maybe, I don't know. Maybe some kind of demoness just cuttin' through the branches and screamin' like the whole world had to come to an end."

"Then what did you do?"

"Well, I just ran. My trousers weren't settled up yet so they fell around my ankles and I tripped in the snow. Just gettin' up and fallin' and runnin' the best I could until I came to this very spot and saw it. All them people layin' dead in the snow all torn up."

Nolan handed the man his bottle of whiskey and cupped his shoulder with the other hand. "Very good," he said. "I think we've gotten farther than anyone else."

Grady looked at the bottle and took it. He took a hard pull and handed it back to the priest. "What does it all mean?" he said. There was sweat now freezing around his temples and his eyes were white as ice.

"Where I'm from there is a fable, Mr. Grady. Women who wail in the wind to tell that death is near."

"What are they?" said Grady.

"The old folks in my country call them *ban síde*. Banshees, in the King's English."

There were now people standing on the steps of the passenger coach, craning their necks and speaking loudly to each other.

"I think I've said enough," said Grady.

"Aye, and I thank you for it. How far to the town?"

Grady pointed up the road. "Just a half-mile up there. Careful, Father, I've heard it is a strange town."

3. The Tale of the Wendigo

Nolan walked through a world that was hushed and frozen, as if he had died in that place and was now passing through some intermedium to be judged and sorted. The road was thick with tamarack trees, and a sheen of ice held at their branches and crackled into the few golden needles that remained, just a tiny, crystalline melody playing to the calm. He drank from the whiskey bottle every few-hundred yards, and he was comforted by the notion that if he fell dead, at least his stomach would not likely freeze.

A gust ravaged a snowbank at the bend in the road, the powder whitening the air and spilling over him like sand. He now stood at a footbridge that lay across an alabaster creek with its wooden deck nestled into the ice as if the two bodies had settled their quarrel until the coming of spring. Here the air smelled of pine-smoke, and as he crossed the footbridge he followed the scent to a clearing where a few cabins hunkered beneath the trees.

There was a calamitous sound in the distance, and he heard an animal wail and scream. He walked to the sound, beyond the cabins to a road that ran like a white scar through the center of a town. A crowd of people had gathered around a toppled cart, and a mule was cast against the structure, kicking as it lay in the road. When Nolan reached the crowd, the mule had found its footing and was beginning to stand. There was a bald man lying in the snow where the mule had lain and his neck was twisted oddly and a redblack stain grew against the ice. The crowd saw Nolan and uncircled when he joined, so that the people now faced him like an audience.

Nolan looked at the dead man and then at the crowd and he felt something must be said but could not determine what. He made the sign of the cross and pressed his palms together, but they just watched him like he was expected to do something else.

"I'm Father Nolan," he said. "I've come for a few days on railroad business."

"The railroad?" An old woman croaked after a wind-filled pause.

"Yes," said Nolan. "I just came in from the station."

The woman scratched at her throat with her knuckles, and Nolan thought perhaps she could also be an old man.

"Ain't no station. Just a place for the trainfolk to shit in the woods. The railroad's brought us nothin' but tribulations," the old person said.

"I'm sorry to hear that," said Nolan. "I'm looking for boarding. Will there be a place to stay?"

"Ain't no hotel in this town," said another man with curly gray hair. "We ain't accustomed to hostin' visitors." The man spat in the snow and bit into a handful of bread.

"I see," said Nolan. "So there'll be no boarding then?"

"Nope," said the man.

Nolan stared at the ground and then gestured to the dead man.

"Well, where did he sleep, then? Reckon he'll not be returnin' to whichever bed he found last night."

The curly-haired man chewed his bread and the elder continued to scratch, as the townsfolk eyed each other like birds on a lakeshore.

A young woman pressed through the crowd, her hair red as sunrise.

"You can stay with me and my pa," she said. "Just a spot by the cookstove is all."

The priest bowed. "That'll be just fine."

The girl's name was Firinne. She spoke fast as if the words were held under some invisible weight and expelled into the air as a matter of physics. They walked through the town and she acted at times like a bureaucrat, pointing to one house and then another, announcing names and occupations as if she were reciting it all from an official ledger. The town ended abruptly at a tiny frozen stream, and Firinne skated across and continued on. Nolan followed, and soon they neared a cabin with a stone chimney that looked no more than an itinerant trapper's hut, with weasel pelts hooked along the front wall.

Firinne opened the door and held it open.

"Pa's likely napping," she said quietly. "I'll put some wood in the stove and get you something to eat."

Inside, the room was sparse and smelled of soup and dirt. The floor was just a mud-cracked bottom with the skins of many animals laid out as if they were warnings for other animals not to enter. There was an old man sitting on a cot in the corner—a wild-looking man with a white beard and eyes with a strange blueness that made him look blind.

"Pa," said the girl. "Yer awake."

"I ain't dead if that's what yer askin'," said the old man.

"I brought a traveler, a priest. He's workin' for the railroad."

The old man eyed the priest for a long time.

"A priest, eh?" said the man, finally. "Reckon yer literate, then?"

Nolan nodded. "Yes," he said. "They made me take a test to prove it."

"Good. Been too long in the company of simple folks. Dostoyevsky?"

Nolan pursed his lips. "What about him?"

"You've read him? The Russian feller?"

"I'm not supposed to, but I have."

The old man smiled, and it struck Nolan that he had more teeth than was expected from a man of his age living in such a town.

Firinne ladled a bowl of soup and laid a bedroll by the cookstove as she promised. The priest and the old man spoke of many things beyond the Northern plains, of politics and war and occurrences in foreign capitals. His name was Halvorsen, and he spoke of being born into a family of trappers with a peculiar intelligence that had never propelled him in any particular direction but here. He read everything he could, from sales catalogs to philosophy, and spoke highly of the railroad as some conduit of knowledge to satisfy his interests. Soon, the conversation turned to Nolan and the reason for his arrival.

"It's the killings you come to learn about, then," said Halvorsen. He looked to Firinne, who was sitting by the window, reading a book with the cover absent from the binding. "Daughter, bring us some of that hooch from the shelf."

Firinne looked up and stuck a dead leaf in the page and folded the book closed.

"It's bad hooch, pa," she said. "Saw Fleming dead in the snow this morning. I know he's been drinkin' from the same batch."

"Fleming's dead?"

"Yessir. Done got himself crushed under his mule somehow. The priest saw it too."

Nolan nodded, then motioned to his bag beside him. "If it's spirits you want," said Nolan. "I've got a bottle to share. I only ask you don't send a telegram about it."

Halverson smiled and his eyes shined in the light of the cookstove. He took Nolan's bottle, and after the first pull he stood as though somehow filled with a potent magic.

"We weren't the first to settle these parts," he said. "The Algonquin lived here before us and set up this place as a trading outpost. Most of them died off from disease—many white folks too. For a while though, we lived together. Some of them turned to our ways and some of us took to their ways, and if we weren't fightin' each other we were learnin' from each other."

He drank again and passed it to Nolan, who had finished the soup and was now seated on the bedroll.

"And what have the Algonquin to do with it?" said Nolan.

"They had a story they'd tell. A thing that came from the cold of winter—the Wendigo, they called it. A hungry ghost of bones and horns, so thin that if it turned sideways you couldn't even see the durn thing. But that creature would tear a dozen men to pieces just to eat their hearts and livers and it would still be hungry. Sounds like a durn campfire story, but if you lived out here long enough and seen the things I seen, well a man starts to wonder about it."

"You reckon this creature killed all them people on the train?"

"I didn't say so," said Halverson. He took another sip and his eyes grew cold, the bottle just dangling from his hands as though it were about to spill onto the dirt floor. He straightened, and then looked at Nolan with those hard eyes. "But if I was Algonquin I'd look you right in the face and insist it was so."

4. The Third Black River Atrocity

It was sometime after midnight when Firinne shook the priest awake.

"Shush," she said, as Nolan sat up from his bedroll. His eyes were unfocused and far away and there were dreams still pooling in his eyes. "Put yer boots on and come with me."

Nolan looked at the girl. She stood over him like some ragged child attempting a robbery. She kicked the boots in his direction and then went to Halverson and listened at his chest as if she knew some way to evaluate his sleep.

Nolan laced his boots and donned his coat and the pair slipped out of the cabin into the frigid night, surrounded by the steam of their breath.

"You've decided to evict me already?" said Nolan.

Firinne turned and placed a finger over her lips. They stood there in the muted sounds of midnight as the stars burned with an unfelt heat that failed at the dome of the sky. The silence grew, and just as Nolan was to speak again, there was a shriek that carried over the town and echoed through the trees like the lonely wail of an animal dying in the darkness. Then another, and yet another.

"It can't be," said Nolan, under a plume of his own speaking.

"It is," she said. "Follow me."

They hurried through the frozen town where icicles hung from the roofs like the teeth of fabled creatures and they crossed the street where Flemming had lain crushed by his mule. With the sounds still calling in the air they went to the footbridge where the trees shrouded nearly all the light from the sky and they now navigated by the glow of the ice alone.

The tamaracks pulsed with an eerie light, and they could hear shrieks from either side of the trail. As they walked, a lighted form appeared in a clearing before them, whirling and twisting in the air. Firinne stood unmoved as the specter wormed above the trail and then tumbled at them like a bird of prey, shrieking its wild dialect as if it came from a place where all sorrow and fury had also been born.

Nolan kneeled and covered his head as the thing passed, but the girl remained standing with her ear to the wind, listening as it flew overhead in a beam of red light and faded into the tamaracks.

"You aren't frightened easily, are you?" said Nolan, peering from his hands.

Firinne shook her head, and as she did so something else bellowed in the distance; something deep and guttural that was felt more than it was heard. A drift of snow spun from the empty boughs as the sound passed, and Nolan could now feel the pulse of it vibrating in his weighted knee like an electric current.

"That," she said. "I'm afraid of that."

They continued on. The trail emptied at a wide place where the snow had hardened into a crystalline plane and there was now moonlight that fell in a silverblue upon that place, cold and luminous like the passing of light through leaden glass. The train tracks ran along the distance and just beyond was a heap of wood and bone-colored canvass, crushed and strewn over the snow.

Firinne held up a hand. Two horses lay dead against the ground, their throats torn and their heads eyeless as if killed for malice rather than predation. There were footprints in the snow that led into the trees, and it wasn't more than twenty yards before they found the first dead man. He lay on his back with his blonde hair flat against the ice and his eyes frozen at the sky. He had the look of a clerk or a lawyer who had run afoul of some fraudulent scheme. Not far from there a man and a woman lay on their sides, cruelly eviscerated and half-consumed. The faces of the dead pinched in horror.

Nolan crouched between the bodies, just watching as if he expected something from them. He was now holding the dagger loosely with his fingertips as it glinted in the snowlight, and he flicked at the collars of the dead to inspect their wounds.

"I'd rather not spend any more time out here," he said, wiping the dagger on the snow. "I've seen enough."

"No," said Firinne, "I don't reckon you have."

She pointed to a line of tracks in the snow, at once cloven and human. They led away from the kill toward the train tracks with spatters of blood on either side like dark rain. They followed the prints until they vanished and all that could be heard were the sounds of ice crackling along the rails and the lonely howl of something mad and hungry calling from the eaves of the world.

Nolan stood looking in that direction for a moment. Crystals grew at the corners of his eyes and glowed like tiny stars.

"The Wendigo," he said. "This is what your father spoke of?"

Firinne nodded. "Yes," she said. "I've heard it every winter as far as I can remember."

Nolan looked at her and then stared at the carnage beyond the tracks. "Go wake the town," he said finally. "It's not right to leave them all night."

Firinne shook her head. "They won't come with that thing howlin' in the trees."

"They'll come if you tell 'em I've gone after it."

Her eyes hardened and she didn't give a response. She just looked at him in a certain way, and there was something in that look that confirmed what he must do.

Nolan ran along the tracks with his hands balled in his coat for warmth. The sky was now a contradiction of snowfall and moonlight, and the trees echoed with that terrible pulsing sound from the thing in the woods. Along the treeline, Nolan found a handful of flesh cooling in the snow. He stabbed at it with the dagger and held it to the moonlight, but he couldn't discern whether it was of human or animal origin.

He continued on. He crossed a frozen creek upon which a fine layer of snow lay like talcum, and it whirled before him in a white mist as he forged across. At the far side of the bank he found another fresh stain in the powder with what looked like a human heart at its center, cold and dark as any riverstone. The Wendigo howled and chittered in the trees as Nolan stooped to look at the heart, and a gust furled the hem of his jacket. He realized now that he was no longer tracking the Wendigo, but was instead being led by the creature.

He stood silent in the muted snowscape. A branchful of powder tumbled onto the solid creek. A gust whinnied through the skull-sized stones on the embankment. Nolan held the bottle of whiskey and looked at it in the dark for a moment, just listening to the forest congeal and turning the bottle over in his hands. The Wendigo cried again, a long and baleful cry like the sound of perpetual dying.

Nolan climbed the embankment, and when he reached the top, he realized that he had replaced the bottle and was now holding the dagger instead. At this place there was no path, nor indication of east or west; only the feral white land. He walked through a grove of firs and climbed a scarp of blood-streaked granite and saw in the moonlight a frozen lake that unspooled before him as if some celestial cloth had fallen to earth. He neared the lakeshore and found a dark trail atop the ice, as though something had been dragged across the lake. He squinted and made out a figure motionless in the starlight, as if a branchless tree grew from beneath the ice.

Slowly he walked across the lake, along the trail of blood and powder. The figure waited for him as if it had always been waiting, and soon he made out its wretched, boney features. The Wendigo lifted its hollow skull and tilted its moonlit horns, showing the cavities of its eyes as it stared from some hollow place where it somehow considered him and knew him. At its feet was a dismembered corpse, headless and emptied of viscera, and Nolan wondered if the thing had stopped here only for lack of material to mark a trail.

The Wendigo chittered and clacked its jaws, and the sound it made was like that of an insect calling in the dark. It stepped toward him, then planted its cloven hooves and repeated the sound.

"What are you, creature?" shouted Nolan, his dagger held before him like some savage offering.

The thing just looked at the priest as if curiosity could somehow exist in those hollow orbits.

"*What are you?*" It said. Its voice was coarse and flat like something boiling from beneath the ice. Nolan couldn't tell if it was just repeating what he had said, or was countering with a question if its own.

"I am Nolan," he said. "A man."

"*I am Nolan,*" said the Wendigo, and tapped at the deadlooking skin that clung to its chest. The thing scooped the hollow corpse from the ice and held it aloft, then righted it in the air beside Nolan so it nearly stood at equal height. "*A man,*" it said, and clacked its teeth together. It let the corpse fold onto the ice and then kicked it away. The body slid along the lake a few yards before coming to a stop, twisted and half-frozen like forgotten prey.

"We are not the same," said Nolan, backing away from the thing as it advanced upon him. "You are a monster. A murderer. You kill for pleasure."

The Wendigo just looked at Nolan and snorted a cold wind at his face. It uncurled its knife-like claws in the space between them, and then swiped them across Nolan's chest. The breast of his jacket tore away, and the bottle of whiskey tumbled from the gash in the fabric and shattered on the ice. The Wendigo circled its snout in the air, the scent of alcohol rising in the cold.

"*You are a monster,*" it said. It reached for Nolan and gathered his shredded coat in it claws and drew the man close.

Nolan pulled back, but was no match for the beast's strength. Instead, he plunged the dagger into the Wendigo's chest and twisted the blade at the hilt. The Wendigo let go and looked at the dagger buried in its leathery skin.

"*Murderer,*" it roared, and brushed the dagger loose with its bony claws. The blade fell to the ice among the shards of broken glass and the Wendigo lunged at Nolan with its claws open and the armory of its mouth agape in the silverglow of the moonlight. Nolan slipped and fell onto the ice with the monster upon him, tearing at the fabric of his coat. Nolan screamed and beat the thing with his fists, but it only pinned him tighter and soon he felt the frigid air on his bare torso as the Wendigo prepared to eat him alive.

There was a shot from somewhere far-off and the Wendigo lifted its grotesque skull, staring madly at the shoreline. Another shot, and this time it fell back in a spray of bone fragments and covered its head with its claws. Nolan kicked his feet and slid backward on the ice until his head pressed against the subtracted corpse behind him. Voices called out, muted by the cold emptiness of that frozen plane and the Wendigo roared and clawed at the air. Another shot sent it tumbling to the ground where it flailed and tried to right itself again. Nolan rolled to his knees and found the dagger lying on the ice and crawled atop the monster, plunging the steel again and again into its mummy-like skin. The Wendigo rocked its head to the side and its horns sliced across Nolan's face. The priest fell to the side as another shot rang out, and then another.

Nolan rolled to his back and felt hot blood streaming over his face. The voices were closer now, and he could hear his name called out as he saw Cassiopeia tilting over the frozen lake and his skin burned in the sub-zero air.

Firinne appeared above him, tucking a badger pelt over his bare chest. He saw Halverson aiming a rifle at the Wendigo, just shooting and reloading and shooting again.

"You were wrong," said Firinne, dabbing at Nolan's face with a wool rag. "Nobody would come. You're lucky my father ran out of whiskey, or else he wouldn't have come either."

Halverson kept firing at the Wendigo as if he had decided to not return with any unspent shells. Nolan rose to his feet, shivering, as Halvorsen searched his pockets for more ammunition.

"If it's not dead now, friend, it ain't ever gonna get there," said Nolan.

Halverson gave Nolan a side glance and then handed the rifle to Firinne. He lifted a hatchet from a loop in his belt and tossed it from one hand to the other.

"You read any Eastern writings, priest?" Halvorsen said. He didn't look at him while he said it, he just fixed his gaze on the creature, folded upon the ice. The hatchet was still passing between his hands.

Nolan was shivering, clutching the beaver pelt with his arms folded. "Yes, some. Why?"

"They got this idea that everything is just made of components, and once you separate it all, you realize it was all just an illusion from the start. Just something made of smaller things."

Nolan nodded in the dark, guessing that Halvorsen didn't actually want to discuss it. Instead, he watched as the man parceled the Wendigo's extremities with his hatchet and laid them one by one on a denim tarp like firewood. When he was finished, the creature's torso looked small and meaningless, like a house that had burned to ashes and all that remained was a solitary chimney without any purpose. Nolan crouched beside the Wendigo's severed head and tilted the skull in his hands. The sockets of it eyes were black like the bottom of a well, and he stared into them wondering where the bloodlust had gone and how it had ever arisen.

5. The Thing in the Crate

It was still daylight when the train finally clanked and hissed into South Boston Station. Nolan nodded to Firinne and motioned out the window to two men standing on the platform. When the train stopped, they gathered their luggage and approached the awaiting figures.

"You look thin," said the monsignor, with his arms crossed over his stomach. "I don't think the frontier agrees with you." Cooke stood beside him grinning like some voyeur. "Who's the girl?"

"Firinne is her name," said Nolan. "She's come to study at the university."

Firinne bowed at the two men.

"She must be well-connected," said Cooke. "Not many women attending the university here."

"She is," said Nolan, smiling. "She knows you."

Cooke's face hardened as he looked the girl over. "I can't say I know her."

"You do now," said Nolan. "She helped you with a problem of great concern."

"This girl?" Cooke looked has if he were being pranked. "She looks barely old enough to leave the house on her own."

Nolan nodded to Firinne, and she pushed a pine crate draped in a wool blanket toward the two men.

"What is this?" said the monsignor. He leaned away from the crate as he said it.

"A gift," said Firinne. "From me and my father."

The monsignor looked at Cooke and then at Nolan, who paddled his hands in the air as if to speed along the exchange.

Cooke sighed and gave an exasperated look as though he had somewhere else to be. He bent forward and yanked at the blanket covering the crate. It didn't unfurl at first, and appeared to be caught on a high point from the object underneath. Cooke yanked again, harder this time and the blanket slipped off and fell to the ground.

Cooke's jaw went slack, and the monsignor clutched the cross around his neck. They stood for a moment, just watching the thing in the crate, then glanced around the station as if suddenly aware there were others that might also see the thing. Cooke tossed the blanket back over the crate and searched the folds with his eyes as though remembering what each contour meant.

"If this is a ruse," Cooke began.

"It is not," said Nolan, running his finger down the scar on his cheek. "The thing is yours to keep—to dissect and examine as you will. One thing you have to know is that it will click its jaws every forty-five minutes or so. I reckon some kinds of hunger endure beyond destruction."

Cooke was taking another look at the Wendigo skull when the train whistled, and he jolted backwards with a start and stumbled onto his knees.

"Careful, sir," said Firinne. "It bites."

The monsignor was smiling. "We'll make a place for the girl while she studies. Cooke will see that she is enrolled for the spring." He narrowed his eyes at Nolan and studied him for a moment. "And what will become of you, Michael Nolan?"

Nolan kicked the crate with his boot and the thing made a hollow click from beneath the blanket.

"I'll not stay long," he said. The train whistled again and he looked over his shoulder at the steam pooling under the eaves of the station. He pulled the white collar from his frock and folded it into his pocket. "One of these trains heads south. I plan on going that way till my hat floats."

Nolan stepped away from the group with his bag in hand and looked over the bustle of the station. The train pistons pulsed and hummed in the platform like the sound of some creature grumbling from afar, and the whistle blew again its mad howl. He smiled at Firinne as a group of passengers disembarked and moved around him until he had disappeared, as if wholly consumed in a sudden and desperate act of hunger.

C.W. Blackwell was born and raised in Santa Cruz, California where he still lives today with his wife and two children. His passion is to blend poetic narratives with pulp dialogue to create strange and rhythmic genre fiction. He writes mostly dark fiction and weird westerns. You can follow him here:
https://www.facebook.com/cwalkerblackwell/

Noir Comedy
by
Charlotte Frnkel

I could tell she was trouble as soon as she walked into my office.

For a start she wasn't wearing a mask.

I adjusted my own Private Investigator mask and watched her face closely as she explained why she'd come to me—emotions constantly skipping and dancing across the damn thing as she talked. Hell, I thought to myself. How is anyone ever supposed to read a person through all that noise?

But all other evidence was pointing towards her being a Femme Fatale. The expertly painted face, the curvaceous figure, the low neckline. And that sultry voice.

"It's my husband, Wilbur Henderson," she purred. "He was found shot dead this morning over the other side of town. Murdered!"

Mrs. Henderson gave a sob that I didn't buy for a minute.

"The police are investigating naturally, but I want to do all I can for poor Wilbur so…"

She looked at me. Pleadingly? So hard to tell without a mask. I stared back at her.

I have to admit I was intrigued. Maybe she didn't love the husband but she apparently cared enough to pay for a detective of her own. I was pretty much hooked, and then came the clincher.

She leant forwards towards me.

"Won't you please help me?"

The broad was showing enough cleavage to audition as a wet nurse.

And like a babe in arms, I fell for it.

We drove back in my car to her place, where she introduced me to six foot six of muscle, otherwise known as "my handyman, Rupert."

But it wasn't his biceps that caught my attention. I swiftly got Mrs. Henderson to one side.

"Say," I told her. "Your handyman's the murderer..."

She put a hand to her mouth. "No! How can you be sure?"

I jerked my head discreetly in his direction.

"Because he's The Murderer," I said. "He's wearing the Murderer's mask."

Mrs. Henderson shook her head. "How clever of you! I must go and phone the police and tell them there's been a positive identification…"

And she walked behind me to go the telephone, while I indicated through gesture and posture how smug I was feeling about solving the case.

Unfortunately I was so caught up in this, her hitting me over the head with a blunt object kinda took me by surprise.

I came round to find myself staring up into my own mask. As my vision became clearer I recognised the person wearing it.

"Rupert!"

He sauntered away and went to stand beside Mrs. Henderson.

I tried and failed to raise my hands to my own mask. But in truth I didn't need to touch it. I already knew which mask I now had on.

"Up you come, you low-life scum."

I was dragged to my feet by the guy who had been restraining my arms. I turned my head as best I could and saw the mask of The Police Officer.

I opened my mouth to speak—to explain about Rupert and the switch.

But I closed it again. What defence did I really have? I was wearing the Murderer's mask—the part was mine.

I had to accept my fate.

And as I was led away Mrs. Henderson gave me a broad grin and two thumbs-up.

What a woman! Enigmatic to the end.

And so here I sit, waiting for that last walk down the hall to the chair.

You may ask, why don't I just take the mask off and do without entirely?

Well, perhaps sometimes you've just gotta be a man and play the role you've been assigned. And perhaps I'd rather die a somebody than live a nobody.

And perhaps that dame had coated the inside of the mask with gum arabic before slapping it onto my face.

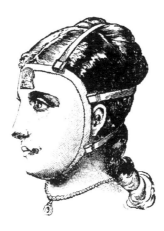

Charlotte Frankel has been writing seriously for some years now—microfiction and humour being her specialities. She lives in the North West of England, and in between all the writing tries to fit in working as a shop assistant.

Glamorous Life of a Sorcery Cop
by
Andrew Johnson

"**A**re you ready for this, Reece?"

"Yes, sir." Holly Reece looked down at the gun on the desk. "I've been waiting months for this moment." Her eyes shifted to the badge next to it, and then to her new captain. "I'm ready."

"Ok. I understand you've been through a lot," the captain said. "But you should know that the Sorcery Division is not like Vice. Or anything else for that matter."

"I understand, Captain Potter."

"No, you don't understand, but you'll find out," the captain said, trying not to laugh. "You'll have your talisman by the end of the day." Reece had barely opened her mouth to ask when another woman entered. A few inches shorter than Reece, she appeared to be Hispanic or mixed race.

"Wanted to see me, sir?" She gave Reece a cursory glance. "Who's the redhead?"

"Wicks, you have a new partner. This is Detective Holly Reece. Reece, Detective Marta Wicks. Show her the ropes, Wicks. How it works in Sorcery."

"Yes, sir." Wicks half smirked as she gave Reece a more thorough look.

Before anyone could say anything else, a desk sergeant ran in. "Sir, we got a report of a body in the park. No immediate cause of death, but they suspect black magic." Despite the seriousness of a body, Reece still wanted to giggle at the mention of "black magic." Potter and Wicks were watching her, though, and Reece managed not to betray her reaction.

"Looks like you two got your first case," Potter said.

Reece leaned against the car and enjoyed the sunlight shining through the trees, throwing splashes of gold and green everywhere. It was a welcome change from the back alleys and general grime of her old precinct. Wicks was less distracted by the scenery. "So, why did they call us?" Reece asked. "And not Homicide?"

"Oh, Homicide will be there. Self-righteous pricks." Wicks grumbled something else Reece could not hear, but got the gist of as they started up the path to where the body had been found.

Reece looked at her wide-eyed. "Uh..."

"You'll find out," Wicks replied. "It's standard procedure to call us whenever there's a mysterious death. Homicide hates us getting involved in 'their' cases, though, and four times out of five we'll get bumped off it."

"Why?"

Wicks finally looked away from the path and stared Reece in the eyes.

"Reece, we have more open cases and fewer arrests than any other division. The other cops look at us like a joke. The magic-using community doesn't like us, doesn't trust us, and doesn't cooperate with us. If you think the gangs have a no-snitching policy, wait till you meet the wizards." Wicks shook her head and kept walking the path.

Reece watched her go and realized that she had not so much been welcomed back to the force after the incident as she had been banished to Sorcery to save the Brass any embarrassment. "You coming, Reece?" Wicks shouted over her shoulder.

The crime scene looked like a typical one, with uniforms milling around. Reece and Wicks flashed their badges and ducked under the yellow tape. Waiting over the body were two men from Homicide. One elbowed the other as Reece and Wicks walked up.

"Hey, Wicks! We was wondering when you would show up," said the guy on the left. He had grey temples and trouble controlling his laughter. "See anything in your crystal ball?"

"What do we have, Riley?" Wicks said to Gray Temples, crouching down to examine the body.

"Male. Late-twenties. No immediate cause of death, but toxicology is working on it. You two may have come all this way for nothing."

As Riley watched Wicks go over the body, his partner stared as Reece. She remembered him from Vice. Soren or something. No, it was Sorenson. "You look familiar," he said.

"Detective Holly Reece." *There, that's out of the way.* Reece watched the light of recognition dawn in Sorenson's eyes. He tapped Riley on the shoulder and whispered into his ear. She could practically hear them both snicker.

Reece tried to ignore them and turned back to Wicks, who was examining a patch of dirt about ten feet away. She picked up a handful and sniffed it.

"He wasn't killed here. This is where they dumped the body." Sorenson tapped his foot next to the body.

"Are you sure about that?" Wicks replied, looking at the handful of dirt in her hand.

"Look, he's in his boxers," Riley said. "And clothes are nowhere to be found. So unless you think he stripped and decided to wander out several miles to the woods in his underwear—"

"Were there any indecent exposure calls? Find any tire tracks?" Wicks said, rising and brushing her hand on her jacket. She took Reece by the arm and led her back to the car. "Call when you need us."

"See you around, Reece!" Riley called after her.

"Worthless pricks," Wicks muttered. "If those idiots just looked around they would see he really was killed there."

"How do you know?"

"Did you see how the ground was dug up there? Our vic stumbled into something he shouldn't. A mandrake field, smelled like."

"Mandrake? The plant?"

Wicks nodded. "Mandrake is one of the best-known aphrodisiacs, among other uses. Big money. And if you're not careful, it kills anyone nearby when it comes out of the ground."

"Then why was he in his boxers?"

"Don't know yet." Wicks shrugged. "Removes any ID."

"So what do we do now?" Reece asked.

"We go see Lelwani."

The hundreds of scents of Lelwani's Apothecary assaulted Reece's nose, but oddly enough it did not smell bad. Shelves full of hundreds of glass jars with powders that Reece could barely pronounce, never mind hope to recognize.

"Lelwani, I need a word with you." Wicks's tone was soft, almost reverential.

A striking black woman came out from the back of the store, casually leaning on a white wooden staff. Despite Reece's training as a cop, Lelwani was more than a little intimidating. She had the body of a model with long dreadlocks that framed her chocolate brown face and piercing green eyes. Reece could not help but feel Lelwani was looking through her. She was grateful when Lelwani turned her gaze back to Wicks.

"*Lachós chibeses*, Wicks. How's my favorite Gypsy?" Reece had expected a Jamaican accent, but was shocked when Lelwani sounded somewhere between Haitian and French.

"*Bonjou*, Lelwani," Wicks replied with a nod of her head. "I need your help. I think we may be onto an illegal mandrake field." Lelwani raised an eyebrow. "A man is dead."

"I am truly sorry." Lelwani shook her head. "I would like to help you, Wicks, but you know I will not reveal my customers. And I know that they would not do such a thing."

"I wouldn't dream of asking you to. Just point me in the right direction. A hint. Anything will help."

"*Yon minit.*" Lelwani made her way to the back again, the sound of her staff tapping on the floor coming out from the darkened room.

"That's it? We ask her nicely?" Reece asked. "She says she won't reveal her customers? We should threaten her with a warrant!" Wicks caught Reece's arm in a vice-grip and dragged her back to an empty corner of the store.

"Did you see that staff she was carrying?" Wicks hissed. "One tap on the ground from that and she can blind you. And if you really piss her off, she could turn you to stone. I've never seen Lelwani fight, but her reputation precedes her. So damn right we ask her nicely!"

Wicks let go and stomped away. They rounded the corner to see Lelwani watching them like a cat. Reece swallowed. *How much had she heard?*

Lelwani raised her chin toward Wicks. "You'll want to talk to Hengest."

"Thank you, Lelwani. Give my best to your husband."

"*Disde yescotría*, Wicks," Lelwani said, as Wicks dragged Reece back to the car.

"So who's Hengest? Do we go meet him now?" Reece asked as they drove away.

"Not yet. I've heard rumors about Hengest," Wicks said. "Kickass wizard. He's supposed to be a little unstable, so before we wander into his front yard, we need to get you all the protection we can."

They walked back into the station. The place was empty as usual, but Reece immediately noticed the smell. "Did we burst a sewer line or something?"

The janitor mopping up the floor stopped and glared at her. "Brown curse."

"Aw, damn!" Wicks sighed. Before Reece could even ask, she offered an explanation. "A brown curse is a petty and really disgusting bit of folk magic. It makes you shit uncontrollably. Not lethal, but really nasty."

Reece made a face.

Wicks nodded her agreement. "Exactly. Someone really pissed off someone else to get *that* thrown at them."

"They're interviewing the poor bastard in the restroom if you want—" the janitor said.

Wicks held up her hand. "No. No, that's all right. Glad it's not my case." She flashed a grin at Reece. "The glamorous life of a Sorcery cop."

"Wicks! Reece!" Captain Potter shouted from the office. Reece fell into step behind Wicks, and closed the door behind her, happy to be out of there. Potter sat at his desk, burning some kind of incense. Standing at the desk behind him was a scruffy-looking man in his late fifties with long hair and a greying beard. He wore an old army trenchcoat and looked like a drifter. Only the staff he carried gave any clue to his true identity.

"Marius." Wicks smiled, stepping up to hug him.

"Marta," he said, patting her on the back.

"Do I get to learn some magic now?" Reece asked. Wicks chuckled to herself, while the Captain Potter guffawed. The wizard,

Marius looked somewhat uncomfortable.

"Any wizard that taught a cop any spell would be dead within a day," he said. "We don't share our secrets with cops." The seriousness in his voice made Reece take a step back.

"Reece, this is Marius. He's a consultant for various Sorcery cases."

"Are you OK to be here? If your kind doesn't exactly like us and retaliations can be—" Reece began.

"She's new," Wicks said with a knowing roll of her eyes.

"I'll be OK. In fact, you're why I'm here." Marius reached into his pocket and pulled out an object that he then pressed into Reece's hand. She turned it over and looked at it. Slightly larger than her police badge, it was some creamy-white wood with a piece of metal set in the middle. Circling it was three lines of text, but not in any language Reece could hope to read. There was a cord on the back, that looked like ordinary nylon.

"Thanks, but what is it?"

"A talisman. Just for you. Think of it like a second badge," Marius said. "Holly and iron for your protection."

"Oh, like my name." Reece turned the thing over and over in her hand.

"Don't spread *that* around," Marius warned.

"What, my name? Why?"

"If some of the others get a hold of your name, they can throw some nasty spells your way. And keep that close. You'll need it." Wicks pulled her own talisman out from underneath her shirt. It looked similar to Reece's but the wood was different, darker, denser.

"Especially where we're going," Wicks muttered.

Captain Potter's eyebrow went up. "You got a lead?"

"Hengest." Wicks scowled.

"Hengest is not to be trifled with. But so far as we know, he's never walked the dark path." Marius tapped his fingers on the desk

"We just heard he may know something," Reece said.

"Do you want me to go along?" Marius asked. "Although, it could make things worse."

Before Wicks could reply, the phone on Potter's desk went off. He snatched it up and listened for a few seconds. "Uh-huh. Yeah. I'll send them right over." Hanging up, he looked directly at Wicks. "Hengest can wait. Forensics has results on your John Doe."

"Great, Homicide will be there. I would rather have dealt with

Hengest," Wicks grumbled as they walked out of the office.

The instant they stepped into the lab, Reece saw Sorenson was already waiting there. Sorenson rolled his eyes and blurted out, "Great, I get them both? Why?"

"They're here because this concerns all of you. As well as Narcotics." The medical examiner did not even look up, but kept flipping through her chart.

"I'm here."

Reece turned at the sound of the familiar voice, and saw a stoic Asian woman come walking in.

"Sylvia Chang," Reece said, trying to keep the contempt out of her voice. She failed.

"Holly," Chang said without so much as the hint of a smile. "It's good to see you again." She turned away from Reece and back to the medical examiner. "What do you have, Kendra?"

"I found some soil samples under his fingernails. They match the soil in the area."

"So he was killed there," Sorenson said. He seemed mystified by the idea.

"Yeppers," Kendra said.

"What about cause of death?" Chang asked.

"No immediately obvious cause of death. But I'll have to run more tests. I did find some blood in the inner ear and—"

"Mandrake. When you pull it out of the ground, it screams. Breaks the eardrums first, then death follows within moments," Wicks said matter-of-factly.

"I did find traces of Mandragora on his hands." Kendra nodded. Chang stepped up to the middle of the group.

"OK. We're all going to have to work together on this for now, so let's try to step on as few toes as possible. Sorenson, you and Riley keep up your investigation. Any clues to our vic's identity?" Reece noted Chang's unspoken propensity for taking point on every investigation she worked. At least some things never changed.

"We have some leads," Sorenson said.

"Wicks, Reece. What about you?"

"We're looking into who may have owned the mandrake field."

"I'll need that info as soon as you get it. It will be a Narcotics matter."

"With all due respect—" Wicks said through clenched teeth.

Chang cut her off. "Illegally grown mandrake falls under Narcotics jurisdiction. If you can find it's being used for magical purposes, then it becomes a matter for Sorcery." Chang stared Wicks down for a few moments waiting for her to protest. When Wicks remained silent, Chang turned to everyone else. "OK people, let's get to work."

Sorenson snickered as he walked out. Wicks stormed out after him and before Reece could follow, Chang stopped her.

"Holly. Are you up for this?" Reece took a breath and turned to face her.

"What do you mean?" Reece knew exactly what she meant, but she was going to make Chang say it.

"You went undercover for a month and fell off the face of the earth."

"I've recovered."

"But you still don't remember what happened."

"It'll come back."

"That assignment cost over eight million—"

"I can handle this, Sylvia. Don't you worry about me." Reece turned and stormed out. There was nothing she had not heard a hundred times before. And none of it made any difference.

Passing Wicks on the way out, she said, "Are we talking to Hengest or what?"

"You're in no shape to do that now," Wicks said. "And neither am I. You want to be at the top of your game when confronting a wizard like Hengest. We'll start fresh tomorrow morning."

"But..."

"Why be in a hurry when that bitch Chang is just going to waltz in and steal it from us?"

She had a point. "Fine. It's gotta be close to five anyway. You want to get a beer or something?"

"Sure. Why not?" Wicks said. "Rourke's Pub?"

"Sounds good."

Despite Rourke's being a cop bar, Reece and Wicks hardly got any welcome from the off-duty police there. The place was not packed, and most were focused on the game on the TV over the bar. Reece did not see anyone she knew, but judging by the looks, they seemed to know her. Wicks got just as cold a welcome, but it did not seem to bother her.

"Over there. They call it the Sorcery section." Wicks pointed to a dimly lit table in the corner. "Reserved just for us, isn't that nice?"

Her sarcasm didn't go unnoticed. Reece grinned and Wicks signaled the bartender. "Two of the usual. You want anything else, Reece?"

Reece shook her head and made her way to the table. Wicks joined her a few moments later with two foaming mugs of beer. She plopped down, took a deep gulp and looked to Reece.

"So, how was your first day?"

"It's been…interesting," she said. "I have yet to meet a wizard who looks like a wizard. They mostly look like any of the bums I met in Vice."

"Things in Sorcery are never straightforward," Wicks said, taking another swig.

"Yeah." They sat in silence for a moment, until Wicks set her beer down.

"If you don't mind me asking, what did Chang want to talk to about?"

"My previous assignment in Vice," Reece said. "We were trying to break up a prostitution ring. I was undercover as a working girl. We were getting close. Then one night, me and three other girls got into a black van and that's the last thing I remember until I woke up in an empty warehouse in Miami with four different girls a month later."

"Wow. A whole month and nothing at all?" Wicks said, reaching for the beer mug again.

Reece shook her head. "Tried therapy and hypnosis, but nothing's come back."

"Wow. That's a hell of a thing." Wicks downed the last of her beer, setting the empty mug at the end of the table.

"Yeah." At first, Reece had tried to remember, but these last few months, she'd spent trying to forget the whole debacle. What had happened during that month? The not knowing continued to haunt her, no matter how much she tried to push forward with her life, the Miami incident always seemed to be lurking in the shadows. She downed the rest of her beer with two gulps. "Another?"

"Definitely." Wicks waved to the bartender.

Wicks and Reece drove down the rural road in silence. It had been so long since she had been out to the country, Reece could not help but feel re-invigorated by the fresh air.

"So how long have you been in Sorcery, Wicks?" she asked, trying to fill the silence.

"Three and a half years now."

"Why did you choose this beat?"

Wicks snorted. "No one chooses Sorcery. At least no sane person should. It's an exercise in frustration." She chuckled to herself, a humorless laugh followed by a sigh. "Shit. I was community outreach officer on the Gypsy Task Force but got assigned here after an argument with Captain Sorenson."

"Captain?" Reece asked.

"Detective Sorenson's uncle, I think." Wicks slowed the vehicle and turned down an old unpaved road on her right. As Reece looked at the trees around her, she realized just how far out in the middle of nowhere they were.

They stopped in a clearing and Wicks killed the engine. The only sign of habitation was the abandoned school bus retrofitted into a shanty about a hundred yards away.

Before they got out of the car, Wicks put a hand on Reece's arm. "Be very careful and follow my lead," she whispered.

They walked up to the door of the bus and Wicks started pounding. "Hengest! Open up. This is the police! Open the door. We want to ask you some questions." There was no response.

"What now?" Reece asked. "We kick the door in?"

"I wouldn't do that if I were you," came a deep male voice. The door flew open and Reece jumped back. Standing in the doorway was a tall man with long dark hair with a touch of gray at his temples. His long beard was also streaked with gray, and sported a few ragged braids. In his right hand was a beautifully carved staff, and finally Reece felt as if she was in the presence of a wizard. His faded poncho, jeans, and muddy boots, however, immediately shattered that impression.

"Wouldn't do what?" Reece asked, trying to sound as nonchalant as possible.

"With my wards, you'd break your foot long before the door gives." Hengest looked Reece over. Then he turned to Wicks. "And Wicks knows I'm out of your jurisdiction."

"I can call the county sheriff," Wicks replied with a nonchalant shrug.

"I would prefer to be cordial," Hengest said. "Lelwani said you might show up. What is it you want?"

"We just want to ask about illegal mandrake fields in city parks."

"They ain't mine," Hengest replied.

"We weren't saying they were. But there was a man killed there."

"Then hire yourself a good necromancer," Hengest said.

"I'm going to pretend you didn't say that," Wicks said. "You know damned well necromancy is illegal."

Hengest sighed. "So what *do* you want, Wicks?"

"Whether you know anyone running an illegal growing operation in the park."

"I'm no herbalist," he said, tapping his staff.

"Please stop avoiding the question," Reece said before she realized it. Wicks looked even more surprised than Hengest.

"The newbie speaks." He looked amused. He stood toe to toe with Reece and was still a good half-head taller. He reached out as if to stroke her hair, only stopped, as if he was feeling the air around her. "Huh, you have no idea what you stepped into, do you, newbie?"

"She didn't mean anything by it," Wicks said. It burned Reece to see a police officer apologize to a suspect. Especially on her behalf.

"Listen carefully," Hengest said. "Mandrake is big business. It could have been anyone. Non-magical folks grow it for cash, like marijuana. Were there glamours over the field?"

"Probably," Wicks said. "But they were broken by the time we got there." Hengest only nodded his head, like he was taking in all the information. But in her head, Reece could hear his voice, as clear as day: *I can give you real answers, Ms. Reece. Come back tonight. Come alone.*

"I can't tell you anything I don't know." Hengest frowned. "But if I hear of something, I'll be sure to let you know right away."

"Sure, uh-huh. Thanks for nothing. We'll be in touch." Wicks jerked her head back toward the car and Hengest withdrew into his school bus.

As they began the drive back to the city, Reece hadn't yet decided if what she'd heard was real. Wicks's cellphone rang.

"Wicks," she said. "Uh-huh. OK. Got it." She clicked it off and dropped it into the empty cupholder. "Whaddya know. Turns out Sorenson and Riley IDed our vic. They are good for something after all. Name was John Nicholas. An IT guy who disappeared from lunch break about two days ago. And here we are with nothing."

"Maybe not," Reece said, and she told her about Hengest's not-so-secret message.

"Reece. Holly." Wicks's tone was measured, as if she was trying to keep her emotions in check. "This is dangerous shit."

"I know," Reece said.

"No," Wicks said. "You don't have a clue."

They returned to the precinct, where every window was still wide open. Reece noticed several cops wheeling in a life-size statue of a woman on a handcart. "Evidence?" Reece asked.

"Victim."

"Someone turned her to stone?" Reece was wide-eyed. The cop nodded, as his compatriots gently set the statue on the floor.

"A wizard of no mean skill." He patted the statue on the shoulder. "Look at that, turned her to solid granite. I've seen people turned to marble or even quartz. Hell, once I even saw a guy turned to basalt. But granite? That takes some skill to get right."

"What will you…do with her?" Reece asked.

"The captain's meetin' with a guy who might be able to turn her back. If not, we'll put her out front and keep the pigeons off of her." He chuckled to himself and Reece looked to Wicks for guidance. Wicks, for her part seemed amused by the whole scene.

"What about her family?"

"C'mon, Reece." Wicks dragged Reece into Captain Potter's office.

The captain and Marius were already having an animated conversation. "But you should remember the Sorcerer's saying, Captain: For the last thousand years, when a wizard was burned at the stake, it was a cop holding the torch. We handle our own problems and keep cops out of our affairs."

"Sir?" Wicks knocked on the already-open door. Whatever conversation he and Potter were having stopped in its tracks.

"What is this about, Wicks?" Potter asked. Wicks went about explaining their encounter with Hengest—including his words directly to Reece. Both Potter and Marius listened with interest.

"I think we should go for it," Wicks said. "If Reece can get Hengest to talk…"

"Are you aware of her history?" Captain Potter asked pointedly.

Reece had been expecting this to come up. "Sir, with all due respect, this is not an undercover assignment. I'm just meeting a potential witness."

"Reece," Potter said. "You don't know what you're in for."

Marius grunted agreement. "He's right. Hengest isn't malevolent, but there could be unforeseen dangers. For him to be able to talk to you like that… It means he found a way around your talisman. It should have kept malign influences away from you."

Reece mulled this over. "Malign. So maybe he didn't want to hurt me. I really think it would be wise to go back and see what he has to say. This seems like something worth following up."

"Would you go with her?" Potter asked Marius.

"That would not go well," Marius said.

"Why not?" Reece demanded.

Marius shook his head. "Hengest is a little paranoid and a bit of a conspiracy theorist. My presence could make things…difficult."

"I could wear a wire or—" Reece offered.

Marius cut her off. "He's probably got enough wards on his place that no wire would record."

"But this could be the break we need," Reece said. Something in the back of Reece's mind reminded her that that last time she volunteered for an assignment, she lost a month of her life.

Captain Potter took a deep breath as if to say something, then clenched his teeth and let it all out through his nose. After a moment, he began again. "If you think you're up to this… But I don't blame you if you don't."

"I'm not afraid, sir." Reece leaned over the captain's desk to look him in the eye. "I can do this."

"You really sure you want to do this?"

They sat in the car at the end of the country road. In the rapidly fading twilight, Reece could just make out the retrofitted bus that Hengest called home.

"Yeah…" Reece realized she was trying to convince herself as much as she was Wicks.

"Hey, remember, we're just talking to a witness," Wicks said. "On our own time. Not official. Hengest has nothing to fear."

Wicks sounded about as sure of herself as Reece did.

"Then let's do this," Reece said, getting out of the car. She told herself that this was no different than any other time she went on an assignment. An owl hooted in the distance and Reece corrected herself: This was definitely creepier.

Just outside the door, she raised her hand to knock but the door opened on its own.

"Come in, Reece," Hengest said from inside. Reece walked in and found the warmth somewhat comforting. Warmer than an old school bus should have been.

"Hengest?"

"Leave your gun and talisman on the table," Hengest said.

"I'd rather hang onto them," she replied.

"Fine, just leave the talisman then. It will disrupt what needs doing."

Reece placed the wood and iron badge on the table and stepped away.

"Now, the questions." Hengest waved her over and indicated that she should sit. "I can feel them welling up inside you."

"Why are you helping me?"

"I think we have something in common."

"Really? And that would be…?"

"Most mandrakers are non-magical folk. Usually looking for a quick buck," Hengest poured a cup of steaming tea. He offered her some but she declined with a shake of her head. He dropped a lump of sugar into his own mug and stirred. "The fact that you've not found them tells me that they do not want to be found. And have the power not to be found. Maybe someone with the power to erase memories."

That had Reece's attention. "Is that possible? Erasing memories?"

"Absolutely," Hengest said. "Like making an undercover cop forget her assignment, perhaps?"

She jerked to attention. "What do you know about that?"

Hengest shrugged. "I've heard rumors, but nothing concrete. But you should ask the more important question first."

"Fine," Reece said through clenched teeth. Clearly Hengest had no trouble reading her. "Can those memories be restored?"

"That depends on how they were taken in the first place, and the skill level of the taker. But you want to know about how this relates to your current case."

"Do you know who John Nicholas is?"

"I've heard his name mentioned," Hengest said. "And I heard he spent a lot of time in Miami."

Reece was getting sick of all the beating around the bush. "Why don't you just tell me!" Her voice was raised more than she meant it to be.

"Because I don't know enough yet," Hengest said, even more calmly than he'd been before. "Which brings us to someone who can give us some answers. Hob, get over here."

Out of nowhere appeared another man. Shorter than either Hengest or Reece, he was bald with a long braided goatee that looked like a rat's tail. He wore a threadbare black trenchcoat and carried a dark staff, that contrasted markedly with his pale white skin. He reminded Reece of some of the scummier pimps she had encountered.

"You said to come alone," Reece said.

"I said *you* should come alone. Hob is a necromancer who owes me a favor," Hengest said. Reece froze. A line was being crossed here and she knew it. She should stand up and leave now. Just get out and forget this whole thing ever happened. After several seconds, she realized she still hadn't moved.

"What can I do for you, Hengest?" the small man asked, digging for some mystery in the pockets of his trenchcoat.

"Reece here has a body and no leads on who killed him."

"You a cop?" Hob asked, eyeing her. He turned back to Hengest. "I don't work with no cops!"

"Sit down, Hob," Hengest growled. Hob stood his ground for a few more seconds before his face broke and his fear showed. He sat down on the couch and pulled out some cigarette papers and tobacco.

"Now," Hengest said. "We all have the same question: who killed your guy in the mandrake field. An answer you can provide for us, Hob."

"Fine," Hob grumbled, rolling his cigarette into a cylinder and licking the ends of the paper to seal it. Satisfied, he slipped the unlit cigarette behind his ear. "But I don't want no shit from the cops about this."

Hob started fishing around in his pockets again, until he pulled out a dead bird, dropping it on the table in front of them. Reece leaned in to get a better look at it. A little sparrow, looked like it had been crushed to death. She looked back up at Hob. "Did you…?"

"Always a price, babe." He looked at his staff, then back to Reece. "What's the dude's name?" Reece took a deep breath, trying to focus on the case at hand.

"John Nicholas." Hob stood up and held his staff directly in front of himself, like some dramatic movie wizard pose. He began chanting in a sibilant-heavy language Reece had never heard before, recognizing only the dead man's name and her own.

Whatever Hob did, it was working. The dead bird burst into a flame with no warmth. In fact, there was a pronounced drop in temperature. Reece shivered as a blue haze formed around the end of Hob's staff. It resolved itself into a human form that Reece recognized as her victim, John Nicholas. He looked around, none too happy to be there, then locked his eyes on Reece.

"Hhhello, Hhholly," he said. His voice was weird. Choppy. Kind of like he was talking through the spinning blades of a fan.

"You know me?"

"Oh, yes." He smiled. He may have had a nice smile once, but either the distortion from the spell, or Nicholas's mood twisted it into something sinister. "I feel your questions, Holly. You can ask me three."

"Who killed you?" Reece asked.

"Lock Covey. Careful with him; he's got some bulletproof magic. This is what you wanted to know? All those questions going through that pretty little head of yours and you want to know who killed *me*?" Nicholas said, laughing.

"I have plenty of questions about the operation you were involved in," Hengest said.

"Sorry, Hengest," Nicholas said. "I wasn't brought here to answer *your* questions."

Reece caught Hengest glowering at Hob, but she turned her attention back to Nicholas's ghost. She knew she should ask about the case, but this was too much for her to resist.

"What happened to me in Miami?" Reece asked.

"Your body was borrowed," Nicholas said.

"Borrowed? How? Why?" Reece asked. "Tell me that."

Nicholas smiled that evil smile again and wagged his blue glowing finger at her. "Questions asked. Questions answered."

"You said I get three questions!"

"And you asked them. Did I know you? Yes. Who killed me? Lock Covey. And what happened to you in Miami? Someone else wore your bones for a while." The ghost turned to Hob. "Now send me on my way, wizard."

Hob puffed out his chest a little in indignation, but with a glare from the ghost, he just spoke his hissing language again. Only a few words this time, and Nicholas vanished like a puff of smoke. The body of the bird had burned down to mostly ash. Hob snatched his cigarette from behind his ear and held it over the smoldering remains.

"Don't smoke that thing in here," Hengest said. "And clean that up." The necromancer shrugged, stuck the cigarette behind his ear and scooped the ash into his pocket.

"Happy?"

Hengest glared at the necromancer. "Now, Hob…Nicholas will leave her alone?"

"Yeah. He's dead and got other shit to do. So do I," Hob said, starting toward the door. He turned back around. "Hengest, next time you gotta deal with the cops, leave me out of it. We're even."

"Don't fret, Hob. You won't be darkening my door again."

Reece couldn't decide if that was a prediction or a threat.

Hengest glared at the necromancer until the door closed and he turned back to Reece. "I hope you got something good out of that."

"I hope so too." Reece grabbed her talisman off the table and walked out the door. Once she was out in the night air, she took a deep breath. This whole experience made her nauseous. She looked up at the stars, as if they could present her with answers. Someone had "borrowed" her body. Her skin crawled at the thought. "How does shit like that happen?" she asked no one. What had they done with her body while they had it? Reece shuddered at the possibilities.

"No," Reece told herself. "I can deal with this." All the months of therapy and work to get back her life, she would not lose it by unraveling now.

"Reece?" Wicks said, getting out of the car. "Did you get anything? Are you all right?"

"I'm fine. We got a name. Let's go!" Reece spoke rapidly, drawing a look from Wicks.

"An anonymous tip?" Captain Potter said, leaning back in his chair, arms crossed over his chest as he glared at Wicks and then Reece. The early morning sun streamed in through his window making him look more regal than any police captain ought to be.

"Turns out Hengest knew someone who wanted to talk," Wicks said. "But not come forward."

"And this anonymous source that gave you this info about your case just happened to be there at the time?" Potter asked.

Reece nodded. "Hengest brought him in."

"Can we trust him?"

"Yes," Reece said.

Potter looked to Wicks who gave a nod.

"OK. All right," Potter said, with a tired sigh. "What was the name you got?"

"Lock Covey," Reece answered.

Wicks slapped down a mugshot on the desk. The man in the picture commanded attention. He had angry eyes enhanced by a vicious scar framing the left one.

"Zachary 'Lock' Covey," Wicks recited. "Quite the man about town. Twice arrested for illegal mandrake operations, as well as attempted necromancy, bunch of assaults, including two with a deadly weapon and he was believed connected to a prostitution ring."

"Prostitution?" Reece asked, but no one seemed to be listening. Was he involved in her former assignment?

Potter picked up his phone. "All right. Let's contact Sorenson and Chang and get moving on this thing."

Wicks and Reece pulled up next to several police cars about a block from Covey's house. The streets had been cleared except for a black woman walking down the street away from everything. It struck Reece as odd. This woman was very nonchalant about the cops gathering around her. She had a bit of a limp, which Reece could have sworn was feigned. And then suddenly it struck Reece that the cane the woman was leaning on was more staff than walking stick. Reece leaned forward in her seat, trying to see her face hidden behind the long dreadlocks. When the woman, perhaps sensing she was being watched, looked up, Reece found herself staring at

Lelwani. Lelwani simply offered a wink.

"C'mon, Reece! Hurry up!" Wicks shouted from ahead.

"I think I just saw…" Reece stopped in her tracks to see Marius standing on the sidewalk in front of them.

"What are you doing here?" Wicks asked.

"I'm your backup. In case Lock Covey tries some kind of magical attack." With that, Marius grinned at Reece, wiggled his eyebrows, took a step back, cast his glamour, and vanished into the crowd.

Reece and Wicks continued on their way, through the center of the street, squad cars flashing their lights on all sides. They found Chang in the thick of it, shouting out orders, her mirrored sunglasses making her look even more of a stone-cold bitch than normal.

Wicks got her attention. "Where's Sorenson and Riley?"

"They're taking point on this. We're here to secure any possible escape routes."

"What do you need us to do?" Reece asked.

"Get out," Chang said without missing a beat. "This is between Narcotics and Homicide now."

"What?" Wicks's hackles were raised. "This is our case too!"

"Nicholas was killed by the mandrake, not by sorcery."

"Yes, but—" Reece started.

"So you have no reason to be here," Chang said. "And quite frankly, you both are in the way."

Reece looked at Wicks and thought she would explode. It was time to get her out of here. Reece quickly took her by the arm and led her away.

"This isn't over, Chang!" Wicks shouted over her shoulder. "I want to bust up that pretty little face of hers! Did you see the sneer on her lips?"

"That would only get you fired," Reece said, hoping they were out of earshot.

Back at the car, Reece half-hoisted, half-shoved Wicks into the passenger seat.

"It's my car, Reece!" Wicks objected.

"You're in no mood to drive," Reece said as she started the car up. She pulled out onto the street and looked at Wicks, expecting the blast of rage to come any minute. After a few minutes, however, Wicks just dropped her head into her hands.

"Again," she muttered. "Another case we've been thrown off of. All because having Sorcery in it would embarrass the department. Sorcery has been a part of police departments since the witchcraft laws of Henry VIII, but in this modern world..."

"It's gonna be all right, Marta." Reece patted her partner on the shoulder. She had seen Wicks angry, but now she just looked kind of tired. Is this what Sorcery does to a person? *And I had thought Vice was corrosive to the soul*, she thought to herself.

"Reece. Holly. This is your first case in Sorcery, but it won't be your last. And you will get sick of other departments horning in on our cases, yanking them away."

"They can't do that all the time and—"

"The brass will support the Sorensons and the Changs on the force because they don't want the shame of any more unsolved Sorcery cases hanging over their heads." Wicks shook her head. "And honestly, I think Sorcery scares them. All that power out there, power that their badges and guns can't control."

"C'mon." Reece pulled into the parking lot of Rourke's "Let's get a beer. Or something stronger."

"Why the hell not," Wicks muttered. "I wish I had your confidence, Reece."

"Listen, according to Hengest's source, considering what Nicholas and Covey were into, Sorcery may well be called in again. Those two might even have been involved with what went down in Miami. Covey has some sort of bulletproof spell on him. They'll take him alive, and then we get our crack at him."

"Miami? So they possibly had something to do with your lost month?" Wicks asked.

Reece nodded.

"Aw damn." Wicks threw an arm over Reece's shoulder and they walked into the bar and made their way to the Sorcery table.

After Reece ordered the usual with a couple shots of whiskey on the side, a bearded policeman sat down at the table with them. She jumped when she realized the cop was none other than Hengest. "What the hell are you doing impersonating a police officer?"

"I'm not," Hengest said. "You just can't see through my glamour like Wicks can." Reece looked to her partner who nodded.

"Why are you here, Hengest?" Wicks asked.

"Just letting you know that things did not go down like you planned."

"Yeah, we got thrown off—"

"No, not that." Hengest jerked his thumb at the TV above the bar. The perky blonde reporter on the screen was standing in the area around Covey's place.

"We are coming live from Fourth Street where just moments ago, police were in a standoff with an armed suspect." The camera panned to the right to reveal Sorenson. "Detective Sorenson, can you tell us what happened?"

"Yes, Amanda. We were attempting to arrest a suspect. When we identified ourselves to him, he opened fire on us. We returned fire and the suspect was hit and killed instantly."

The reporter asked Sorenson a few more questions, but Reece was no longer listening. "Killed?" She looked at Hengest, who was already getting up. "How? I thought he was supposed to be bulletproof."

"Other forces were at work. I disagreed with this plan, but it was how things went down. I am sorry you didn't get your answers," Hengest said.

"You—" Reece started.

"This wasn't my decision. But we handle our own troublemakers." Hengest spread his hands out apologetically. "I thought you deserved to know."

"Reece..." Wicks started.

"No! We were supposed to arrest him and so we could find his connections to the Miami prostitution ring and—"

Reece. Hengest was in her head again. *Powers beyond us both chose to allow Covey to die. Our community takes care of our own problems. Just know this is far from over, and if you're patient, you will still get your answers. I'll see to that. I like you, Reece, even if you are a cop.* "I'll be in touch." With that, Hengest turned and walked out the door.

"Reece," Wicks said again. Reece pounded the table a few times and struggled to hold back the tears. She felt Wicks's hand on her shoulder. "Welcome to Sorcery, Reece. There are no happy endings here."

Andrew Johnson was born in Lancaster County, Pennsylvania and currently lives in northern Arizona. To date, his fiction has been published in magazines like *Tales of the Talesman* and *Nebula Rift*. In addition to writing, he is also an avid photographer and a woodcarver.

Insomnia
by
Stephen R. Smith

Thirty-two years and a detective for twenty-one of those. He'd lost count of the number of homicides. John Barrick wished he'd known how good he'd had it as a beat cop.

John opened the back door of his cruiser. Reaching in, he grabbed his prisoner's hands by the zip tie binding them behind his back and dragged him roughly out onto the ground. The car's suspension wheezed at the change in load, re-leveling itself.

There was no going back now.

Barrick pulled the limp figure's head back by the hair and snapped a sim cap under his shattered nose.

"Wake up, Stanton." He shook him, pushing the cap into the man's nostrils until he recoiled from the smell, wake up.

Stanton coughed and sputtered, hands straining against the binding and head twisting behind the wide tape covering his eyes. He struggled and managed to get his feet underneath his body and propelled himself upright.

"This doesn't smell like the cells." His speech slow and calm, "I want my legal representative."

Barrick unclipped the heavy gun he'd hung on his belt, and prodded the unsteady man in the back with it. Stanton moved hesitantly away from the prodding, puzzled at the whining sound that followed each jab in the spine.

"I'm tired of catching you, Stanton." John's body ached with fatigue as he pulled the prisoner up short before a half-meter square opening in the ground. "I keep putting you in the box, and you keep coming out and doing the same shit time and again."

Stanton grinned, broken teeth bloody behind cracked lips. "That's the beauty of virtual. I can do twenty years of that standing on my head, and when my time's up, you're just a little older and none the wiser. Twenty years in a bit box don't mean shit to me out here. It's just the economics of the new justice system. Don't beat yourself up over it."

Barrick had seen Stanton convicted seven times since he'd been on the force, each with a twenty-year term in virtual lockup; fully immersive confinement with the realtime clock turned way down. The prisoners rode out the whole sentence, but the taxpayers got to save the expense of a full-term crate in a big house somewhere with all the amenities. Economical. Mostly effective, except for with the Stantons of the world.

Barrick clipped the gun back on his belt, and gripping the other man's shoulders, propelled him forward until one foot hovered over open air. He kicked the other foot out violently from under him and stepped back as Stanton dropped ten feet down into the darkness.

"What's this, pre-v isolation?" The voice was still calm above the sound of him pushing himself upright again in the darkness. "That's against protocol. When my lawyer hears..."

The rest of his words were muffled as Barrick wrestled the heavy wooden lid into place over the hole. Unclipping the heavy framing nailer, he leaned into it, listening to the whine as the igniter primed and enjoying the satisfying pop as it discharged steel framing spikes through the lid and into the crate below.

Once the clip was emptied, Barrick wiped down and tossed the nail gun on top of the crate before filling in what was left of the hole and spreading the remaining dirt.

As his cruiser climbed the gravel road back to the highway, Barrick eyed the towering paving machines at rest behind him. In the morning, they would lay down a forty-meter wide stripe of concrete and asphalt, locking the door on Henry Thomas Stanton for the very last time.

While they worked, for the first time in thirty-two years, John Barrick knew he'd be asleep.

Stephen Smith realized early in life that his path was going to be forever engaged in the business of the future. From creating in code, to imagining possible tomorrows in prose, the future is never far away. The founder of a successful consulting and software development company, and an avid programmer and technophile, Stephen is equally fluent in the language of men, and that of machines. In his spare time, Stephen speaks of himself in the third person, and maintains 365tomorrows.com, featuring a new piece of flash fiction daily, on the wire since 2005.

Social Situations
by
Kimber Cam♀cho

Kenth sat at the table out front of the Terran-style café in one of the seedier social districts of New London, being "even more inconspicuous than usual, Kenth" as Rillam had drawled before fruffling his blue-streaked dark curls, turning up the collar on his dramatically anachronistic blue and black jacket, and pasting a cold, dark scowl upon his striking face. He'd then turned away to saunter over to a mixed group of beings gathered near a mobile food stall, taking on an entirely different manner and gait between one step and the next, giving absolutely no sign that he was in any way affiliated with the ordinary looking man he was leaving behind at the café table. The usual.

Granted, even though it had only taken less than a quarter cycle—three Terran months—to *become* the usual, Kenth would have been lying if he said he didn't like being in the eccentric orbit of the brilliantly unusual person that was Rillam Cavish, Freelance Investigator (*never* to be confused with a "private detective"). Sometimes, Kenth wondered precisely how eccentric his orbit was, but then again, he was a Med-Tech, not an astrophysicist.

The precise words "Freelance Investigator and Consultant" had been imprinted on the card Rillam had given him when they first met aboard the transport ship *Aldrin* heading for the Rim Colonies, and it had provided fodder for conversation when Kenth's brain had stalled out in shock at the tall, then auburn-haired, stranger rattling out a string of suppositions about Kenth only minutes after they'd been introduced. Very nearly all of them dead-on, too.

Less than three days later, Kenth had been embroiled in an—apparently—freelance murder investigation and soon thereafter had saved his new, slightly mad friend's life, helped bag the killer, and ended up with his portion of their shared cabin on the ship refunded to him as a reward. By the time they reached the Rim Colonies, Kenth had completely changed his mind about joining his cousins at their place in one of the older established colony outposts. Sure, the outpost needed more medically trained people, as well as a slew of other skillsets, but how could that compare to the world that had opened up for him upon meeting Rillam Cavish? How could he ignore the opportunity to feel like a useful, dynamic individual instead of an invalided-out ex-marine? A formerly up-and-coming front-line med-tech who could no longer trust the steadiness of his dominant hand, let alone a gammy leg that occasionally dumped him on his arse with almost no warning? The answers to these questions, at least to Kenth, were obvious.

Those answers had led to Kenth sitting in that café, watching Rillam expertly slide into one of his alternate personas. Most of these personas as effective as full-on costume and make-up changes might have been, because he was just that talented; he seemed to almost *become* someone else. It had brought impressive results in Kenth's reasonably brief experience, as well as proving almost as entertaining as the choicest media on the vidnet feeds.

Rillam's walk as he approached the group had become the confident stroll of someone deadly in their own right, holding himself in a way that those who knew what to look for would recognise as a person ready to react to anything, while the casual observer would likely see only a good-looking male human in rather retro clothing walking across the street. Kenth watched for who noticed Rillam first, and who said or did something about his approach, as well as who—if anyone—suddenly had business elsewhere. Kenth was doing more than being Rillam's audience; he was his back-up and his escape plan. Not that Rillam seemed ready to fully trust that Kenth was more capable than he seemed, but Kenth knew they were getting there. It had taken time to fill in all the things their sudden connection had skipped past, for their almost instant friendship to settle and solidify. Assisting with Rillam's various consultations and cases had gone a long way toward making that happen.

Their current case had led them to this district of New London, where Rillam was certain he could get some crucial information from beings who generally didn't divulge much of anything to the authorities when questioned. If he could engage those beings in the persona of someone quite the opposite of a peacekeeper or port official, Rillam's expectation was that he could learn something more concrete about the missing person they were seeking, a Menaru female named Castazi Bool—as well as the criminals who were most likely responsible in some way for her disappearance, along with the possible murder of another, which had led them to seek Bool. With a bounty hunter, which was the role Rillam was portraying, answers otherwise kept back might be had for the offer of a few credits; peacekeepers didn't pay for information.

It didn't take long for Rillam to get into the conversation—in fact, he somehow managed to get himself brought in by one of the participants—and then Kenth could only watch and continue to regret that Rillam hadn't wanted to use their personal comm channel. Kenth couldn't argue that it could possibly be detected, but it was a pretty unlikely chance. Still, Rillam only had one shot at getting information from this group and Kenth was still relatively new to Rillam's *modus operandi*. So, Rillam went in and Kenth watched from across the way, stewing in mixed concern and admiration.

The group was, indeed, mixed. Three humans were interspersed among the group—one male, two females—and read to Kenth as ex-military, probably mercs now. One hulking Lonai, bristling with sharp-edged scales, crouched on powerful haunches wearing nothing much but a complicated network of strapping and pouches, as well as dozens of curved knives. The Lonai was probably male, wearing an insignia on his chest and back that must surely have been from one of the local guilds—the more likely were the port guilds of stevedores, in-system pilots, or maintenance staff—and the vaguely saurian being was tracking on Rillam the moment he came close enough to no longer be considered a passer-by. The last four of the group were solidly built beings Kenth had not seen the like of since he'd been stationed out near Groombridge 34, and it was only because of his previous exposure to other Oubek-anat that he could tell these four were a family group—though the term "family" was a loose translation and "shield brothers/sisters" would come just as close—and all four bore guild insignias, along with at least three different types of weapon each.

With that kind of diversity in this setting, Kenth hoped Rillam didn't set off an incident that might get them both dead, or at least arrested if they survived. He didn't reach back to touch the stunner he had in a low-profile holster in the small of his back, but he wanted to do. He had reconfigured it from a typical personal stunner to one that was lethal on its highest setting, though that would give him far fewer shots possible before the charge ran out; however, sometimes only a few strategic shots were needed. About the moment he had the thought, he heard suddenly raised voices as one of the human females grabbed Rillam by a handful of his jacket's shoulder.

Not moving yet, Kenth waited, hearing the blurred edge to the female's voice—inebriated on something—and when the other female tugged her back, loudly chastising her for "always starting shite, Doni, fecking hell", Kenth relaxed a little. Rillam's body language remained solid, confident, and he waved away whatever "Doni's" companion said about the incident. More talking ensued, the Lonai leaning closer to rumble something in his gravel and growl voice, and a quick exchange amongst the other human male and two of the Oubek-anat. Gestures, head tilts, ear flicks, one tail-thump from the Lonai that Kenth could feel along the ground, even across the street, and Rillam nodding casually all the while, as if it was all just another day for him.

Then, though Kenth couldn't hear what was said prior, the whole group went silent; all faces turned to one of the Oubek-anat, whose head ridge had risen as xe backed up a couple of steps and faced Rillam with a snarling series of sounds in xyr own language. Kenth only understood the last few words, which he was almost certain made a phrase that translated roughly to *"redeem your insult with your claws"*, or in more simplistic terms, "it's on, you little shit, fight me." It was part of a series of cultural rituals among the Oubek-anat that Kenth had learned enough about to hopefully avoid getting into a fight when he and his squaddies mingled with the Oubek-anat forces.

"Couldn't keep that mouth in control another five minutes, could you?" Kenth muttered as he rose and vaulted the café railing to not-quite-run across the street. "A spirited mosey," his old assistant med-tech Jill would've said sardonically. He only ran when absolutely necessary, given the random nerve misfires that still sometimes plagued his bad leg—it was better, by far, than when he'd been invalided out, but those hasty battlefield regens were notorious for leaving the flesh whole and the nerves confused. Luckily, today it was cooperating, and he didn't even have a limp as he strode over to possibly rescue, possibly join his impetuous, yet brilliant, friend in a fight.

"Of course I wasn't insulting you," Rillam said as Kenth came within earshot. "This is a negotiation, not a social situation; keep your personal issues at home, citizen."

If Kenth hadn't been in the process of hurrying over, he'd have face-palmed and sighed loudly. By all the old mythos, Rillam was proving too often to be a blithering idiot at social interaction.

Though he'd had no actual plan when he started over, Kenth quickly weighed their options and thought fast. He'd have to take a chance his memory wasn't too faulty and that these Oubek-anat truly followed their old customs, rather than just doing them lip service with such ritual phrases. Even if they *were* the sort Kenth hoped, it would still be a big gamble whether Rillam would go along with it—he was certainly clever enough to catch on, but he had a more-than-healthy amount of pride with his ego—or if he'd blow it and they'd end up having to fight for their lives or run for it.

"Every situation where thinking beings cross paths is a social situation, *citizen*," argued the Oubek-anat who'd taken exception to whatever Rillam had said, as well as to his most recent insensitive statement. "You will make reparation with claws and blood, or I shall carve it into your hide."

The other three Oubek-anat ranged themselves behind their companion, looking ready to hold Rillam down for the process if need be. Kenth had time for one deep breath before he was shoving shoulders and elbows aside—in the case of the Lonai he was merely pushing himself past, since Kenth's mass was easily a quarter less in comparison.

"Stop!" Kenth said in his best grabbing-the-grunts'-attention sort of voice. He moved quickly, but didn't run, only strode to Rillam and stood in front of him, slightly to one side, facing the Oubek-anat sombrely. Lifting his head proudly, posture strong and settled, Kenth held out his left hand, palm up. "This is my *mou-zuna*, and his wrongs are mine to balance. I am Vanner."

Rillam made a small noise, one Kenth couldn't really interpret without seeing his friend's face, but he didn't say a thing or move away, which Kenth counted as a small victory. In the background of his attention, Kenth noticed that the rest of the group, muttering in varying reactions, were shuffling away, giving them a wide area for whatever was going to happen; however, after a moment or two, it was plain that none of them seemed inclined to actually leave the area. Except for the food stall proprietor, who was already steering the slightly ramshackle stall off down the street.

The disgruntled Oubek-anat's four reddish-gold eyes focussed upon Kenth, then Rillam, and back to Kenth. "Your people have the *ʒuna* bond? It is not the same as your…" Xe turned to the other three, murmuring something in their own language, Ana-keki.

"Co-habitation contract," one of the three muttered.

Kenth shook his head. "No, it's not the same. As you know, a co-habitation contract is limited, can be broken on a whim, and means much less than it should." He reached back without looking, to put his hand upon Rillam's chest. "The *ʒuna* bond is for life. Unbreakable."

The three Oubek-anat all made soft sounds, like breathy grunts, and the fourth one who'd taken offense at Rillam did the same with a lowering of xyr head—they didn't have multiple sexes, really, unless they wanted to have young. Half-lidding xyr eyes, the Oubek-anat sounded less angry, but still gruff. "I am Bouket'nektat. You have no other *ʒuna* here, Vanner?"

"No, we are new," Kenth explained, lowering his hand from Rillam's chest to curve his hand around the man's hip, keeping him in place, as well as being sure where he was if things took a turn for the worse. "He is unfamiliar with your people, Bouket'nektat. I take the lack on myself for not teaching him what little I know." Rillam made a sub-vocal sound, as if he had been about to argue, but caught himself. Kenth shook his head the tiniest bit, digging his fingers into Rillam's hip a bit.

One of the other Oubek-anat touched Bouket'nektat's shoulder before speaking quietly. "Curiosity, Vanner. I am Bouket'atekit. Is your *mou-ʒuna*… is he *ʒemsha*?" The other two made sounds that seemed like chastisements, but quietly, their hands tugging on Bouket'atekit's tunic as if to pull xem back.

After a short few syllables that sounded in tone very much like *"shut it, I'm doing the talking, here"*, Bouket'nektat said, "It is not necessary to answer, Vanner."

Having been frantically trying to remember what *ʒemsha* meant, Kenth started to try and play it off like it was no problem, but then the memory kicked in. Hooking a finger in Rillam's nearest belt loop to pull him a little closer, Kenth inclined his head with a put-on look of reluctance. "Uh, well… yes, he is *ʒemsha*."

After Bouket held up a three-fingered hand, the Oubek-anat conferred in murmurs and whispers, all in Ana-keki, with a lot of rapid, urgent whispers from Bouket'atekit. After only a few minutes, Bouket'nektat made shushing sounds and gestures—surprisingly universal, those—and turned back to Kenth with another commonality amongst many species: a heavy sigh. "Vanner, given the circumstances, I understand the…issue…and I agree. We can balance the offense between us."

Kenth turned his head to glance at Rillam, who lifted his brows in question, and whispered, "Don't interfere." Rillam's lips parted, a little of the agitation he must have been hiding peeking through for just an instant before he pressed his lips together and nodded once. Bending down, Kenth pulled his jackknife from its pocket in his boot and unfolded it slowly. "I am grateful for your understanding, Bouket'nektat."

The Oubek-anat drew a slender little blade from some hidden pocket or slit in xyr tunic, the knife was delicately designed, the handle and blade both curved in opposite directions to form a shallow *S*. "Vanner has given offense. Bouket's honour can be cleansed in blood."

Taking another quick bracing breath, Kenth hoped he was remembering right when he used his own blade to make a small cut in his palm, cupping his hand to keep the slow, slight welling up of blood in the bowl of his hand.

Bouket'nektat made a rough sound, like a grunting growl, and did the same with xyr own knife, then touched the tip of xyr blade in the blood pooled in Kenth's hand. Xe bowed shallowly to Kenth after a moment and Kenth echoed the gesture, dipping his own knife in the small puddle of dark orange blood.

"Blood cleanses," Bouket'nektat said solemnly, shaking xyr knife so the small gloss of blood was flicked onto the ground. "We have both shed our offenses and are now balanced again. Good fortune to the Vanner's *zuna*, grow and prosper."

"May your own *zuna* have every good fortune." Once he'd done the same with his own knife, Kenth hesitated, adding quietly, "My kin call me Kenth," though he knew it wasn't necessary.

"Vanner'kenth," Bouket'nektat repeated, closing xyr hand into a fist. "We are now known to one another."

Catching the forefinger of his uninjured hand in Rillam's belt loop again, Kenth urged him forward, then shifting his arm inside of Rillam's jacket to rest around his lean waist in a more typical manner. "This is—"

"Liam," Rillam said quickly, before Kenth could say his proper name. He put his arm around Kenth's shoulders in return and his previously almost blank features shifted to a very good expression of apologetic humility. "I regret my offense."

Bouket'nektat nodded again and Bouket'atekit made a soft sound that Kenth suspected might be laughter, but Bouket'nektat didn't acknowledge it. Instead, xe said, "Vanner'liam. We, too, are now balanced and are known to one another."

Rillam gave a short dip of his chin, glancing at Kenth for guidance, and then said nothing more at Kenth's tiny hint of a headshake.

"Bouket'nektat, before we part ways, I would ask a question," Kenth then said cautiously, keeping to a politely neutral tone, aware that it might be wiser to bid them farewell and leave before their luck turned for the worse, but still…

"My answer will depend upon the question, Vanner'kenth," replied Bouket'nektat evenly.

"I find that to be only fair." Kenth glanced at Rillam, whose brows had risen over eyes intent with anticipation; he had already guessed where Kenth was going, no doubt. "We are seeking information. In fact, that was the reason my *mou zuna* sought you and the others out."

All four of the Bouket family group looked curious, though Bouket'nektat still had a cautious stance, as well, but xe made a subtle gesture of agreement. "I suspected there was more to the matter than it seemed. Very well, then. If it is information we have, it may be shared."

Kenth turned to Rillam, whom he noticed had been practically vibrating with eagerness as soon as he'd sussed out Kenth's intentions. When Kenth tilted his head in an encouraging gesture, Rillam spoke in a low, intense tone. "There is a group of beings who have been paying, and sometimes coercing, members of the local guilds to help them smuggle illicit goods."

Bouket'atekit made a soft sound and asked in an equally low voice, "Would the being you were asking after earlier—Castazi Bool—be one of those being paid or those doing the paying, Vanner'liam?"

Smiling in obvious pleasure at Bouket'atekit's catching onto his earlier purpose, Rillam replied, "I know Bool was contacted by one of those I'm seeking and, I suspect, may have taken them up on their offer. However, though she signed on for her shift, Bool has since vanished, which might mean she *didn't* agree to work for them. Either she jumped ship at Mars or is in hiding. Or…" He gave a regretful shrug, revealing a social delicacy Kenth had rarely seen him demonstrate he knew how to employ.

"Or…perhaps…you worry that something less pleasant has happened to this being?" Bouket'nektat hazarded, evidently understanding the implications in Rillam's unfinished sentence, xyr reddish-gold eyes going from Rillam to Kenth and back, head tilted enquiringly.

Rillam made a little sound of happy surprise, inclining his head. "Exactly my concern, Bouket'nektat."

"Then, your offer of credits for information on Castazi Bool was not as a bounty hunter or collector's agent, but in the service of bringing to justice such beings as those who would incite her to attempt smuggling?" Bouket'nektat asked.

Kenth fought a snigger at Rillam's only barely wiped away pleased expression—obviously he'd hoped to be taken as exactly that sort of person, so was just as obviously pleased to have got it right. Instead of calling him out on it, Kenth took a deep breath and took a chance on upsetting his self-satisfied friend by telling the truth. "Yes. We are, indeed, hoping to serve justice, Bouket'nektat. We are independent investigators who assist the Metro Peacekeepers in some of the Serious Crime Division's difficult cases. About a quarter cycle ago, a young Degnite was caught smuggling and, though they insisted they'd been forced to do it via threats to their loved ones, there was no proof. They were killed only days after being sent to the detention facility. Their family came to us… Asked us to do what we could to discover the truth and, hopefully, salvage the honour of their dead kin. We hope to produce the proof the SCD's people need to apprehend the beings truly responsible. That trail led us to Castazi Bool, whose trail led us here."

The Oubek-anat nodded slowly, eyes focussing on Kenth and then Rillam for a long few moments before xe turned to xyr *zuna* to speak a few rapid sentences in Ana-keki. Kenth couldn't quite catch it all, but the gist was something about trust and answers. Perhaps they had lucked out in more ways than one. The responses from the other three members of the Bouket family group seemed positive.

Kenth glanced at Rillam, giving the smallest dip of his chin to reassure him, which shifted Rillam's subtly questioning expression to one of anticipation.

Bouket'nektat finally turned xyr attention back to Kenth and Rillam, speaking quietly after a glance about them. "We have often worked with Castazi Bool. She contacted Bouket'atekit not long ago for advice on this very matter."

Bouket'atekit moved slightly forward, saying even more softly, "I will share all I know, if you will promise to try to save her…if it is still possible."

Rillam spoke before Kenth could do so, but his voice was solemn and resonant with conviction. "I will do all in my power to help her, if, as you say, it is possible. Please share everything. Any smallest detail might be more important than you realise."

Before Bouket'atekit could begin xyr tale, Kenth gently suggested they find a more private place to talk, just in case. Though he thought the Bouket *zuna* shared some worried glances, all agreed. They adjourned to a secluded corner booth at the nearby café—Rillam knew the owner, it turned out, and said she could be trusted, which was why he'd parked Kenth there to wait in the first place. The discussion lasted a good long while, fortifying drinks and snacks were ordered along the way, and Rillam's whole demeanour was astonishingly mannered and direct without being overbearing. Kenth was impressed anew.

As it happened, Bouket'atekit's information was incredibly useful, as Castazi Bool had shared much with her co-worker, fearing the very thing that seemed to have happened—her disappearance.

"Amazing," Kenth breathed, keeping his arm around Rillam's waist, his friend doing him the great courtesy of not arguing while walking along with him past the café and around the corner, they continued on toward the nearest lift to the mag-lev platform.

Once well away from the area and approaching the lift, Rillam let out a big gusty breath and his arm tightened around Kenth's shoulders. "That was…" He seemed to lack a proper descriptor.

"A fecking lucky turn?" Kenth offered, knowing he ought to be furious with Rillam, but finding himself bubbling up with something else, something far more like astonished humour. Seemingly one of their usual responses to danger, regardless. It ought to trouble him more, he supposed, but didn't follow the thought any further as Rillam's reply distracted him.

"Yes. Oh, yes it was that," Rillam agreed, shaking Kenth within the curve of his arm with an excess of zeal. As they both stepped onto the lift and the clear sides slid up to enclose them for the five-level ride upward, Rillam turned to Kenth with a slowly increasing grin. "You were brilliant, Kenth."

Brows high, Kenth tilted his head, looking up at Rillam in pleased surprise.

Laughing out loud, Rillam shook his head and just rocked Kenth from side to side again, as if he couldn't find a proper gesture to convey whatever he felt—which seemed very like his usual post-investigation triumphant glee, actually. "Amazing, Kenth."

"You're stealing all my best lines," Kenth protested with almost genuine earnest, since he did tend to compliment Rillam freely on his regular shows of brilliance. Rillam snorted himself into something closer to a giggle than a laugh, and Kenth couldn't help joining him, tittering like a schoolboy.

Once on the platform, they stood near the bench instead of sitting, and yet neither moved away from the other, even when Kenth carefully dug into his pocket for the mini first aid kit he kept there. Kenth couldn't stop smiling and, he noticed with a few brief glances, that Rillam seemed to have the same affliction. Kenth's shoulders moved as he barely resisted more giggles, popping open the small white and red soft-sided box to fetch out a little tube of antiseptic wound sealant.

Even though he huffed out a soft bit of nearly-silent laughter, Rillam kept his arm around Kenth's shoulders, watching him quickly and efficiently tend to the small cut in his hand. "You told them I was your spouse," Rillam said while Kenth tucked the first aid kit away once more.

"Yes." Nodding, Kenth looked straight forward, rocking on his feet once before sliding his arm around Rillam's waist again; thumb returning to Rillam's belt loop. It felt… comfortable.

"And what's *zemsha*?" Long fingers tapped lightly upon Kenth's far shoulder.

Blushing a little, Kenth snuck a glance over at Rillam, seeing the upward curl at the corner of his mouth and the uneven lift of his eyebrows. Kenth licked his lips and muttered, "It means…uh…essentially… 'Carrying the egg.'"

Deadpan, face gone still, Rillam didn't actually ask, "Basically, you told them I was pregnant."

"Yep." Kenth made a little 'that's about it' sort of face, shrugging.

The low hum of the mag-lev approaching didn't at all drown out Rillam then saying, "Getting a bit ahead of yourself, there, Vanner'kenth."

Kenth looked up at Rillam in confused surprise as the doors to the first mag-lev car opened nearby with a mellow *"bong bong bong"* to announce the fact, though only a handful of people got off and moved on without pause. Moments later, only Kenth and Rillam occupied the platform. Rillam slid away from Kenth's side to enter.

At the open doors, Rillam turned back and gave Kenth a brows-up expectant look. "Coming, *zuna?*"

Kimber lives in California and has been married to the same wonderfully talented partner for a surprising number of years. She's been making up stories most of her life; from crayons on construction paper to word processing programs. A voracious reader, Kimber also enjoys a wide variety of music, and has dabbled in other artistic endeavors like drawing and sculpting. She regularly participates in writing-oriented AO3, Dreamwidth, and Tumblr communities.

Veuve Noir
by
C.A. Harland

There is a place where dreams and reality blur into a single, pleasure-filled haze. Where the air is thicker than the water, and the water runs with honey. Where there are no rules or limitations, and all pain, pleasure, and paradise bows down in the name of the queen. They call it *Silk*.

Silk was the kind of joint that leant its name to its clientele, or the other way around. Never in the same place twice, it was the elite of the elite. If you could afford to know where *Silk* was going to be, you could afford whatever they were selling inside. Butterfly dust, bee venom. Heck, even aphids' honey was on the menu there. Or so the rumours went.

See, my partner and I had been on *Silk's* trail for months. Following one dry lead after another. Like leaves in the fall, our clues on the elusive club were dead and cold, slowly being plucked away by the wind and the night. And the body count had continued to grow. Never mind the unlicenced honey, or the black market powder, those were enough to shut *Silk* down for good, but the thing that had the force in a bloody hive, was the seemingly endless trail of bodies that *Silk* left in its wake. Whatever the bastards were doing in there, Funnelweb and I were going to find them.

That was until Funnelweb went missing. The last message I had from him was a web note to say he'd found a new lead on *Silk*. Some old scarab across town who carted deliveries to the club's newly chosen locations. It hadn't taken much to get him to talk. He was a tough old bastard, for sure, but I could hold all six of his legs down, and still have two free to make my point. There's a reason they like arachnids for the force.

And so, after months of searching, I finally found *Silk*. The webbed dome was silver in the moonlight. Dew beaded on its threaded sides like sweat on the pelt of some great beast. I could hear the cicada song from outside, and smell the sickly sweet perfume of the honey that dripped from the ceiling.

The rhinoceros beetle at the door lowered his horn, but I flashed the scarab's invite, and he waved me through. The air inside was even heavier with smells, carrying the pounding of the music. Moisture clung to the bristles on my legs, making them stand up. Silk fibres threaded around my claws, pulling me deeper into the bowels. Bugs of all kinds filled the main floor, while moths with painted eyes and velvet wings served drinks and drugs in equal measure.

I flagged down one of the moths. She pranced over to me, batting her feathery antennae.

"What can I do you for?"

"I'm looking for a spider, name of Funnelweb. I heard he came in here."

She gave a smile and a flick of her wings. "Not a lot of names in here. But I'm sure whatever your friend wanted, we can find one for you too." She took a step closer, the butterfly dust on her chest sparkling in the light.

She was holding out on me. Stalling. I couldn't tell you how I knew. Call it an eighth sense. "Someone here knows where I can find him."

The moth pouted. "Maybe you should talk to the boss." She nodded to the bar at the back.

I followed her direction and came face to face with a dame the likes of which I've never seen before. Her skin was glossy black and shone like lacquer in the dim lights of the club. She sauntered over to the bar on legs as long as they were thin, and looked up at me with eight of the most luminous eyes I've encountered.

"What can I help you with, Huntsman?"

I shook my head clear of the sudden stupor. "How'd you know my name?"

She gave a slight narrowing of her eyes. The barest touch of a smile. "Oh, it's my business to know. I've been hoping you would come, detective."

I almost smiled back. "You have?"

"Oh, yes. Ever since your partner was here. He told me so much about you, detective. I've been just dying to meet you."

I tried to reply, to ask about Funnelweb, but the words didn't quite make it out. The dizzying fugue state had returned. The pulse of the music seemed to swim in her eyes, and the lights danced across her skin. She placed two glasses on the benchtop between us, and as she turned to reach for a bottle of aphids' honey, I saw a striking swath of red down her back.

"Have a drink, detective. Let's talk about your investigation."

"Who are you?" I managed.

She slid a glass of amber liquid across the bench with one delicate claw. "You can call me Widow. And I'm going to take good care of you."

C. A. Harland started drawing from the moment she could hold a pencil. With a head full of characters, it seemed only natural to sketch them out. It wasn't until years later that she also started writing them down and turning them into stories. In 2012 she completed a Fiction Writing course. It is through the support of the fellow writers from this course that her debut novel *Sol.Terra* was completed.

Mysterious Circumstances
by
A.R. Collins

1.

I was the one who discovered the body of my brother Andrew. It washed up on the Brough of Birsay causeway one morning in October, when the sky was red and the wind was sharp, too early for anybody but me to be there.

The ruined settlement on that tiny island had always spoken to me. I loved it even more than the mysterious Ring of Brodgar, or the Standing Stones of Stenness; even more than Maeshowe, where I had spent hours at a time watching for the fabled Hogboon; far more than the legendary vanishing island belonging to the Finfolk, which for a few childish years I had hoped to find; more than the beaches where seals basked in the summer and autumn, and I imagined the beautiful men and women within their skins, hiding there until we slept on Midsummer's Eve.

As much as I loved all those stories, I had never actually found the proof. The Viking settlement, though, I knew to be real. My connection to it was real too; I was descended from the settlers on my mother's side. When I found Andrew on the path to their village, a place I considered an old friend, it was hard to believe. He lay sprawled across my path, the blood almost washed from his face, a clear dent in his skull that marked the killing blow.

At first, I blamed him. Whatever had killed him—demons, the sea and the rocks, the ghosts of our ancestors—it must have been due to his lack of care and respect. He used to swim miles out to sea and stay there long enough to make our mother think he'd drowned. He used to stay among the Viking ruins long after everyone else had gone and the causeway was barely visible beneath the churning waves. He used to laugh at Aunt Emma's stories of ghosts and demons who had walked the islands for centuries.

"Haven't you grown up yet, Karen?" he said once, when I tried to warn him. "You're too old to still believe in ghosts and Finfolk and those mound-dwelling...whatever you call them."

"Hogboons," I said. "And I'm not too old to believe in high tide and sharp rocks and drowning and freezing, now, am I?"

I remembered such arguments as I stared at his lifeless body, but by the time I'd roused the occupants of the nearest house, cold tears were biting into my cheeks. I could barely speak. Eventually I got the farmer's wife to call the police, but I couldn't tell her why.

"She's very upset," she said. "Please just come, and we'll try to get her talking."

There was one other time that I knew of the police being needed for something serious, on these quiet and happy islands where everybody knows everybody. That was to do with my family as well. My Aunt Emma disappeared. They searched for days, and tried to track down family and friends she might have gone to, but there was no trace of her. At last it was decided she must have been killed and carried away by the sea, probably by accident, possibly not.

The difference with Andrew was that he had been washed up, not away, so we knew he had died from a blow to the head. Well, there were plenty of those to be had in a rough sea. I accepted his death as an accident through all the time that my mother had to be dragged out of bed in the afternoons, forced to eat and reminded that she still had me.

Then one day, she got up before I made her. She met me in the bathroom doorway, and said, "I'm sorry, pet. I'll be normal for you now. Come down and I'll make breakfast."

"Are you sure?" I asked.

"Of course I am."

I sat at the kitchen table and watched her work, and for the first time in weeks, I had a moment to think. I wanted to talk as well. No one had really talked to me about my brother's death.

"Do you think it's right?" I asked. "What they said about Andrew?"

"What do you mean?" Mum asked.

"That it was an accident...he was swimming or he slipped on the causeway or whatever."

"It'll do you no good to think such thoughts, Karen."

"But I was thinking...honestly I was...what if it wasn't an

accident?"

"How could it be anything but?" said Mum. "Why would someone want to...to do that to your brother? And besides, you know what he was like."

"Not all the time," I said, "and definitely not at night. I don't remember him doing anything dangerous in the dark, with no one around."

"If no one was around," my mother said, "how would anyone know what he was doing? Let it lie now, and eat your breakfast."

I did as I was told, but I wasn't satisfied. I chewed over my thoughts with my food until I was sure I knew what to say next.

"Why haven't Finn and Uncle John been round?" I asked.

My mother stiffened. "You know Uncle John and I don't get on."

"Even so," I said. "He's your brother! And you like Finn. So do I. We went to see them when Aunt Emma went."

"I'm nicer than John. I went to see him; he hasn't come to see me."

"I remember that. I remember thinking how strange it was. It was like they weren't surprised she was gone. Uncle John didn't even seem sad. Finn was sad, but he wasn't surprised."

"That was a long time ago," said Mum. "More than half your lifetime. You can't possibly remember how it really was."

"I can," I said. "Andrew thought the same thing. He told me." That was at least half a lie. Andrew hadn't told me anything, but nor had he disagreed with me when I'd told him my thoughts all those years ago. "And you thought so too. I know you did."

"I thought no such thing," said Mum. "If you must know, I wasn't all that surprised myself."

This was news to me. It seemed the most significant thing of all, and I was desperate to know more.

"Why not?" I asked.

"Because John was a tyrant where Emma was concerned. You have no idea."

"Then you don't think she drowned? You think she ran away? But no one ever found her – not a trace of her!"

"She must have covered her tracks too well."

"So you think she's alive?" I asked. "And hiding?"

"Maybe."

"But what about Finn? Mothers don't leave their sons to

tyrants."

"Sometimes they do," said Mum. "Anyway, John's no tyrant to Finn. Not that I know of, anyway. Well, if Finn was being tyrannised, don't you think he'd do something about it?"

"I think he'd come to see us if Uncle John would let him," I said, "at a time like this."

"Perhaps he's waiting to be invited."

"Can we?"

"Not yet," said Mum. "I'm not ready, Karen."

I didn't believe her. I was suspicious of everyone, and I was sure my mother wanted to stop me from asking Finn and Uncle John questions. I'd always had questions about Aunt Emma, and now I had them about Andrew as well. I was becoming convinced that the same thing had happened to both of them, and what had become of their bodies was entirely down to chance.

2.

It was Uncle John who answered the door.

"Karen," he said. "We intended to come and see you, but we didn't know how much time your mother would need. In fact, I didn't know if she'd see *me* at all."

"I don't suppose you want to tell me what that's all about?" I asked.

"Oh, just silliness," he said. "Come on in."

"Is Finn here?"

"Aye."

I followed Uncle John inside, and up the creaky wooden stairs to Finn's bedroom. His door was open and he was hunched over his desk with his back to us.

"Finn," said Uncle John, and Finn looked over his shoulder. When he saw me, he turned all the way and got clumsily to his feet, banging his knee and knocking over his pen pot as he did so.

"It's only me," I said, ducking through the low wooden doorway as he flinched and cursed over his hurt knee. I picked up his pens for him.

"Thanks," he said, still looking at his knee. "I'm doing my homework. Miss Kerridge told me to ask if you want any work sent, but I didn't know if..." He took a breath. "People keep asking about you. I'd have come sooner, only I didn't know...and Dad said..."

"*What* did he say?" I asked, after checking that Uncle John had really gone.

"Nothing. Just that you and Aunt Rachel might not want visitors." He forgot his knee then, and looked at me. "She doesn't like you seeing Dad, does she? Does she know you're here?"

"No."

"Maybe you should have rung and asked me to come to you. Well, you're here now. Can I get you anything?"

"I want to know something," I said. "When your mum disappeared, what really happened?"

"What?" He stared at me a moment, then started rolling up his trouser leg to examine his knee again. "I'll have a bruise tomorrow. Do you think it feels tender?"

"I'm not feeling your knee!" I said. "Answer me, Finn."

"How do you expect me to know?"

"You wouldn't have avoided the question if you didn't know something," I said. "Anyway, it's obvious. I've always known there was something fishy about it."

"If you've always known," said Finn, "then why are you asking me now?"

"Because of Andrew."

"I'm sorry about Andrew." He smiled at me then, and gave me a hug that melted away the years. I hadn't felt so close to him since Aunt Emma was around. Then he pushed me gently away, and said, "But I don't see what he has to do with Mum's disappearance."

"I think the same thing happened to them both," I said.

"Oh, no," said Finn, shaking his head. "No, Karen, definitely not."

"How do you know?"

He went quiet again, and stooped to roll down his trouser leg.

"You've got to tell me now you've said that."

For a few moments more, Finn said nothing and wouldn't look at me. Then suddenly he straightened, grabbed my wrist and said, "Why not? I don't know why it has to be kept secret from you, now I think about it."

He pulled me out of the room, and I only just ducked in time to avoid the low beam. All of a sudden he seemed desperate to tell me, or to show me. The stairs groaned under our heavy footfall, then we came to a halt outside the cupboard underneath the stairwell.

"Remember how Dad always kept this locked?" Finn asked.

"Of course," I said. "We found the key one day, remember?"

He looked amazed. "*We* found the key?"

"Yes!" I was furious with him for forgetting. It had been our last real fun together. "It was under the biscuit barrel. I stood on your shoulders."

"Oh aye," said Finn, "I remember."

"But there was nothing in there."

"That's what we thought. Do you remember how angry Dad was? He snatched the key from me...or you...and locked the door and told us never to try anything like that again."

"I remember," I said. "It worked on me – I was terrified. But not on you?"

"No," said Finn, "not on me. It was obvious there was something in here, and all I could think was that I *had* to find it. It was more than just curiosity. It was taking me over, like...well..."

He tailed off, but not because he couldn't think of the word; he just didn't want to say it. I said it for him, in a breathless whisper.

"Magic?"

"Now I remember," he said, the ordinariness of his voice breaking the spell. "This is why we don't tell you."

"You have to now!" I said. "What did you find? No, wait... I think I can guess."

How can I describe my excitement? Whatever I had always claimed to believe, this was the first time I'd dared to hope it really might be true. But I wasn't just excited. I hated Finn in that moment, and I hated my mother too when I realised she must have known.

"Go on then," I said. "Where was it?"

Finn frowned at my petulance, but he answered my question all the same. He walked the two steps that the cupboard allowed, kicked at the floor in one corner, and upended the floorboard there. I peered into the darkness, and as soon as I saw what he had done, I grabbed him and hurled him out into the hallway, then fell to my knees like a person at prayer.

"There's nothing there now," Finn said behind me.

"Of course not," I said, and got to my feet. "Then why bother to show me?"

"So you'd believe it."

"This doesn't prove anything."

"No," said a voice behind us, and I remembered how frightened I had been when Uncle John found us in that same forbidden cupboard all those years before. Now here he was again, reaching between us to shut the door.

"She's seen no proof, Finn," he said, "so she still can't believe it."

"But I *do* believe it, Uncle John!" I said.

This was what I had deduced: my Aunt Emma was a selkie, forced to marry Uncle John because he had found and hidden her seal skin while she bathed on the beach in her human form. All the legends said that the hidden skins were found by the children born from the union of selkie and man, so naturally Finn had found Aunt Emma's skin. Without it, she had been unable to return to the sea. With it, she'd had no desire to stay, not even for her human son.

"If you saw one," said Uncle John, "you'd know you'd never believed up until then."

He turned and walked through the nearest doorway, into the kitchen. He didn't seem angry. Finn let out a sigh of relief.

"What else do you know?" I asked him.

"Nothing," said Finn. "What else *is* there to know? Don't you see how it couldn't be what happened to Andrew? He was no selkie—we can be sure of that."

"Can we?" I said. A delicious idea was forming in my mind, and without another word to Finn, I followed Uncle John into the kitchen.

"Would you like something to drink, Karen?" he asked.

"I want to know more," I said. "Is it why you and Mum don't talk?"

"It's why she doesn't talk to me," he said. "She doesn't approve of the practice... thinks it's cruel or patriarchal or something."

"Well, it's both, isn't it?" I had always thought so, however much I loved the legend.

"I'll make us some tea. How's Rachel been keeping?"

"Terrible for a while, but she's on the mend now. Uncle John, could Andrew have been a selkie too?"

"You and your ideas!" he said. "Of course he wasn't a selkie, and even if he was, how would that make sense of his death?"

I drew breath to answer, but couldn't. I had been fixated on the idea of Andrew and Aunt Emma suffering the same fate, but of course they hadn't; that was obvious now. Still, it didn't disprove my theory. Andrew couldn't have been all selkie, of course, but perhaps he wasn't all human either.

"Who's our father?" I asked.

"Richard McBride," said Uncle John, still making tea, "as you well know. All the story of how your mother met him and married him and he died in your first year is true."

"How do I know it's true? I don't remember him."

"Everyone else does. Ask anybody. I'm sorry, Karen, but there's nothing otherworldly in you besides that imagination of yours."

He put two cups down on the kitchen table, and seated himself in front of one. Feeling myself deflate, I sat down beside him and blew across the steaming surface of my tea.

"I'm sorry you're not one of them," he said, "and neither was your poor brother. That is, I'm sorry you feel like this about it. But those bull selkies are a bad sort, Karen, if you really believe in them. Better to know that your father was a good, honest man who loved his wife and his bairns."

"What about the females?" I asked. "They're not all like Aunt Emma, are they...just doing as they're told and waiting for someone else to find their skins?"

"I don't know, lass," said Uncle John. "So say the legends."

"The legends were written a long time ago," I said, "by men. I don't believe that selkie men have power over human women, and human men have power over selkie women. It just doesn't make sense."

"Aye," said Uncle John, "you're probably right there."

By this time I was itching to leave, for yet another idea was forming in my mind.

"Thanks for the tea, Uncle John," I said, and jumped to my feet. "Would it be all right if Finn came out with me?"

"If you like," said Uncle John. "What's the hurry?"

I didn't tell him.

3.

"Isn't this where you found him?" Finn asked, as we dragged our feet over the Brough of Birsay causeway, our hands shoved into our coat pockets to avoid the cold.

"What if it is?" I said. "Is there anything to be scared of now? Look, the seals have all gone."

"What's that got to do with anything? I'm not scared of seals."

"Maybe you should be. Maybe they're not all like your mum."

He stopped walking, forcing me to stop too, and gave me a look. "What are you getting at?"

"Just listen a minute," I said. "Imagine you're...no, *I'm* a selkie. And I've taken off my seal skin to lie around on the beach."

Finn started to giggle. "I don't want to imagine that, Karen!"

"Take this seriously!" I said. "Don't imagine what I look like. Imagine how I *feel* when I find some stupid man has stolen my skin and expects me to marry him. Do I let him get away with it?"

"Well," said Finn, "no, *you* don't."

"Too right I don't! So why shouldn't some of those selkie women be like me? I think your dad was lucky Aunt Emma went along with it. It can't be right that all selkie women are like her. Do you see what I mean?"

"No," said Finn. "Why don't you just *tell* me what you mean?"

"I mean, maybe some of them are more like the Finfolk. You know...aggressive, violent, evil if you like... But I can't say I'd blame her."

"Blame who?"

"A selkie who found someone stealing her seal skin. I couldn't exactly blame her if she stopped him by lashing out and hitting him over the head with a rock or something. Maybe she didn't know how hard she hit him. Maybe she didn't *mean* to kill him...or then again, maybe she did." I took a moment to digest this idea. "But anyway, that could be it, couldn't it? That *must* be it!"

"I don't know," said Finn. "I suppose that *could* be it. Or maybe he just had an accident, like everybody thinks."

"I know better," I said.

"Okay," said Finn, "so you've worked it out. Now you know."

He was starting to annoy me with his obvious attempt to humour me, which was entirely his fault, and with that jealousy still lingering, which was entirely mine.

"I *don't* know for sure," I said. "But I'm going to find out."

"How?"

"Talk to them, of course. I bet you can call them, can't you?"

"So that's why you're dragging me into this," said Finn. "Well I'm sorry, Karen, but I can't call selkies from...well, from wherever they've gone."

"You're lying," I said. "You're one of them!"

"Only half," he said, "and it doesn't work like that. You know the legends. They don't say anything about it working like that, do they?"

"No," I said, calming down considerably, trying to clear my head so that I could remember what the legends *did* say. "But there's a way to summon one."

"You mustn't."

"Why not?"

"Well, because...all sorts of reasons!" said Finn. "What if they're dangerous? You already think one killed Andrew. And even if one did, why should she tell *you* about it?"

"She can't," I said, with all the triumph of a child who has won a silly argument. "It's only males that can be summoned, isn't it?"

"Well then what's the point? What can *he* tell you? Anyway, it's probably not true."

"Then where's the harm in trying? Why am I still talking to you about it, anyway?"

On that note, I turned away from Finn and ran home to my books, to see exactly what the legends had to say on the matter.

I found out that a selkie man could be summoned by what the legends called an "unsatisfied woman" wishing to make contact, and as far as I was concerned, this described me exactly. The time of year didn't matter, but the time of day did, and that took some thinking about. It had to be at high tide. At first, I decided to forget my idea of performing the ritual at the Brough of Birsay, where seals were often sighted and where I had found Andrew (surely, I thought, more evidence that my theory was correct). If I were there at high tide, I'd be stuck there all night.

Then I started to think about where else I could go, and how many people might be around, and even if they weren't I'd worry about them turning up and spoiling things. In that light, the Brough of Birsay seemed like the perfect place. I went back there before the tide got anywhere near the causeway and spent two or three hours hiding from people behind the ruins, so that no one staying until the last minute could make me go back with them.

Though I had lived in Orkney all my life, I had never stood alone on a shrinking island in the height of winter as the sun went down. I thought I was used to the cold; it turned out I didn't know the meaning of the word. When the sun had set, I could see the artificial light of the mainland in the distance, but of my immediate surroundings I could see nothing. All I could hear was the roar of the sea. There was no one on the island with me, the causeway was covered, and the cold was eating away at my fingers. I walked around with my hands shoved under my armpits, determined not to regret my decision. I had no way of knowing when the tide was at precisely its highest, so I would just have to guess. It didn't take me long to decide that, yes, now was probably the time.

The ritual itself seemed simple enough. All I had to do was cry seven tears into the sea, and crying should have been easy. I thought about Andrew and my sadness, and how much worse my mother's was, and how I had lost something special when Finn and I stopped playing together just after Aunt Emma went, and now I knew the truth about that, I could have beaten Finn half to death, and I was wrong to feel that way because it wasn't his fault he was half selkie, but it *was* his fault he'd kept it from me. I thought about these things until I could no longer stand being trapped with my misery in such cold and darkness as I had never known before.

But I couldn't force myself to cry.

I turned away from the sea and stumbled through the darkness until I tripped over the low wall of some ruin or other. I lay there for a moment until I was sure I wasn't hurt, then found the corner that most shielded me from the wind and curled up inside my coat. I knew I would never sleep there, and even if I could, I probably shouldn't in that cold. I wished I had never gone, and soon enough I started crying. When I realised it, I was so overjoyed that I almost stopped.

I jumped to my feet, ran to the water's edge, fell onto my hands and knees and tried to cry into the sea. This was impossible. I couldn't stop the tears from going into my mouth, or rolling down my neck, or going wherever they pleased. Some were washed away by the icy spray; did that count as crying into the sea? Whether it did or it didn't, how could I possibly count how many of my tears went in? If the number exceeded seven, surely the ritual wouldn't work.

The ritual wouldn't work. That was the truth of it. By now I was so frustrated with the whole thing that I was sure it wouldn't work even if I got the process right. I got to my feet, ready to cry the rest of my tears freely, when suddenly I thought I heard a voice call my name.

Could it possibly be a selkie? I dried my eyes with my gloved hands and peered out to sea. A small, yellow light was approaching me. Then I heard the buzz of a motor, and my name again.

"Karen! Answer me!"

It was Uncle John. I started crying again, with relief this time, and I hurled myself into his boat the moment it was close enough.

"Stupid girl!" he said, fighting to steady the vessel as it rocked with the violence of the tide and of my entry. "Do you still think your brother didn't die of foolishness?"

"How did you know I was here?" I asked.

"We didn't," said Uncle John. "None of us thought you'd be stupid enough to try anything here, at this time of night, at this time of year. Your mother's worried half to death!"

"You knew what I was doing, then," I said. "I'll kill that son of yours."

"He may have saved your life by telling us."

"Oh, Uncle John...how do you did it? How did you ever find her?"

"I was lucky," he said, "if you want to look at it like that. What made you think that silly ritual would work anyway? It's supposed to be for women who...well..."

"*Unsatisfied* women!" I said. "Well, isn't that what I am?"

"You don't understand, Karen," he said. "You don't understand anything about this, which is why you need to stop playing around with it."

"I need to know," I said.

"Know what?" he asked. "What happened to Andrew, you mean?"

"Yes!"

"That's not what you're after. Why can't you be contented with what you *do* know? Haven't we given you reason enough to be proud of your heritage?"

"The Vikings were rapists and thieves and murderers," I said, and slipped into a sulk.

4.

I sought out Finn at school one lunchtime in order to abuse him.

"I should be able to trust you! How dare you go telling tales on me? Why did you have to do it? You don't really believe they're dangerous. You just want to keep them all to yourself."

"Your mum rang up in floods," Finn said. "It's the first time she'd contacted Dad in years, she was that worried. We all were."

"I'm never talking to you again," I said, and meant it, but it wasn't because of what he'd told Uncle John. It was because of what he *hadn't* told me and, more than that, my silly wish that his secrets could have been mine in the first place.

I didn't actively go looking for selkies after that. I didn't have the heart for it. I even started doubting that Aunt Emma really had been one. All right, so Finn had found some kind of coat under a loose floorboard and then she'd run away. No one had to be a selkie for that to happen.

Once I'd reached this conclusion, I decided to hate Finn even more, and for half a year I honoured my vow of never talking to him again. As I saw it, I did some growing up in that time. I happened to gain a greater understanding of what the term "unsatisfied woman" really meant, and then decided that all my earlier ideas had been nothing more than childish nonsense.

When I broke my resolution regarding Finn, it was because I was taken off guard. He jostled me awake one night from an extraordinarily deep sleep, and as soon as I opened my mouth to enquire (I'm sure I had no intention of screaming or anything like that), he clamped a sweaty hand over it and said in a stage whisper, "Hush now. You don't want to wake Aunt Rachel."

"*Why* don't I?" I said, once I'd prised his hand from my mouth. "What's the matter with you? You'll suffocate me. Why are you breaking into my room in the middle of the night?"

"Your window was open."

"That doesn't answer my question."

"So you're still angry with me," he said. "I hoped you'd be over it by now. But that's why I'm here. I want to make it up to you, Karen. Get some more clothes on."

"Why?"

"It's Midsummer's Eve."

"So what? Why can't you answer questions anymore?"

"Oh, come *on*!" said Finn. "You know the legends better than anyone."

Midsummer's Eve. After a moment's thought, I started to understand. Them! I got out of bed and made my way over to my wardrobe, saying, "If this is a joke, Finn Sorenson..."

"Listen to yourself," said Finn. "Like I'm here with my dad's boat in the middle of the night, when I could be asleep, when I've never played a trick in my life, because I'd rather start now than make it up with my only living cousin, because I'm *so* happy she hasn't spoken to me since before Christmas that now I want her to hate me even more!"

I had on my trousers and jumper, and was struggling into a stout and awkward pair of boots. Seething with annoyance, at them and at Finn, I said, "I didn't know you had your dad's boat, did I?"

"I brought her all round the coast and left her moored at Skara Brae. We're going to the Brough of Birsay."

Skara Brae is a Neolithic settlement on the mainland. I knew that some of its people must have been my ancestors, though we couldn't trace ourselves to them as we could to the Vikings. On that night, Finn and I walked through the site with only a feeble beam of torchlight to stop us from falling into any of the sunken houses.

"What happens if kids get caught going out in people's speedboats?" I asked, as we boarded.

"It's the middle of the night," said Finn.

"I'm surprised at you. Do you do this often?"

"I normally go on foot, all the way up to the Point of Buckquoy."

"What, the Brough of Birsay car park?"

"All right," said Finn, "if you'd rather call it that. But there's only ever one who goes to shore there."

I touched his arm. "Your mother?"

"Aye."

In Orkney, the sky is never completely dark in the summer, and it didn't take Finn long to drive the boat along the coastline and up to the Brough of Birsay. The temperature was comfortable and the sea was calm. Finn took me to the site of the causeway, now many feet below the water, and we dragged the boat onto the land. It was hard work for me, and until Finn seemed satisfied that the boat was safe, I could concentrate on only my effort.

It came as a relief to free my hands, straighten my back and raise my head. Before I could even start remembering why we were there, my eyes took in their surroundings, and I stood dumbfounded. Through the incomplete darkness, I could see the shapes of many women and a very few men all over the tiny island, most of them bathing in the moonlight, some strolling through the damp grass with a large garment slung over their arms. Their seal skins, I thought. They had to be. At any rate, it was the only sign of any kind of clothing. Bar Finn and me, everyone in the vicinity was quite naked. I suddenly felt embarrassed, and looked around for Finn.

I heard him before I saw him, when he let out a bark exactly like that of a seal pup. I probably assumed it *was* a seal pup, but when I turned in the direction of the sound I saw the silhouette of Finn's coat, trousers and heavy walking boots. I ran over to him.

"What are you doing?" I asked.

"Shut up," he said, and barked again.

Moments later, the black surface of the sea was broken by an indistinct shape. It moved towards us, gracefully at first, and Finn held his breath as it approached. Then the movements became clumsy as the creature hauled itself onto the land. At last, Finn let out his breath in a long sigh of contentment. It was a seal, of course, and by then I had worked out exactly which seal.

"Finn," I whispered, "aren't there others like you who come here?"

"Of course not," he said, as the selkie barked joyfully, then rolled over onto her back and began to climb out of her skin. "Who *does* that these days?"

"Well," I said, "your dad."

"I'm the only one, Karen."

The words were still on his lips when he broke into a run and hurled himself into Aunt Emma's arms. I watched them for a moment, all at once touched by the reunion, wondering whether I was dreaming, and longing to go and greet Aunt Emma myself. But I didn't want to spoil their moment. I started thinking about Andrew, and wondering if I could possibly find anything out.

I turned round to look at the other selkies, and was startled to see that several of them had moved closer to me, and even those who hung behind were looking at me, hugging their skins to their bodies. I felt hostility in their stares, and started to back away, finally turning when I sensed Finn and his mother close behind me.

"Aunt Emma!" I said, grabbing onto her arm. "I never thought I'd see you again."

"Karen?" said Aunt Emma. "Can it be? Oh, I never would have recognised you if you weren't the only girl in the world to call me Aunt Emma! What are you *doing* here?" she added, sounding almost displeased, at the same time pulling me into a tight hug.

"I brought her," said Finn.

"Oh, my darling," said Emma. "Why?"

"Aye, boy," said another woman's voice, low and threatening, and I turned to see that a dozen or more selkies in human form had gathered close around us. "Why?"

5.

"She's my cousin," said Finn, trying to project his voice across the tiny island, but hampered by Aunt Emma's arms around his shoulders and chest as she held him to her. "So was her brother. He was killed here last autumn. She's been trying to find out what happened."

"Why should showing us to her be of any help?" asked the selkie woman.

"She's the boy's cousin," said a new voice, and the largest of all the men came forward from the crowd. "She is of the clan of Sorenson, therefore so was her brother. Was he of age, lass?"

His voice was gentle yet authoritative, kind yet guarded. He was tall and well-muscled, far stronger than the spindly young men around him, the human version of the biggest and most blubbery bull seal who ever basked. He was just what I had imagined an alpha male selkie to be. In front of me was the very core of all my fantasies, so naturally I felt far too shy to look at him. Even if he'd had clothes on, I would still have felt too shy to look at him.

"Murchadh asked you a question," said the female.

"What?" I said. "Oh...almost. He was seventeen."

"When once the clan of Sorenson had settled here," said Murchadh, "and discovered our race, it became tradition that their sons and their nephews should steal the skin of a selkie and force her into marriage. It may be that this rite had something to do with your brother's death. Is that why you have come?"

I couldn't answer him. I had only known for a short time that Aunt Emma was a selkie. I never dreamed there was a whole history of selkie marriages in my family. I looked at Finn, and said, "Did you know about this?"

"Dad mentioned it," he said, "but it's not a tradition anymore, Karen. He was the first one to do it for a couple of hundred years at least."

"That's true enough," said the selkie woman, the note of hostility still in her voice. "It took them long enough to learn that we don't always take it lying down. But one day, they learned."

"Then it's happened before?" Finally I was able to look at the male, wanting him to confirm the conclusion to which I had leapt. "One of my ancestors was killed when he tried to steal a selkie's skin?"

"That is not what Ailsa said," said Murchadh.

"But it's what she implied!"

Murchadh looked at me for a moment. Then he turned to face the selkies behind him, and asked in a voice that reached to the far end of the island and beyond, "Can anyone tell this girl anything about her poor dead brother?"

For a moment, the only sound to be heard was the quiet roar of the sea. Then Ailsa stepped forward.

"I may have seen them," she said, looking at Murchadh.

"Address the girl, Ailsa," he said.

I looked at her. "Them?"

"That's what I said," Ailsa said to me. "It was the autumn, as you said, when the ordinary seals come to breed. I was with them. There was a boy, or a young man if you like, who may have been your brother. And a man with him."

6.

"What man?" I asked.

"Probably a relative of yours," said Ailsa. "He was telling the lad about selkies, saying we were real and true and, as a man of the line of Sorenson, your brother had a right to us. If I was going to kill anyone, lass, it would have been him."

"What happened?" I asked. "Did they try to steal a selkie skin? Did another selkie kill Andrew? Are you sure it wasn't you?"

I took a step towards her, but Finn touched my arm, and that stopped me. Goodness knows what I thought I was going to do to her anyway.

"It was nothing to do with me," said Ailsa. "I was keeping my skin on, at least until they'd left. But there must have been a selkie's skin around somewhere, because the man was urging the boy to take it. He wouldn't, and he tried to walk away. The man tried to stop him. He tried to stop him with his hands, lass. They argued on the causeway. They argued violently."

"So maybe that's why Andrew fell," Finn said to me. Then he looked at Ailsa. "Did you see what happened?"

"No, lad," she said. "Sorry."

It didn't sound to me like she meant that, so I decided to doubt everything she had said.

"Why should I believe you?" I said. "I think he tried to take your skin and you killed him to get it back!"

"Why should you think that?" said Ailsa. "You don't know me, but you do know your brother. Would he do a thing like that?"

"I... I don't know," I said, thrown by her sudden gentleness. "He never believed..."

"Ailsa has told you the truth, lass," said Murchadh. "I know she would not lie. Nor would anybody here."

"We are not humans," Ailsa added.

"Karen," Aunt Emma said gently, "it seems to me that you know now who's responsible."

"What are you going to do, Karen?" asked Finn, full of anxiety, which must have been for his father. I realised then that Aunt Emma was right. She may have spoken out of hatred, but even so, she was right.

"What *can* I do?" I said. "There's nothing the police can do about hearsay from a selkie. Even if they believed me, it could never be proved that Uncle John had anything to do with his death. And I still don't know what happened, anyway. Did he fall, or was he pushed?"

"Dad wouldn't do that," Finn was quick to say.

"Not on purpose, perhaps," I said, and I found I believed that whatever happened, Uncle John had not done anything out of malice.

I felt better having learned more about Andrew. And it was all thanks to Finn. No matter how hard I had investigated on my own, everything I found out was because of him.

7.

I had no choice but to wait while Finn had the rest of his quality time with his mother. I lay and looked at the sky, thinking, wondering why I didn't have more to say to the selkies all around me. As a child, I had imagined I could talk to them for hours.

One of them spoke to me, though, just as the sun began to rise. It was Ailsa. She lay down beside me, on her front like a seal, and said, "I told you the truth. Do you believe me?"

"I suppose," I said.

"I'm sorry about your brother."

"Thanks."

"What did they say your name was?"

"Karen."

"Karen Sorenson?"

"No," I said. "Karen McBride."

"Ah, then at least one of your forefathers was a mortal man."

"Nothing wrong with that."

"Of course," said Ailsa. "Don't get me wrong. I was just thinking… Do the daughters of the clan of Sorenson ever marry selkies?"

"I don't know," I said. "The legends don't seem to think that's an option, but I never did believe all that male dominance stuff."

"Maybe selkie men don't get trapped into marriage because human women are kinder than human men."

"I don't want to stereotype men," I said. "Anyway, Finn's kind. So was Andrew."

"Finn's half selkie," said Ailsa. "And Andrew must have been a little bit selkie too, you know. Just like you."

I couldn't think of anything to say to that, so we went on lying in silence until Finn was ready to go home. As I got to my feet, I took one last look around, assuming that I would never see the selkie colony like this again. As it happened, several of them were back in their seal skins. Murchadh was in his, his large and shapeless silhouette dominating the landscape, his call drowning out all others.

Whatever I had been looking for, there was now no more to find.

A. R. Collins lives in England, and teaches English language and literature to small groups of teenagers, a job which she loves. Exposed to children's classics from a young age, she has always loved stories, and wanted to write her own before she learned how to write. Her writing website and blog can be found at http://arcollins.weebly.com/.

Virus
by
Stephen R. Smith

The flickering neon promise was the same as always: *Rooms by the Hour* and underneath flashed *Vacancy*.

I knew what I would find inside.

The locks on the double front doors were burned away completely leaving a meter-wide hole in the surrounding glass, soft bubbled edges that were very recently molten.

I pushed one door open with the barrel of my pistol and stepped into the lobby. The small room reeked of antiseptic cleansers layered with floral air conditioners. Neither masked the smell of roasted hair and flesh.

Behind the front desk a thin figure in a grey suit lay in an androgynous heap, head burned completely off. It wouldn't matter how fast the meat wagons got here, they could grow back an arm or a leg, scrape the latent personality and experience from the brain and reprint a clone if the kill turned out to be unrighteous, but without a head this life was lost for good. Working the front desk at a whore house, it was unlikely whoever it was could afford backup.

Up the stairs to the second floor, I passed room after room where the scene played out the same: doors kicked off hinges, hookers and clients alike in various states of undress lay in torched heaps, some in their beds, some near the doorway no doubt investigating the noise, some halfway to the bathroom or bedroom window, their desperate attempt to escape cut short by the merciless hand of death dealt at apparent close range.

He was in the last room, standing staring at her body where it lay motionless on the bed. He turned slightly as I entered, the weapon hanging limply at his side. The virus had turned more than half of his skin black, polished and shiny, the far side of his face infected top to bottom giving him the eerie appearance of a man half in shadow, even in this light.

She was dead. Skin turned completely black, joints shattered where her death throes had broken the crystalline flesh in the last few moments of life.

"They must have made her a carrier, kept her isolated until she infected me." He waved absently at her. "I was her only client in the last three weeks, she was saving herself for me." I remembered the body at the front desk, his opening salvo of questions. "They must have let it off its leash once they were done with her." One side of his face creased into a smile, the dark side frozen, the resulting expression appropriately grotesque. "No loose ends." He fished in his pocket and produced my badge. "You'll be needing this," he said as he tossed it to me. I caught it left handed without looking, brailled its surface reflexively and slipped it in my hip pocket. "We're not done here."

I knew what he'd started I would have to finish. We stared at each other, like figures on either side of a funhouse mirror, he regarding what he'd looked like before the infection effectively ended his life, I was looking back at what I had become in the days while I was being reconstituted. The carnage between then and now making us two very different people.

"Not different," he read my mind, "we're the same." He weighed the blaster carefully, studying the purpose-built simplicity of the weapon as though seeing it for the first time. "And if they came for us once, they'll be coming again."

I knew he was right. Knew I was right. He met my gaze and held it. I wondered if the sadness in his eyes was echoed in mine.

"Thank god for backup." He raised the barrel and pushed it under his jaw, once more the grotesque smile in the instant before the particle blast erased it for good.

"Thank god for backup." I repeated.

A Study in Augmentation
by
Melissa Swanepoel

Jenna shut her staff locker, dumped her upgrade scrubs in the anti-static bin, and ducked out the back entrance to get outside without having to interact with any of the rest of the team.

NewMecha was a new clinic and a fresh start, away from the facts and rumours of her situation—but to them, Jenna was just the new augmentations clinic. As such, she was supposed to be building rapport with the rest of the staff, but while that had seemed a worthwhile if challenging pursuit when she first signed on, after today, it seemed an insurmountable challenge.

"Good work in there, today."

Ahh, wonderful. Of course Connor was out here smoking and not the least bit shaken by what was said during their last refit. What *he* said, as a matter of fact.

"Yeah. Thanks, I suppose." Jenna felt her gloved hands clench even as she fought back the urge to say something that might get her in trouble, or blacklisted. Something like, '*not bad for prototype,*'—but after fuming about Connor's offhand remark about their patient all day, Jenna didn't have it in her to throw a verbal punch—or herself under the bus. Not when it could very well land her back on the unemployed roster and the good graces of the very few willing to sign on a prototyper.

Jenna adjusted her stance to lean less heavily on her brace-wrapped left leg, and the implants whirring away in her left shoulder creaked at the shift. She was two weeks in at NewMecha Clinic, and if she could just get herself home, she'd be able to transfer most of her first pay cheque and finally download the software upgrade she'd been waiting for—saving for, to be honest.

"You've got a gear-thumb, that's for sure," Connor joked, taking a drag from his cigarette, unaware of exactly how true what he'd just said was. After all, they only ever saw one another in the pit, scrubbed and robed and gloved up, when they were working together to refit implants, run system resets, or embed new neural relay seed layers.

"Right," Jenna said, too tired of him, of today, to grin at how true that sentence was, and at how stupid Connor had—yet again—revealed himself to be. How blind. "See you tomorrow." She turned away, cutting what Connor thought passed for conversation short, and then headed out into the pedestrian flow.

For a moment, Jenna considered her options for getting home. She was cutting it fine in so many different ways—money and time being the worst of them. She barely had enough for the upgrade as it was—if she splurged on transport home, she might not be able to buy what she needed to keep herself fed for the next week. Hunger would lead to loss of focus, which would lead to loss of job—no go there.

If she elected to walk home, she wouldn't have to choose between a full week's worth of groceries and her at this point critical update, but she knew that her time was running out on getting the updates she needed. She glanced at her wrist mount:

23:20hrs

It was only an hour's walk to home—40minutes if she hustled and took every short cut she'd found between here and there so far.

With a nod, Jenna chose and set off at a brisk pace. Time to put one last set of paces on her current configuration.

In so many other worlds of different outcomes, Jenna chose a different path. She splurged on transportation, or walked slower, or walked faster, or chose an altogether different route.

But in this world, Jenna chose to cut through Tunning Square at close to midnight, and in this world, Jenna stumbled, quite accidentally, on the following scene:

A woman, perhaps in her early thirties, like Jenna herself, standing tall and arrogant even as she was herded back towards the mouth of the alleyway Jenna had wormed herself into via a rotten divider gate.

And now Jenna had a choice once more: go back the way she

came and get herself home, stick to the plan—or involve herself. She gritted her teeth and clenched her fists and hunkered in a dark corner to wait, to see what was what. For all she knew, things weren't as they seemed—and that would be a point of convenience, since Jenna was on a tight schedule.

From where she waited, crouched, she could hear a clear and rather posh voice make some sort of demand—and then the dark laughter and razzing catcalls that sound like a terrible outcome in the making.

Jenna sighed and started moving forward in the shadows, because now she knew things were exactly what they seemed: some silly night-time tourist in the net of one of the packs of predators with nothing better to do than ruin someone's night—or life.

Creeping until just shy of the light that shone a circle on the ground by the alley mouth, Jenna waited for a break in the woman's imperious questioning—something about a boy and a murder?—and then stepped forward.

"Evening all," Jenna said mildly. "Hope I'm not late," she said to the very surprised and somehow delighted-looking woman. "Shall we get going?" she asked, trying to de-escalate the situation, maybe get everyone on board with the plan of her and her "friend" just walking away while the shock of her appearance numbed responses.

"Oh, now, that's something," the young man at the front of the pack said, his eyes flicking to Jenna, specifically her neck. "What a night, my beauts," he said in hushed tones over his shoulder at his mates.

Coming to stand to the right of the woman, who was also looking her over with bright, inquisitive eyes, seemingly oblivious to the situation they were both in now, Jenna cleared her throat and tried again:

"My friend and I—"

"—Are trespassing." The head of the pack crossed his arms. "Not exactly wise, considering what you are, but oh, so convenient." His grin was a flash of cruel intention.

The stares at her neck, the time of night, and the location clicked for Jenna: not just a pack of ruffians, but specifically a pack of a *scrappers*.

Well, shit.

The scarring creeping up the side of her neck was not as bad as it could be, and often read as an elective upgrade instead of what it really was, but it was still visible, hence her flipped-up collar and scarf. In her haste to make her way home, it seemed those two barriers had shifted just enough to expose her neck—and her augmented nature. Jenna should have expected something like this—but then how could she have anticipated walking head on into a scrapper altercation?

New job, she thought. New turf, new threats. High time to break in the streets, probably. Jenna's mouth pulled into a grim line as she readied herself.

"Ohh, we can spot one of you lot a mile away," the leader continued on with a jaunty sort of confidence, as if this were a fun challenge, a distraction.

"What luck for us, then, to have found such an expert," the woman spoke up then, her voice still loud and clear, with a sort of confidence that almost pulled agreement from those who heard it. Her words wore enthusiasm and charm, while underneath Jenna could detect an icy disdain. Jenna raised her eyebrows at the woman's matter-of-fact adaptation to Jenna's presence and the nature of the gang's intent. "We'd like to ask you some questions about recent scrapper gang activity in this area," the woman continued, but it was as if she didn't exist.

"What's it then," the lead scrapper said over her, stepping toward Jenna, his eyes calculating, appraising, more like. "Got yourself a little tweak for your eyes? Maybe some extra RAM so you can outperform real people and steal their work?" He didn't seem too upset at the latter possibility—more like a businessman evaluating a competitor's portfolio prior to a violent acquisition.

He was close enough now that Jenna could have lunged for him—but she didn't. His words were nothing new in her reality, and his assumptions were not going to arm him against her in this.

Quite the opposite, in fact.

"If you tell me now," he crooned, "maybe we keep your corpse a little prettier for the identifying, yeah?"

"This is your last chance to cooperate—" the woman started again.

He rolled his eyes, expression thick with annoyance. "New deal, babe. How about you go home safe and sound, and we'll just get on with stripping this clunker for parts."

The woman frowned, glanced at Jenna, then stared defiantly

back at their antagoniser. "How about you—" she started to counter, but didn't get far.

The scrapper's patience snapped. His fist came forward, the hilt of a cable knife clasped tight, ready to drive pommel to temple.

Even as his fist tracked closer, Jenna was moving to intercept, and the woman was ducking out of the way, surprisingly agile, surging back up—

And *headbutting* her attacker.

Jenna nearly stumbled from surprise, but didn't—instead she stepped between the woman and the very surprised scrapper as he lurched backwards, just in time to block retaliation when it arrived in the form of another scrapper on the attack, this time a lad with hooked blade.

Jenna may not have had the words for her anger with Connor earlier, but she had the fists, the blows for it now. Her right hand reached out to grasp the offending wrist on the down swing, then slid and curved around the attacking arm; she felt the twist and her body reacted without her even needing to think about it, bringing up her left elbow to snap the head back with a loud crack of a chin strike. As the newly limp scrapper fell back, she spun, opening her left hand and extending it to deliver the hard blade of her palm to the throat of the next attacker, who fell back gasping and choking, retching and wretched.

Behind her, the woman regained her composure just as the first attacker lurched forward for another go, trying to sidestep Jenna and her left arm.

Jenna, however, wasn't going to allow him anywhere near the woman at her side—her right hand shot out in a lightning movement, grabbed the back of the leader's collar, and used their joined momentum to spin him into the V of her left arm, and *squeezed*.

He struggled, thrashing, but with his lungs' access to oxygen much restricted, and his brain's access to blood even more so, what must have been planned as a masterful counter-manoeuvre was as effective as a tissue in a gale.

Beyond the theater of his defeat, the other two attackers were slowly, unsteadily picking themselves up, the last unscathed member putting a trembling hand on each of them.

The woman stepped briskly forward, righting the tumble of her dark curls with a rake of her fingers. She smiled brightly at each of them, before turning her attention to the man still feebly fighting Jenna's hold. She had a dark red mark on her forehead and a glint in her eye.

"What's your name then?" she asked, pointedly conversational and cheerful.

Jenna's captive struggled in her grasp, tried to dislodge her grip once more, tried to bite even, but she had his neck in her metal crook, and simply tightened her hold even further, making him wheeze.

"Hh-hh-hh," he tried.

"Oh, dearie me," the woman said with a little shake of her head. "Doctor, if you'd be so good as to let him have a lungful of air?"

Jenna's eyebrows flicked up in surprise, but she relaxed her arm a fraction. Her captive gasped in air, his hands scrabbling weakly at the steel vice around his trachea.

"Splendid," the woman said. "Now: name, please?"

"G-g—Geti."

"Hello, Geti, it's a pleasure to formally meet you. Please have your friends stand down, or my friend here will—well, do you really want me to finish that particular sentence?" She smiled a smile that would've been charming if it hadn't shown quite so many teeth.

"Back off, you lot. I said back!" Geti hissed hoarsely, his one hand ineffectually pawing at Jenna's elbow and the other gesturing weakly.

"Thank you," the woman said, utterly sincerely. "Now, back to questions: have you heard of anyone killing augmentation recipients and purposefully destroying the implants?"

Jenna restrained her surprise even as Geti gaped at the woman. He then struggled to position himself to make eye contact with Jenna. "Is she for real?"

Jenna snorted and raised her eyebrows at the woman, who rolled her eyes. Jenna tried to control the urge to grin, and only partly succeeded. The result was lopsided and impish and made Jenna feel like she was in on some delightful secret.

"Do you really want to drag this out, Geti?" the woman asked their interrogation suspect pointedly, who heaved a harsh breath. Jenna's throat almost ached in sympathy. "My question?" she prompted again.

"Makes no sense," Geti croaked out. "Why ruin salvage? Why go to all the trouble?"

"There was a boy found, recently," the woman continued. "Body ruined—flesh and implants alike. There were two more before him—a woman and a man, in similar states. Does that ring a bell at all?" She looked expectantly from one scrapper to the next, and Jenna watched as those sharp eyes ticked over their faces, their bodies, cataloguing details to the smallest degree, it appeared.

Geti frowned darkly at the question, and Jenna noticed the rest of his gang seemed similarly taken aback—almost affronted.

"Hmm," the woman hummed, and her hands steepled at her chin briefly, as if she were lecturing at a university and had just been presented with an absolutely unexpected answer by her students. "So, no stories like that? No roving gangs of scrappers gone too far? Not even accidentally?" she pushed. With a quick swoop, the woman got in Geti's space, looking closely at his face. Her eyes narrowed after a moment, and she glanced up at Jenna. "Maybe stop crushing his windpipe for now?" she suggested.

Jenna shrugged and decided she was done with him altogether. She dumped him from her hold, and he shuddered and shivered on the ground. After a cautious moment, the unscathed scrapper darted forward to check him over and help him to his feet.

Once upright, Geti's eyes glimmered with the yellow of the streetlight, and his angry stare landed on Jenna even as he answered the woman. "Everyone makes mistakes the first few times—cut the wrong joint, pull the wrong cable, forget to collect some of the scarring network. But no one makes that their M.O. There's good money even in the botches—less than perfect removal can still be worth the effort of finding a buyer. But leaving it to rot and rust?" Geti shook his head, and his mates joined in. They seem disturbed by the idea.

"Wasteful," the girl holding a hooked cabling knife said. She looked at Jenna as she said it, then asked the woman: "You sure you don't want to cash *that* in?" There was an ugly mark blooming on her neck, and a grudge thinking about doing the same in her eyes as she glared at Jenna.

"You—" the woman began hotly, but Jenna stepped forward ever so slightly into readiness, a reminder of events not long past.

"—Are welcome to try," Jenna finished for the woman. She watched the girl's eyes as they travelled, taking her in properly—the barely-there sweat at her brow and temples, the disarray of her hair, the way her scarf hung open and her collar sat askew, broadcasting her scarring and its pale gleam. Those eyes traced the flex of her arms and her legs, saw the steel-toed boots and the fists ready to find skin and flesh and bone once more. Jenna could feel a buzzing anticipation in her body, in her implants, as if every fibre, natural and mechanical, were queuing attacks, just in case.

"Boss?" the girl asked Geti, unsure.

"Not them," he rasped. His mates were visibly relieved. "Not here and not now." They gathered themselves, and then Jenna and her companion watched as they slunk off into the gloom beyond the lampposts.

"Well," the woman said at last, rocking on her feet briskly. "That wasn't as useless as it could have been." She turned to Jenna in a sudden move, her hand out—

Offering a shake.

"Name's Elle—Elle Cunningham."

Jenna took the hand on autopilot and shook it. "Jenna West."

"*Doctor* Jenna West," Elle corrected her and Jenna stopped shaking her hand.

"How do you arrive at that?" she asked, her curiosity piqued. It had been so long since she'd been anything but an augmentation technician—at least three years, now.

"Oh, just something I noticed." Elle smiled a self-satisfied little smile.

That sounded like a load of bollocks, but Jenna found herself frowning, wondering at the answer all the same.

"You're also not contradicting me—unless you're happy to let me continue uncorrected?"

"It's not wrong," Jenna said at last. "Just out of date." After a moment, she remembered to let go of Elle's hand. Jenna flexed her left arm and checked it for damage, trying to parse beyond the usual connection static. "Are you hurt?" she asked Elle, trying to move past the confusion in her thoughts. "That was one hell of blow to the head."

"I'm fine," Elle said, flapping a hand.

"And I'm not convinced," Jenna said drily. She felt a twinge deep in her hip, and her face went still. Oh god, she'd lost track of the time—of everything. Her thoughts raced even as she became aware of a long list of grievances her leg had been logging during the unexpected exertion. "Are we done here?"

"Yes, I suppose." Elle peered at her curiously, as if taken aback by Jenna's sudden change.

"Good—then we should get back to mine so we can patch up."

Elle frowned at her, and tilted her head. "I told you, I'm fine—"

"Yes, well, I'm not." Jenna took a steadying breath. "And, I think I'm going to need your help."

Elle hailed them a cab once they'd made it back to the better-lit part of the city. It was a good thing, too, because Jenna's leg had started locking up, the knee reluctant to swing, and there was a persistent ache in her chest, although that could have been due to nerves.

Jenna didn't want to find out if that were true, and besides: her focus had narrowed to getting home, checking out her leg, and connecting for her update. If she'd had any choice in the matter, she would have been alone for all of that—but in her current state, she needed help walking. She'd likely need help with the rest of it too.

Jenna bit her lip nervously. Adding Elle into the mix, while necessary, felt momentous and open. Unguarded.

Well, Jenna thought. Maybe it wouldn't be necessary. Maybe it would be a superficial bit of interference and she could send Elle on her way and sort it herself.

It was not.

By the time they got to Jenna's bedsit, got inside and got Jenna situated at the tiny kitchen table in her tiny kitchen, her leg had completely stopped functioning, only emitting a sort of vague, internal humming vibration, as if putting forth a great personal effort to accomplish not much at all.

Jenna scowled at it through her pants leg after ripping open the brace and roughly tugging it away from its supportive position, and remained lost in a fuming frown until finally Elle's fidgeting grew obvious enough to pull her focus back to the present.

"Next steps?" Elle asked, and there was a hesitant, helpfulness about her, so unlike the voraciously curious and careless person she had been up until Jenna's need for help. Her eyes were scanning first Jenna's face, then her body, looking for obvious sign of injury.

"If you're injured, shouldn't we have taken you to—"

"No, I don't need a clinic, just—" Jenna cut her off and took a deep breath. "I will need your help performing a hard reset on my leg, Elle."

"Your…leg," Elle repeated. She frowned, her whole face pinching.

Jenna nodded. "Hand me those scissors?" She chucked the brace she was still holding aside.

Elle looked where Jenna had indicated, and grabbed the scissors from the magnetic plate that held them. She handed them to Jenna even as she said, "Why would you need to do a hard reset on your—"

Jenna sheared her trouser leg down her left side, and Elle's eyes widened.

Gleaming between them lay Jenna's leg. Even unresponsive, there seemed to be an air of movement to it, in the same way that sports cars and running shoes always seemed poised for action.

Jenna had suspected Elle's sharp eyes had sussed out her arm, and possibly some of the more intricate, deeper implants—but she'd been right in thinking the leg had flown under her radar. The fact that she'd needed her brace today due to stabilizers running sluggish pre-driver update had likely added to that illusion.

Camouflaged in plain sight—fix hiding under flaw.

"Oh," Elle breathed. "Oh, there's more to you than meets the eye."

Jenna huffed a humourless laugh. "Or less," she said darkly. "Here," she handed the scissors back.

Elle set the scissors aside, her eyes still transfixed by Jenna's leg. Jenna followed her gaze as it flowed from the high peak of the hip seam peeking out above the waistband of her briefs, a pearly net of scarring and subcutaneous relay mesh, down to the broad swaths of cabling inside metflex sheaths, visible yet encased, then to the knee, a complex joint millennia in the evolving here simplified into a ball socket joint with a hard 135 degree range of motion. Past that, Jenna's lower leg consisted of more cabling, these strands thinner, more densely packed leading to the ankle, another engineering marvel recast in metal and polymer and manufacturing design branding ethos. Her foot was the newest component, gleaming brighter, its design more minimalist, the shapes of the toes neatly seating together to make a nimble, responsive wedge—or at least, they would if they were currently capable of processing their environment.

Elle looked up at last. "You—" she began, then stopped. "What do you need me to do?"

"I'm late on a pretty vital update, and that little altercation did not help matters." Jenna looked up at her and took a deep breath. "I need you to help me perform a reset on it so I can get it to a state where it will allow an update—can I ask that of you?"

Elle nodded, her face serious even as her eyes shone with interest.

Jenna nodded to herself and said, "Underneath my bed are three sectional cases—bring the two nearest the foot of the bed here, please." She added, "And towels!" as Elle dashed to her bed, her movements nimble and swift and purposeful and everything Jenna currently wasn't.

She clenched her fists and tried to put that feeling aside. It wasn't helping, and it wasn't new, and it wasn't fixable, not right now. No, right now her leg needed fixing, and she had enough tools to accomplish that job, even if she'd need a spare set of hands, and— well—

Elle hadn't run screaming or disgusted, hadn't even politely bowed out and left Jenna to her own meagre devices, and she would have been well within her rights to do any of those things, to be frank. Many others had backed away from helping for catching much less of a glimpse of Jenna's augmentations.

Scattering that train of thought, Elle returned with a carry case in each hand, trying to manage the weight as evenly as possible. She set them down with a bit of grunt, then watched with keen eyes as Jenna thumbprint-keyed open both of them. Unlocked, they rolled open, tool trays lifting up as the kits splayed wide, sanitizing vapour wisping into nothingness.

"Oh," Elle's eyes lit up with delight, already pulling on a pair of the nitrile gloves included in the kit. "I see you bring your work home with you."

"No escaping it when it's part of you," Jenna said without thinking, reaching for one of the towels had placed beside her. She positioned a towel under her unresponsive leg with much shuffling, then pulled on her own set of gloves as she reached for a tool resembling a medical grade crowbar.

"I'm so glad to meet someone who understands that aspect of—

" Elle started, then stopped as Jenna glanced up, confused. "Oh, wait, you mean that literally."

Jenna stared, caught off guard by this woman who seemed curious and at home all at once in a situation most people preferred to pretend didn't exist. Jenna felt a frown go to war with the moment before a laugh, and the resultant skirmish produced a sort of bemused, perplexed outcome, Jenna's mouth oddly paused mid-open, and an odder chuck of sound escaping through it.

But then time and urgency reasserted themselves, and Jenna blinked, and the strange moment was gone. She snorted. "Right. So, uh..." She looked down at her leg, the thing that actually needed attention, and didn't look up to meet Elle's eyes for a moment, still caught up in a moment that had come and gone and left something indelible behind.

Jenna firmed her thoughts, her focus. Whatever it was that had happened, had been left behind—it didn't matter. What mattered was getting her implant components functional again, before the rest of her status could begin to deteriorate.

Despite her leg currently pitching the biggest fit, there were certainly components at far greater risk. Her left arm, the internal assembly of collar bone and tissues surrounding her shoulder socket, and aortic assembly implant were all in peril as long as this deviant process was allowed to continue affecting her leg.

Jenna's jaw tightened as her left hand spasmed. If they didn't reboot the leg soon, whatever run-error had taken root in the leg's processors could very well make the neural relay jump and infect her thoracic unit.

"What do you need?" Elle asked, and Jenna pursed her lips.

"Hold this." Jenna handed her a cable spreader. "I'm going to force this cabling up and away from the NR housing, and I need you to position it to hold the cables apart when I take this lever away. Can you do that?"

Elle rolled her eyes. "I'm sure I'll manage to perform such a complex task."

Jenna rolled her eyes right back at her. "Just get ready." And with that, she slipped the slimmer edge of the crowbar along the taper lip of one bundle of cabling, where her IT band would have been had she still had it. With some pressure, she got the lever to sink a thumb's length in, and then adjusted her grip. "Ready?"

Elle nodded, only remembering halfway through to close her

mouth.

Jenna heaved back with as much force as she could, and her quad stand-in cabling moved the merest amount. Jenna grunted, half in pain, half in frustration. She clenched her jaws and kept at it, fighting the stasis of her unresponsive implant, her right arm's muscles aching and complaining, and her left a persistent buzz of strain.

"Jenna—" Elle's voice was tight.

"I know," Jenna gritted out, not needing to see her leg opening up, slowly but surely—she could feel it distantly, through a sort of numbing static, for which she was momentarily very grateful. Cracking open a leg like a crate without that influence would have been horrendously painful otherwise.

"Almost far enough," Elle murmured, holding the spreader at the ready, fingers steady even as her voice trembled a bit. "There—"

Like lightning she pushed the wedge bracket in and *into*, and Jenna jerked in surprise. The crowbar clattered out of her hands, but the wedge settled into its place, fulfilling its purpose, and Jenna bent forward to heave a few deep breaths.

"A little warning next time?" Jenna asked at last, and Elle ducked her head sheepishly.

"Apologies."

"It's okay." Jenna took another deep breath and her back muscles trembled—from exertion or stress, it didn't matter. Everything felt raw and overused right now.

"Okay," she said at last, and again, "okay." She sat back up. "So, next we'll need the second kit—inside there should be a blue vial and a clear vial—we'll want both in a minute, but above those is a small, slim set of rods. We want the middle one." She watched as Elle's gloved fingers held up the rod in question.

"What's this for?"

Jenna quirked a grim smile. "The hard reset. If you look inside the cavity we've created, there should be a small hole the same diameter as—"

"Oh my god, is this a joke?" Elle asked, her face going slack. She sat back on her haunches and fixed Jenna with a shrewd look.

Jenna frowned at her. "I need you to insert—"

"You *cannot* be serious." Elle almost seemed upset.

Jenna's frown deepened. "But I am. Look—" she started before Elle could start again, "I didn't design this system, and I'm not responsible for whoever it was decided to put the access point for hard reset behind the cabling that stiffens when a hard reset is necessary." The number of conflicts of design in prototype units always left Jenna shaking her head—when she wasn't shaking with anger.

"No, but—" Elle tried to interject, holding up the reset pin as if that said everything that needed to be said—but Jenna pushed on:

"I'm just the sod who needs a hard reset. Now, please. Before whatever code iteration malfunctioned mirror-clones itself beyond its local origination." She swallowed around the panic that sentence wanted to bring with it.

Elle's mouth clicked shut, then opened: "What does that mean?"

Jenna closed her eyes. "It means please reset my leg before whatever disabled it spreads into my thoracic implant." She blinked her eyes open again.

Elle's face drained of colour. "Oh—god—"

"Just—"

Elle slotted the little bit of metal into place and drove it home with the pad of her thumb.

Jenna's leg jerked ineffectually, then went completely lax—only the weight of her leg's cabling kept the wedge pinned in place, all tension gone, just under two stone of dead weight metal attached to her body via complex seams.

"How long?" Elle asked, seeming a bit breathless.

Jenna tried to ignore the feeling of "missing" a part of her. Her left leg normally fed her brain enough data that she could forget that something that she'd been born with was nowhere to be found, but in moments of neural silence like this, Jenna was achingly aware of the altered state of herself. "About ten seconds should do."

Elle nodded, and they waited, silently, together, until—

A crawling sensation trickled up Jenna's neck and into her scalp, her skull, followed by her leg initiating: a waltz-pattern of vibrations cycled three times, *b̃-b̃-b̃, b̃-b̃-b̃, b̃-b̃-b̃,* and then a series of clicks and whirrs played out, each accompanied by a testing flex of a different section of Jenna's leg.

She gently took the reset rod from Elle's fingers, and then removed the spreader wedge just in time for the quad-cabling to contract and settle back into place.

Finally, after her foot had flexed and pointed itself and checked its range of motion, her leg fell silent. A moment later, Jenna registered a building internal pressure. She clenched her jaw and closed her eyes as that pressure bubble burst—and flooded her leg with a cleansing rinse. The pressure pushed it all the way to the surface via the complex channels and layers of her interlaced components, where it felt warm and cold at the same time—her leg's best approximation of "wet," it seemed—and seeped from the surface lines where those components layered against one another. It was a dirty blue, like water used to wash new denim, and it soaked into the towel she'd placed so strategically at the start.

When Jenna opened her eyes, Elle was staring at her leg, and had obviously dipped her gloved fingers into a blue patch on the towel. She had pinched her thumb and forefinger together and pulled them apart, as indicated by the thick, viscous strand of cleanser that now strung them together.

"Fascinating," she said, startling Jenna, who'd been expecting a rather different response. Elle blinked and met Jenna's wary gaze. "So," she said.

Jenna waited, still poised for that other response to finally arrive, yet unsure what was coming.

Elle wiped her fingers back on the towel, then pulled her gloves off. "The quality of your implants is professional grade—but the designs leave much to be desired for optimization—so, prototypes." Elle tapped steepled fingers against her lips as Jenna stared at her, as she continued with, "Making you what is colloquially referred to as a 'prototyper'—thought of as unstable, untrustworthy, and unsafe. Terrible attachments of meaning to an otherwise useful designation."

Elle paused, her eyes ticking over Jenna. "Multiple implants, all on the left side—likely the result of severe bodily trauma. Likely war, given your skillsets—doctor and unarmed combatant—likely Chechnya, given the timeline. Sound about right?"

Jenna gaped at her, which Elle seemed to take as an affirmative.

Elle nodded down at Jenna's exposed implants. "Your leg, your arm, and some component of your thoracic organ set." Her eyes tracked all over Jenna's face, then to the scarring on her neck, then to her eyes again. "Anything else?"

Jenna felt her eyebrows raise and finally found her voice: "Did someone surgically remove your tact?"

"Congenital defect," Elle answered without missing a beat and accompanying hand flap. "But, you are right—apologies for the bluntness of my curiosity."

"But not for your curiosity?"

"Oh, I never apologise for that," Elle said with a bit of a charming grin and what could have been a wink.

Jenna felt supremely unbalanced, even though she was still sitting down. She blinked up at where Elle now stood, rocking up and down on the balls of her feet with something like a nervous energy.

"Of course, it is late and I have offended you." She unclasped her hands from where they'd been behind her back, and tucked them into her pockets. "I can show myself out and be on my way – "

"No," Jenna said at once, quite surprising herself and Elle as well, if her quizzical look was any evidence.

"No?" Elle asked, her rocking slowing to a halt.

"It's late," Jenna said, then grimaced at how simple she must sound. "I mean—taxis stop picking up in this neighbourhood after midnight, and same goes for any ride share service you care to try. Your options are walking and—well, that's it, I'm afraid. And I think you've seen for yourself that that's not really an option in this part of town."

"I can handle myself," Elle sniffed, but made no move to head towards the door.

"You don't need a body full of scavengable tech to make you a tempting target. Take my couch—it pulls out into a cot—and in the morning, you can catch a bus or a cab, and not your death."

"That is very—you're sure?" Elle asked, seeming a bit nonplussed by the offer. Possibly she'd expected to be thrown bodily from the bedsit for her rambling and personal observations of Jenna's situation—but beyond the tactlessness of the delivery, Jenna had sensed no vitriol, no spite, not even pity. Elle had gathered the facts of Jenna and stated them back to her plainly with no judgement. It had been—refreshing, oddly enough.

Jenna blinked at the thought, and said, "I would sleep much better knowing you are safe for the night." Jenna'd already seen Elle's ability to get caught up in curiosity and forsake safety—and it really was an unfriendly time of night, especially in this part of town. There was a different urge at work as well: she didn't just want to keep Elle safe—she wanted to keep her close. The events of the night so far had been absolutely mad—but they had nothing on

Elle, on the fact of her existence, and Jenna was half afraid that she'd blink and they'd be gone, un-happened, just imagined by her faulty wiring and loneliness feeding on each other. "Please," she said at last, and hoped she didn't sound like she felt, confused and hopeful, and confused about feeling hopeful. She desperately wanted time to process the blur of the night.

Elle's eyes narrowed. "Unexpected," she murmured after a moment, almost as if to herself.

"What is?" Jenna asked, flexing her left foot and trying not to sound like she was hanging on Elle's answer.

Elle's gaze snapped back to focus on Jenna, as if she'd been a long way away. She gave a little shake of her head, setting her dark curls bouncing. "Nothing—or at least, very little on this green earth," she said with another dismissive flap of her hand. "So, alright, fine, yes, I'll stay—what next?" She indicated Jenna's leg. "That's not finished, is it?"

Jenna pulled her mouth to the side even as she reeled internally. "Not quite. I need both those vials I mentioned earlier—one's for me, and one's for the leg—and also two fresh syringes. And, sorry, you said you'll stay?"

"Yes," Elle said, already moving to gather what Jenna had asked for. She paused in the middle of pulling on one fresh nitrile glove. "Why? Changed your mind?"

"Nope—not at all—just…checking. Thank you."

"I believe it's convention for me to thank you," Elle said stiffly, not meeting Jenna's eyes quite dead on as she handed over the implements with her gloved hand. "So, that. To you." And with that she clammed up, and Jenna was grateful to have a task to be absorbed in.

Jenna still felt a wave of nerves under those sharp eyes, and tried not to let it show or affect her hands as she extracted a full dose from the blue vial. The needle was large, less of a puncturing tip and more of a docking attachment.

Jenna pulled her briefs down over her left hip, trying not to blush under Elle's unwavering gaze as she worked a silicone plug free from a groove port. Once it was out, she slotted the syringe home, and pushed the plunger slowly, pushing the viscous, gel-like liquid into the waiting cavity.

"It's a refill. For what just happened. Anti-static gel and dust repellent," Jenna said, needing to fill the silence in the room. "Since we forced a reset, small particles may have contaminated deeper, more sensitive layers. The pressurised flush uses the inner circulatory system to mitigate any contamination we may have caused."

Elle nodded and continued to watch as Jenna pulled the syringe free and re-plugged the port, then wiped the top of her leg down with a fresh towel. It came away faintly blue. "And this clear one?" Elle held up the vial against the light and examined it.

"That one's for me." Jenna held out a hand to take the vial and the accompanying syringe. This needle was much finer, although still not what Jenna would consider a beginner jab. "It keeps my immune system from noticing there's a neural relay to reject inside me." She pulled another full dose, and then rearranged herself so she could lift her unaugmented right buttock off the floor. "Hand me one of those little alcohol wipes?"

The wipe was cool against her skin, and then the needle was hotly sharp as it punched through into fatty tissue. Jenna grunted, then pushed the plunger with her right thumb, breathing tersely through her nose. She then had her brief internal struggle, the same she always did, when she had to pull the needle free, the usual anxiousness compounded by being watched.

"I would have thought you'd be accustomed to administering injections," Elle remarked, her voice carefully neutral.

"To other people, yes. I try to avoid having to do this to myself. I am not," Jenna ground out, finally removing the needle from herself, "a fan."

"It's not the pain," Elle said, as if to herself.

Jenna snorted. "Of course it's not the pain. It's never the pain."

"Then what?"

Jenna shook her head, not sure she had words for the functional panic of unattached fear whenever she did this for herself. Jenna released a breath. "Help me up so I can bin this mess?"

Elle helped hoist her to standing, then offered her a plaster for her puncture site. Jenna accepted it and got the barely bleeding hole covered. She walked stiffly, her steps ginger on her newly rebooted leg. It always felt a bit tight after, like jeans gone through the wash, and needed about a half mile's walking to wear it back in. She was never sure whether it was physical or psychosomatic.

Jenna tidied up, hyper aware of Elle still watching her. At last she ran out of things to do turned to face Elle.

"So. Um." She gestured helplessly at the small space she called home. "Make yourself at home. The loo's through there—" she pointed, "—and there are extra blankets and pillows in the closet beside it."

Elle nodded, her eyes caught on Jenna and not following her pointing.

"I need to get settled for the night so I can run my update—will you be alright for the night if I do that now?"

Elle nodded again.

They set about their separate routines—Jenna ate a packet of oyster crackers so she wouldn't wake nauseous from updating on an empty stomach, and Elle spent fifteen minutes in the bathroom with the door shut before emerging looking exactly the same as she had when she entered, saved for having untucked her blouse from her suit pants and removed her shoes.

There followed some very formal "good nights", and then the flat fell silent.

At last Jenna lay back in bed. Pulling a battered ethernet cable from her bedside table drawer, she plugged it into her cervical port. She reconfirmed her update download, transferred the payment out of her account, and lay back, ready for the download to happen. A triple buzz announced successful connection, and she felt the initiating hum. Relief flooded her, and Jenna closed her eyes.

She slipped downward into darkness.

The next morning dawned bright and awkward and early.

Jenna stuttered awake to the sound of Elle clattering about in the kitchen.

She barely remembered to unplug herself from the ethernet cable before sitting up, not wanting to upset her guest first thing in the morning. Replacement limbs were one thing, but she'd yet to meet anyone unfazed by cranial implant interfacing, and that was including herself –

"Was your update successful?" Elle asked, turning around with a bag of ground coffee clutched triumphantly. "I assume it was the update happening via your cranial cable attachment, and not some sort of recharge mechanism?"

Jenna blinked and stared. She opened, closed her mouth.

"…Yes?"

"Excellent, then you can come be functional and tell me where you've hidden what passes for a coffee maker in this place."

"So, what's the next step?" Jenna asked, pushing down on the plunger of her French press. It was a battered metal and glass little thing that she'd found in the cabinets after she'd moved into this particular bedsit. Despite its age and unknown origins, it had helped her wake up many a morning.

Elle was busily tapping away at her phone. She'd spent the better part of the morning so far filling Jenna in on her role in the investigation into the murders she'd mentioned to the scrappers last night. Apparently, she'd also been up all night on Jenna's couch, researching and reaching out to her contacts regarding next steps. Sleep seemed not to be a priority for Elle, which explained why caffeine was.

"Well, first we went low," Elle said, accepting a mug of hot, just pressed coffee. She looked comfortable and fresh, if rumpled, after a night on Jenna's tiny fold-out set. "Next, let's try high." Her eyes were focused somewhere far away as she doctored her mug and took a sip, and Jenna saw that peculiar, almost sinister-seeming focus it seemed she got when she was running other people's potential actions through the planning engine of her brain.

"'We'?" Jenna asked.

"Of course—you've been instrumental to my progress on this case with less than twelve hours of involvement." She smiled impishly. "You asked me to stay last night. Don't tell me you're ok with not knowing what happens next."

Jenna took a breath to speak, then closed her mouth. A moment later she blew out a gust of half-answers unworded. She'd spent a fair portion of her own night post-update completion tossing and turning, wishing the morning wouldn't mean the inevitable: this interesting thing being over, this interesting person being gone.

But, real life rarely gave you what you wanted, she knew all too well, and she'd resigned herself to returning to the mundane complexities of her life with what little grace she could muster. She wouldn't intrude on Elle's life any more than she already had, and she wouldn't foist her difficulties on this woman who obviously had more important things to involve herself in. "I'm sure you must know and have connections to many who are more qualified—"

"Pffft," Elle said with that flap of her hand. "Are you in or out?"

Jenna blinked, then nodded, her lips pressed tight. She held her hand out for a shake. "In."

Elle's eyes lit up as she shook Jenna's hand. "Brilliant."

Jenna smiled to herself, poured her own cup of coffee and blew on it to cool it for drinking. She felt far less composed than Elle looked this morning—she'd slept deeply, but not all in one piece.

The reboot last night had rattled her hard, inside and out, leaving her exhausted and jittery with nerves all at once. As for the upgrade, the download had taken most of the night, fraying the edges of her sleep, but vital, and so she had endured. She could still feel it settling into place, and despite her small snack, she'd still woken to a patina of nausea, a feeling akin to a hangover.

And yet, standing in her kitchenette with coffee in hand and Elle in reach, Jenna felt oddly calm, if nonplussed. She'd forgotten to throw on her sweats she normally wore to cover her leg and arm even when alone, and was in sleep shorts and shirt only. Somehow, when covered in layer after layer of clothing out in public left her feeling raw and exposed, here, under the laser scrutiny of Elle's curiosity, Jenna felt…fine. Good, even. Comfortable, and wasn't that preposterous? She hadn't felt *comfortable* for going on three years now. And here, with a near-stranger she'd fished out of a fight just the night before, suddenly she was just that.

She shifted her weight to her left leg, felt the series of smooth adjustments it made to accommodate her weight and fine-tune her centre of gravity, felt the deep-tissue tingle of data relay.

Her tiny space seemed larger and also fuller with another person in it—although this might have been a function of the identity of that person, as any time her landlord dropped by to "check on her", every inch of the place seemed more cramped than usual, and somehow void all at once.

When Jenna returned from her musings, Elle was busy thumbing away at her phone again (still, really), her coffee already drained.

"Ah, there you are," she said without looking up. "Best to get ready, I should think—we have an appointment in an hour."

Jenna frowned. "What? With whom?"

"CEO of Exagon. Drink up—I've a cab fetching us in ten."

Jenna gaped at Elle as she popped off from her perch on the

counter and made her way to the miniscule bathroom. After a moment, she shrugged, drained her coffee, and then went to rummage for something to wear.

"Mr. Irving will see you now."

Jenna looked up from where she'd been studying a wall fresco-cum-sculpture of the tree of evolution. At the tip of the *sapiens* branch, and artist had rendered a fanciful version of a thriving Exagon brand augmented person. Jenna scowled at it.

Elle finished tapping out a message on her phone and then bounced to her feet. "Splendid."

Tall office doors swung inward, and they stepped through into a brightly lit space roughly six times larger than Jenna's entire bedsit, including bathroom. She felt her mouth pull to the side and tried not to let it—they were here to get what information they could from this "Irving", not have fits about a boastful company's boastful excess.

"Mr. Irving, this is Elle Cunningham and Jenna Weston to see you." The assistant's eyes and artful scarring caught the light unnaturally in the office, and Jenna wondered at the cost of the no-doubt top-shelf implants that skull held, so very different in quality and origin to her own.

"Errich, please," Irving said, stepping forward with a welcoming smile and holding his hand out to shake theirs. Elle kept her hands firmly tucked in her pockets and only nodded at him. Jenna shrugged and held her hand out and immediately regretted it: Irving took the shake and managed to turn it into something like a courtier's hold on a lady's hand, something to bow over.

Jenna clenched her jaw and roughly turned the hold back into a handshake, then dropped his hand.

"What can I do for you ladies, then?" Irving asked, his good-natured smile still firmly in place, although his eyes flickered at Jenna's show of disdain.

"You can answer a few questions for us about some recent deaths," Elle said, and Jenna raised her eyes to the ceiling. They were definitely going to get thrown out.

Irving frowned, his smile slipping. "I—there must be some mixup, I'm afraid. I was given to understand—"

"—That we're here as potential investors, yes. That'll be a favour I called in." Elle's smile was smug.

"Well, no favour will keep you here." Irving reached for the intercom, presumably to rid himself of their presence.

"I wouldn't follow through with that, if I were you," Elle said, her voice slipping into that cheerful conversational tone Jenna was beginning to think of as "sweetly threatening."

"Or what?" Irving took the bait, his hand pausing above the intercom.

"Or nothing." Elle shrugged, spreading her hands. "I would just assume you'd rather not involve the police right as you're opening your next round of investment. These things have a tendency to murk up the waters when you least want them to." Elle's expression was a study in open, earnest simplicity.

Irving scowled. "I have nothing to hide from the police—"

"How wonderful! Neither do I. Let's have them put in for a warrant to come and kick up some dust, shall we?" Elle suggested brightly.

"And why should they want to do that?"

"Because I'll tell my connections at the Met all about how you didn't want to answer some very basic questions, and how suspicious I found it all." Elle's eyes glittered. "My word tends to carry some weight, with the right ear at the other end of the line." She dipped her head to the side, mock-considering. "Or, you can answer my questions, and we can leave, and you can continue your investment round unimpeded." Her head tipped to the opposite side. "Choices."

There was a beat of silence, and then Irving straightened his already very straight tie. "Very well, ask your questions, then."

"Are you aware there's been a series of murders of augmentation recipients within the last few weeks?"

Jenna watched Irving closely as surprise ticked across his features.

"Has there? How terrible."

"Yes, I'm sure you care deeply about people you profited from and whose deaths you won't be impacted by," Elle said dryly. "Can you tell us if anything's changed within the field of influence of your company recently? You're the biggest player in London when it comes to implants; surely you have your finger to the pulse?"

"If you're suggesting we're somehow responsible for these

senseless crimes, I'm afraid you've not done your research." Irving leaned back against his desk. "Exagon has recently launched an internal research division for determining new measures for longevity of use for our clients who elect to undergo augmentation as well as improving lifespan for our volunteer prototypers."

"How very big of you," Jenna noted dryly.

Irving frowned at her, and turned back to Elle. "Satisfied?"

"Hardly." Elle took up a slow, pacing stroll around the office, her eyes scanning everything before them relentlessly. "Autopsy of the victims revealed they all had Exagon neural relays, although strangely they did seem to have mixed branding when it came to the actual hardware. Care to comment on that?"

"That's preposterous—we would never put off-brand hardware in with our NR nets. There's all sorts of incompatibility issues that could crop up from doing that—run-time errors and that sort of thing."

"Those could be patched up, though," Jenna pointed out, and Irving started, as if he'd forgotten she was there.

"Yes, but why build in the expectation that things will go wrong for our brand while lining the pockets of our competitors?" Irving crossed his arms.

Elle dipped her head in acknowledgement.

"Why no universal linking system?" Jenna asked, surprising herself.

Irving scowled at her. "Why do the work for no profit? There's no patent-depth to be had in universality."

"Longevity and lifespan," Jenna quipped, "or is that research just for show? Universally interactive relays would make people's lives easier if they live with large-scale implants," Jenna said, her left fist clenching by her side.

Irving's eyes flicked down to it, noted the gloves she wore, and then he got a peculiar sort of smile. "Ah, not just an enthusiast, but also a customer. Tell me, how likely are you to recommend Exagon brand implants to your friends and family?"

"—Jenna," Elle said softly. She was suddenly standing beside Jenna, the fingers of her left hand gently touching the back of Jenna's right arm, a reminder, an anchor.

"Piss off," Jenna said, just this side of heatedly, trying to rein herself in even as she glared at Irving.

"Oh, not an electioneer, then. A *volunteer*." Irving smirked.

"You're very welcome for your life."

In some other world, Jenna punched the smirk right off his face.

In some other world, Jenna never went overseas on a mission to be anywhere but home. In some other world, she did, but didn't stumble, because that detonation was a few clicks further away from her. In some other world, her left foot followed in the cleared path tread-marks of her squad ahead of her. In some other world, Jenna's left leg and arm were still attached via blood vessels and sinew and flesh and bone.

Jenna didn't often think about those other worlds, but right now as her fist curled in on itself and her blood churned in on itself, one of those worlds was a mere decision away.

"Funny that you have no implants of your own," Elle mused, and while it didn't sound calculated to bring Jenna back from the brink, it did.

"Not necessary, and besides, we encourage diversity here at all levels." Irving smiled beatifically.

"You mean you outsource the implant-requiring specialisations to your underlings and take advantage of their willingness to adapt," Jenna said, a little more in control of herself. "Do you make them give back the implants if they leave?"

"It is company property," Irving said with a shrug.

"Gosh, that all sounds so elective." Elle pursed her lips, and her eyes turned hard as she stared at Irving. "I want a tour of your new R&D department."

"And why do you think I'll agree to that?"

"Because you're still researching, not developing new technologies yet—you said it yourself, it's just been established, and you're fundraising." Elle lifted her eyebrows pointedly, and Irving shut his mouth on the breath he'd taken, presumably to argue. "You say you're looking into longevity—prove it. Show me the evidence that your company is invested in the opposite result from the crime scenes that brought us here today."

Irving's eyes narrowed. "Fine," he snapped. "Ten minutes with one of the researchers, tomorrow."

"A tour of the lab, today," Elle countered, calmly. Irving took breath to argue, and Elle's eyebrows rose eloquently, once more. "Willing or warrant," she said, and Jenna could tell she revelled in the man's consternation.

Jenna couldn't deny she felt something similar.

"Fine," Irving said at last, shoulders slumping.

"Perfect," Elle said with saccharine smile. "Ta for the assistance, you've been *so* kind. Jenna?"

"Right." Jenna turned to follow Elle out, her whole left side buzzing with frustration and awareness—and a punch she hadn't thrown.

The research and development was tucked away in a lower floor, beneath the car park, and the lift ride down was long and tense.

Irving had pawned them off on his assistant once more, who now played escort duty to them with the air of someone who had many other things to do, and now found herself with one more. Her name was Jasmine, and she could have won medals for her middle-distance stare.

Jasmine had had them sign NDAs—standard, Elle had proclaimed, before signing with an unreadable scrawl. Jenna had shrugged and put her signature down; if Elle had a loophole prepared for circumventing documents like these in the course of her inquiries, it didn't matter what Jenna saw or said.

Now they descended into the bowels of the building, the lift slowing to a stop at strategic points for Jasmine's voice and thumb scan.

"No retina scan?" Elle scoffed, poking fun at what seemed like an unnecessarily complicated security screening.

Jasmine blinked at her, but it was Jenna who shook her head and answered: "Implants can cause shifts in retina reads, and if the scan incorporates the implant, it can be more closely duplicated."

Jasmine blinked at Jenna, seeming to focus on her for the first time. *"You* have retina grafts?" she asked, and the disbelief was palpable. Retina grafts were costly, elective, and much sought after procedures. When coupled with a RAM interface, they allowed for photographic memory, bio-digital scanning, and all sorts of filtered vision options.

Jenna smiled grimly, and it was answer enough.

"Oh, a *technician*," Jasmine said then, as if all were right in her world again.

"Doctor, actually," Elle corrected, and Jenna shot her a glance but didn't say anything.

Jasmine for her part, tossed her head and shrugged, disinterested in the extreme.

After a final descent, lengthened by the chilly mood in the air, the doors opened.

"Ten minutes," Jasmine said, her voice cold and somehow aggressively disinterested.

Elle glanced at her phone, then strode into the lab. "Morning!" she said brightly at two lab techs, the only people in the room. "Don't mind us, we're just conducting a bit of corporate espionage." She beamed at them, her eyes ticking all over them. The techs frowned in confusion, looked at each other, and then glanced around themselves, as if seeking answers.

As Elle started her questioning, Jenna let herself absorb as much of the space as she could. It was brightly lit, clean, and she could tell that great pains had been taken to make the space as contaminant and dust free as it could be without putting everyone in repellent suits. Certainly, there would be deeper chambers within this facility where true clean rooms housed raw, exposed neural circuits and relays, the beginning compositions of Exagon's next leaps forward.

Her leg hummed as she shifted her weight to it, and Jenna pulled her mouth tight. Just over three years ago, her implants may have been in this—or a very similar—building. Field test-ready prototypes, waiting for the right set of circumstances to deliver them a host.

Jenna forced herself to breathe through the tightness in her windpipe, around the complicated lumps of *foreign* in chest. Her heart rattled her thoracic components as it beat, and for a moment, Jenna was profoundly aware of how made she was.

She tore her eyes away from the clean work surfaces and focused on Elle, who was continuing to hurl question after question at the technicians while Jasmine stood nearby, arms crossed impatiently.

Elle didn't seem to be getting far, and everyone seemed distracted (or in Jasmine's case, disinterested), and so Jenna drifted away from the conversation.

The lab, to her eyes, was far emptier than she'd expected. If it weren't for the dearth of projects at workstations and the absence of good hiding places, she'd have sworn everyone had decided to creep into dark nooks and wait out their visit.

"Come back here," Jasmine said, suddenly just behind Jenna. "You're not allowed to wander off unaccompanied," she said crossly. Behind her, the lab techs had turned to face this new commotion, and started forward to join them.

Just beyond them and out of sight of her three observers, Elle motioned frantically at Jenna, throwing her hands up as if miming pulling much longer hair than she possessed from her head—or perhaps some sort of whirlwind of chaos.

Oh, Jenna thought. She glanced at her surroundings—she'd drifted over to a workstation where an array of polished surgical steel tools gleamed in stacked trays, sterile and ready for use. All right then, she thought, and smiled curiously at her three chaperones. "So, what do you do down here—"

She flung her arm out to indicate the space behind her in general, an all-encompassing sort of motion—a motion that, quite unfortunately—and very specifically—encompassed the balanced tiers of trays. The resultant clang and clash were accompanied by runs of smaller, sharper sounds as delicate instruments and tools scattered, clattered to the floor, rolling every which way.

"Oh god—oh, I'm so sorry!" Jenna put her hands to her mouth and dropped to her knees to try and tidy up, and that had the desired effect of everyone darting forward and down to try and help as well as stop her from causing more of a mess.

"For godssake," Jasmine snapped, but the techs were busy tidying, and Jasmine was trying to wrangle Jenna, and behind them all, Elle darted off, her feet silent, in the opposite direction. There was a wall, white as everything else, that Jenna only saw as Elle slid around the corner of it and disappeared.

It took a solid five minutes before anyone thought to look up from the task of sorting implements that had to be discarded—even minor scratches or nicks in sharp surfaces ruined the surgical integrity of them—and those that could be re-sterilized.

"Just chuck the lot, why don't you?" Elle said suddenly, from where she was leaning against the lab table nearest the mess. Her arms were crossed, and to all the world she seemed as bored and unimpressed as if she'd been there the whole time. She could have given Jasmine a run for her money in the disinterested department. "We're done letting you waste our time, by the way," she said coldly to Jasmine.

Jasmine stood, straightening her suit jacket, her too-perfect eyes narrowing. Her crisp lines were a bit rumpled.

Jenna stood and gave her sheepish smile-shrug. "I *am* sorry," she said, only half fibbing. Upsetting a prep station, even though it hadn't been by accident, still plucked at the memories of her nervous student days. Remembered embarrassment coloured her face.

Jasmine clicked her tongue. "Clean this up," she said unnecessarily to the technicians still doggedly trying to salvage what trays they could. "We're going back up."

Jenna and Elle followed her into the lift and up into the surface world once more.

"So, what exactly did that accomplish?" Jenna asked, taking a sip of the latte Elle had handed her shortly after they arrived at a café a scant few block from Exagon's headquarters. It was creamy and richer than anything she'd eaten or drunk in a long time, and she took a moment to savour the smoothness of the frothed milk on her tongue before swallowing. "Getting a look at their R&D can't have been worth much—they definitely had advance notice we were coming."

Elle snorted. "There's nothing they can hide without making it more obvious that something's missing. At least not to me," Elle grinned and took a sip of her own frothy coffee. Jenna had watched, almost mesmerized, as Elle had poured what seemed like a fatal dose of honey into the already brim-full cup. "What?" she asked when she looked up, catching Jenna mid grin-inducing thought.

Jenna tried to stifle what felt like a laugh. "Nothing—I just— had this image of you as a hummingbird, living on nectar and flitting about." A single giggle escaped, and Jenna pursed her lips to keep another from doing the same.

Elle rolled her eyes and threw a stir stick at Jenna, who recovered enough to dodge it.

They both caught sight of a small child a few tables over, watching them with shocked, disapproving eyes, far more the adult than either of them in that moment.

They burst into a fit of laughter simultaneously, made worse by desperately trying to subdue it. They managed—then didn't—then regained some composure.

"As to your question," Elle said with a stern, back-to-the-matter-at-hand look, "we did get a good look at their working quarters.

They're setting up for some rather large implant experiments." Elle paused thoughtfully. "They also never intended for us to look behind the curtain, so to speak." She flashed Jenna a grin. "That was a masterful distraction, I should say."

Jenna felt herself flush, then half frowned at the feeling. She'd not expected that remembered embarrassment to linger like this.

"Thanks to that," Elle continued, seemingly oblivious to Jenna's confusion, "I wasn't stuck speaking with those two decoy techs. I got a good look at the benches they'd moved in-process projects to before we arrived. Lots of locked doors, too, behind that divider wall—and a few personnel desks."

"Oh?" Jenna asked, snapped out of her self-questioning spiral by intrigue. "And?"

"They *are* studying longevity—at least, one of them is. Aaron J. Weiss. Piles of data and notes on and in his desk." Elle sat back and watched Jenna process her words.

"Well, that corroborates their story then, doesn't it?" Jenna asked half relieved and half disappointed. She'd hardly known Irving, but she would have been surprised by even the smallest grain of truth in the flood of his smarmy words.

Elle had a peculiar sort of smile as she asked: "Nothing about what I said…strikes you as odd?"

"A researcher with piles of data." Jenna blinked. "Unless your point is that it's Too Normal or something—"

"*Piles* of data, I said." Elle tilted her head pointedly, as if willing Jenna to catch on.

Jenna lifted her hands. "And?"

"Hand written, physical copies of notes in a data-secure facility?" Elle raised her eyebrows.

"…oh," Jenna breathed at last.

"'Oh,'" Elle echoed.

"He doesn't want them stored with the rest of the research."

"Nope," Elle said, her eyes widening for emphasis. "Our friend Aaron is doing a bit of data gathering on the side, I expect."

"Wait—why would he leave them out for anyone to just stumble upon them?" Jenna asked.

Elle shrugged. "Possibly because they were all cleared out at a moment's notice and he couldn't kick up a fuss about being made to leave his work without calling attention?" Elle tipped her head, considering. "All I know is," she said, dipping her hand into her coat pocket, "that it's been an hour and Exagon hasn't rung me to demand the return of this."

Elle's hand emerged holding a small field note book, about the size of a travel-size diary or planner. It was grubby, like all field notebooks were if they were used for their intended purpose.

Jenna gaped at her. "You stole that?" she hissed.

"Pocketed it," Elle said, proud as a cat with a cream moustache, precisely enunciating each consonant, as if savouring them.

"You daft—what if—"

"No one's called, no one's reacted," Elle pointed out. "By now their staff will have been back at their posts, projects, and desks—and Aaron J. Weiss will most certainly have checked for the book of notes he'd left on his desk. If Exagon knew about his notes, if he was comfortable reporting its absence, don't you think I'd have received a strongly worded text at the very least? A disapproving email, even?"

Jenna wove her fingers together in a loose knot in front of her mouth and stared at the book on the table. "What's in it?"

"Not sure," Elle said.

"Oh," Jenna said, a bit deflated. She slumped back from where she'd been creeping towards the edge of her seat.

"It's written vaguely, with lots of shorthand and references," Elle said with a defensive tone. "I suspect I'll have to read a fair bit of it before it starts to make sense."

Jenna stared thoughtfully at the book that lay between them. "Well," she said at last, "It's just as well—I'll have to go on shift in a bit, so I'll be getting out of your hair." She gave Elle a sort of rueful smile.

"Out of my—?" Elle scrunched her face up in a frown. "Don't be preposterous. You've been invaluable to my work so far in this case. You might take a bit to catch on mentally—"

"Oy!" Jenna sat up straight, stung—

"—but you have a fantastic intuition for the physical," Elle continued, and Jenna closed her mouth on the rest of her reaction, charmed despite herself. "And you are welcome to join me in deciphering this—well, attempt to join me, I should say—although, you may catch small fragments I might not and inspire me by accident."

"Gosh, you make that sound so tempting," Jenna said, her tone sarcastic to the marrow, although she was surprised to find that the thought of watching Elle work her way through this next, albeit less exciting, chapter of the mystery was nevertheless just that: tempting.

Elle lifted her eyebrows at Jenna as if she could see past the sarcasm. Maybe she could.

Jenna's mouth quirked ruefully to the side. "Some of us have work, though," Jenna said regretfully, all pretense at sarcasm dropped away. Anything with Elle sounded better than administering routine maintenance to other augmentation recipients in various degrees of discontentment with life and their lot in it.

"I have work," Elle protested, mock-affronted.

"Job work," Jenna clarified. Elle had been explaining her work to Jenna on and off throughout the morning. As far as Jenna could tell, she was something of an expert on demand, working as a consultant in various fields, frequently within the domain of odd and unsolved crimes. The way Elle talked about it, it seemed exotic, exciting—perfect for someone so full of energy, so easily bored. To Jenna it sounded absolutely mad and left her feeling a little dull. She smiled a sad little smile, feeling the differences between their worlds. "Fired-for-not-showing-up work. Lose-the-roof-over-your-head-if-you-can't-make-rent work."

Elle hmmed in response, toying with her last remaining stir stick, unconcerned with such prosaic things, it seemed. "Honestly, I think you'd be better off losing that hole you hang your hat in." She flipped the little stick through the air, and tracked it as it flung itself into the rubbish bins just past their table. "If you ask me."

"But I'm not," Jenna retorted, side-stepping the sting of the insult. Elle's bluntness did not seem like judgement—or, rather, it didn't seem personal. Normally, when people talked about Jenna's situation, be it her housing or her implants, there was always a not-quite-hidden barb of judgement embedded somewhere. Sometimes it was dressed up as pity, which could sink under Jenna's skin nauseatingly, twisting in like a corkscrew.

Elle's remarks, however, seemed more compartmentalised than that. Of course, Jenna had seen Elle make her remarks personal by now, but while she'd seen it aimed at others as a weapon, she'd yet to experience that herself. She glanced down at her watch. "And if I leave right now I'll only be ten minutes late."

"Or you can use the car I just called."

Jenna blinked. "How did you know I needed to get back to the clinic?"

"You've been checking the time compulsively for the last thirty minutes or so. Hard to miss, really."

"Right," Jenna said slowly. "You don't miss much, do you?"

"Not usually, no," Elle said with an odd sort of grin.

Jenna stood, shifted her weight to her left leg, feeling the hum of the metabolic processes deep within its metal bones. "So," she began, but was interrupted:

"Of course," Elle said a touch hurriedly, "we still don't have our killer." The sentence, for all the words it contained, was tinged with hope. She stood too, now, and together they started walking slowly towards the café door.

Jenna found herself grinning. "I suppose we don't. You do have an entire diary to decipher." She put on a melodramatic voice: "Entry 107: Dear Diary, today I went to the grocery store and purchased Not At All Suspicious Amounts of Bleach."

Elle sniffed, a proud air to the tilt of her jaw as they passed through the doors. "Shouldn't take that long, I expect. Serial killers love to be found out, love performing for an audience." A father and young daughter both gave them astonished looks as they passed through.

Jenna's grin widened, and she said, "Well in that case, it'll probably be more like: 'Entry 14: Dear Diary, today I decided to become a serial killer—I think it'll suit me, and I've been meaning to find a new hobby that'll get me out of doors. I'll need a code—hence forth 'research' will refer to finding my next target, and 'development' to their demise. I'll be unstoppable, aha ha ha ha,'—and so on."

Elle rolled her eyes, but Jenna spotted a bit of a suppressed smile, just enough that she could tell Elle was amused.

"As I was saying, it shouldn't take long—join me after?" Elle asked. A car glided to a halt in front of them, and Elle checked her phone, then nodded at Jenna: it was the car she'd called for her.

Jenna smiled, lit up inside by the invitation. "Wouldn't miss it for the world."

She got in the car and it pulled away. "NewMecha Clinic, designation EXG 7," she gave her destination, then had a moment of absurd panic—she hadn't gotten Elle's contact information, and Elle hadn't asked for hers—

Her phone gave a buzz: incoming message. Jenna stared at the screen, which provided an originating number and the following:

Knew you'd forget. I hope you don't mind that I've taken the liberty of connecting us. After all, we still have a killer to catch.

Jenna smiled to herself and tapped out a reply:

Not at all. Keep me posted?

Elle's reply came within a moment:

Headed back to mine as we speak to begin reading.

Jenna felt a thrill—she wondered what Elle would find after deciphering the diary. She wished she could be there to watch it unfold.

Rotation was different this time. Jenna was antsy to be done, to be back and helping, or at the very least following along over Elle's shoulder, but she was also deeply focused on the details of each patient's case, more so than usual.

She stole quick moments in between patients to check her phone when she could:

Slow going here—lots of pointless lists

And:

He keeps a tally of money he gives to the transient population—performative nobility? Self-worth issues?

And:

Vaguely interesting bit about brand combination—did you know there've been independent attempts at studying it? Not enough volunteers willing to mix their brands to make a go of it though.

Jenna could feel Elle's mood wax and wane with each text, each little window into the workings of her mind.

For her part, she paid close attention to the components of the people she was tending to, and sure enough: neural relays were Exagon brand, one hundred percent of the time—and while the hardware followed closely in branding presence, Jenna did take note of one patient in particular who broke the pattern:

He was a boy in his late teens, sullen and resigned to being on her table, receiving a treatment for implants beyond what most would elect to receive. His right arm, much like Jenna's left, was replaced, although she could tell it was a newer unit by the absence of hinge abrasions—and yet there were calluses about his attachment points that hinted at a longer term of use.

Jenna frowned. "How long have you had this implant?" she

asked, noting that the implant date field was blank in his admitting papers. If she hadn't been curious about the lifespan of his implants, she might never have known to look. Now, the closer she looked, the more signs she saw of a hard life—at least, hard post-augmentation.

The boy shrugged, his brown skin ashy next to the bleached grey of the clinic robe. He was thin, but wiry, with short nails, dirt ground into them. "Just here for my shots," he mumbled, and Jenna pursed her lips. He looked like he could do with a good meal—or several.

"You're new to this clinic, yeah?" Jenna asked, trying to make conversation, lighten the mood, anything to dispel the tension growing in the room, behind their words. "Where were you before this?"

The boy shook his head, and Jenna backed away from that topic. Might be an uncomfortable question—could be an unpleasant memory. She prepped his shots, and then had to track down his input ports since they weren't where she expected. "You have multiple brands integrated here," she said, finally finding the port and pressing the first injection into place. "It's…unusual. Who did this?"

The boy shrugged his good shoulder again, not making eye contact.

"How did they sort out the NR interference?" Jenna probed, but the boy was silent. She administered the second injection, noted the boy's flinchless ease when it came to the pain, and tried one last time: "You're a pro at this, I can tell. Did you make these mods?"

The boy seemed taken aback by the suggestion, but quickly wiped his reaction from his face. "Don't know what you're talking about, miss," he mumbled again. "Can I go now?"

Jenna sighed and motioned for him to enter the dressing cubicle. She left the room as decorum demanded, and when she returned, noted that several of her pre-dosed syringes were missing from their now *un*locked case.

She sighed, shrugged, and logged it as a contaminated batch disposal—this clinic was low on the rungs of people giving a shit anyway, and it wouldn't be the first time their shipment arrived unusable. The loss wouldn't affect them much, if at all, and doses like the ones taken could make or break someone's mobility post-augmentation. And besides—while she hadn't been in this boy's position herself, she could only and far too easily imagine a similar set of circumstances that would have her stealing her next, vital maintenance doses.

As she stood staring at the log, waiting for her last patient of the day to enter, something turned over in her mind. Distantly, almost as if it were happening to someone else, Jenna made a connection.

She hit the intercom, barked out, "I've had a personal emergency: cover the rest of my shift!" grabbed her things, and bolted.

It wasn't until she burst out onto the pavement that she remembered to dial Elle, ignoring a long queue of unread messages in her rush to get to the street.

Elle answered on the second ring. "Are you on your way?" she demanded.

"What?" Jenna asked, flinging her arm out to try and stop a cab—it barrelled past, uninterested in someone flailing madly in front of an augmentation clinic. Jenna strode irately up the street, trying to distance herself from the no-go zone. "I think I figured out who he's targeting, and why," she began.

"Me too," Elle jumped in. "I'm on my way now—are you?"

Jenna swung her arm out at another taxi—no luck. "It's homeless protoypers—wait, what?—I don't—I'm trying to catch a cab, but no one's up for it—wait, you're going where?"

"To the arches—he's got a pattern, it's all in the book—and his usual hunting time is now and there—makes perfect sense, it's almost centrally equidistant to the three killings so far—"

"Don't you dare run into that on your own," Jenna said harshly, trying madly to spot a taxi that she could hail, still walking further and further from the clinic. The arches were a series of disused transit tunnels, exposed by floods, on the edge of the city. London's homeless population frequently used them as a means of getting about without being hassled by the police.

"Too late, I've just arrived!" Elle chirped cheerfully. "So, get your arse over here—"

The line went dead. Not hung-up out of cheek dead, but dropped signal deadline.

Unable to connect dead.

Jenna blanched, whipped around and then stepped into traffic, into the path of a taxi all set to ignore her.

It screeched to a halt.

"*So* kind," Jenna said, all teeth, as she flung herself into the passenger seat, wrenching the door shut behind herself while the driver was still recovering from the shock of nearly hitting her, already scrolling for a navigation point. "There," she said, before he could start yelling at her with the breath he'd just taken, flicking her nav-point to his guidance console and fixing him with a stare she'd honed in desert combat. "Take me there."

It was late afternoon, and the sun had baked the stones of the entrance to the arches into bricks that even now were pushing their oven-like heat into the air around them. Jenna's skin prickled with the remembered blaze of her battlefield home, even years distant from her now, as she stepped out of the taxi and into the mirage-flickered air.

The driver jabbed a finger at the meter, ready to be done with her. Jenna clenched her jaw as transferred her credits for the overpriced ride—a surcharge for her behaviour, no doubt—and the taxi driver drove off with not so much as a by-your-leave.

Jenna put the driver out of her mind, and turned to survey the path before her. The entrance to the arches was a dark puncture in the otherwise uniform of the radiant heat and reflected sunlight of the stone walls. A cool, damp, breath-like push of air issued forth from that maw of an opening, like an exhale from a decaying throat. A shiver ran down Jenna's spine.

She took a step forward, then stopped. There was no doubt in Jenna's mind that this was where and how Elle had lost signal, by running into the tunnels. If she went any further, she might lose signal, too—and then what? But she didn't have back up she could call, and she didn't have time for emergency dispatch to decide what to do with her and her report about someone she barely knew running off into the catacombs under the city.

What good was a phone in this situation?

Muttering a few choice four-letter words under her breath, Jenna made her decision and set off at the fastest walk she could manage, headed into the dark mouth of the arches.

Inside, beyond where light and heat dazzled, Jenna found herself wishing for the first time that her augmentations were more extensive. Night vision would have been welcome right about now, she thought grimly—not to mention heat tracking.

Instead, she had her paltry normal senses to rely on—diurnal-specialised eyes, her right hand and foot for touch, her nose and ears.

Her eyes could barely make anything out, and she stopped to wait and see if they would adjust to the gloom and become useful. Touch was useless—she couldn't track by blind feel and didn't know what her surroundings were supposed to look or feel like undisturbed. Her nose would not help her here; the urine-and-dung reek in the air clouded out all other, useful information.

And all her ears could pick out was a rush of white noise, like soft static covering all ambient sounds that may have been useful—

Oh, no, wait—

Jenna blinked, frowned. That…was actually her replacement limbs.

They were *buzzing*.

Jenna touched her right hand to her left arm, but couldn't feel the buzz that way. On impulse, she lifted her left hand and passed it through the air in front of her—and yes, there was buzzing, like static made touch—but more importantly, there was a patch in the air where it seemed…denser, somehow.

Jenna passed her hand through the air again.

No, not a patch—a direction.

Jenna turned to face that way, and plunged into the vibrating darkness, listening for the first time and trusting in what her metal bones were saying.

Walking as quickly and as quietly as she could, Jenna followed the thread of the path, trying not to mind that the further she went, the more she felt like her bones were being rattled. She found herself continually checking her left side with her right hand, just to make sure—but the buzzing never progressed beyond something her augmentations 'felt' and passed along like gossip on her neural relays.

She covered quite a distance, and her eyes grew a little more at home to the dark. Jenna clung to that little bit of clarity, trying to keep her other senses from being swamped by this new addition. It felt like her whole head, her whole body, had been filled with metallic wool and was singing like a flicked tuning fork. The more she "listened" to it, the more it was all she could "hear," rendering her deaf to her surroundings.

That would not do.

Jenna shook her head, refocused on feedback from her other senses. The cool and clammy air, the decomposing smell, the grit underfoot. She felt the buzzing recede, a bit, and heard some of the ambient sounds of the arches start to register again. Good, she thought, and continued forward.

Despite managing to reallocate the buzz as a feeling and not a sound, Jenna nearly missed the words spoken behind it as she rounded another curve in her path:

"And you think you're the one to stop me?" It was a dry, rough voice, laden with disbelief and malice.

"There was nothing good on, so, yeah, why not?" And there was Elle, sounding blithe and arrogant, just like the first time Jenna heard her voice—

Which meant she was probably outgunned again, if Jenna were to place bets.

She crept along the side of the narrow turning path her body had felt its way down. She became aware of an open expanse ahead of her—and then saw that it was lit dimly, although even the light from some failing overhead flicker bulbs seemed like suns after the darkness.

Now she could clearly see Elle, standing nonchalantly and completely at home in the centre of the decrepit room, flood stains and worse around her—

And their killer.

Well, he had to be—he had an assortment of tools on a belt slung over his shoulder that Jenna recognised and wished she hadn't, and beyond that he had a gun. Trained on Elle.

No weapon, Jenna thought, angry at herself. No plan.

Fantastic.

"I wish you hadn't interfered, my dear, but now…" The man shrugged, sweat bright on his high, exposed forehead, bringing the gun higher and aiming—

Jenna flung herself forward, gritting her teeth against the stiffness in her leg and the buzzing that felt, here, like it could shake her apart screw by screw.

She hadn't been far from Weiss to start, and collided with him a moment later, sweeping her left arm under the gun and up, sending the shot meant for Elle up to bury itself in the soft and rotten ceiling of the catacomb.

Jenna twisted the rest of her motion, trying to get Weiss down and controlled—and then—

Stopped.

She struggled against the sudden stillness of her limbs, but felt locked into motionlessness, trapped within the cage of—

Her neural network, Jenna realised. She ground her teeth together as Weiss stood up. She was hunched over, and he was chortling, a sort of proud and pleased little huffing laugh.

"Jenna, what—" Elle shouted, and Jenna heard her move closer then stop. Jenna could see that the gun was aimed at her once more.

"Oh now, what serendipity," Weiss said, bending to examine Jenna, who was having a bit of difficulty breathing. She tried not to think about what might be happening in her chest, where her aortic assembly helped her heart do its job. "Look at you—Exagon brand prototyper. How appropriate—and convenient."

"Convenient?" Elle asked, and Jenn heard something that seemed like anger or fear beyond the cool delivery of her voice. "What are you doing to her?"

"It's just a stasis field—keeps neural relays busy while I get my work done." Weiss chuckled again. "I'm in no shape to overpower my test subjects, after all."

"So you trick them into accepting upgrades or modifications or whatever, for the low, low price of unwilling experimentation?" Elle asked, her voice now like banked coals.

"It was the only way to get some answers," Weiss said, his voice matter of fact. "The company wasn't going to let me study brand combination, and I wanted to know what would happen." He straightened up from his casual inspection of Jenna's frozen form.

Jenna tried to clench her fist, and couldn't. Tried to straighten, and couldn't. The more she thought about moving, the less she did—like some sort of electronic boa constrictor, tightening down on her executable movement plans. Whatever her motor cortex was trying to send, her relay circuits were intercepting and tying up.

"I wanted to know what happened with all sorts of combinations—so I set up my own experiments with my own subjects. So many prototypers down here, willing to do just about anything for their next rejection preventative doses."

"You're monstrous," Elle noted.

"Scientific," Weiss pushed back.

"And so, what, the experiment backfired and you needed to cover it up? Destroy the evidence?" Elle asked harshly.

"Oh, oh no," Weiss said, earnestly. "It worked—beautifully. Integration is possible—and preferable."

"What?" Elle asked, disbelief in her voice.

Jenna could only listen, but inside the cage of stillness, her mind raced at this revelation.

"Diversification allows for resilience when exposed to all sorts of threats—including infections at the attachment sites. Even rejection—it turns out that when the body is presented with many different types of neural relays, they're not all active simultaneously, which means the body cannot single one out to reject. It's rather beautiful," Weiss breathed.

"Then why—" Elle began, and Weiss cut in:

"Why end the experiment? Why dispose of my test subjects?" Weiss shrugged. "Do you really think I could go public with my findings without facing the wrath of Exagon? Do you think they would approve of my experiment? My methods? My findings?" Weiss sighed. "I would lose my position at best—more, likely," he added darkly. "The company is not a kind employer."

"I take it back—you're not monstrous. You're a coward and selfish, a pathetic smear of humanity's worst offerings," Elle said.

Shut up and run, Jenna wanted to yell at Elle, but could only rage against her position, trying to find a way out of this predicament. She blinked, still frozen, as a thought pierced her turmoil: her aortic assembly had movable parts, too, but since she hadn't pitched over dead yet, she could only assume it hadn't been locked down like the rest of her. Did her implants queue functions meant to be autonomic? How long did she have left then?

And she could blink, she realised. She blinked again in surprise—but moment she tried to blink on purpose, the interference got in the way and stopped it happening.

Beside her, Weiss lifted his gun again. Distracted by the threat of him, Jenna blinked again—and made a connection.

"And now, sweetheart," Weiss was saying, "it's time. Say good bye to your friend—"

Jenna could see him take aim from the corner of her eye, could track the tightening of his finger on the trigger—

She didn't think about it, didn't plan it—she got out of the way all together, and just let herself react. Weiss was within arm's reach of her, and so that's just what her right arm did, reaching out with a wild, haymaker of a blow, connecting, punching the gun to the side, followed by her toppling ungracefully over onto him in a confused series of reactive thrashes. Her left arm, bent as it was, seemingly recalled a set of motions implemented less than a day previously, and managed to get itself around Weiss's neck, her right hand positioning itself, instinctively, and then—

The moment was over. Awareness of what she'd done and what she could do next crashed over Jenna, and the more her frontal cortex sang its plans, the more they were shut down.

But this time, there was a vital difference:

Jenna's surge of activity had surprised Weiss into dropping his weapon as much as her sloppy disarm had, and since she'd gotten her arms around his neck in a fairly decent chokehold before she lost the edge of her muscle memory, her dead, frozen weight was now immobilising Weiss beyond recovery.

In short, Weiss was gunless and soon to be breathless.

"Well," Elle said from where she'd been pinned by the gun's aim until moments ago. "That's one hell of a turnabout." She walked forward, kicking the gun even further away as she did, and then crouched close to where Weiss struggled in Jenna's frozen grip. "You all right, Jenna?"

Jenna grunted, then sucked in a breath, her jaw locked.

"Good, because the police should be here any minute, I should think." Elle stood and turned a torch on and shone it about the area. "Aha," she said, and strode off towards a corner.

"Won't do you any good," Weiss rasped. "You think you look like the heroes here?"

Elena ignored him, saying instead, "Jenna, I'm going to turn that stasis field emitter off—ready?"

Jenna grunted in the affirmative, and a moment later there was a harsh, snapping, tearing sound as Elle destroyed something out of Jenna's field of vision. The tangle of blocking interference fell away from her nerves, her limbs, her chest. She pulled in an achingly deep breath.

"Christ," she gasped, and tightened her grip on Weiss even more as he renewed his struggling, trying to take advantage of the momentary disorientation of the switch. "You all right?" she asked Elle.

Elle laughed delightedly as the distant sounds of sirens permeated the darkness around them. "Never better."

It took hours to sort everything out—Elle and Jenna were questioned separately, together, and multiple times by exceedingly confused officers. "Hang on—you met *yesterday*?" they kept asking, and Elle and Jenna kept answering, yes. Yes, yesterday. It was difficult not to cap that answer off with a shared grin.

Weiss tried to kick up a fuss right at the start, claiming he'd been the one to call in the cavalry—but when Elle's contact, Detective Inspector Nguyen stepped forward with a very pointed look indicating the contrary, Weiss clammed up.

"It's a shame he's gone silent," Elle said to Jenna as they sat on the back edge of an ambulance. They'd both been thoroughly examined by now, and had been cleared of medical issues resultant from recent events. "Still, I expect they'll manage to find something—I've pointed them in the right direction with that diary and there is the gun—and, why are you smiling like that?"

Jenna's smile grew even wider, if that were possible. "I had my phone in my pocket during all of that."

"And?" Elle's eyes widened in delight. "Oh—"

"On record," Jenna said, smugly pleased with herself.

"Oh, that is—just perfect," Elle said, joining Jenna in a wide beaming smile.

Eventually, they were free to go—with the understanding that they'd be called upon likely multiple times over the next week to provide input, observations, and testimony. It was beginning to edge towards light again, and the adrenaline of the night had worn thin.

"Mine's closest," Elle said, and Jenna didn't argue. Somewhere inside her exhausted brain, it felt like balance—and like hope.

Jenna woke roughly twenty-four hours after passing out, bewildered by her unfamiliar surroundings—then not. Elle was splayed out in an arm chair—she'd obviously slept and woken at least once, if the change in her clothes was any indicator.

Jenna got up stiffly, discovered the loo for herself, and then went back to the couch, hardly parsing her surroundings.

When she woke again, Elle was already up, poking about the kitchen.

"If you're wondering what that strange feeling in your stomach is, it's probably hunger," Jenna croaked, sitting up. There was a glass of water on the table in front of her—it hadn't been there when she went to sleep. She drank it down in one long pull. "Food?" she suggested.

Elle stilled her nervous prowling in the kitchen.

"Food," she said, very, very seriously.

A newspaper thumped down on the table in front of Jenna's breakfast plate.

They were in a café not far from Elle's messy, roomy, lived-in flat. Elle had ordered coffee and an obscene amount of food, which they were facing together with grim determination. "I forget to eat sometimes, during," she'd said. "Well, let's fix that, then," Jenna had said, and they'd tucked in together.

"What's that?" Jenna asked now, around a mouthful of eggs. She felt far less coherent and rested than Elle looked—but she suspected Elle always looked effortlessly arranged.

"Headlines," Elle said.

Jenna looked back down and scanned—then got sucked into reading:

EXAGON INT'L UNDER REVIEW [cont'd pg. 12]
Early reports this Wednesday indicate that biomedical and augmentation giant Exagon International may be on precarious footing. Insider access details --

The article went on to outline several key ethics conflicts and the need for review of their research and findings sharing procedures. It ended with a statement to the effect that the company was withdrawing from this current investment round to lick its wounds.

"And this." Elle layered another paper down on top of the first. This time it wasn't the front page, but the headline had the fork dropping from Jenna's suddenly numb right hand:

One Size Fits All? Aug'd Entrepreneur Swoops In to Fill Void Left By Dominant Brands

"What—how—when?" Jenna asked. Her lips felt numb, and the

world seemed distant, separated from her by shock. Elle's voice was clear beside her though.

"The 'why' of it's probably a bit more useful: I, um," and Elle looked uncustomarily sheepish for a moment. "I may have exaggerated the need for review and warrants after our visit to Exagon headquarters in my report to the Met."

"You sabotaged their investment round," Jenna breathed.

"Yes."

"Why?"

"I don't like monopolies when it comes to—well, anything, really." Elle smiled brightly. "Also I don't like their bedside manner," she added as she wrinkled her nose. "And besides, if they were putting money into longevity research, it was likely because they saw a threat somewhere—likely a smaller business with an ethos beyond making the most money fastest. Weiss's research was established essentially to disprove the need for universality. By getting all of that discredited—"

"You made room for something else."

"Clear the dead weight and see what rises to the top." Elle tipped her head and grinned. "That works in all manner of situations, you know," she said.

"What do you—"

"Move in with me."

"Elle—what?"

"Stay with me," Elle said, and if she hadn't squirmed under Jenna's shocked stare, if she hadn't pinked slightly and looked terribly unsure and hopeful and preemptively devastated, Jenna would have said no without hesitating, just like she'd said no to others before.

"You're serious," she said instead, and heard the exact same range of emotion reflected in her own voice.

"Yes," Elle said simply, and without artifice. "I can give you reasons if you want them—but I think you can think of your own."

Jenna blinked at her. "We barely know each other—"

"And we've already stopped a serial killer." Elle grinned, and Jenna didn't even try to fight the urge to join in.

"It's quite a start," Jenna said slowly, testing the feel of the idea. She was just a little frightened of how right it felt—which only made it seem more exciting.

"Who knows where and what it could lead to?" Elle mused.

Anywhere, Jenna thought. Anything—and the possibility, the potential of it poured over her for a moment, into her. "All right," Jenna said with a nod, just as Elle opened her mouth to continue her persuasion.

Elle's mouth snapped shut, then opened again. "Really?" she asked, and there was that hope again, that soft underbelly.

Jenna smiled and held her hand out for a shake. In so many other worlds of different outcomes, Jenna chose a different path. She played it safe—for her, at least—and stayed on her own. She chose a better travelled road with expected and expectable outcomes, or perhaps even an altogether different route.

But in this world, Jenna said, "Yes,"—to anywhere, to anything—but more importantly, to Elle. Her path chosen, Jenna set off down it.

She didn't look back.

Melissa Swanepoel lives in Austin, TX and has trouble writing 3-4 sentence bios about herself. She much prefers stringing together less realistic sentences about people that do not exist. Melissa spends an inordinate amount of time upside down and sounds regrettably foreign no matter where she goes.

Noise on the Wire
by
Damon L. W⸋kes

"**I** understand you've been in here before, Mister Walker. Facing the same charges, in fact."

Walker's thin, pale face suddenly burst into life. "I was innocent!" He thumped his palms on the table, his cuffs making a tremendous noise as they hit the wood. "It's been proven in court. If you think you can bully me into some—"

Inspector Rees lifted his hands. "I'm not here to do anything of the sort. I'm just making sure you understand the situation." He took a drag on his cigarette. A cheap brand: like sucking on a teabag. He tried to look like he was enjoying it. "A lot of people have some very funny ideas about these interviews. They've heard of some...old techniques and got it into their heads that they'll be forced to give a confession. It's important that you know that's not the case and, since you've been here before, I imagine that you do." He smiled. "As you say, you've been found innocent once already. Cigarette?"

Walker took one from the offered pack. Rees slid his book of matches across the table. Walker struck one, not quite able to get his wrists far enough apart to perform the task naturally.

"I'd take those off you, but the boss would have my hide if he found out. And he would." Rees nodded at the quietly humming device sitting on the edge of the table, against the wall. "You know what that is?"

"I think I've seen a wire recorder before, yeah."

"Just making sure." Rees smiled again. He was supposed to build a rapport with the suspect, make out they were on the same side. Clearly Walker was having none of it. "Obviously a recording's no good to us unless you know you're being recorded. Transparency's our watchword."

Rees smoked for a while, waiting to see if Walker would say anything on his own initiative. He didn't. Rees sighed. Conveniently, it led into what he planned to say next. "Walker, things aren't the same as they were last time. A man is dead." He let the words hang in the air. "You were the one who provided the...organism...that killed him. Now, I'm not forcing you to say anything. If you just want to stay quiet, that's your right, but..." he blew a plume of smoke at the ceiling, "I'm telling you, things are different now. Beyond what happened to Moss, the laws are changing."

Walker's sunken eyes were staring now. Rees held the silence, just letting the reels in the wire recorder hum softly in the background. He'd got him now. He could tell just by the look.

"What do you mean?" Walker asked at last.

"Well..." Rees allowed himself a nervous laugh. There was a lot riding on this interrogation. "Here's the thing. It sounds strange, when you're looking at manslaughter already, but there's growing concern about the, er...the ethical issues of your line of work. The RSPCA in particular has been trying to extend the Animal Protection Act to xenofauna. It's been in the works for a while. They're really just waiting for the right case."

What little colour there was in Walker's face seemed to have drained out of it.

Rees leant forward, putting a hand on the suspect's shoulder. He had been specifically instructed not to, but the medical advisor could go suck a lemon: Rees needed this confession. "I know you weren't involved with what happened in that basement," he said, locking eyes with Walker. "You just provided the...specimens. You weren't around for the fights. I worked that other case—the collector with that phony license—and I know you'd never have dealt with him if you'd been able to spot the forgery. There's no way you knew what Moss was doing." It was a lie, of course. Everyone knew that Moss was a brute. He'd been running dogfights his whole life. He'd be doing it still if Walker hadn't sold him something better, and if that *something* hadn't put him in the morgue. Walker had known full well what was going on, but Rees had to give him a way out. In order to secure an "All right, I did it," he had to provide a "but..."

Walker said nothing. He just sat there, his forehead quietly collecting beads of sweat.

Inspector Rees leant forward. "We found the apparatus you used to reach the Alterworld."

"That's all legal."

Rees barely managed to suppress a grin. That meant there were things that weren't. He'd have to look into that later on. "It's legal," he acknowledged, "but the equipment we've found—the cages, the snares—it links you solidly to everything that Moss was doing. And since he's dead, you'll be the one to take the fall."

Walker said nothing, but Rees knew he was about to crack. He waited.

"Last time..." Walker reached up with both hands to scratch inside his ear. "Last time I had a legal...legal...representative."

Rees was suddenly very aware of the wire running through the machine. The noise it made as it slid from one reel to the other. If Walker demanded a solicitor, that was it. The interview was over. Rees knew he had to go all in. "We can bring someone in if you want, but there's something I have to tell you." He lifted his briefcase onto the table. Walker hadn't been impressed by the wire recorder, but if this didn't catch his attention, nothing would. He took the device out and set it on the wood between them. "Do you know what this is?"

"It's a Ferniot counter." Walker looked nonplussed. "Anyone who's been in the Alterworld could tell you that. Without one of those, you might walk into an ALICE hotspot, and..."

Rees switched on the device and pointed it at Walker. The thing registered a few blips, and Walker's eyes widened. Even that was a thousand times what should have been expected outside the Alterwold. Then he stretched his arm forward, letting the sensor head hover about half a foot from Walker's chest. The device screamed.

Walker jumped to his feet, chair toppling behind him. His eyes were like golf balls. The cigarette dropped from his mouth.

Rees switched off the device and set it back in his briefcase without closing the lid. "It was the xenofauna you sold Moss," he explained. "The eggheads at the University think it's some kind of defence mechanism. One of the creatures you brought back from the other side...it releases ALICE when threatened. Or maybe it's just heavily contaminated. We're not sure of the details. What we do know is that it got away when the fight broke up, and we haven't seen it since. It's loose, Walker. It's loose in the city." Rees hadn't often found himself appealing to a suspect's conscience, but Walker knew what he'd been doing. He knew what he'd done.

"It's…" handcuff chain rattling, Walker picked up his chair and sat back down. "It's not contaminated."

This was it. Rees stubbed out his cigarette on the corner of the tabletop. Now that Walker had started to tell the truth, it would be harder for him to lie, even if he changed his mind.

"I…knew Moss," he admitted. "I'd known him for a long time, and I knew what was going on. But you have to understand, when I started going after xenofauna for collectors, there was never any idea they might…feel. Nobody was even sure if these things were properly alive! And now that it looks that way, now that I've sunk everything I have into the business…" He stopped, looking down at his cigarette, still glowing on the concrete floor. "Moss paid good money," he said at last. He was quiet after that.

"There are people who can help you," offered Rees. "At the University, they're looking into ways to reverse the effects of ALICE exposure. They can try and fix this, but first we have to make sure it can't affect anyone else."

"Okay." Walker took a deep, slightly ragged breath. "I was there when it happened. I didn't want to see the fight, but Moss insisted on it. Said he wanted me to see what happened so I'd know what to bring him next time."

Rees gave Walker another cigarette, this time lighting it for him. Walker took a drag. "So Moss has all the fauna lined up in cages in that basement. Obviously I've seen them all before. I gave them to him, didn't I?" His voice was apologetic. "There are maybe a dozen from the first layer, some the size of rabbits, one the size of a pit pony, a few in between. But these are common, you know? Collectors are getting bored of them, and so a lot of the punters have already seen them at menageries and that. But Moss knows this is going to happen, he knows he's not the only one starting to run these fights, so he's prepared. See, he paid extra for something more. He paid for something from the second layer."

Inspector Rees sat and listened. If he'd wanted to, he could have just broken Walker under the weight of the evidence. There was a lot of it. A whole lot. But a little tact went a long way, and now it was starting to pay off. Walker was starting to talk about things the force had never passed on. Things that backed up what the boffins could only guess. Things that tied him to the crime. And there would be more to come.

"I know that's illegal," Walker admitted. "But it was just the once, just for this one guy. And everybody does it from time to time...all those really strange specimens they 'just happened to find' somewhere in the first layer?" He sneered. "Most of the time they're unremarkable. Rare, but unremarkable. But this one was different. Because I'm there, looking in the cages, and I realise it doesn't look anything like it did when I found it: different number of limbs, different shape head, different vents on the neck. And I try to point this out to Moss, but he just elbows me in the gut, and I realise he doesn't want the punters to know it's different, doesn't want them to know it's...not stable."

Rees had lied when he said they hadn't seen the creature since the fighting ring scattered. At least three witnesses had got a very good look at it, and this backed up exactly what they'd said.

A clump of ash dropped off the end of Walker's cigarette and onto the table. He wasn't really smoking it anymore. "I didn't just decide to help Moss out on a whim," he explained. "I knew him. We'd been in the same circles for a while. I'd never liked him, you understand, but I knew he had the money coming in, and I knew he was always looking for something different. Something more."

Walker stopped again, but there was something there. Rees decided to press him, just a little. "Go on..."

Walker breathed deeply. "Moss had a dog once. This black, hairy thing: not big, but vicious. Called it 'Shuck,' and it lived up to the name. It's hard to know what's true and what's just gamblers' stories, but what's certain is the thing was mad. Moss made a bundle off the fights, right up until one night he went in to get it from the kennel and found it had gnawed off its own leg. Just for the taste of blood. Moss said he had to destroy it: not because it was lame, but because he knew at that point it would kill him if he ever let it out." He paused. "If I'd thought I was giving him anything that could think, I'd have... I'd have not..." He trailed away.

Rees couldn't let him clam up again. "Anything you know could help save lives. What happened when the fight started?"

"At first? Nothing." Walker stared at the table. "The first two or three went much as you'd expect. Moss got his money from the bets. But then, once the crowd was keen, he went to bring out that creature."

Walker had begun to shake. Rees genuinely wasn't sure how to approach him now. He'd as good as got a confession out of him, but he needed all the information Walker could provide. If pressed, would he make the effort to talk, or just break down? Rees waited. He'd seen what had happened to Moss: what was left of him. He was surprised Walker had held together this long.

"I don't know how it happened," he continued at last. "Moss went to bring that thing out and then, all of a sudden...it was Shuck. Only twice the size, with eyes like hot metal and stump still bleeding."

Walker stopped again. He hadn't said much. Rees wasn't bothered. They'd brought in a lot of people who'd turned up at the fight, and under pressure they'd all told that some story: the three-legged dog with glowing eyes. Still, it had affected Walker more than most. Rees knew he had to calm him down. "It was the ALICE," he said, gently. "Just the ALICE."

"Eh?" Walker stared at him, or rather past him.

"In high enough concentrations, it makes people hallucinate. Someone cries 'Shuck' and suddenly everyone sees it."

Walker's cuffs hit the table again, and Rees jumped. "That's not what it was!" the suspect bellowed. "It's not! It's not!"

Rees stared at him, still trying to gauge the situation.

Walker calmed a little, surprised by the sudden volume of his own voice. "Moss never told anybody about what really happened with Shuck. Not anybody but me. What came out of that cage...that was Shuck as Moss remembered him. As only Moss could remember him. The thing changed. It changed to what was inside his mind."

There was a sudden click as the reel of wire ran out. Perfect timing, Rees thought. There was more he wanted to know—for the most part, Walker hadn't said anything the force wasn't already aware of, and certainly nothing they didn't already suspect—but it would have to wait. Walker was pale and trembling. He looked like he might pass out. There would be another interview, another day.

"Thank you for your cooperation," said Rees. "I promise, we'll do everything we can."

He carefully took the reels of wire out of the recorder and stowed them in the custom-sized pocket of his briefcase. Then, he left the room, making sure to lock the door behind him. Down the hall, he paused to re-open his briefcase and wave the Ferniot counter over himself. It was definitely reading something, but no more than the hazard pay was worth, and definitely worth the results. The boss would be pleased.

Rees made his way through the building to the lobby, and into a deafening buzz of activity. He'd been doing this job long enough to know when something was wrong.

"Rees!" The Superintendent pushed through. "Where have you been? James Walker's being taken to the Royal Hospital now. If the doctors are right, this may be our only chance to get anything out of him."

"But I just..." Rees didn't bother finishing. Instead, he ran back to the interrogation room, fumbling his keys in the lock. There was no way Walker had reached the lobby before him, let alone made it into an ambulance before he even got there. The lock clicked, and Rees shouldered his way through.

The room was empty. Empty, that was, except for the two chairs, the table, and the wire recorder. He unlocked his briefcase, took out the twin reels, slotted them into the machine and waited for it to rewind. He hit play.

"...ster Walker. Facing the same charges, in fact."

Silence.

"I'm not here to do anything of the sort..."

He skipped ahead.

"...different now. Beyond what happened to Moss, the laws are changing."

More silence. Rees shut the machine off and felt his face go cold. Had he really just been sitting in here, talking to himself? The alternatives somehow didn't seem any better. Turning the machine on again, he skipped forward, searching for something specific.

"...ollector with that phony licen..."

"...to reach the Alterw..."

"...links you solidly t..."

Then, he heard the clunk of him setting the Ferniot counter down on the tabletop. "Do you know what this is?" The question hung in the air.

Silence.

Silence.

Recorded on the wire, the counter screamed.

Inspector Wolf
and the Hill of Beans
by
Shondra Snodderly

The sheepskin was killing me. It held the dank stench of something that had been in storage for years and never been aired out. And it was crawling with fleas. I had a thick coat of lanolin worked into my fur to hide my scent from the sheep, and it should have been pulling double duty by keeping the fleas out. But several of the more industrious ones had found gaps big enough to slip through safely and were happily chowing down on my sorry hide.

And to top it all off, it was the middle of summer.

I would have killed to be able to wash off in a cold creek and sleep off the heat of the day in some quiet, shady place. Instead, I was spending it in the open, greasy, itchy, and miserable, wearing not one, but two thick coats that were more suitable for the freezing dark of winter than a summer day in a meadow.

But this was a favor for a friend, so I stayed where I was and waited for her flock to make a move. They didn't, of course. They hadn't moved from the meadow on their own in the three days I'd been watching them. I thought about trying to chase one and make something happen, but I reminded myself that Bo Peep was paying in food and shelter. Babysitting a lazy flock was a lot less dangerous than trying to poach something from the royal forest. The game enforcers there did terrible things to trespassers.

To take my mind off the heat, I snapped up a mouthful of grass. It did not taste nearly as good as the sheep made it seem. I spent the rest of the day with a tongue coated in grass blades and a gut full of self-pity. Never in my life had I been so glad to see the sun go down.

Bo Peep herded her sheep to their pen with an air of command I'd only ever seen in garrison captains running soldiers through field exercises. Any sheep that stepped out of line received a quick smack on the backside with her crook. The whole process was over in less than half an hour. Impressive, considering the size of her flock.

"Oh, no you don't," she called to me as I tried to enter the pen. She pointed at the door of her cabin with her crook. "New sheep goes in the house."

I sped off before she decided to use that crook on me.

Her cabin was small but cozy. There was a loft bed in the rafters, a cushioned rocking chair by the fire, a larder, and a bin for uncarded wool. A tub of steaming water waited by the hearth. I shook off my disguise and hoped the water wasn't too hot this time.

Bo came in from putting the sheep away, rolled up her sleeves, grabbed a bar of lye soap, and got to work scrubbing the lanolin out of my fur.

Afterward, I shook out my fur, she drained the tub, and we both settled down to helpings of lamb stew she ladled out of a pot on the fire. I would have liked my lamb raw, but I also wasn't about to complain about a free meal.

Not when I had better things to complain about, anyway.

"Your sheep are only disappearing on market days, right?"

"That is correct, Mister Wolf."

"Then why do I have to be out there every day? Why not just on market days?"

Bo set aside her bowl and leaned forward in her chair. "Because if a thief is responsible, he might be watching the flock. And wouldn't it be mighty suspicious if there happened to be one extra sheep in the field every market day?"

She had a point, but she couldn't blame me for trying. That coat was the worst thing I'd ever had to deal with.

"What if it's not a thief? What if they've figured out that you're killing some of them off every now and then and they're masterminding an escape into the wild?"

She scoffed. "Sheep are too stupid to mastermind anything. And they would never survive on their own. That's why there are shepherds."

I licked a bit of gravy from my empty bowl. It was a good stew, even if it was full of cooked meat. "In my experience, no animal would choose to be eaten over getting to live."

"Of course not," she said. She scooped up our bowls and took them out to the trough to soak. When she came back in she grabbed up an armload of wool for carding. "But sheep are only good for two things. Food," she said with a nod at the pot, "and warmth." She dumped the wool into a basket by her chair and sat down to work.

"A good sheep knows its place in the natural order, and sticks to it."

She tore into the wool with vicious strokes of her carding combs, but her gaze kept straying to the window, out where her sheep were huddled in their pen, safe for the night. Her eyes started doing that shimmering thing that human eyes do when they're about to cry. I decided it was time to change the subject.

"How was your last trip to the market?"

Bo dropped the carding combs into her lap with the wool. "You wouldn't believe it. The miller came by my stall. Bought nearly everything I had."

"That sounds like a good thing."

"Oh, it was a good day for business, but you should have heard him. He picked over everything I had. 'Only the best for my little Gerta,' he said. 'Such a clever girl. Could like as to spin straw into gold, that one.' Feh! Made me sick to my stomach. Talk like that is going to get him in trouble one of these days."

"Most likely," I said. The moon rose outside her window. I felt a longing to get out and stretch my legs, but standing in that field all day had worn me out. I yawned wide and rested my head on my paws.

"You know, I saw Mary there, too. Tried to get her secret. Her sheep never leaves her side. Silly thing probably thinks she's its mother."

"What did she say?"

"She just smiled and said it was love. As if I don't love my sheep. I dare you to find someone in this entire kingdom who treats their flock as well as I treat mine. She's just holding out on me, is all."

"We'll figure this out, Bo. Even if I have to spend the entire summer in that stupid sheepskin."

She smiled a little and picked up her carding. "I'm sure it helps that you're getting paid in hot meals and a warm place by the fire."

"Well, it doesn't hurt." I didn't tell her I would have done it for free. Why take the chance she'd take me up on that offer?

As predicted, nothing happened until the next market day. I saw Bo off with her cart of clean, combed wool and trudged into the meadow to mingle with the flock. The sun had barely baked off the mist that hung around in the early morning and it was pleasantly warm out, even with my sheepskin. I started to doze.

Then I heard a sound rising up out of the forest, slow and sweet. In my half-asleep stupor, I figured it was the wind blowing through the trees, but then it picked up into a tune that tugged on my memory. I had heard this song somewhere before, and I almost dismissed it as the song from some mountain dweller, but the effect it was having on the sheep gave me pause.

One by one, the sheep turned toward the source of the sound and headed off single file to the woods. They never made a sound.

I fell into the back of the line and kept my head down. If someone was watching, I didn't want them to have too good a look at me before I'd gotten a good look at them.

The meadow disappeared behind us, and the cool, dark, familiar forest closed in around us. The sheep took no notice. It was getting close to lunch time. Bo would be coming back with whatever money she had made from the market and what goods she couldn't sell this week. The thought of food set my stomach to growling. I hadn't eaten since the night before, and I wasn't going to get to eat until after the sun went down. Sheep were dumb, but they weren't that dumb. Seeing another sheep chowing down on a hunk of meat would set them to wondering what was up. So I tried to ignore the fact that I was at the back of what was essentially a very long lunch line.

We walked for most of the morning and into the afternoon. The sheep didn't tire, didn't make a noise. If I hadn't spent an entire week with them I would have doubted they were real.

Our destination was a clearing with a makeshift pen that was little more than sticks in the ground with bits of string tied to them. A sneeze could have taken it out, but the sheep filed in just as they would for Bo at the end of a long day of grazing and they all went right to sleep. I ducked my head and waited for the musician to show himself.

I didn't have to wait long. He was preceded by the stench of magic that burned in my nose like the smell of hot peppers stewing in a tavern kitchen. From the sound of the footfalls, the thief was inspecting each sheep as he made his way through the crowd. He muttered under his breath as he went. I still couldn't see him through the crowd. I was tempted to go looking for him, but that would give me away. For all he knew I was an ensorcelled sheep, sleeping through all of this without a clue. I would just have to wait.

Finally, he came up behind me and stopped. "Well, now, aren't you an ugly thing? No wonder she's been keeping you in the house at night. You'd probably scare all your little friends if they saw you in the dark."

He chuckled to himself as he moved on to the next sheep. I caught a glimpse of his belt as he passed. A simple pipe hung from it. Anyone else would have thought of it as ordinary, but it smelled anything but ordinary. The sight of it told me exactly who I was dealing with.

"Piper," I growled.

Piper spun on his heels, head swiveling back and forth in search of his accuser. Normally I would have been annoyed, but being overlooked gave me an advantage this time. I walked up behind him, caught his shirt in my teeth, and dragged him down to the ground. The air left him in one big whoosh, and his belongings scattered in the grass and the dirt.

"I thought they snapped your pipe when they ran you out of Hamlin."

"Hello, Wolf." Piper glowered up at me from the ground. "I suppose you'd know all about being run out of towns."

"Why are you stealing Bo Peep's sheep?"

"Isn't it obvious?" He spread his hands out in the grass. "I'm just trying to survive, same as you."

I bristled at the accusation, but I reminded myself that this one needed to be handed over to the authorities. That was the way you were supposed to do it. "Unlike you, I know how to make an honest living."

He laughed, loud and ugly, right in my face. "A wolf? Honest? That'll be the day!"

I leaned in real close so that he could count every one of my teeth. The laughter died in a weak cough. "I believe I asked you a question."

"And I believe I gave you an answer," he said with a lot less bravado. "I'm taking only what I need to survive. At least this is a victimless crime."

"Victimless," I barked. "These things are her livelihood. Each one is a blow to her profits. Profits she works hard to earn, unlike someone here I could name. You're essentially taking food out of her mouth."

Piper shrugged and put his hands up in a gesture of surrender. "Couldn't she just write it off as a charitable donation?"

I shook my head at his audacity. Even while I had him dead to rights, he was still trying to find a way to weasel out of taking responsibility. But my work was done here. I had discovered the source of Bo's mysteriously disappearing sheep, and I had the culprit under my paws. All I needed to do was take him back and let the town guards deal with him.

"You know what? Let's go ask her." I took a mouthful of his filthy shirt in my teeth and dragged him back down the trail the sheep had taken to get there. By the time we arrived at Bo's house and I dropped him at her feet, he was exhausted, sore, and the knees of his already threadbare pants were worn completely away from crawling the entire distance.

She looked at him like he was a pile of dead squirrels on her good linens and then back at me.

"Mister Wolf," she said, "this is not my sheep."

The guards didn't waste any time responding to Bo Peep's call for assistance. It probably had to do with her pretty face and complete lack of fur and fangs. They carried him off between them since he was too tired to even stand under his own power. I watched from the shadows under the water trough outside Bo's little house. The guards had never been fond of me, and if they spotted me, they might make trouble for Bo.

After they left, I led Bo through the woods to where the sheep were just waking up from whatever trance Piper had put them into. As soon as they were free from his spell, they wasted no time trampling the makeshift pen and tasting the various belongings Piper had lost in the tussle. Bo rushed over to one that was chewing on a leather pouch.

"Spit that out, you troublemaker. You don't know what kind of beans those are. They could make you sick!"

I stopped digging the hole to bury Piper's pipe at the mention of beans. "What do they look like?"

Bo pulled one out and held it out between her thumb and forefinger. "They look like regular beans to me."

I went over for a look. They did look like normal beans, but the stench of magic rolling off them burned my nostrils and left me lightheaded.

"Close that up. Give it to me. Don't let any of them spill out."

"Why?" She pulled the drawstring tight and hung it around my neck. "What's wrong with them?"

"I'm not entirely sure," I said. "But if Piper had them, it can't be anything good."

Bo leaned on her crook and glared at one of the sheep who thought it was sneaky enough to make it out of the clearing without being noticed. "I suppose not," she said. "So what are you going to do with them?"

"Same thing you do with any Class Three controlled magical substance," I said. "I'm going to turn it over to the king."

The king's palace dominated a hilltop that let it gaze out over the rest of the kingdom. The towers rose higher than any other building I'd ever seen, and all the stonework shimmered like an opal in the sunlight. Colorful, embroidered banners in purple and silver hung from every window, and the shingles on every rooftop were the deep purple of the sky after sunset. This was supposedly the tallest human-made structure on the entire continent.

It was all too flashy for my taste. All the glitter and expensive colors only served to paint a target on the castle that screamed "attack here first". If it were up to me, it would be a well-stocked fortress, sturdy and square. That was a much better place to protect a royal family. Personally, I would have been happy with a shallow cave or a rocky overhang. Maybe the occasional nap by a friend's fire. But it wasn't up to me. And rumor had it the king was a dandy who cared more about appearances than tactics, so the palace definitely matched his personality.

Two guards stood on either side of the gate, each holding a halberd loosely in his hands. They were dressed in shining silver armor and purple tabards like they were part of a matching set. They looked just as embarrassed as I would be in the same getup. As soon as they saw me, though, every trace of relaxation disappeared from their demeanor. They brought down their halberds on level with my nose and glared at me through their visors.

"That's close enough, cur."

I twitched an ear and reminded myself I was here on important business. "Stand aside," I said in my most authoritative voice. "I have urgent business with the king."

The guard on the left barked out a laugh, and it wasn't a pleasant one. "What sort of business would the king have with something like you?"

"Besides," said the guard on the right, "his majesty ain't seeing anyone today. Supposed to be spending the day getting fitted for some new outfit or another."

Lefty elbowed Righty hard in the side. "Shut up. That's no one's business but the king's."

"But if he didn't want anyone to know, why'd he tell us?"

"Just shut up, would you? Let someone smart do the talking."

"Yes, please," I said to catch their attention again. "Could I speak to the smart person here, please?"

Lefty didn't seem to appreciate my comment because he trained his halberd on me once again. "Hey, didn't I tell you to shove off?"

"No, you didn't."

"Oh. Well, then. Shove off!" He jabbed at me with the halberd, but I held my ground.

"I can't leave. Not until I've seen the king."

"King ain't seeing anyone today," said Righty again, with a careful look at Lefty.

"And even if he were, he would have no interest in having his time wasted by some common street mutt."

"Listen, you clanking buffoons," I growled. "Your stupid kingdom is in very real danger. If he does not take immediate action, you could all be facing catastrophe before the month is out."

Lefty leveled a skeptical gaze at me. "Oh, yeah? What sort of danger is it, then?"

I pawed the pouch off of my neck and spilled the contents on the cobblestones for them to see. If they had been properly trained and educated, I would have been rewarded with some level of concern and appreciation. Instead, the guards laughed loud and long and ugly.

"Beans?" Righty clutched his sides, nearly dropping his halberd and narrowly missing smacking himself in the face with it. "That's what we're all in grave danger from?"

"They're magic beans," I said, trying to regain some semblance of control over this situation.

"Sure," said Lefty with a sneer. "And I'm the king's second cousin."

Righty turned to him with a look of awe. "Are you really?"

"Oh, shut up, Daniel! Are you still here, dog?" Lefty suddenly seemed to remember I was there and jabbed his halberd at me. The tip cut into my shoulder, drawing a surprised and pained yelp from my mouth. "Go on. Get out of here before I turn you into a rug for my hearth!"

I picked up the beans and ran before he could make good on his threat.

"The nerve of them!" Bo thrust an armload of firewood into the hearth rack. She gave it a good, hard kick to settle the logs and sat in her rocking chair to card more wool. "If it had been me, I would have given them a piece of my mind right then and there. That's no way to treat a citizen."

"But I'm not a citizen, Bo." I tore a strip of meat from the leg of lamb she had found for me in her larder and worked it over in my teeth. "And besides that, I'm a scary wolf. For all they knew, I was trying to trick my way in so I could eat the king and his son."

Bo shook loose a clump of wool from the pile she was working over that night. "That's ridiculous. You've never harmed a human in your whole life. Right?"

"Of course not. That would be suicide."

We sat in silence, listening to the crackle of the fireplace and the scrape of carding combs against wool.

"Perhaps I could take the beans to him," Bo mused. "He might be willing to hear me out."

"No good," I said between bites of lamb. "He's supposedly busy with some new outfit. The only people he seems interested in seeing are his tailors."

I shook my head. "I only have one lead, and he's wasting away in the king's dungeon."

Bo stared down at her work like she could pick an answer out of the fibers. "What about his supplier?"

I rolled onto my good side and licked at the wound on my shoulder. It wasn't deep, but it still stung. "His supplier?"

"Whoever sold him the beans in the first place, of course. He ought to know what they're for."

"But I don't know who that is." With my stomach full, my next priority was warming it by the glow of the fire.

"Ask Piper. He'll know."

"I would, but he's holed up in the castle, and the guards won't let me past the drawbridge."

Bo nodded and picked up her carding combs again. After a few minutes of combing and picking out burrs, she looked back up at me. "What if the guards didn't know it was you?"

The mischievous gleam in her eyes told me all I needed to know. "Oh, no."

Bo and I set out on the next market day, her in her favorite dress with the fluffy petticoats and me in the damned sheepskin. There was no lanolin in my fur this time, but she had tied the skin down so none of my wolf fur showed through. Now there was nowhere for me to reach in with a paw to get at the fleas who had crawled under my disguise.

"Quit scratching," Bo said under her breath to me. "You're going to give yourself away."

"But it itches. And we're nowhere near the gates. The guards won't notice a thing." But I put my foot down anyway. It was hard to see in this getup, and she had probably seen something I couldn't.

"It's not the guards I'm worried about," she said. "It's the other people heading for the gate. All it would take is one person to see something is off about you and the guards will be told."

She had a point. Any human who saw a sheep reach up with a hind leg to scratch itself like a dog would be understandably suspicious. I promised myself a good, all-over scratching as soon as I was able to ditch the sheepskin.

The line was a long one, and the sun was playing among the ridiculously tall spires by the time we reached the gate. By then I was ready to crawl out of my own skin as well.

"State your business," said the guard at the gate in a bored tone of voice. It was probably the hundredth time he had said those words that morning, and he'd probably say them a hundred more before he was able to go back to the barracks for supper and a good night's sleep.

Bo gestured to the pushcart with one hand. "I'm here to sell my wool at the market, same as every week."

The guard passed his eyes over the cart but stopped when he got to me. This was a different guard from the ones I had met on my last visit. "You've got a friend today, I see."

"Yes. Poor thing's been feeling rather sickly, so I thought a change of scenery would perk him up."

The guard scribbled something onto the board in his hand. "I'll say. If you want my opinion, you ought to take him to the butcher. Probably get better use of him."

If my ears hadn't already been flattened by the sheepskin, I might have folded them back myself. I choked back the growl that bubbled in my throat. The guard gave me a sharp look.

Bo was quick to rescue me. "Oh, listen to that. He's still congested, the poor thing. Fell into the creek a few days ago and hasn't been quite right since. I'm afraid he'd make a poor supper for anyone."

The guard went back to his board. "I'll take your word for it. Shame, though. Even meat as tough as his might have been a welcome change from the gruel they feed us at the barracks. Let me know if you change your mind. I'll pay you better than what he's probably worth."

"I'll keep that in mind," Bo muttered. I stared at the guard's ankle and wished it wasn't so well armored, or that it wouldn't give me away to bite him. He could have used a quick lesson in manners.

"Market's been moved, by the way," he said as he gestured for the door to be opened for us to pass through. "King's having some sort of parade to show off his new outfit. Follow the signs and you should be fine."

"What a jackass," I muttered as soon as we were out of earshot.

"At least he didn't cancel the market day outright." Bo stopped pushing the cart so she could scan for the signs she was supposed to follow. "I probably won't do much business today, but I'll still be able to catch up on all the gossip."

"I meant the guard."

She patted my head. "Of course you did."

The alternate location for the market wasn't even a square. He seemed to have picked the darkest and most claustrophobic alleyway possible, probably to encourage people to attend his parade. And in such close quarters, everything had started to pick up a mingled scent of wilting flowers, day old fish, and sweating bodies. I almost preferred the smell of the sheepskin. Almost.

"It'll be a miracle if anyone fits in here, let alone finds the place,"

Bo said as she forced the cart into the little open space she could find for her wheels.

"Who on Earth are you talking to, Little Bo Peep?"

I looked up to see Bo's shoulders tense and a smile crack her face. "Hello, Mary."

Mary smiled down at me. "I see you brought a friend today. Honestly, honey, when you came to me for advice, I didn't think you were going to copy everything I did." Her laughter rang out like little silver bells, but Bo flinched at the sound like it was glass shattering.

"This one's feeling rather poorly as of late. I've only got him with me so I can keep an eye on him. Can't have him mingling with the healthy sheep, now can we?"

The lamb that had been prancing around Mary like some sort of living maypole skipped over to investigate me. I didn't think my costume would hold up to such close inspection, even by a sheep, so I let out my deepest and most raspy "baa" in an attempt to scare it off.

It didn't work on the lamb, but Mary used her crook to pull her lamb back to her side, probably out of fear that what I had was catching. "I can see that." The look she gave me probably could have withered a bouquet of summer wildflowers. Then she was back to more important matters.

"I'm sure you've heard about the miller's daughter by now," she said, the sunny smile thawing her features out again.

"Yes. Her father bought out most of my wool and sang her praises the entire time. I thought I'd be sick."

Mary hooked her arm through Bo's, using her crook to keep the lamb well away from me as we all made our way down the alley to an open space for Bo to set up shop. "Well, word has it the king caught wind of her talent and moved her whole family into the palace. And wouldn't you know it, she's actually turning straw into gold for him!"

Bo gasped. "No! I thought it just the bragging of a foolish old man."

"It's true. Turns out precious little Gerda really can spin straw into gold. Personally, I don't believe it. She's probably using witchcraft, or made a pact with a demon."

We had come up on Bo's market space, and there was a convenient alley right behind it. I waited until the ladies were busy setting up their stalls and slipped into the dark to shed my sheepskin.

After a good, all-over scratching, I set off through the network of the castle town's alleys in the direction of the palace. Even with the buildings that hung out into open space, the palace wasn't hard to track. The spires were visible from just about anywhere inside the walls. I was sure it was a stylistic choice. The king did love getting attention, and what better way to stay on everyone's minds than by keeping the palace visible at all times?

Only a few guards were still patrolling the courtyards around the palace, and they were easy to evade. They were all baking under that armor. Their only thought was probably to a cold dunking in the nearest trough once their shifts were over.

I had never been inside the walls of this castle—or any castle, for that matter—so I had no idea where the dungeons would be kept. But luck seemed to still be with me because I could hear a familiar voice singing some shepherd's tune. The sound led me around to the back side of the castle, where a row of windows lined up at ground level across the wall, each with sturdy iron bars to keep whatever was inside from getting out. Or maybe that was to keep anything on the outside from getting in.

Piper was behind the middle window. I found him sitting on a low bed, picking over a bowl of gruel and singing to himself between slurping bites.

"You have a great voice," I said to him through the bars. He startled and dropped his bowl on the floor. His watery lunch splattered all over the stone floor. "It's a pity you didn't decide to become a bard instead."

"What are you doing here? Come to gloat?" Piper glared up at me with all the dignity he could muster for a man with gruel all over his shoes and pant legs.

I lay down and put my head on my paws. "Seeing as you're my first official arrest, I thought I'd come and see how you're being taken care of. Please tell me they beat you on a regular basis."

He kicked his bowl at the door. "You're wasting your time. I have nothing to say to you."

"I admire a man who sticks to his principles. Too bad for you you're not one of them. What can you tell me about these?" I pushed the pouch of beans off my neck and pulled it open for him to look.

Piper gripped the bars and hauled himself up for a better look.

After a moment of intense scrutiny, he looked me straight in the eye. "I'd say that not only are you bound and determined to see me starve, you intend to mock me the whole time."

"Don't play games with me, Piper," I growled. "My patience is already worn thin. What were you going to do with these beans?"

"What does anyone do with beans? I was going to eat them with a cut of that mutton you cheated me out of."

I brought my face closer to the bars and bared my teeth. He had the good grace to lower himself to the floor. "Nobody eats magic beans, Piper. They plant them."

"Not those beans," Piper said. "He told me he'd only give them to me if I boiled and ate every single one. I swore a blood oath not to let a single one get into the ground."

"Did he say why?"

"No. He just insisted I eat them."

So the supplier did know about the beans. "Who did you swear this oath to?"

Piper glared at me. "Why should I tell you? What have I got to gain from it?"

"Because," I said as if I were speaking to a bothersome pup, "if these are the beans I think they are, we are all in a lot of trouble, dungeon or no dungeon."

"Yeah? And what would a wolf know about magic beans?"

"You'd be surprised what gets said under the cover of night." I didn't tell him that most of my information came from digging through trash heaps outside of taverns. I'd dealt with enough humiliation for a whole lifetime, let alone one short week. My pride wouldn't stand up to another blow.

"What could possibly get me in a dungeon?" He was putting up a good show, but I could see the fear simmering behind his eyes. I decided to play on that.

"Oh, all kinds of things. Have you ever seen a castle ravaged by dragon fire? They say a dragon breathes flames so hot they melt stone so it runs like water. All that's left of those castles is a congealed puddle of stone. I shudder to think what happened to the poor sods locked up in the dungeon. You can bet the jailers didn't bother to let them out while they were fleeing for their lives."

Piper examined his cell, no doubt imagining the walls melting around him like bright orange snow under a springtime sun. "Do you really think the beans could bring dragons?"

"Don't be foolish. Who ever heard of a dragon being summoned from a bean?" He blew out the breath he'd been holding. "My bet is on giants. They're not much better, you know. Could crush an entire castle under one foot if it offended them. Which do you think is worse, being crushed alive, or buried under molten rock? Oh, well. I guess we'll find out soon. Enjoy your sentence."

I got up to leave, but Piper thrust his arm through the bars of his window, reaching for one of my paws to stop me. "Wait."

"Yes?"

"I can't tell you how to find him, but I can give you a name and a place."

The Goblin Market wasn't a fixed place. It never turned up in any one place long enough to get a permanent spot on any map. I suppose that was useful for keeping the town guards away, but it meant a lot of headache for someone new to the market. If you didn't know someone who knew where they were going to pop up next, you were out of luck.

I thought I might be able to get a lead from the miller's daughter. If she was trucking with demons or practicing sorcery to spin straw into gold, she would have to have had dealings with the market, either to meet an affable demon with the necessary skills or to buy the spell or components to do so. And lucky for me, she was being housed at the castle while she worked her miracles for the king. I just hoped he didn't decide to bring her along on his wardrobe exhibition.

I doubted the servants would have wanted to lug all the straw up any flights of stairs any more than they would have wanted to haul any amount of solid gold downstairs, so my guess was that Gerda was on the ground floor.

While I was sniffing my way around, however, I caught sight of a gnarled little man hobbling off in the direction of the outer wall, muttering to himself and clutching something close to his chest. I decided to investigate.

Our chase ended at a drainage grate at the castle wall. The little man had crouched down to remove the grate, only the item in his hand was preventing him from getting a good grip on the grate. I wondered what could be so important that he couldn't just keep it in his pocket while he worked.

"Stealing from the palace is grounds for execution."

The little man rounded on me in a rage, spluttering and scowling before he even laid eyes on me.

"Stealing? I'll have you know I've never stolen a thing in all my life." He held out his tightly closed fist. "I'll have you know I bargained for this. It was a fair transaction. Not that that's any of your business."

"Must have been a lousy bargain if you can hold the entire payment in one hand like that."

The little man sneered and opened his hand. A plain copper locket tumbled down the length of a fraying piece of twine. Garbage. Nobody would miss it.

The man saw this in my expression, because he drew himself up to his full height, which was barely tall enough to look me in the eye, and explained. "See? Of course, a savage like you would never understand the true value of something like this. You look at it and see junk."

I rolled my shoulders in approximation of a shrug. "Isn't it?"

"Wrong! Wrong!" He danced in place and gathered the necklace back up in his hand. "You look at this and you only see the price you would get for it in the marketplace. But there's a deeper value to it for those who know how to look."

"Enlighten me."

"This is the first piece of jewelry owned by a future queen. And what's more, it was the last thing her mother gave her before she died. The emotional value is what's important here. Something like this could cast a powerful spell, and in the right circles, could fetch a handsome price."

So, the king was marrying Gerda into the family to keep her gold-spinning ability in the palace. Only she wasn't the one doing the spinning. I could only imagine how he'd react if word got out. "You're the one turning straw into gold."

"Well of course I am! Did you honestly think she was? That silly creature couldn't spin in a circle without someone holding her hands to guide her. Now, if you're through harassing me, I have important business to attend to."

He turned back to the grate, probably trying to figure out how to lift it without letting go of the necklace.

"Business at the Goblin Market?"

He glared at me over his shoulder. "You're awfully nosy, aren't you?"

"And loud. Did you know a wolf's howl can carry for miles? I wonder what would happen to your trinket business if the king were to find out his future daughter-in-law is conning him. That can't be legal, can it?"

This seemed to grab his attention. He darted a glance at the palace, then at the grate, and then back at me. "What do you want?"

"I need a guide."

The Goblin Market was held on nights when there was no moon. Not because it was magic and only appeared on those nights, but because it was easier to conduct business of a particular nature under cover of darkness. I waited in the bushes with my reluctant new friend, who sat in a miserable huddle under a nearby tree.

At exactly an hour after what would have been moonrise, a swarm of black-clad folk flooded the streets, setting up tents and stalls. Within minutes, the dark and silent street was transformed into a bustling center of commerce where the only official language was the jingle of coins changing hands.

The little man pushed past me as soon as he saw the lights go up. "There you have it," he said. "Our business is concluded. Stay here for a few minutes before you do what you came here to do. I can't think what would happen to my reputation if anyone figures out I helped you find the place."

And just like that, he was gone.

I did as he asked, and as soon as I felt enough time had passed, I put my nose down and got to work.

Surprisingly, the entire market didn't stink of magic. Only a small number of stalls were selling legitimate magical items. Some stalls had two or three real pieces as display items, but the rest were as fake as my sheep disguise. The few legitimate stalls and tents had brutes standing guard against shoplifters. I sniffed around those only until I caught someone's attention, and then I moved on.

One stall had emulated the legitimate magic dealers by hiring huge armed guards, but the flying carpets he claimed to deal in were only special in that they had come from a country across the sea. They were beautiful, but they were by no means magical.

The tent Piper told me to look for was at the end of the street. It didn't stand quite straight, as if the person setting it up wasn't tall enough to get the tent entirely onto the poles. A dirty wooden plaque sat outside the flap that read "Crooked Lane Antiques and Curiosities".

There were no guards outside, or even inside, though the whole place reeked of enough magic to make my head spin. Maybe this guy didn't need muscle to protect himself from thieves.

The inside was smoky with three kinds of incense burning in the center of the tent. Shelves lined either side, packed to overflowing with various items that would be considered trash if they had been seen anywhere else. Any one of them could have brought down kingdoms in the right hands.

"No, doggy. Shoo! No treats for you no scraps. Go on now."

At the back of the tent, a plump little man sat on an overstuffed silk cushion. He held a crystal goblet of wine in one hand and waved the other at me the way a woman might flap her hand at problematic chickens.

"It's a good thing I'm not here for food, then."

To my disappointment, he didn't seem surprised that a talking wolf had shown up in his tent. He set aside the goblet so he could reach out and take my face in his hands. "Is this one of my enchantments at work?"

I wrenched my face away from him, baring my teeth in warning. He had already insulted me twice in the few minutes since my arrival, and I was getting pretty tired of people treating me this way.

"Do I look like I have any trinkets on me?"

He shrugged. "You could easily have been given a potion or had a spell cast upon you. It is very likely you are a messenger from one of my more discreet clients. They are known for such stunts. Tell me, who has sent you?"

"Nobody sent me. I got your name from the Pied Piper of Hamlin."

"Ah, yes. How is Piper? Is he enjoying his new flute? They are so hard to come by, but I gave him a discount for his beautiful playing."

"With any luck, it's broken, same as the first. He's currently gracing the king's dungeons with his presence and his voice."

"Such a shame." I got the feeling he didn't mean the thirty drowned children. He reached for a tome that lay next to his goblet and scribbled something in the margins. "I hope you are not here to hold me accountable for his actions. My clients assume full responsibility for whatever use they put my items to. They sign contracts, and these will hold up in court if you wish to take it that far."

I sat back on my haunches and caught his eye. "What about the beans?"

For the first time since I walked into his tent, he paled. "What beans?"

"These beans." I pushed off the pouch again and pawed it open, careful not to let any of them spill out. "Piper says you made him swear a blood oath not to plant any of these."

He held out a hand like he could ward them off. "Please. Close that bag. You will doom us all."

"Why?" I pawed at the dirt floor, churning up loose dirt. "Will they make me rich? Are they poison?"

I paused for effect. "Will they violate an important treaty?"

"Did the king send you?"

"I don't work for the king. Consider me a free agent. One who doesn't like seeing his friends put in danger."

"Close the bag, please. I will tell you what you need to know."

I pulled the drawstring tight with my teeth. "Talk quickly."

The man waddled over to a shelf full of magical items and dug around among the antiques and trinkets until he found a large bag with a tightly tied top. He set it down in front of me. The contents carried the same stink as the beans in my pouch. "These things have been a burden ever since they found their way into my inventory," he said.

"You mean you didn't take them on by choice?"

"Of course not. What possible benefit could there be in a war with the giants? I've been getting rid of them a little at a time. They lose all their power if they are boiled and eaten. So I sell them as additives for soups and stews. Most times I invite myself to dinner to make sure they're all eaten."

I looked at the sack. There were still enough beans in it to grow a forest of magic bean stalks. "Why not just boil them all at once, then? Get it all done in one go?"

He shook his head. "And what would happen if one undercooked bean got into the dirt? I can't take the chance that they could still retain some magic if they're boiled and not eaten. And I have no wish to spend a week eating all those beans at once."

I could see his point. There was definitely more than one comfortable serving in there. "But you didn't watch everyone," I said.

"Whatever else you might think of him, Piper is a man of his word. He promised me he would eat the beans with his next meal."

"To be fair to him, he lost the beans before he could make good on that promise. Is there anyone else you might have given these beans to and not watched them eat? Like you said. All it takes is one stray bean to doom us all."

He flipped through the tome, studying the pages as he went. "No, there is no one. No one except..." His voice trailed away and he put a hand over his mouth.

"Who?"

"He wasn't a customer. I never got his name."

"Just give me a location. I'll figure out the rest."

The Crooked Man had been between towns when he came across a starving boy on his way to the market to sell his family cow for food money. He knew the boy wouldn't make it before the market closed, and that the cow was too far gone to be of any value, so he filled a pouch with the beans and traded them for the cow. The boy promised he'd eat the beans with his mother that night, and the Crooked Man turned the cow loose in the nearest pasture.

Before I left to track the boy down I got a cart and hauled all the beans to Bo Peep's place. She put them in her larder and swore that not a single bean would leave it until I returned with the king's guards. Then I set off on the trail of the boy.

It wasn't much of a lead, but he was the only one that the Crooked Man couldn't account for. I hoped the boy hadn't gotten it into his head that he could save his family farm with them.

Then the ground shook so hard I rolled into the nearest ditch, my hopes dashed.

When it was safe to walk again, the skyline was broken by a huge beanstalk working its way up into the clouds above. The leaves that sprouted threw entire villages into artificial night, and I was sure the roots had made refugees out of more than one family.

At least I didn't have to waste time trying to track him down by scent.

The distance I had to go to reach the beanstalk was too great to cover before anyone got it in their heads to try to climb the thing. I could only hope it was too steep or too slick to get a good grip.

I reached the farm where the beanstalk had taken root, and was surprised to discover that the farmhouse had not been upended in the excitement. It stood defiantly on a hill of dirt churned up by the roots of the stalk, and at the bottom of that hill, a woman sat, sobbing into a handkerchief. The boy's mother, no doubt.

I stopped a polite and nonthreatening distance away and cleared my throat. "Excuse me, ma'am."

She shrieked and looked around for the source of the voice in the gloom. I sat up straight and spoke again. "Would you happen to be the mother of the boy with the magic beans?"

"My Jack?" She looked stricken. "Is he in trouble? Please. He didn't do this. It was all my fault. Take me in, not him."

"Wait. Slow down. What's all your fault?"

The woman bit down on her knuckle. "I was just so angry that night. Old Bess was all we had left of any value. Those beans he brought back wouldn't have lasted us more'n a day or two. I knocked them out of his hand."

"Where is Jack now?"

Her darted glance toward the clouds told me all I needed to know. "That's all right. We can still salvage this. Just as long as he doesn't take anything while he's up there."

Then from above us came the most godawful squawking and flapping noise. Feathers floated down like ungainly snowflakes all around us. I closed my eyes.

"Or maybe we're all going to die."

"Jack!" The boy's mother rushed over as the biggest goose I'd ever seen in my life crashed to the earth. The boy perched on its back. "What's going on? Where did you get this bird?"

"Mother!" Jack leaped down from the bird, careful to hold onto a thick rope he had wrapped around his arm and tied to the goose. Under his other arm was a golden harp that dragged the ground behind him. "I've fixed everything. This bird lays golden eggs. We'll be living like kings by the month's end."

"And the harp? Why would we need a harp if these eggs could pay for our every need?"

"This is no ordinary harp, Mother. It tells me it's a princess under an evil spell. If we can free her, we really will be royalty. Everything is going to be better now. Aren't you proud?"

His mother darted a glance at me, no doubt hearing my hope that Jack hadn't taken anything while he was up there. "Jack, where did these things come from? Surely these valuable things were not lying around without an owner."

Jack stared down at the ground. "No. They weren't."

"Oh, Jack. Who did you take these from?"

"It's all right, mother. He's a monster of a man. I did these two a favor by taking them. Now he can't hurt them anymore."

She took the hand with the rope into her empty hands and squeezed. Jack gritted his teeth at the pressure. "What if he comes after his missing things?"

He stared up at the top of the beanstalk, and a look of understanding washed over his face. "Where's the ax?"

"Are you seriously thinking of fighting off an angry giant with an ax?" she called after him as he scurried off to the wood pile. The goose honked in Jack's mother's ear.

"Of course not," Jack said as he reemerged, ax in hand. "I'm going to chop the beanstalk down before he gets here."

I'd heard enough. It was time to step in. "Jack, look at that thing. There's no way you're chopping it down before the giant catches up to you."

He looked down at me, apparently unsurprised that a wolf was trying to give him advice. I guess he'd seen enough fantastical things while he was up in Cloud Country that this seemed normal. "I definitely won't if I don't try."

"But think about it. Let's pretend you do succeed. When that beanstalk falls, it's going to fall on people. There's no way it won't. Those people will die. Do you really want that on your conscience?"

"What about all the people the giant will kill when he gets here? That's bound to be loads more than from one beanstalk falling over."

I rubbed at my nose with a paw. "Okay. So let's say that you don't manage to do it in time. Let's pretend the giant is on the beanstalk when you finish cutting it. He falls to his death. His brethren find out about it and come to pick up where they left off from the last war."

"What war?" Jack's mother had been looking back and forth between us during our conversation. Now she wrung her hands together and looked skyward. "They wouldn't really come down here, would they?"

"They could come any time they want to." I said this to her, but my eyes were on Jack. "It's the treaty that keeps them up there."

Jack furrowed his brow, but he rested the axe head on the ground. "What treaty?"

I moved until I was standing between Jack and the beanstalk. If he decided to make a move toward the beanstalk, I wanted to be able to stop him. Then I sat down to tell them what I knew. "From what I can piece together, humans and giants moved freely between the realms. But a theft set off tensions, and the giants decided to conduct raids on human lands."

"But we fought them off, right?"

"Are you kidding me? Have you heard the stories? Giants are practically indestructible."

Now it was Jack's mother's turn to look confused. "I don't understand. Why did they stop if we couldn't fight them?"

"Because we figured out how to kill them."

"And we slaughtered them, right?" Jack's whole face lit up at that. I shook my head. The kid would make a great soldier one day.

"No. Just two."

"Two?"

I tossed my head. "Think about it. Giants are huge and slow and tough. There's not much that can hurt them. So they don't need to have kids as often as, say, rabbits. When one dies, it's a pretty big deal. You, the tiny, squishable, insignificant humans, killed two. That was a pretty big deal to them."

Now Jack's mother was picking up on the thread. "So they agreed to stay up there if we stayed down here," she said slowly.

"Yes."

"And Jack broke that treaty by going up there and stealing from the giant."

We all gazed up at the clouds as if we expected the giant to materialize.

"Exactly."

She rounded on the boy and cuffed him over the head. "Jack, you bone-headed louse. You've gone and doomed us all! Isn't it just fitting that we'll be the first to be crushed when he gets here? You won't have to live long enough to see the damage you've done."

Jack cowered and covered his head. "I did it for us, mother. How was I supposed to know there was a treaty?"

Before she could respond, the air was split with the roar of a thunderous voice.

"FE FI FO FUM."

A foot thrust its way down out of the clouds, seeking purchase on the beanstalk. Jack hefted the ax, but his mother caught him by the shirt collar before he could move. "Oh, no you don't. I won't see murder added to the list of charges against you."

She turned to me. "Mister Wolf, there must be some way out of this that doesn't end in bloodshed. Please, help us make things right."

The other giant's foot had found its way onto the beanstalk. It wouldn't take him long to climb down. I racked my brain for something that would stop the giant, make him want to leave peacefully. "Do you have a sword?"

"I thought we were ending this without bloodshed," Jack said, his face pale as the moon on a winter night.

"Do I look like a soldier?" Jack's mother asked. "The closest thing I've got is a walking stick by the fireplace."

"Go get it. And let's pray this giant's vision is just as poor as the ones in the stories."

By the time the giant reached the ground, we were assembled. Jack's mother held her son with his arm twisted behind his back. I suspected the pained look on his face wasn't acting. The boy would probably face some stricter punishment after this was over.

If any of us came out of it alive.

The giant squatted down to take in the scene better, looked around as if searching for something. The goose honked and ran over to him. "There you are, Ferdinand! And my harp, too."

He gathered up both in his arm. The goose nestled close to its master. The harp was swallowed up in the giant's grip. It suddenly made sense for the giant to have a magic harp. There was no way those humongous fingers could pluck the strings. At least, not in any way that would create a pleasant sort of sound.

"Greet him," I muttered so he couldn't hear. "Like I told you. Good and loud."

"Oh. Right. Um, greetings, cloud dweller."

The giant looked at us as if just noticing us. He pointed a finger the size of me at Jack. "There's the little thief. Hand him over. I have business with him."

Jack's mother gave me a helpless look. I nodded back up at the giant, urging her to keep going.

"I have apprehended this thief. He will answer to the human courts for what he's done. You have recovered your missing things. Go home, and we will never speak of this again."

"Go home? This thief has broken the treaty. No human was to set foot in Cloud Country."

I nudged Jack's mother with my head, playing the part of a hungry pet looking for a handout. "Remind him of the war," I said.

"Oh, right. Are you really so eager to go to war again? Have you forgotten the fate of your brothers?"

He leaned in close so he could glower at her. Any other human I knew might have wilted under that stare, but she was a mother protecting her child, and that seemed to give her strength. "We will never forget them. Would you risk the lives of your people over one criminal?"

She didn't need any more prompting from me. Her anger was enough to carry her now. "You won't find us so easy to trample, giant."

"Oh, no? And why is that?"

"Because I am descended of the Tailor." She waved her crumbling wooden walking stick as if it were the finest masterwork steel sword ever forged. The giant reared back. Good, I thought. They still remembered the Tailor up there in Cloud Country.

"The Tailor?" His eyes darted back and forth as he did what passed for quick thinking among the giants. "So what?"

She looked at me, helpless again. "So what," she whispered. "What do I say to that?"

"Remember the needle," I said. I had no idea what the Tailor had done with the needle that scared the giants so badly, but hopefully, they would remember. Barring that, I hoped they were too scared to ask for a demonstration.

"Do you really think he died without passing on his knowledge? We've had a century to improve on his fighting technique. If you bring a war to these lands, you'll lose a damn sight more than just two men. That I promise you." To emphasize her point, she jabbed at him with her walking stick. He flinched with every thrust.

The giant hugged his stolen property close to his chest, his face creased in misery and confusion. Finally, his survival instincts won out over his pride. "If I go back and I say nothing to the council, you promise no more humans will go up there?"

"I swear on the Tailor's memory," she said. I nodded. That was a nice touch.

He pointed at Jack. "And he'll be punished?"

She glared at her son, whose head was hung low enough that I couldn't see what was going through his mind. "Have no doubt about that."

The giant huffed out a sigh, turned his back on us, and started the long climb back up the beanstalk.

Jack sagged in his mother's grip in spite of his twisted arm and laughed. "Wow. I'm glad that's over with."

"It's not even remotely over, Jack. When I'm through with you, you'll wish I'd given you to the giants instead. Get in the house. We have work to do."

I believed she would carry out her word, so I left them to it. In the meantime, the king needed to be informed about what had gone on there, and perhaps informed about his guards' handling of the whole situation.

I never got to talk to the king. He had shut himself away after his parade went badly. It turns out that if someone is trying to sell you something you can't see, they might be con artists. The poor man had strutted around the main square with absolutely nothing on and become an instant laughingstock.

The captain of the guard, on the other hand, was very interested in talking to me. He had heard about the beanstalk sprouting up, and unlike his subordinates, he had a bit of knowledge about the kind of trouble it could have caused. As soon as I was done with my story, he assigned a squadron to go and take the beanstalk down piece by piece, with orders that no man should so much as reach a hand up into the clouds as they worked.

A few days later we sat on a hill overlooking the valley and watched as the men worked at the base of the stalk. It wasn't enough to cut it down. The root system was hearty enough that it could just grow back. The pieces would have to be dug up and burned to ensure we held up our end of the bargain. Same with the beans. Bo had gladly handed them over when we went to fetch them. She was worried that some of her more mischievous sheep would break into her larder and eat them while her back was turned.

"Was it really as big as the stories say?" He didn't look at me, but kept his eyes on the work carrying out below us. I nodded anyway.

"Bigger, if that's possible. I still can't hold all of him in my mind."

He mulled this over in silence. "Then I'm glad they stay up there and leave us in peace and safety down here."

I grinned up at him. "What? No desire to test your mettle against a giant?"

The captain allowed himself a small smile. It was nice to see he had a less serious side. "There's bravery, Mister Wolf, and then there's stupidity. Only a stupid man picks a fight he isn't reasonably sure he can win."

"Fair enough."

"Speaking of bravery, I have spoken with the king, and he is impressed by what you've accomplished in spite of your limitations."

"Anyone could have done it," I said. "They probably could have done it better than me, too."

"But they didn't. You did."

"I was just sniffing around in the right places at the right times. It was mostly luck."

"That may be, but his majesty wishes you to continue 'sniffing around', as you put it. He has authorized me to confer upon you the title of Royal Inspector. You will be able to come and go as you please, as long as it's in the best interests of the kingdom. And to look into matters on his behalf from time to time."

"Of course." There was always a catch to these things, wasn't there? "And I suppose his majesty already has something in mind?"

He shrugged. "The tailors who embarrassed him have disappeared without a trace. My best men have been unable to find them and bring them back to stand trial." He probably wanted his money back, too. If the tailors were carting it around with them, the weight of it would no doubt slow them down.

"Does he want these men back dead or alive?"

"Alive, if you can help it."

The captain held out a wide leather collar with a gold tag attached. Engraved on it were the words "Royal Inspector". The light from the setting sun turned it a fiery red. It was tempting.

Taking the title would mean helping more people like Bo, whose problems were "too small" for the local guardsmen to take care of. But it would mean having to answer to the king from time to time, whether I liked his assignments or not.

"This all sounds very nice, but I have just one question before I accept."

The ghost of a smile played on his lips. A wolf, making demands of a king. It must have all seemed very rich. "And what would that be?"

"Does his majesty pay in meat?"

Shondra Snodderly hails from historic Saint Joseph, Missouri. When she isn't busy managing a chaotic household or baking sweet treats to share with her friends, she can be found wrestling various story ideas onto the page. Her other works can be read on Smashwords and listened to on Youtube. She has also been published in the anthology *Phantasmical Contraptions and Other Errors.*

Trouble
by
Ariel Pt🔍k

To Marshal Harv Fletcher, trouble was like a storm. It was a change in the air, clouds massing on the horizon, the rumble of thunder that shook your bones and the very earth beneath your feet, the flash of a lightning strike. Sometimes you could see it coming. Sometimes it sprung up out of the blue, and your only option was to salvage what you could from the squall.

This one was building like an electric charge, and it was close, and in just the direction he was headed. Fletcher looked, felt, and calculated. A few miles ahead, give or take a little. There was a dusty little town in the area, if he recalled correctly, a town just big enough for a main street and a saloon.

Not surprising.

"Come on, Ty," he said, glancing over the back of his horse. "Duty calls. Hyah, Ranger!"

The dust that rose in their wake hovered on the air like clouds.

There was a dusty little town where Fletcher recalled. It had a main street, and the saloon was in an uproar. He left Ranger at the post outside, made sure his badge was on prominent display, and entered the storm.

The hush did not fall immediately. One man glanced away from the fight and saw him, slapped his partner on the shoulder until he looked as well, and in gestures and whispers the knowledge spread, and with it, stillness. This was part of his territory, his guardianship, and many of these people knew him. Those who had been cheering the fight on began to shuffle toward corners, ducking behind the brims of their hats and the drinks they hadn't managed to spill. Others who had been watching in fear or uncertainty breathed relief.

Soon only the brawlers themselves were still moving, too focused on their fight to realize or care what was happening in the rest of the room. The cards and chips scattered across the ground told Fletcher a little of what might have started this. He unholstered his gun, checked it, and pointed it at the ceiling.

BANG.

The fighters broke apart, one rolling under a table to take cover. The other scrambled upright, fists cocked and one eye already swelling shut. It took him two long beats to focus on Fletcher as the source of the gunshot, another to spot the badge. By then Fletcher had already put the gun away.

"All right boys, no more. Job Greene?"

"'E started it," the man spat, gesturing at the one unfolding himself from beneath the table. "'E cheated me. I didn't do nuthin'."

"I'm not here for this, and even if I was that'd be something for you to tell a judge, not me. I'm here because I've got a warrant with your name on it. You skipped court, Greene. Now, you come quiet with me, and we'll get that taken care of, all right?"

Greene wasn't thinking of coming quietly. Fletcher could see the calculations clicking like rusty gears behind his one clear eye. Trouble rumbled in the air, a low warning growl of thunder. Fletcher didn't see a weapon on the man or any signs of a hidden holster or blade. He did see Greene's eye dart to a chair within arm's reach and to the tiny stage against the wall closer to Greene than Fletcher. Fletcher thought of the door behind that stage, the exit into the alley between this building and the next.

"Resisting arrest won't help your case," he warned.

Greene hesitated. The thunder built, the charge in the air hummed, and Fletcher ducked almost before the man scooped up the chair and hurled it with a wild shout. It shattered against the wall behind him. Those nearest him jumped, shouted, threw up their arms against the splinters and violence of the motion. Fletcher straightened; Greene was already scrambling up onto the stage.

He was a fast draw and a good shot. He had a clean line of sight right to Greene's back. But Greene wasn't trying to kill him, just run, and Fletcher had other means. He turned and strode out the main door just as he heard the smaller door bang open against the wall. There was a terrified scream, a grunt, and a thud. The storm faded. Fletcher walked calmly around the side of the building.

Greene lay unconscious in the alley, the recipient of a very gentle tap on the head courtesy of Ty. The bear snuffled in Fletcher's direction. It was a satisfied sort of snuffle.

Got him.

"That you did. Come on, let's get this one back to the city and report all this."

This wasn't difficult.

"No, and I'm glad," Fletcher said, picking his quarry up and draping him over the bear's broad back. "We could do with an easy break now and then."

Storms are coming.

"Yeah. Yeah, they are."

Ashes to Ashes
by
Jessica Augustsson

The sun beat down on the desert landscape and the suit's coolant system wasn't keeping up well. Sweat beaded on his forehead and he had no way to stop it from running into his eyes, stinging and blurring his vision. The situation wasn't improved by his breath fogging the helmet's glass.

"They should install a window squeegee in these things," he muttered.

His radio crackled. "What was that, Recruit? Didn't catch that."

"Uh, nothing, ma'am." He stood up straighter but resisted the urge to salute. "Just, uh, clearing my throat."

"All right. If you're done where you are, I want you to head to quadrant 18T before we wrap up today."

"Yes, ma'am. I'll head there now."

There was nothing but hard sand out here. The first settlers had set up camp nearer the coast, and he was not clear on why the surface expedition needed to come out this far. The expedition team had been here for weeks and still found nothing that would prohibit colonization, but he guessed the United Delegation had their reasons. He was relieved that there had been no complications. The end of the expedition would mean the end of his year-long field duty requirement, finally making him a full-fledged member of the diplomatic corps. He looked forward to spending his days away from all the other recruits and working instead in the xenoforensics lab. Anything was better than being *outside*. His roommate Josh had had some choice tales to tell about the time his suit's airflow system had broken down entirely, and he'd been a three-hour hike away from base.

The recruit grimaced at the thought and then winced as the facial movement caused another stream of saline to flow into the dry cracked creases of his eyes.

"Owwwwwtchhhh…" His exclamation turned into a hiss. He stretched his neck and contorted his face in an attempt to press his cheek up to the helmet's inner surface to wipe away some of the moisture when the ground disappeared beneath his feet.

He landed with a thump and scrambled to get his bearings. Before him, a concave sloping wall of yet more sand. Behind him… He shrunk back. "Ohmygod ohmygod ohmygod!"

A pile of blackened bodies of strange proportions and odd and somehow revolting joints that bent backward. He could feel his heart pounding as he turned back to the wall and forced himself up it. The sand gave him little purchase, sliding past him as he made his way out of the pit, and it seemed like he was struggling forever. But finally he reached the top and ran a few steps before falling, exhausted, soaked through.

"Recruit, re— Report. Is ev—ight? Repeat—verything all right?" His commander's signal was breaking up. What he *could* hear, though, sounded both angry and worried. "Rec—spond. Repeat, please respond."

He sat a moment longer, slowing his breathing. When he looked back toward the pit he'd fallen into, there was no sign of it. Just flat sand stretching out to the horizon. What a story he'd have for Josh tonight. Or maybe not…

"Yes, ma'am. Sorry, ma'am. Just stumbled. Low on fluids, I think," he responded, saying the first thing that popped into his head.

"Get back here, then. Day's over."

She hadn't heard his panicked tone. Or didn't care. "Yes, ma'am. On my way."

Constance stepped out of the temp-controlled enviro of the burping, steaming hypertrain onto the platform and the baking air wrapped itself around her head like cotton wool. She gasped at the sudden heat and the taste of hot dust filled her mouth, dried her lungs. Putting a hand up to shade her eyes, she peered at the world around her. People always said that a dry heat is more bearable, but Constance wasn't so sure she agreed, her energy being seemingly leached away just standing there. Even though the sun was setting, ripples of heat still rose from the sands, distorting the two pale moons in the sky.

She made a face as she felt sweat roll down the small of her back. Sighing, she took her suitcase from the porter and proceeded through the station to the camel-drawn cabs that waited past the windows on the other side.

Just as expected, someone was there to greet her. A short, local man wearing a thick woolen sweater—clearly a long-time colonist— held up a sign with her name.

No sweat on his brow. She sighed again and trudged up to the carriage. It might be hot temperatures to her, but to the locals, it was the winter season, and therefore cold.

"Ms. Hart?" the small man asked, giving her a warm smile.

"Yes. Pleased to meet you," she replied dutifully.

"My name is Ahmad and I'll be your escort. Let me get that for you." He gestured to her bag and Constance was too tired to argue. He opened the door for her to step in, before hefting the large suitcase onto the carriage roof.

Inside the carriage, the greater gravity of the planet impelled Constance down into her seat a bit less gracefully than she would have liked. She reminded herself that she needed to be cautious until she got used to it. She soon smiled in relief, however, as cool air massaged the back of her neck and her forehead. She opened her purse and retrieved her datapad. *Might as well read up a bit on the way to the excavation.*

The settler village of Amheida on Hurghada Prime had grown up around a large, natural oasis, nomadic tents gradually being replaced by mudbrick huts, and then two or three-storied hardened adobe houses made from the mineral-rich sand mixed with the clay found deep beneath it. The first builders—who had traveled here on their rickety second-hand cargo ships retrofitted to support several families long enough to reach deep space—had always been careful to replant vegetation even as they used it, and in so doing, the oasis had grown.

When the United Delegation first arrived thirty years ago with a colony ship from Earth, the small town was already well established, though hopelessly primitive according to the new arrivals. But, the colonists found a few reasons to stay: the curative effects of the lothan blossom, the sunny climate, and the excellent gin that could be made from the seedpods of the jinzo palm that spread its roots right out into the waters of the oasis.

The UD's exploration prior to colonization had also found that the distant moon, Malo, was rich with the same strange mineral that was found in minute amounts in the sand of the planet. The mineral was malleable and easily mined, but hardened incredibly when mixed with the clay of the planet. With this discovery, skyscrapers sprang up, rails were laid for the steam hypertrains, and channels were dug to bring the coastal waters into the growing city for irrigation.

The United Delegation was less concerned than the first settlers had been about *preserving* nature, and more adept at *manipulating* it. At great speed and not without a great deal of success. The meteorologists constantly monitored the atmosphere, helping the scientists to make use of every bit of information, such as finding distant clouds so they could be seeded in order to collect the rainfall for use in the city.

The extra water required huge cisterns which were placed some distance from the city, and dug deep into the clay, which both helped to keep the water cooler and kept the surface landscape from being scarred by eyesores. Once there was a group of five or six cisterns together, a new location around the perimeter of the city was chosen. It was during the excavation of a new cistern that the pit was discovered. And the alien bodies within that pit.

Constance pushed the hotel room door shut behind her against the hubbub of the hotel's other guests and felt immediate relief. She always did do a little better on her own. Not that she didn't *like* people, but they sapped her energy, and she always needed time alone to recharge. She kicked off her sandals and enjoyed the cool feel of the terra cotta tiles on the soles of her feet. Spreading her toes to stretch the tendons, she walked toward the balcony, dropping her heavy pack onto the desk. She noted with some pleasure that her suitcase was already here, placed neatly beside the wardrobe. It was a relief not to have it delivered after she was in the

room. It was always frustrating when arriving in new places…should one tip the bellhop? If so, how much? And Constance
was only ever able to hand money over awkwardly. She felt like such
a dolt.

With a smile, she pulled aside the filmy drapes and looked out
the large windows. There was a clear view of the oasis, surrounded
by jinzo palms and shimmering amidst the dry dunes, while the light
from the sun, even lower in the sky now, sparkled diamond-like on
the waters of the channel leading out toward the sea. Constance
turned her back on the strange landscape and peeled off her blouse,
thoroughly damp by now. On the bed, the bath towels had been
shaped into a heart and crimson flower petals had been strewn
about the bedspread. She snorted and grabbed a towel, heading off
for the bathroom and stepping out of the rest of her clothes along
the way.

She turned on the shower and set the temperature to tepid—
nothing too hot in this weather. What she needed was to cool down.
She let it stream down her back and over her ample bottom and
thighs. She was often self-aware that she was not thin; never had
been. But, except on bad days, it didn't matter to her. She would get
on exercise and health food kicks every now and then, but then a
case would come up, and all thoughts of her body disappeared and
the mysterious details of the case would consume her. That was
what she was best at, after all. Solving the most confusing of
puzzles. And that was both her blessing and her curse. She was good
at her job and knew it, and she took it very seriously. But being good
at it meant that she had to go to distant places to investigate, talk to
the people involved and see the crime scene itself. Which is why she
was here, among all these people, instead of in the comfort of her
own living room.

When the UD colonization of worlds began, there was an unspoken
rule, which later became law, that if any alien civilizations were
found, the star system would be left undisturbed and any
colonization plans would be abandoned. This could be problematic
as colonization was, unsurprisingly, an expensive undertaking. Also,
while the old SETI program's list of planets in the HabCat—the
Catalogue of Habitable Stellar Systems—had been added to over

time, worlds that could sustain life—particularly human life—were few and far between.

Sentient alien life had been discovered on four planets the UD had considered colonizing. The species were not space-faring, however, and no attempt had been made to contact them. The UD had decided, to study those species from afar until they decided it was safe to make contact then. Two planets had some mammal-like life, but after careful study, these were deemed to be less intelligent and colonization had proceeded successfully. The alien animals were unconcerned and went about their business. And on Jokash, the icy, mountainous planet, a white-furred, catlike creature seemed to have somewhat tamed itself, becoming friendly with the human colonists there. They were herbivores, larger than domesticated Earth cats, and seemed quite content to come in out of the cold mountain forests of Jokash as often as they could get away with.

But no sentient life had been found on Hurghada Prime. Now, with the discovery of alien remains, the UD was debating what steps to take. There were no rules about what to do if an alien civilization was discovered on the planet *after* colonization had begun. Nothing like this had occurred before.

Constance was still a bit confused as to how she could help in this case. Usually she was brought in on clear or potential murder cases. But an alien civilization? She was no xenobiologist and she was certain that there was more to it. Her clients rarely liked to share all the details of a case before she arrived, but they had been even more closed-lipped than usual on this one. She had a meeting set with the ambassador to the UD, hopefully she would get more useful information then.

Constance peered down into the roped-off excavation, glad for the cooling, nearing-twilight air. The setting sun was still quite bright, however, and she grumbled under her breath at the signs of boot prints that had clearly trampled the whole area. A pristine crime scene would have been too much to hope for, she guessed. A dark-suited, crouched figure at the foot of the hole jerked his head suddenly in her direction.

"Ah, Ms. Hart! It's good to have you here." A smooth voice behind mirrored aviator shades drifted up to her and she watched as he unfolded himself and stood upright, offering his hand to help her down into the pit.

"Inspector Turjuro." Constance was relieved she'd managed to not gasp. She transferred her evidence bag to her left hand, placed her right hand in his with slight embarrassment, and stepped down heavily, again with less grace than she wished. "What's the situation?" *Damn it all*, she thought. *Why did it have to be him?* She had forgotten that he worked for the UD now. Six years ago at an interworld law enforcement conference, she and Gabe Turjuro had both had a little too much to drink and a little too much naked togetherness, and to make things worse, Constance really liked him and respected him. A lot. She suddenly felt like an angsty awkward teenager.

"You're familiar with the case?"

"Somewhat, yes," she said, thankful that she'd brushed up a little on the coach. She swept her bangs aside with her fingers and knelt down to get a closer look, placing her evidence bag beside her. *Focus! You love your job! You're good at it.* "Quite a surprising find, I understand. But what I don't yet know is how I can help. Your employers weren't very revealing."

He shrugged. "This is Hurghada Prime's first indication of any previous inhabitants. The UD Ambassador wanted to ensure that everything was done properly, visibly. They and the university were very excited when RainWater Works, Inc. first realized what they'd found and stopped their digging immediately." He pointed to the enormous boring and drilling machines, now empty and still, beside the pit. "Professor Clarke himself came out from Akhenaten City to investigate before any official excavation began."

"Clarke is here?" The admiration the inspector had for the university's dean of archeology was understandable. Dr. Itzak Clarke was known throughout the galaxy for finding the first alien civilization. He toured all the major universities, promoting xenoanthropology and xenoarcheology.

"He's been a guest professor at Akhenaten U for the past decade or so. Ostensibly while he helps them 'set up' their xeno department."

Constance nodded. "I'm obviously behind the times. Last I heard, Clarke was on Ganymede, examining inner-ocean species. But there must be more to this. Did Clarke find something?"

"Well..." Turjuro slid his glasses up and indicated the pit. "Professor Clarke's initial tests indicated that this area was not an ancient burial site, as was originally speculated, but rather a mass grave."

"I still don't—"

"Look here." Turjuro pointed to the hardened remains. "According to Dr. Clarke, these are recent. They are not more than a few decades old, despite the apparent mummification."

"Was there a fire?" The remains in the pit looked charred. She reached out with a gloved fingertip, and the surface of the body was hard like glass. Her finger came away blackened with what appeared to be a coal-like dust. The skulls of the bodies were slightly elongated but narrower than human skulls, and though these skeletons looked to be humanoid, the hip and knee joints were more reminiscent of a small horse or deer. The feet were made up of three long toes and a heel spur. They seemed to be designed to run fairly quickly, with as little of the foot touching the hot sand as possible.

"It sure looks like it, and Dr. Clarke thinks so, but I'm not yet clear on how or why. Clarke took one scraping but he mentioned the fire hampering his carbon dating. He said he would hold off on further testing until after you arrived to see the scene."

She wrinkled her brow. Even though she knew her way around the lab, advanced forensics wasn't really her area, and now it seemed she might need to get a fire expert out here too. "So what happened—why are they here? And where are the living ones if these only died semi-recently? And how did UD or the first settlers not encounter them?"

"Indeed. And so you see, we have several mysteries. If we can solve one, perhaps we can solve the others." Turjuro's nut-brown eyes darted towards her and she thought she detected a glint of enjoyment in his face.

Constance stood up again, brushing the clay from her trousers. The sand and clay around the whole area was freshly dug, as RainWater Works had just begun preparing the site for another cistern. She nevertheless took a took a sample of the loamy mixture. Scrapings from the humanoids could be taken later in the lab. She sidled around the edge of the pit, leaning as far over into the center as she could, looking closely, hoping to find…something. Anything that might provide information. As she made her way back around toward Inspector Turjuro, the setting sun, for a split second, glinted off something shiny.

Constance paused, moving her head back and forth to find the spot again. *There!* She found the position where the sun glanced off the object and leaned in toward the bodies to get a closer look. It was an object about the size of her fist, looking to be made of the same clay as that in the pit, but it had been painted, fired and glazed, and it was that glaze that had caught the sunlight. *Some kind of bird?* As her eyes got used to the dimmer light, she decided it looked to have dropped out of the hand of the smallish corpse above it. *A child's toy?*

"Gabe," she called out, forgetting all protocols. "Hand me my bag." Constance held out her hand but did not look away from the small object. She did not see Gabriel Turjuro smile at her, eyes ablaze with admiration, as he handed her the evidence bag.

Donning a glove, she grasped the clay bird and popped it into a small manila envelope.

She nodded. "All right. I'm ready for a closer look. The remains can be moved to the lab. And if forensics finds anything, let me know, will you?"

Constance entered the laboratory, her brain all abuzz with questions. What were these aliens and how did they get here? Why was there no trace of them until now? For that matter, why was there no trace of them anywhere else on the planet? Were there some still alive? What happened to them? If Dr. Clarke was correct in it being a mass grave, then they all must have died at the same time. So what had killed them? The evidence pointed to a fire, but if so, how did it start? Was it deliberate? Accidental? All these questions, and many more, were zipping through her head as she was helped by one of the interns into surgical gown, cap, and mask and shown into the inner rooms where most of the remains had been brought from the excavation site. Each body had been tagged, numbered, and placed carefully here in a particular order to indicate where they had been located in the pit. Not everything had been moved yet, but Constance was impatient to get started.

"I understand Dr. Clarke took samples from the dig site to determine the age of the remains," Constance said to the intern at her side, who nodded agreement. "Did he do any other tests?"

"No, detective. Only the carbon dating, which indicated the incident took place recently. Not more than fifty years ago." The intern fiddled with his glasses; he looked nervous. Constance peered at him. Though he was greying at the temples, he had one of those faces that disguised his age; he could have been 30 or he could have been 60. She realized he'd been following her every move. *Has he been sent to keep tabs on me?* The thought made her uncomfortable. She wasn't usually so paranoid. "Dr. Clarke only took a scraping from the surface, but his sample was too small to do more testing. And as soon as he learned that the remains were possibly only a few decades old, he stopped any further disruption of the scene until a more official investigation could begin. In fact, it was he who put in a request to the UD ambassador to have you brought here."

Constance grimaced in confusion. *Clarke is a scientist. He knows that a surface scraping of an object in a recent fire will get a recent carbon-date reading no matter how old the object inside. And why would a worlds-famous xenoanthropologist have any reason to know about a murder investigator, let alone request me for what initially seemed to be an archeological dig?* But then, she reluctantly had to admit to herself that she *had* had a few cases that had received some media attention. She hated that, frankly, because it meant people were always asking for interviews at inopportune times. Well, all times were inopportune when it came to interviews, in Constance's opinion. She preferred to be left alone.

"Let's begin there, then," she said, happier to have a jumping-off point. Knowing where to start could often be the most difficult part of a case. Once the remains were thoroughly examined, any possible clues would present themselves to her, and she could follow the paths they led her down. "Let's get some random surface sampling from various remains and run them through the mass spectrometer—see if we can confirm Clarke's findings and also see if anything else turns up that might indicate why they died. If we find something, we can go from there. Later on, we can do a full autopsy. I'd like to get Dr. Clarke involved if I can."

"Yes, detective." The intern moved as if to get started.

"Wait! I'm being rude. What's your name?" Constance felt like kicking herself.

"Gíslason. Einar Gíslason." He held out his hand.

Shit. This was Dr. Clarke's second in line, and here she'd been, treating him like a trainee. She cursed her obliviousness. "Oh, I'm so sorry, Dr. Gíslason. I thought you were an intern and—" She shook his hand.

He stopped her with a casual wave of his hand. "No need to be, detective. I'm eager to work with you." With that, he turned on his heel and departed to get the samples.

She let herself feel stupid and embarrassed for a moment, just to get it out of her system. Then she breathed deeply, sighed out the insecurity and frustration and moved toward the newer skeleton. She hoped to glean something insightful from the bones, but after poring over them for nearly two hours and finding nothing significant externally, she gave up. She turned to the clay bird she'd found at the dig site.

It was rust colored with the wings and eyes painted with a dark blue pigment. At first glance, it seemed to be made of the same clay and sand mixture as the earliest settlers' adobe huts. Constance tried to get a scraping, but her tool made no mark in the hard glazing. She placed the entire bird into the industrial mechanized microscope and turned up the magnification. She would have to get some samples to compare, but it appeared as if the glaze might contain the hardening mineral from the asteroid—the same material used to construct Amheida's skyscrapers.

Constance chewed on her lip. There was otherwise nothing interesting about the bird other than where she had found it. She imagined the child who had held it so tightly, even in death. After a moment, she sniffed and shook her head. This wasn't the time.

She should have it tested for DNA which might appear on the surface. But it would have to be sent back to Earth to check for possible DNA in any skin oils that may have touched it, and that would take at least two weeks. Perhaps they could test the pigment and the glaze as well. But there was no point in sending it yet. There might be other things requiring further testing on Earth, so for now, best to store this in the evidence vault on her ship in orbit around the planet. She placed the bird back into the evidence envelope, sealed and labeled it. She pressed the Lamson button near the door and listened to the whoosh of air as the pneumatic pipeline pushed a cylinder pod to her location. In went the envelope, she returned the cylinder to the tube, and punched the button. She disliked having to rely on the primitive post system on the planet for getting things to her ship, but she didn't have many other options.

Gíslason came through the door just then, looking a bit grim.

"What do you have for me?" she asked, hoping for some helpful information.

"I'm sorry, detective. The spectrometer found nothing unusual—nothing that doesn't naturally occur on the planet already."

This case is determined to annoy me. Right now, her so-called clues didn't seem to be leading her anywhere helpful. Where were the paths that usually made themselves so clear to her? "Let me have a look."

There were no anomalous spikes in the graph he handed over. This was not her area of expertise. Even so, sometimes fresh and questioning eyes, in their attempt to understand what they did not, had helped her spot seemingly insignificant things of the sort the experts she'd consulted no longer bothered paying attention to.

Not to denigrate the experts. In their work overall, oftentimes those things *were* insignificant, but in her work, a tiny bit of information that appeared trivial could crack a whole case wide open. This time, however, it didn't seem to be the case. Frustrated, she scanned it into her datapad and filed it with her other notes, giving the printout back to Gíslason.

"Can you tell me about the original scans of the planet?" she asked. "I'm wondering how it is the UD missed this in the first place."

Gíslason clenched his jaw briefly. Constance noticed. *Was he nervous or upset about something?*

"I don't really know much, Detective Hart. Planetary scans are made from orbit. If no structures or living animal life is found, exploration proceeds to surface expedition. I'm not sure of what that entails."

Constance shook her head. "I'll have to find out from the ambassador. I'm meeting with her tonight…" Meetings on Hurghada Prime were like everything else here—formal and subject to very particular protocols. She'd remembered to bring the necessary ball-gown, but was not looking forward to the inevitable small talk.

"I'll get what data I can on the scans, detective, and have them ready for you tomorrow."

Constance couldn't repress the gasp this time, as she stepped out of the lift and into the glass-walled corridor framing the lights of Akhenaten City spread out beneath her. They glistened stunningly off the ever-changing surface of the Hapi Channel running through the center up from the oasis. She took a deep breath to steel her nerves and looked at her own reflection in the enormous windows. The royal blue silk fell gracefully to skim the floor, cleverly hiding the flat sandals she'd worn in lieu of heels, knowing she might have to stand around all evening practicing her idle chit-chat skills. She touched the carnelian beads at her throat, a gift from her mother before she'd died, and the coolness of the stones felt reassuring against her skin's hot flush of trepidation.

She approached the ambassador's flat, scanning for a doorbell, when the door opened before her. The sounds of a chatter-filled room spilled out into the corridor, and Constance felt surrounded, almost bowled over, much as she had with the planet's heat when she'd first alighted from the hypertrain. This was more than just a small meeting. *There must be a hundred people here!*

"Chief Detective Inspector Constance Hart, First Grade, Intergalactic Police Department."

The disembodied introduction quieted the hubbub, gathered the attention of the assembled guests, and everyone turned to stare at her.

Constance wished she could turn invisible and float away. Placing one foot in front of the other, she stepped through the doorway, but wanted nothing more than to flee back down the lift. Then *he* swooped in to her rescue and people turned back to their conversations. "Gabe! I—I mean Inspector Turjuro! So glad to see a friendly face," she gushed, realizing she'd been holding her breath.

"You look ravishing!" And he leaned in and whispered, his breath tickling her neck. "You really don't need to be so formal with me, you know."

Goosebumps of delight spread across her skin and her breath caught in her throat once again. Before she had a chance to react, he turned toward the crowd and led her further inside. "Come, let me introduce you to the ambassador."

Around the periphery of the room, tables were set with crystal glasses, expensive flatware and silver utensils laid out to exact measurements. A large seating chart was hung on one wall. Exactly the thing Constance hated most about formal events. They were usually rather old-fashionedly organized into alternating male-female order, particularly on planets like this, where holding onto past technologies and traditions was foremost. She hated seating charts. If she was lucky, she might be placed near Gabriel, but more likely, she'd be surrounded by strangers.

In the center of the vast ballroom, couples danced, and surrounding them in small clusters, other people chatted. The orchestra played a somewhat Glenn Miller-inspired tune, and waiters held aloft shining trays of sparkling wine—Hurghada Prime followed the strict CIVC rules which still disallowed anywhere outside of the Champagne district in France to use their sacred appellation. Constance was reminded of a theft in Reims she'd been called in on several years ago. The grateful vintner had promised her a lifetime supply of his wares in payment. She smiled at the thought as she watched the glasses of bubbly liquid disappear quickly among the crowd.

A tall cocoa-skinned woman in a gorgeous emerald shantung silk emerged from the middle of one of the clusters and seemed to float across the floor toward her and Gabe. Trailing her was an older man, slightly shorter, pale with bright orange hair and beard. Constance ran through her internal lists of characters. Ambassador Rachael Böhm Loveland-Hubbard—Rachael Love, as she'd been known in her early teens as a child actress—was the daughter of a privileged-but-bleeding-heart heiress and her working-class inamorato. Rachael had attended the finest schools, to be sure, but she was shrewd, and had taken well to navigating dangerous political landscapes and calming heated tempers quickly.

The ambassador reached out to Constance with both hands and clasped her arm tightly, as if greeting an old friend. "Chief Detective, I'm so glad to welcome you here. I've heard so much about the important cases you've worked on, and I don't think there was anyone else more fitting to help us with this delicate matter."

Constance had only enough time to smile before the ambassador continued. "This is the Regional UD Corporate chairman, Joshua Gorland. His parents were some of the first settlers." She turned to him. "Chairman, you know Inspector Gabriel Turjuro."

The orange-haired man nodded and thrust out a hand to Gabe and then to her in turn. Constance thought him very pale to have lived on such a sunny planet for his entire life.

"Inspector." The chairman nodded at Gabe and turned to Constance. "Detective, we are overjoyed to have you here. I was thrilled at the ambassador's request to bring you in on our case."

The ambassador's request? Not Clarke's? "Very nice to meet you, Mr. Chairman." Constance shook his offered hand. "But I'm not yet sure how I'll be of any help. I'm no expert in any of the areas this case seems to encompass."

"Aha!" he retorted. "But you are a master puzzle-solver, are you not?"

Constance was caught between wondering if she should feel flattered or skeptical when a silver tray drifted by, conveyed by a tuxedoed waiter. The ambassador took a glass in each hand and offered one to her. "Come, gentlemen! Let's not overwhelm our guest. It's a party. Here, darling. Don't leave me to drink alone with these indelicates."

"Thank you." Constance took a sip. Champagne—sparkling wine, she corrected herself—was not her drink of choice, usually resulting in a terrible headache. *Just one glass won't hurt,* she decided.

"What about you, Inspector? I've heard you can keep up with the best of them." The chairman raised his glass and took a gulp.

Gabe's smile didn't falter, but his muscles tensed and the air chilled between them. "I don't drink. Not anymore."

The chairman scoffed. "So boring. A party's not a party without settlers and off-worlders racing each other to the bottom of a bottle."

Gabe stiffened more, and Constance noticed the tips of his ears turning red. The ambassador came to the rescue. "Stop being so snide, Joshua. I've never met an off-worlder *or* a settler who could drink *me* under the table! Now be a dear and go find Marshall for me. I want him to arrange the seating so the inspector and Detective Hart are beside me at the table."

The chairman looked like he was grumbling under his breath, but left to do as he was told. Constance looked at the ambassador again, appreciating her diplomatic skills all the more.

"Ambassador, I want to thank you for meeting me."

Constance, Inspector Turjuro, Ambassador Loveland-Hubbard and her assistant Marshall sat in the ambassador's private office off the ballroom while waiting for the dessert course. It was a welcome respite to be away from the hubbub, if only briefly.

"Please, call me Rachael. And can I just start with how much I love your dress. It's gorgeous."

Constance blushed. Throughout the evening, she had gradually been able to relax. The ambassador had been formal but kind, and there was definitely a sincere sense of respect—all of which had eased the stress Constance had been feeling when she'd arrived. "Thank you. As you can imagine, it doesn't get many occasions to be seen."

"Well, I think you should wear it more often, then." The ambassador pressed a button on the wall and a panel opened up revealing a small wet bar. "Martini?"

Constance grinned. "That would be amazing. As filthy as possible, please."

"Allow me." Gabriel took up the bottle of gin. "You three have a chat."

"So gallant." The ambassador winked at her assistant suggestively. Something was going on there, Constance noted. "By all means." She sat down beside Constance on the davenport and Marshall sat in the armchair beside them. "Now, you must tell me all about your case on the Starletta Mavin-Jones murder. It's been all over the news."

Inspector Turjuro—*Oh hell, she might as well call him Gabe too!*—placed chilled martinis before them both, went back and collected Marshall's, and his own glass of seltzer over ice and sat down opposite them.

"Well, I couldn't possibly talk about Starletta without mentioning her butler." Constance smirked and took a sip of the martini, letting the cold salty sweetness of it slide down her throat as she pondered where to begin.

"Here we are."

"Thank you for walking me home, Gabe." Constance leaned against the door and looked up at him. She felt tipsy, but good. Not drunk… Just brave.

"I'm just down the hall, you know." He smiled and tipped his head in closer.

"I know. I'm glad." She felt warm all over.

He smiled but said nothing.

A thought occurred to her. "Why did you say you don't drink?

At the party?"

Gabe's smile faltered. "I—I'd rather talk about that later. Not n—"

She interrupted him with a kiss. He returned it almost immediately. His lips felt so good, making hers tingle. His tongue probed. She lost herself in his sweet mouth and fumbled for the key to the door.

Gabe broke off with a breathy laugh. He looked happier than he had since...she didn't know when. He helped her insert the key into the door and they pushed their way in, kissing once more. Constance didn't remember when they'd started again. Gabe flipped the deadbolt behind him and they kissed their way to the bed.

"We don't really have time for this." Constance tapped her pen on the conference table. "I need to examine those bodies."

"I know you're not a fan of these updates, but they're protocol. Better to get through it as quickly as possible so we can get back to work."

Constance noticed the "we". She knew Gabe was not careless with words. She tap-tap-tapped her pen more fiercely. Gabe put his hand on hers, and she whipped her head around. He had just the hint of a commiserating smile, and his eyes were kind. She let her annoyance go. *He really is beautiful, dammit. And he was beautiful last night, too.*

"It's going to be okay."

Constance clenched her teeth and nodded. He was right. Still, she couldn't stop wishing this were over already.

The temperature in the mostly empty glassed-in conference room was not as oppressive as the outdoor heat, but the streaming sun warmed the room to a point beyond Constance's comfort. She sat stiffly in the leather swivel armchair and tried not to wiggle too much for fear of making that horrid squeaking sound leather chairs inevitably made at exactly the worst moment. To her right, Gabe smiled when she finally picked up the folder Gíslason had prepared for her and fanned herself.

"What?"

Gabe shook his head, still smiling. "Nothing really. I was just thinking about something the locals say. 'You never get used to the heat. You just get used to being sweaty.'"

Constance snorted and thought about her little flat in London. She lived in the same building as another well-known detective, though he was fictional. It pleased her to share a building with the egotistical Belgian even if their addresses were not quite the same, since Whitehaven Mansions was the name given to the Art Deco building on Charterhouse Square where the famous series based on Agatha Christie's stories had been filmed. Nevertheless, as gorgeous as the building was, the sweeping curved windows leaked heat like nobody's business. And with the English being English, new-fangled window technologies were still forbidden in historic buildings, so her flat always felt chilly when it wasn't the height of summer, and she'd grown used to it. *Give me too cold over too hot any day.*

"…made him stay before! I don't know how you did it, but you're going to do it again. Why didn't you tell me about this sooner?" Dr. Clarke, and the chair of Regional UD Corporate surged into the room on a wave of emphatic discussion, their words trailing off as they realized they were no longer alone. Constance found the exchange curious filing it away for future reference. Marshall, the ambassador's assistant, followed them in and closed the door.

"Good afternoon, detectives. I hear you have some news for us?" The UD chairman sat opposite her—*Why can't I remember his name?*—and a seething Dr. Clarke flopped angrily into the chair two spaces away from him. Marshall moved around and sat perpendicular to Constance at the end of the table.

Constance glanced sidelong at Gabe, who responded with a raised eyebrow. She nodded and cleared her throat, opening the folder she had received from Gíslason. "We've got the results of the scans, both our recent ones as well as those of the initial UD expeditionary scans from space. They show a number of similar tunnels across the surface of the planet." She laid out the scan images across the table before them.

"Ah, yes." The chairman looked cool and more relaxed than he'd been at the party. "Those were examined and found to be completely natural."

When he offered nothing more by way of explanation,

Constance turned to Dr. Clarke. He sat up from his angry slouch and looked more closely at the pictures. "They were found to contain clay-sand mixture with enough mineral to harden the surface. When there was no sentient life found, they were believed to be a naturally occurring phenomenon, much like lava tubes on Earth, though we could not tell how they came to be. Now, it seems, we might have to reconsider."

"I notice none of the original scans include this area." Gabe indicated the pit as being very far off the edge of one of the pictures.

"That's standard," the chairman replied. "Scanning an entire planetary surface is an enormously expensive and time-consuming affair. It is also unnecessary. Strategic places to scan for signs of sentient life are determined based on temperatures, presence of water and other resources. This has worked extremely well for decades now."

"Have any of the tunnels been excavated, examined?" Constance felt there was something here, but couldn't quite catch the thread that would unravel the case for her.

Dr. Clarke frowned. "Not to my knowledge. We would ha—"

"Some were used for the cisterns." The chairman interrupted. "RainWater Works thought it would save time digging, and we gave them the go-ahead."

Dr. Clarke looked at the chairman wide eyed. He clearly had not heard this before.

"And nothing else was found?" Constance directed the question at them both.

"Of course not!" The chairman seemed to be trying to sound convincing, reassuring, but his tone was growing louder, shriller. "We would never have gone ahead with official colonization if we'd found anything."

Constance decided not to read too much into his reaction. It was not strange for him to be nervous about potential lawsuits for not being careful enough. But why were bodies found here and nowhere else on the planet? Not even traces? *Is it because they aren't there, or because no one really looked for them?*

"Is there anything else?" The chairman looked at his watch.

"Yes, actually." Constance pushed across the results of Gíslason's carbon test. As you suspected, Dr. Clarke, the surface of the bodies shows recent charring, yes. But with careful scrapings, your assistant found that beneath is another layer of charring that is decades older, and beneath that, the burnt substance is much older still."

At the mention of Dr. Gíslason, the UD chairman tugged at his tie.

"Multiple fires?" Dr. Clarke's eyes grew brighter, more interested at this information. "This must be why my initial testing was so inconclusive. There was little time for preparing the samples as carefully as I'd have liked, which is why I wished to retest. But multiple fires! I hadn't considered that. How can such a thing have occurred?"

"Gíslason also contacted an expert in tunnel and underground fires. Her opinion was that though fire-related deaths in enclosed spaces like that usually are due to inhalation of the toxic smoke, the initial images of the opened pit indicates the aliens likely died in a much quicker way. Such as a flashover-type fire. To be able to tell more though, she would need some additional information about weather patterns and temperatures, as well as any potential fuel sources."

"So we'd like to go back to the pit, now that all the bodies have been removed, and have another look." Gabe gestured out the window in the rough direction of the discovery.

Constance nodded before adding, "And we are hoping that a more thorough examination of the bones might tell us something more."

"I'd like to be a part of that, if I may." Dr. Clarke was leaning forward now.

"Of course. This is what we were hoping. We'd like to start right away."

"I have a lecture to give this afternoon. Can it be delayed a few hours?"

Constance fought off the urge to roll her eyes. "I'll have Dr. Gíslason schedule the autopsy for this evening at 6pm at the lab. We'll see you there." She looked over at Marshall, who had put a thoughtful fist to his mouth and gotten a very far-away look. "Marshall? Does the ambassador have anything to add?"

With a minute jerk that only she seemed to notice, he came back to himself. "Not at this time, detective, but I'll let you know if we learn anything."

"Is there anything in particular we're looking for?" Gabe asked, snapping on his rubber gloves.

Constance squinted in the bright sunlight and felt the blazing heat penetrate the fabric of her clothing, stripping it of the remaining coolness from the conditioned air of the carriage. "I've been thinking about the surface scans. It wasn't exactly clear about the scale of the tunnels, but I have this hunch…"

The pit had been closed off from access once the bodies were removed to the lab, and it now looked like nothing more than a large bowl-shaped concavity in the sand, the surface smooth and black from fires throughout the years. Though he seemed less interested in the tunnels, she had to echo Dr. Clarke's questions about the fires. How could there have been several of them and, more importantly, what could have caused them?

Gabe helped her down into the depression as he'd done her first day, and they began their search…for what, they didn't know.

"According to the weather data sent to us by Chairman Gorland, the planet's climate getting cooler. Apparently, while a good deal of the cooling is due to man-made changes, there is some speculation as to whether it's part of a cycle."

"Hmm…" Constance moved toward the back wall of the pit. *Gorland, that was his name. Joshua Gorland.*

"Scanner's not showing much." Gabe frowned at his handheld device—Earth-tech, not UD issue. United Delegation did not spend money on top-of-the-line tech not directly related to colonization. But Gabe had been a cop long enough to know there was no sense not using the best available tools. "Nothing to indicate what this cavern, might have been used for."

"I suspect they built underground to escape the heat, though. What do you think?" Constance wiped a sleeve across her forehead.

Gabe looked over the tops of his aviator shades at her and grinned. "It's what you would've done, yeah?"

"You're damn straight." She was at ease with Gabe again. Teasing, joking. It was good. Let her concentrate on her work instead of his perception of her. "Hang on, what's this?"

Gabe came up behind her where she faced an inner wall of the pit. "Oh, is that—?"

"A tunnel opening." Constance fetched a small collapsible spade from her bag and she and Gabe began to widen the narrow hole.

"Looks like. The entrance. Collapsed in on itself." Gabe grunted each sentence as he dug.

They finally cleared enough to crawl in. Constance dropped the shovel and turned on the bright LED flashlight on her datapad. Shining it into the dark tunnel, she saw the tube was still completely intact and she went inside.

"Whoa! Hold on there! Wait for me. If that thing collapses on you—"

"You can call for help."

"I'm not letting you go in there alone."

Constance smirked. "Fine. But bring your scanner."

The farther they went into the tunnel, the cooler it became. Constance turned to look behind her. The entrance wasn't that far away. "Strange that it's this cool already, isn't it?"

Gabe nodded. "Maybe your theory was right. This tunnel looks like it's just the right height for those aliens to stand upright in."

"My thoughts exactly. And notice this tunnel is straight and not sloping, as the fire expert suggested would fit the conditions of a tunnel flashover."

"So we have a piece of the puzzle, but we still don't know how the fire started or why there was more than one."

Ugh, thank you for stating the obvious. She continued away from the pit, wondering why she was annoyed and agitated. Probably she'd just been too hot. The air farther into the tunnel almost felt damp now, and cool, like a cellar. With so much sun and heat on the surface, it was hard to imagine this could be possible. It was a respite from the heat, but her head was starting to pound, and she felt vaguely dizzy, nauseous.

"It smells a bit strange in here, doesn't it?"

Constance sniffed the air and as she took another step, her foot slid forward out from under her and she landed hard on her opposite knee. She yelled, both in unpleasant surprise and stabbing pain.

Gabe was there beside her. "Are you okay? Let me help you."

"No, no. I'm fine. Be careful, it's slippery here." Constance held back the tears. She was embarrassed and angry with herself. Her knee throbbed, as did her head, but she clenched her teeth against the pain and made a show of feeling around her on the ground, as if looking for something she'd dropped. It was a fruitful feign, at least; she discovered that there was moss growing all over the inner surface of the tunnel. She could not remember seeing it anywhere else.

She allowed Gabe to help her up and she took a sample of the moss, put it in a container and jammed it into her bag. She gave her shirttails a hard tug. "Let's go just a bit further. Are you still scanning?" That sounded harsher than she'd meant it.

Gabe peered closely at her, but she pretended to ignore him so he wouldn't see her tears, and he gave an almost imperceptible shake of his head and sighed. "Um, yes. Scanner's still going. Hard to get a good idea of what all we're picking up down here, though. I'm no scientist. I'll put the data in for better detailed analysis when we get back, and we can get Gíslason to have a look." His tone was colder now.

What changed? What did I do?

Further examination of the tunnel revealed nothing obvious, and the smell grew stronger. As did Constance's nausea. When she nearly stumbled again, Gabe jerked his hands toward her as if to help, and then put them down again, pretending not to notice.

"Look, Con, I really think we should go back. We don't know for certain what's in this air, and my scanner is limited. I'm getting a headache, and that's not a good sign. And Dr. Clarke will be expecting us soon."

Constance nodded, more than ready to accept this defeat. They headed back, with much less conviviality than they'd had when they'd arrived.

In the lab, she placed the container of moss in the compressor-cooled refrigerator next to various other samples that still needed testing. She snorted derisively. *I'm surprised they're not still using ice boxes.* After a moment, she wondered why she was so annoyed. She needed to clear her head before the autopsy. She wished she could talk to Gabe, but something felt a bit off now.

Constance sat in the hotel bar nursing a glass of Octomore. The UD was paying, after all. Mostly she was just inhaling its scent. She had always liked the smell of whisky more than the taste. She was hoping Gabe would show up. She wanted to… *Apologize? Explain?* She wasn't sure. But she wanted to fix whatever had happened between them in the tunnel. Her head had ached terribly for hours, and clearly the air in there had been affecting them both. She hadn't yet had time to talk with Gíslason about the results of their scans or his analysis of the moss, which he'd indicated he would do following the autopsy.

The autopsy. The autopsy had been something of a disaster. Once Gíslason had gotten his scalpel past the hardened charring, the corpse completely disintegrated. Just sand. And once it began to collapse around his entry point, the whole body just crumbled in like a carefully balanced line of dominos.

Dr. Clarke was furious and insisted they begin again, and that *he* be the one to perform the procedure. Gíslason smoldered quietly, but acquiesced with no verbal objection. *He's a good sort,* she thought. *An assistant accustomed to letting his superior shine.*

But the second autopsy mirrored the first. The entire cadaver became a simple pile of sand.

A third body was tested, this time using a laser scalpel. The same result.

Could this be why no other bodies had been found? They had all fallen apart. Or were there other bodies out there, where the planetary scans had not discovered them? It felt like they were running into wall after uninformative wall.

Her datapad flashed a calendar reminder of the 6am meeting with Chairman Gorland and Clarke and the ambassador, and when it faded away. It was almost midnight. Gabe wouldn't be making an appearance. She wondered where he was, feeling distinctly jealous of whomever was sharing his company tonight.

She downed the rest of the Octomore, thumb-printed her tab for the bartender, and went to bed alone.

Einar Gíslason was annoyed as he waited for the results from the mass spectrometer. Clarke was becoming impossible. It was one thing to keep him here, working on this backwater planet for more than half his career, but now Clarke was starting to question his work. He was tired of waiting, tired of being the obedient assistant. He'd already made up his mind, and told Josh as much, but this evening's autopsy had been the last straw. He was determined to say yes to the professorship offered by Sally Ride University on Titan.

Yet the sand had given him an idea. A clean way out.

The machine pinged and the printer gishhhgossshhhgisshed and presented Einar with a sheet of paper.

He rolled his chair across the floor and fetched it. "Yes! Thank you, silicon 32 isotope!" He kissed the paper, rolled it up with all the other printouts from the day's research, as well as the analyses and findings from the inspector's scanner and popped them in a pneumatic tube pod and whooshed them off to Clarke. He hadn't read them all yet himself, but there would be time in the morning before the meeting to let Clarke know what they said. First, he wanted to check the moss specimen Detective Hart had brought in. The sooner he got all the tests done, the sooner he could hand off the rest to Clarke and get himself off this planet for good.

He scrawled a note and sent it to Josh. Pushing the button that sucked away the pod gave him a sensation of the pneumatic air pulling a weight off his shoulders. It was the first hope he'd had in years. He whistled as he pulled on a new set of gloves and sauntered over to the refrigerator.

As he opened the door, there was a very strong and terrible smell.

A flash; he was flying; nothing.

His lips were soft. She relished the feel of his skin on hers, her cheek on his chest, his leg draped over her hips, his—

The phone rang, startling them both.

"Is that yours or mine?" Constance giggled, fumbling around in the dark, but her hands didn't obey. The ringing continued, but no matter how she pressed the buttons, they did nothing.

Ring ring. Ring ring.

Constance jerked awake.

Her bed was empty. Her datapad flashed at her. She jabbed the answer button with vague disappointment. "Hello?"

"Detective Hart, this is Marshall with Ambassador Loveland-Hubbard's office. We apologize for waking you, but we need you to come to the lab right away. There's been a death."

She threw on her clothing from the day before, grabbing her bag and weapon, and hurried out the door. She ran down the hall and was about to knock on Gabe's door when it opened.

"You got the call too? The ambassador's assistant?" He looked disheveled and a bit bleary-eyed but at least temporarily alert.

Constance nodded. "Let's go."

The lab building was surrounded by police vehicles, steam billowing, lights flashing and reflecting in the windows, making the whole area look like a patriotic holiday tree. But for one window. The glass was shattered and black smoke and grit surrounded the blown-out frame. Constance had seen similar patterns in a case she had worked some years back on Mars while tracking down the Wonderland Bomber.

Gabe spotted Marshall craning his neck, looking for them. Constance waved and Marshall beelined in their direction.

"Thank you for getting here so quickly." He led them to a police coach and they all stepped inside. "There, now we have some privacy."

"What happened?"

"There's been an explosion in the lab."

"What? What happened? Was it intentional?" Constance remembered the heartbreaking horrors she'd encountered in the Wonderland Settlements, and was not looking forward to reliving such a thing. So much blood and destruction. She shook her head to clear out the memories.

"We're still determining whether it was intentional. But we don't think so. The logs only show Dr. Gíslason as having been working."

No!

"Fuck!" Gabe breathed a shaky sigh. "We saw him just hours ago."

Marshall nodded. "We spoke briefly with Dr. Clarke a few minutes before you arrived. He mentioned Gíslason had been frustrated with the results of the autopsy and had wanted to stay and run some final tests on the sand and the items you found?"

Constance could tell that they were being interrogated. She nodded her answer, though. And chose her next words carefully. "This afternoon, we made scans of the tunnel connected to the pit where the bodies were found. Some distance within the tunnel, we found the inner surface covered with a kind of moss. I took a sample with me back to the lab."

The piercing look Marshall gave her now convinced her he was no one's assistant. Or at least that it was not his primary job. But then his demeanor relaxed somewhat. "Look, we had to ask, but I'm convinced neither of you are involved. That said, I still have to follow protocol." He took up a radio and thumbed the button. "Ambassador, you can come in now."

Rachael Loveland-Hubbard, dressed in jeans and dark blue leather jacket and looking remarkably ordinary, climbed in the rear door.

"Hello again. Let me reintroduce you," she said jerking her head toward Marshall. "Thomas Marshall Beresford the fifth. Private investigator supreme and my assistant and partner for the past twelve years. It was his idea to bring you in, Detective Hart, based both on your impressive case history and your, uh, personal history with Inspector Turjuro here, who we knew had been assigned to investigate by the UD."

Gabe stiffened and Constance felt her face getting hot.

"Oh, please don't be angry. I don't mean it as an affront. I meant only that I suspected you would work well together."

Constance remembered again something Gíslason had said. "But I was led to believe Dr. Clarke was the one who had requested me."

"Well, yes," replied Rachael. "That's sort of true. He came to me insisting that he wanted an independent investigation into this whole thing. He wasn't thrilled with the high-profile nature of most of your cases, but your reputation of skill and integrity convinced him that you were the best for the job."

Constance shrugged. "I don't play favorites. The results are what they are. But why didn't you investigate the case yourself?" She directed this last question to Marshall.

"My parents were subversives working against UD. They would never have trusted anything I told them."

"But your fairness is exactly why Marshall wanted you here," Rachael continued.

Gabe looked at his feet. Constance flicked her gaze to the ceiling. Marshall looked at Rachael and broke the uncomfortable silence.

"Before...what we believe to have been an accident…" Marshall cleared his throat and began again. "Before the accident, Dr. Gíslason sent all his latest data to Dr. Clarke. Clarke forwarded the information to us and we're sending it to your datapads. When we've all had time to run through what evidence is left, I can tell you more, and I'm hoping you can help. The sand of the corpses, from what we can tell, inspired Gíslason to do a whole new batch of testing. Instead of carbon dating, he tried silicon dating the remains and it would seem he put their age at approximately eight thousand years old."

"Silicon dating." Constance couldn't stop a smile. *It seems so obvious now.* "So they *are* from long before the planet was colonized."

Marshall nodded. "But the thing is, we found Gíslason's corpse against the opposite wall of the refrigerator. The door was blown off its hinges, and his body was blackened and charred in the same way as the bodies in the pit. What concerns me, though, is what caused the explosion."

"It's not the heat. It's the cold!" Gabe said.

Rachael and Marshall both whipped their heads toward him.

"Yes! And the gases." Constance saw his train of thought as a clear line connecting each point in the case. She pulled up the information on her datapad. "Whatever it was that was giving us a headache."

"Yeah," Gabe agreed. "Knocked me right out. I had to go back to the hotel and lie down after we did the autopsy. I was out cold and didn't wake up until Marshall called."

"Silane, or something like it," Constance read, keeping her face neutral. All her prior jealousy and annoyance dissipated entirely. Her heart nearly leapt into her throat. He had gone back to his room alone as well. "Your scans from the tunnel measured small amounts of a gas that bears some chemical similarities to silane. That's what smelled so terrible. But this says the gas is highly explosive. That it can autoignite at 21 degrees Celsius, or below as the pressure or amount of oxygen increases and/or the temperature decreases. Was it that cool in the tunnel, Gabe?"

His eyes crinkled and the corners of his mouth went up as she said his name. "Not quite. But definitely approaching. So where was the gas coming from. The moss?"

"I suspect so. That would explain the refrigerator explosion. It would have been mostly air-tight, and definitely cooler. About 4 degrees Celsius. Once Dr. Gíslason opened the door, the influx of oxygen is probably what made it explode."

"I'll send this theory to our forensics and science team. And see if we can get another sample from the tunnel." Marshall began tapping on his datapad.

"If the cooling weather patterns go in waves or cycles depending on the orbit and the distance from the sun, and the gas is auto-igniting, that could explain the different ages of the charred layers. I kept looking for the heat to be a reason." Gabe's eyes were lit up now.

Constance nodded. "Especially after reading the notes from the fire expert. That heat could cause flashovers. But it was the cooler temperatures all along. And the UD's terraforming has increased the rapidity of the cooling. Marshall, warn your team to take precautions. That tunnel could potentially burst into flame at any time."

"Gíslason solved the case without realizing it," Gabe said.

"Not without your help."

"I wouldn't have figured out any of it on my own."

Rachael and Marshall were smiling at them. Constance raised her eyebrows in query. "This is why we wanted the two of you working together. This dynamic. I apologize that the circumstances have turned in this direction. Dr. Gíslason will absolutely be missed, and there are many who are convinced he was the true genius behind Dr. Clarke's work for the past decades. But I can see that Marshall had the right instincts about you."

Marshall yawned on cue, and Rachael stood. "All right. I think this is it for now. I guess it was premature of us to bring you down here tonight, but I'm glad you came. You've put the clues together and we can now give our teams the leads they need to continue. Now there's only one last thing, but that will have to wait until tomorrow."

"I waited in the bar for you last night." Constance glanced out the carriage window at the lit-up darkness of the city.

"You did?"

She nodded and looked at him. He had a goofy smile plastered across his face. It made her smile too. "I did."

They came to a stop outside the hotel and he held out his hand. She took it.

The hot conference room once again. Constance didn't feel as bothered by the heat now. Or perhaps Gabe was right. You just get used to being sweaty. She looked at the clock on her datapad.

"It's a quarter past. Where is everyone?"

Gabe shrugged and just then Chairman Gorland entered looking disheveled, upset.

"Look, uh, it's just me this morning. I've got some final information for you."

"Final—?" Gabe began, leaning forward in his chair.

Chairman Gorland held up a hand. "I would have preferred this remain internal to the UD, but the ambassador and her assistant impressed upon me the…uh, gravity…of the situation. Additionally, I trust Inspector Turjuro and he trusts you, Detective Hart, but I'd like it if this didn't go further than this room."

Gabe leaned back, and Constance could see his face. He seemed to be as clueless as she was at this moment.

"Einar Gíslason and I were both UD recruits on the surface expedition team. We were roommates and friends. We were more than that, but we kept it hidden. The UD frowned on…fraternization.

"He had an accident on the last expedition—fell into a pit. Almost didn't manage to get out, from what he told me. He didn't tell anyone about what he saw there, though. I could tell he was keeping something from me. Something that was eating away at him."

Constance realized she was holding her breath and let it out slowly.

"I was young and stupid and cruel then. I taunted him about it until he finally told me about the blackened alien bodies he'd found in that pit. I felt betrayed, not only because he had kept a secret from me, but because my parents were among the first settlers. On some level, the planet felt like ours, and now he was telling me it belonged to someone else?

"We fought. It was ridiculous. But he made me promise never to tell anyone. Mostly, I forgot about it. He went on to work as an apprentice in xenobiology under Dr. Clarke, and I joined UD corporate. During that time, Clarke published some of his most famous theories. But once Einar finished his apprenticeship and planned to go elsewhere, Dr. Clarke put in a request to UD to try to persuade him to stay. It was then I knew that Einar was the real thing, and Clarke was using him. But the UD wanted to keep Clarke happy—they needed his clout to bring home a deal with the company that supplied asteroid-mining machinery. I had a big promotion hanging in the balance right then. I was selfish. I told my superiors that I'd known Einar back when we were recruits; that I thought I could convince him."

Chairman Gorland shook his head and swallowed. His eyes glistened with tears.

Constance could guess what happened. "So you blackmailed him into staying. Told him you'd tell his story of finding the pit."

"If he'd fought me on it, I never would have gone through with it. But he stayed. When this new pit was found—"

"Wait, this wasn't the same pit?" Gabe asked.

"No. Our expedition was never in this area."

"So there could be more."

"Possibly. I'm not a scientist. But the issue was that if these bodies were recently dead, the whole colonization process would be called into question. A few weeks ago, Einar got an offer from the university on Titan. He was leaving. I had let Dr. Clarke know, to prepare him, to give him time to find a new apprentice. He was angry. Wanted me to talk to Einar again—insist that he stay. But I didn't begrudge Einar this opportunity, this chance at freedom. I was only concerned about the age of the bodies endangering the colonies.

"Last night, Einar sent me a message. He told me how the bodies had turned to sand. And that he'd dated them and they were several thousand years old. The UD was safe, the colonies were safe... My job...was safe." Chairman Gorland finished, hands splayed apologetically. He turned and stared out the window.

Constance kissed Gabe again and hugged him, her arms looped around his back. The platform practically sizzled and the hypertrain burped steam all around them.

"You've told the ambassador?" she asked.

He nodded, his eyes glistening. "I have. She and Marshall are tying up loose ends. Dr. Clarke won't lose his job, but he is likely going to be reduced to part-time lecturing. There's going to be a memorial, both for Gíslason and the aliens."

"Aliens. I guess, really, they're the natives."

Gabe gave a half-smile and nodded in thoughtful agreement. He looked at her, eyes flicking back and forth between hers. He leaned in and kissed her again. "A month is too long, dammit. I wish I could come with you now."

"I know. We both have to wrap things up. But I'll see you soon on Green Lakes Station. And then you'll tell me the whole story? Why you stopped drinking, why you're ready to give up on working for the UD, everything?"

Gabe nodded again. He swallowed. "It's because of you. I love you. I have since I met you. I was a fool for not realizing it the first time. I'll explain better when I see you again."

Constance took a breath but the lump in her throat prevented her from speaking. She covered his mouth with many rapid kisses, squeezed him hard to her, and jumped onto the train before the tears started pouring.

She found her seat, bit her lip and waved. This was harder than she'd expected.

Once on her ship again, she set the environmental controls to 19 degrees Celsius and stripped off her sweaty clothing. Flopping down into the pilot's chair, she set a course for London, Earth, and picked up the post she'd sent herself from the planet. Opening the evidence envelope, the glazed bird fell into her hand. *Oh! I'd forgotten.*

She rubbed the last of the char from its smooth surface and put it up on a shelf, gazing at it thoughtfully for a moment.

By the sweat of your brow, shall you eat bread till you return to the ground, she remembered the verse. *For out of it were you taken; for dust you are, and unto dust shall you return.*

Jessica Augustsson is a speculative fiction copy editor, grammar nerd, eclipse chaser, part-time writer, and a bit of a geek. As a spec-fic copy editor, most of her writing can be found nestled among the words of other authors, but she can't help typing out a few of her own stories now and then. As for spec fic in her own life, she was voted by her Idaho high school class to be the most likely to go live on the moon; when she was 20, she moved to Sweden so she guesses that's pretty close.

If You Love Something
by
Stephen R. Smith

Judy knelt on the pavement, struggling to process the confusion of the moment. The scene before her was all too familiar, as was the woven mass of tubing and wires snaking off into a sea of blinking lights and chirping boxes.

Stretched out on the asphalt before her was a man, his eyes unfocused and staring towards the stars. A dark grey blanket had been laid across his torso from one shoulder to the opposite hip, wide tape of an even darker grey securing it both to his uniform and the ground beneath him. Her eyes traveled across her husband's still form, from the trickle of blood striping his cheek to the point beneath the grey fabric where he became unfathomably thin. There were dark marks forming on the grey where the fluids they were pumping into him were defying all attempts to keep them from seeping out again.

Farther up the street, a white jet of flame sent molten alloy and smoke streaking into the night as a crew began cutting open what must have been the assailant's vehicle. A long length of track sprawled abandoned on the pavement where it had been jettisoned in mid-flight, followed by the deep rift the ATV's unshod wheels had torn in the ground before being turned almost sideways and forced to a stop. Smoke billowed from the fatal wound a rocketeer had scored in its armor.

A hand clasped at hers, snapping her attention back to the man on the ground, his eyes suddenly focused and riveting.

It was the voice of another officer nearby though that broke the silence.

"Ma'am, we've got tissues in the tank already, clone's pretty much eighty percent complete, but we need you to authorize the transfer." The uniformed figure stopped in front of her, but she wouldn't unlock her gaze from her husband's. "Ma'am—we've only got a few minutes to move here, it took a while to get you here, and he's in worse shape than last time." He paused, shifting his weight from one foot to the other. "Ma'am—the unit's all ready and if we don't get the transfer done now, we're going to lose him, and if he dies, we can't bring him back." The voice was quiet for a long moment before he spoke again, trying too hard to sound optimistic and failing. "Hell, he's gone through this half a dozen times already, he could probably do the procedure himself if he wasn't so banged up."

Judy looked up at the anxious face of the man fidgeting before her, then around at the scene. A medivac vehicle hovered a few meters away, just on the other side of a circle of light being cast by a clutter of hastily deployed equipment, all of it straining to keep her husband alive. Again. She knew exactly how this would go, the months it would take to grow the last of him, the physiotherapy he'd need to learn how to use a newly grown body he'd only been able to keep intact for a year this time. The memory lapses, the bits of him that wouldn't come through, and the haunting nightmares of all of these accumulated moments of finality.

"We've been here too many times before. You don't get him back this time." Her husband clenched his eyes shut as she spoke, tears joining the other fluids streaking his face, his hand squeezing hers.

"Ma'am—I've got orders from the Chief, we don't have time—"

She cut him off abruptly. "Last I checked, Sergeant, the Chief wasn't wearing his ring, so you can tell him we're done. You can call our Union rep if you want to argue, but in the meantime, turn him off. Turn all of this shit off, and leave us alone."

A weary hand gradually cooled in hers, and as she looked into his eyes, she saw a peace there she hadn't seen in a long, long time. She had no choice but to let him die tonight, this one last time.

The Game of Logic:
A Tangled Tale
by
G.H. Finn

Sunday, 14th[th] August 1936.

While the spires of Oxford may not have been dreaming, they did seem to slumber lazily as they basked in the sunshine. The few steam-powered airships drifting silently through the tranquil sky puffed smoke into the aether but left the world below undisturbed by their passing.

Mr A. Underland Esq.—Alistair to his friends—was rather hot about the face as he pedalled his velocipede toward the university, and firmly wished he hadn't habitually followed his mother's parting advice to always wear a vest—but it was too late to worry about that now. He avoided the busy street containing *The Walrus & Carpenter*, his favourite pub, and instead headed down a quiet side alley. He was already perilously close to missing his appointment and undergraduates did not keep senior lecturers waiting—at least, not if they hoped to one day become faculty members themselves. Steering his velocipede one-handed, Alastair glanced at his watch. He grimaced and muttered "I'm late!", feeling more than a little like the White Rabbit. Then he couldn't help but smile, as it struck him this was remarkably apt considering he was currently on his way to examine some effects of the late Charles Dodgson.

It tended to annoy Alastair that among the general public, Dodgson, better known as Lewis Carroll, was often regarded as merely a writer of whimsical nonsense for children. At least in the cloisters of Oxford University, Charles Dodgson—who had died in 1898, almost forty years previously—was still respected and admired for his consummate skills as both a mathematician and a logician. As a child in his nursery, Alastair had been very fond of Alice's adventures but as a young man he also had developed a love for Dodgson's works on logic. Alastair considered himself very lucky to have been asked to write a biographical article about a man he regarded as something of a hero, even if it was only for his college's student newspaper. It was perhaps even more fortunate that one of the more doddering of the elderly Masters at the college had by chance remarked that he possessed a jumble of Dodgson's old effects and papers, stored for posterity but for many years forgotten, mouldering away in his museum of a house. Alistair was aware that the aged academic had a reputation for being "a snapper up of ill-considered trifles" but had never suspected that these might include any of Dodgson's private writings. Apparently, these papers included some personal correspondence with another professor of mathematics, but Alastair's informant could remember no further details.

To his great delight, Alastair had, eventually and rather reluctantly, been given permission to come and sort through these relics of Dodgson's to decide for himself if any might be helpful in writing his article. While he knew that in all likelihood he would find nothing more exciting than a ledger of household accounts, secretly he hoped he might stumble across some unpublished mathematical theorem—or perhaps even the manuscript of another Alice chronicle! Alastair still occasionally read his favourite stories, *Alice's Adventures in the Underworld* and *Alice Through the Scrying Glass*. He would dearly have loved to have found an unpublished *Alice* novel.

Arriving at his destination several minutes later than the firmly stipulated two o'clock (and amidst a steady stream of perspiration), Alastair was unsure whether to be worried or relieved that his octogenarian benefactor had not bothered to wait for his arrival. On the front door, placed under a brass knocker that had been sculpted to resemble the head of a bandersnatch, was a sheet of paper bearing the words "Punctuality is the politeness of kings. Louis XVIII," beneath which was written "I see no reason why your lateness should be the cause of my own. You are welcome to use my house to conduct your research in my absence. Ignore the cat. It being the Sabbath, my servants have been granted a day of rest, thus you must be prepared to fend for yourself. The chest you are interested in has been placed in the drawing room. Do not venture into the back garden. The snark is not kept tethered and does not like strangers.

Let yourself in and try not to make too much mess." The note was signed with an entirely indecipherable flourish that seemed to have more in common with a hieroglyph than a signature.

Alistair opened the heavy front door and as he entered his sense were assaulted by a wild array of gleaming brass cogs, delicate silks, spellcast iron and intoxicating spices. With more than a hint of trepidation, Alistair walked further into the hallway of the elderly academic's house. At first he thought his apprehension was due simply to the mild embarrassment of being given the run of the property by a virtual stranger, coupled with an irrational fear that he would inadvertently destroy some unique and valuable antique while trying to find the drawing room. But further consideration of the matter made Alistair realise two things. Firstly, that it was not entirely irrational to fear that he might indeed knock over a priceless Greek urn, scuff an ancient Egyptian sarcophagus, or shatter an exquisitely fragile jade carving of some Taoist alchemical formula, for the house was filled with such things, more than half of which had at one time probably been looted from countries the Britannic Empire had conquered and ground beneath its feet. All in the name of spreading civilisation, of course. Secondly, Alistair decided that the danger of damaging relics was not the true cause of his unease.

There was something about the house…something he could not describe. A brooding shadow seemed to hang over the place, and the atmosphere inside the Victorian town-house hinted at mysteries of a subtle and enigmatically disturbing nature. But Alistair eventually managed to convince himself that all this was probably no more than his overactive imagination coupled with an unpleasantly nagging case of indigestion, no doubt due to eating Scotch eggs too swiftly before pedalling like a madman to arrive here.

He decided to find the drawing room and get to work immediately. The sooner he began, the sooner he would finish and could leave this place. He wanted to get back outside and into the sunlight without unnecessary delay. But even so, as he pondered which of the many doors—some ridiculously large, some unfeasibly small— might lead to the drawing room, Alistair could not help but cast his eyes along the walls, pause to glance at shelves and stop to peer into dusty display cabinets, filled with an assortment of trinkets including an umbrella, a watch, jewels and rings.

The old chap certainly has eclectic tastes, thought Alistair as he noticed an unbelievably small Hookah pipe, *Getting that thing to hubble-bubble must be a lot of toil and trouble.* He glanced at a *wunderkamercast* and found that the cabinet of curiosities was filled with a seemingly random collection of items—a small stuffed Wolpertinger snarled eternally, frozen in a pose that displayed its fangs, wings and antlers to notable effect. A row of shoes adorned a small shelf, next to models of ships that stood gathering dust. Alistair noticed they included a Russian ship, the *Demeter*, that had run aground at Whitby, the legendary *The Flying Dutchman* and the infamous *Marie Celeste*. A collection of old death warrants, bearing royal seals pressed into their scarlet wax, mouldered in a haphazard pile. A hand-bound dissertation on cabbage growing in the Carpathian Mountains had been propped next to a collection of small marble busts depicting every male monarch of England since the time of the Anglo-Saxon heptarchy, right up to the recent coronation of Charles III. The small, withered corpse of a Fijian mermaid, pickled and preserved in a jar of alcohol, bobbed sadly, turning its sightless eyes toward him.

So lost in idle wonderment was Alistair that he nearly jumped out of his skin when a gargantuan shadow fell over him. But the young man gratefully relaxed once he realised the awful shadow was merely cast by sunlight hitting the taxidermied (and sadly moth-eaten) head of an Albanian jabberwock, mounted on an oak-panelled wall. A lithographic print titled *The Cannibal Tree of Madagascar* showed an unfortunate native being engulfed by the tendrils of a hideous and monstrous plant. Beneath the illustration was a sealed glass tube, labelled "Do NOT allow to germinate." It contained three thorn-covered seed pods. On another wall, a huge and rusty headsman's axe hung grimly. The blade was a work of art, depicting an interwoven design of hearts and crowns.

Alistair thought it was a pity to let the weapon fall apart due to decay, then he gulped as he noticed the reddish-brown marks on the blade were not in fact rust but rather old stains, dried upon the metal. Turning away, he tried door after door and found them locked. But at last he came to the drawing room. Like the rest of the ramshackle abode, this room too was filled with oddities and marvels gathered from every corner of the globe. A Gothically styled writing desk, carved from the heartwood of a Peruvian tumtum tree, stood against one wall. For some reason it reminded Alistair of a raven, but he could not decide why.

He was tempted to explore the numerous and freakish curios that lined the room, but then his eyes fell upon the tea-chest set beside a large, antique table, veneered with tulgeywood and partially covered with a crocheted tablecloth that was far too small for so large a piece of furniture, but which was nevertheless of exquisite design, being made from the finest quality fractal lace. Enthusiastically, he turned his attention back to the subject of Dodgson's artefacts.

A short while later, all trepidation now forgotten and replaced with boyish excitement, Alastair was seated at the table. He went to some pains not to scratch the delicate surface as he steadily began unpacking the contents of the battered leather trunk he had recovered from the bottom of the large tea-chest. Alastair began by carefully removing one item at a time and attempting to devise some system for cataloguing his finds, but quickly gave up on this idea.

He realised he first had to work out what it was he was trying to examine. There were several books with titles he had never before come across, such as *Svartblót, Liber Mortum, Myrkbok, Kitab al-Azif, Unaussprechlichen Kulten* and *Megin ok Ergi* which he stacked neatly at one end of the table. The only volumes in English were a leather-bound copy of *The Dynamics of an Asteroid*, a handwritten translation of *The Egyptian Book Of The Undead,* and an old treatise upon the binomial theorem. There were also many sepia-tinted photographs, most probably taken by Dodgson himself, which Alastair placed carefully in a pile of their own.

There were batches of handwritten notes that Alastair was sure would warrant closer attention, but for now he assembled them into a heap in front of him. And then there were letters, private correspondence mostly, between Dodgson and someone who might have been a colleague of his—judging by a quick glance, it was indeed some professor of mathematics but whether one who had taught at Oxford or elsewhere, Alastair could not judge. The letters bore no address and for the most part were signed simply "M."

Amongst the letters was a sealed, blank, black envelope. Alistair looked around the room until he spotted an ornate letter opener on the corvid writing desk. He swiftly went to fetch it and was impressed to discover it had a vorpal blade, which he quickly used to slice open the envelope. It contained nothing but a small brass key with a skull-and-crossbones design embossed upon it.

Finally, there was a most singular item. At the bottom of the tea-chest, Alastair had discovered a life-sized clockwork dodo. He lifted it out of the tea-chest and set it upon the table. It was a beautiful yet bizarre automaton fashioned from a mechanical mixture of copper, brass and iron components. Alistair noticed a keyhole set between the bird's short and flightless wings. Remembering the key from the envelope, he tried it and was delighted to find it was a perfect fit. Eagerly, Alistair wound the robot dodo's mechanism, feeling the internal springs coil and tighten with every turn of the key. When he could twist the key no further, Alistair stood back to watch.

At first nothing happened. Alistair had expected the clockwork motor to animate the automaton, bringing the artificial bird to life. But it remained dead. As dead as a… *But wait!* thought Alistair. It was moving! It was alive.

The dodo flapped its short useless wings and strutted up and down on its squat legs. Glass eyes peered over the bird's oversized beak and something behind the amber lenses seemed to watch Alistair with an uncanny intelligence. Suddenly the bird crouched down and fluttered its mechanical feathers. Alistair could clearly hear the sounds of gears whirring and cogs revolving inside the dodo's body.

Goodness gracious me! thought Alistair. *It's going to lay an egg!*

But Alistair was mistaken. The mechanoid had certainly been designed to produce an egg, but when it eventually finished its robotic clucking, no egg lay upon the table. Instead, from within its artificial body, the dodo had deposited a heavy, ovoid glass bottle.

Then the metal bird's internal springs wound down, its gears stopped turning, its cogs became silent, and it was dead once more. Alistair stared at the dodo, having the odd sensation that while it was certainly dead, somehow it was dreaming. But he shook his head at the silliness of the idea and turned his attention to the unusual bottle.

Curious, thought Alastair, as he bent to examine the strange glass vessel and saw that while the bottle held no liquid, on careful inspection it had been most thoroughly stoppered, and sealed both with lead foil and wax. *More and more curious.* Alastair had had the bitter lessons of accepted grammar beaten into him while at prep school. Looking through the glass darkly, inside the bottle, Alastair could see a sealed paper envelope, inscribed with the simple instruction, "Read Me."

Not being at all sure what to make of the mystery bottle, Alastair peered at it on the table and stroked his chin. While, unsurprisingly, the items arranged before him did not seem overly likely to conceal a hitherto unknown novel about the amazing Alice, they still might contain many deep insights into Dodgson's life and works. They were also decidedly weird. But there really was only one way to be sure whether any of them may have any use at all. And so Alastair resolved to work his way through his finds, one by one. He was tempted to start with the photographs, as he felt they could perhaps be examined more swiftly than the various writings, but he rejected the notion on the grounds that they were also less likely to shed any light on either Dodgson's mathematical research or his literary endeavours. At first glance, the notes seemed rather unclear, if not decidedly cryptic. They would require quite some time to study properly. Nodding to himself, Alastair resolved to begin by reading the letters from Professor M.

Alastair suddenly shivered. He looked around his and saw nothing, but he could have sworn he was being watched. For a moment, he thought he heard an eerie purring but decided he must have imagined it. He couldn't see a cat anywhere, though he remembered the note on the door had mentioned one. But what did it matter? Pulling himself together, he returned to the task in hand.

While Alastair was not always the most organised of men, he was reasonably diligent and methodical. He began by sorting the professor's letters into date order. Then, with the earliest first, he began to read. It quickly became apparent that Charles Dodgson and the professor must have held each other in high regard, either academically or intellectually, and it seemed they may perhaps have been good friends, for in the course of the correspondence, M had suggested Dodgson might like to play a game of logic and deduction with him. The professor would pose a problem the solution to which, if Dodgson were to solve it, would lead Dodgson to the location of the next clue.

What a jolly old fellow, thought Alastair. *I wish more professors were like him.* In Alastair's own experience, most members of the university staff not only did not possess a sense of humour, they vehemently objected to their students doing anything that might be considered enjoyable under any circumstances.

Something in the shadows at the far end of the room caught Alastair's eye. All that was set there was an old winged armchair. Yet for a moment, just for a moment, he was sure he had seen a huge, disembodied grin floating in mid-air above the chair. Something about that smile had seemed…unnatural. It worried him briefly, but he dismissed it. Just a trick of the light. Nothing more.

Reading further, it was obvious Dodgson must have accepted this amusing challenge, for the next few letters each contained complex riddles, mathematical puzzles, codes, cyphers and perplexing problems of the most baffling nature. How Dodgson had unriddled these mysteries remained unknown, *Unless...* thought Alastair, *Perhaps the handwritten notes might shed some light on this?* But regardless of the methods he had employed, clearly Dodgson had indeed solved M's enigmas—and Alastair suspected he would have thoroughly enjoyed the process of doing so. He also wondered whether the professor had been pleased to have his conundrums picked apart so easily, or whether M would have felt annoyed that an intellect existed to rival his own? Judging by the letters, the professor certainly was something of a genius when it came to plotting out cunning mental tricks and traps. At times, his writing suggested a hint of intellectual arrogance. Yet it seemed Dodgson had always been able to best M in this game of wits.

Good for him, thought Alistair. *He always was a mental giant. The artful Dodgson never needed one of those new-fangled thinking machines to do his work for him. Difference engines, similarity engines, indifference engines… What is the world coming to? All Dodgson ever needed was a pencil and paper.*

At last, Alastair began to read the last of the letters from the mysterious Professor M.

In it, M congratulated Dodgson on how well he had played their game thus far, and then, rather than immediately present another puzzle, Professor M began to expound upon a somewhat disturbing subject. At least, it would have been unsettling were it not so obviously a joke. It had to have been a light-hearted addition to the game. Surely it must...

At that moment, Alastair was distracted by a pencilled addition to the inked writing of the letter. The professor's habitual M had been circled on this particular sheet, a line drawn from it, and in the margins in what looked very much like Dodgson's handwriting was a question mark and the comment "Why does M. never sign his name?" This meant very little to Alastair, although for some reason he had a nagging feeling that maybe he should know the identity of Professor M. Then again, Oxford was always awash with so many doctors and professors, it probably wasn't of any distinct significance.

M had introduced a new topic into this last letter. It would have been scandalous if it were not framed purely as an exercise in logic. The professor had begun by asking a question.

"Have you given any consideration to the problem of how one might commit the perfect crime? From the standpoint of the logician, it is a most interesting subject upon which to formulate an analysis."

While Alastair would admit that, from an entirely abstract perspective, the question was harmless enough and might be interesting to idly speculate upon, nevertheless there was something about the change in the tone of the writing that subtly disturbed him. The professor continued, expanding on his theme and offering a few hints as to his thoughts on how a "Perfect Crime" might be constructed—from a purely logical and hypothetical standpoint, of course. As ethically questionable as the subject may have been, Alastair did find M's suggestions compelling, but there was a far more startling revelation to come. Having once introduced the subject, within a few paragraphs the professor went on to state that he had, theoretically, devised a method for committing such a "perfect" crime. He then stopped short of explaining the details of his theorem, however. There was a trace of sardonic mockery in M's writing as he all but boasted of this artfully crafted master plan, constructed upon simple logical premises, yet which he also described more than a little challengingly as being "an unsolvable enigma."

Alastair frowned and again wondered where he had heard of a Professor M before. He shook his head and returned to read the closing paragraph of the letter:

"Would you like to know the details of my perfect crime? Would you really? The question in my mind remains, are you worthy to know this frumious secret? I propose a final round to our game of logic and deduction. If you solve my greatest riddle (and with this you will either sink or swim), you will be led to a message in a bottle—you will most certainly recognise this if you are clever enough to find it. In my final letter, I shall withhold no secrets, rather I will lay all information before you, demonstrating exactly how a man might commit a perfect crime. Yet despite this, I most decidedly assure you, the crime is of such a nature that even with evidence fully provided, it will never be solved. Here is your puzzle."

The rest of the sheet of paper had been torn off, but Alastair found he was not overly interested to know what the professor's last riddle may have been. Whatever it was, it was perfectly obvious that Dodgson had solved it; the proof was standing on the table before him. Alastair sat in uffish thought, staring at the strange sealed bottle with its enigmatic envelope nestling inside it.

And then another mystery occurred to Alastair. Having deduced the solution to M's final puzzle, why then had Charles Dodgson not opened the bottle?

Alastair let his eyes wander around the room as he pondered the question. A discarded top hat lay on a chair at the far side of the table, surely newly purchased as it still had a price-tag attached. A steam-driven tellurian orrery chuffed on a small shelf, it's planets revolving around a central sun, which gyred and gimbled with remarkable precision. On an opposite shelf, a wizened and sorry-looking Hand of Glory stood, the candles formed by its fingers burnt down to little more than stumps. On the far wall stood the embalmed remains of a borogove, which sadly now looked to be dreadfully decayed and far from its habitually preferred state of mimsiness. A tarnished brass lamp stood on a nearby shelf, with a worn label attached to it, reading simply, "Do not polish". But Alastair barely registered any of these items, lost in his own thoughts.

The young man frowned and stared again at the letter. All he could see was "Read Me."

And at that moment, he decided that he would.

Somewhat hesitantly, he broke the scarlet wax seal around the top of the bottle, removed the cork and vainly attempted to reach the envelope inside. A strange but not altogether unpleasant fragrance emanated from the bottle, filling his nostrils and almost making him sneeze. It had a heavy note of perfume. Absentmindedly, he wondered if the letter inside the bottle had been written by a lady, for surely a gentleman would not have scented his writing materials in such a fashion? Unless perhaps he was a foreigner? Alastair was sure there were plenty of European professors with a surname beginning with M... Maybe a Professor Medici or a Professor Machiavelli or some such? A hint of the orient had seemed to suggest itself amid the pungent miasma that assailed his nose. A Professor Ming or perhaps a Professor Manchu? It seemed unlikely... After a few moments spent in a fruitless attempt to reach the envelope by alternately inserting a finger into the neck of the bottle and then, abandoning this approach, turning the bottle upside down and shaking it, he eventually decided that the simplest course of action would be to break the bottle. He glanced at a large teapot left standing at one end of the table, failed to notice the slight sound of gentle snoring coming from within, but decided he would be likely to smash the china pot if he used it as a bludgeon. Instead he reached for a heavy candlestick that had been conveniently left upon the far side of the table. Remembering that he had been instructed to avoid making a mess, he first carefully wrapped the bottle in a fold of the tablecloth then struck it sharply with the base of the candlestick. Nothing happened, but a second harder blow produced a satisfying splintered cracking sound. Cautiously Alastair placed the open top of the tea-chest under the table, unwrapped the table-cloth from around the bottle and let the combination of broken glass and sealed envelope fall into the otherwise empty chest. Then he reached carefully inside and retrieved the envelope, which he found was held shut by a blob of black sealing wax bearing the imprint of a skull, with the word *memento* and a larger ornate *M* embossed beneath.

Alastair's curiosity could not be suppressed any longer. He swiftly broke open the seal, opened the envelope and removed a sheet of paper from within. Once again, his nose was assaulted by a pungent aroma. He felt sure he could detect the scents of sandalwood, attar of roses, cinnamon, frankincense, patchouli, musk—and beneath these, some acrid cloying after-scent that he could not put a name to.

He began to read.

The paper bore a single word as its heading: Martyrio.

Alastair had no difficulty in recognising this as a Latin term for "testimony", in particular that of a martyr about to be put to death. He considered idly that the term was perhaps grammatically incorrect when used in this way, but he gave it no further thought and began reading.

> To Whomsoever is reading these words,
>
> Logic, that sweet sibling of mathematics, has long been an interest of mine. My fascination for the subject is due not only to its stimulation of the cerebral processes but also to logic's purity of form and its oh-so-useful practical application to the problems of

the manifest world. As with mathematics, logic is pure in that it is entirely free from petty human illusions such as fashion, compassion, sentiment or morality. Rather it rests upon the application of laws greater than those found in either church or courtroom, laws that are rooted in intellect and science rather than in foolish faith or the judgement of twelve good mental weaklings on a jury.

Moreover, logic can—as I shall demonstrate—be bent to serve the will and purpose of its master, regardless of whether such a purpose be deemed *moral* or *immoral* by the lesser intelligences of the general populace. To this end, let me present to you a conundrum that has vexed me for some years: How might one commit a perfect crime?

I suggest you make yourself comfortable and read on, as through the medium of this letter, I intend to show you.

Before applying logic to solve this problem, let us first define and agree some terms and parameters.

i)   For a crime to be perfect, it must be a crime recognised in law, or by some other self-inflating and objectively irrelevant authority such as religion. Preferably, it will be deemed a crime both by church and state. For our purposes here, a crime is not a crime unless it be near universally accepted as such.

ii) The crime must have a manifest reality and the crime must actually occur. I therefore preclude from this discussion petty "crimes" which have no tangible basis in the physical world (such as verbal blasphemy, treason or slander) and also any "crime" which may be deemed to take place only in the heart and mind of the individual or in any other way to lack a concrete nature.

iii) For a crime to be perfect, it must be unsolved and must remain effectively unsolvable.

It has been argued that "a perfect crime" would be one that is undetected and undetectable. This I refute. Such a crime would certainly be agreeable, and fit with the concept of a perfect crime, were it not that it would be scientifically unverifiable. If a man claps his hands in an effort to frighten away lions, this we may consider to be logical. If no lions appear, logically the method may be a sound one. But should the man claim that his clapping drives away lions from his home in London, we should scoff at him and his method, rightly pointing out that an absence of lions does not prove that his clapping has driven them away. So too, a man claiming to have developed a methodology for committing a perfect crime cannot simply state that he has done so and offer the lack of the detection of his crimes as proof of their perfection, otherwise he would run the risk of being considered either a simpleton or a lying fool.

I therefore add further conditions to my definition of a perfect crime:

iv) At least one person besides the Master Criminal must be aware that the crime has been committed.

This stipulation will help to ensure the scientific validity of the method. After all, one should hardly simply take the word of a self-proclaimed Mastermind of Crime as I, or rather they, may, of course, be lying. In a puzzle of logic, one must always be on one's guard against statements which may later prove to be false.

v) It would further be desirable that in addition to at least one person knowing of the commission of the crime (whether by directly witnessing it or by deduction), ideally there should be undeniable physical evidence of the crime—yet naturally, this evidence must be such that it cannot be used to prove the identity of the perpetrator of the perfect crime, or as I might immodestly refer to him, the Perfect Criminal.

Whilst in theory, many crimes might be suitable for the purpose of our little experiment, let us not trifle with inconsequentialities. Let us set the stakes of this game high. Let us assume that the perfect crime must be at the apex of all criminality. Let us choose for our crime nothing less than that most manxome of crimes: murder.

How then may our Perfect Criminal commit a murder and yet remain unfettered by any undue fear of detection?

Let us first make a few assumptions about our Mastermind.

Let us assume that he is no ham-fisted, galumphing bungler apt to leave behind a mass of readily understood clues to his crimes. Let us assume he is a man of high intelligence and diligence, possessed of no small measure of guile. Let us assume he is educated to the highest degree, well placed in society and canny enough to work, primarily, through intermediaries and that he is thus able to still further reduce the already limited risk of detection.

Should then our Master criminal be afraid of being caught in the perpetration of a crime? Should he fear that he might leave some unfortuitous item behind at the scene of his activities, such as a misplaced monogrammed glove, a feather fallen from his pet Jubjub bird, or a carelessly dropped calling card bearing his address? No, for he has a veritable army of lesser criminals to carry out his orders while he, like any prudent general, remains far from the field of conflict and concerns himself primarily with strategy.

Should he fear the risk of some whiffling betrayal by one of his deputies? Not if he is canny enough to ensure very few men know his true identity, and also to arrange that those slender few who could identify either his name or his face are themselves in far greater fear of him than ever they would fear a hangman's noose.

If then our Master Criminal may justly feel himself safe from the risk of discovery by the victims of his crimes, and if likewise he may understandably feel unendangered by the humdrum, tweedling investigations of the denizens of Scotland Yard, who then *should* our Master Criminal guard himself against?

In certain Chinese schools of thought, and likewise among the ancient Manichaean philosophers, there exists a concept of a natural law of opposites. For there to be night, so then must there be day. For there to be darkness, so too must there be light. If there is such a person as a Master Criminal, so, inevitably, must there one day come a Master Detective.

While our Master Criminal may justifiably fear no ordinary policeman, being himself of an extraordinary nature far beyond the reach of normal men, it would only be prudent for our Master Criminal to guard against the possibility of his discovery by an equally extraordinary detective, one whose wit and knowledge, training and temperament, skills and powers of reasoning are close to being a match for my own. Such a Master Detective might yet see through any obfuscating fog I employed to baffle lesser minds. If he were to apply his superior abilities unceasingly, forgo food and sleep until he'd solved a problem, then he might eliminate six impossible things before breakfast and thus be left with the truth—no matter how improbable it might seem that anyone could truly be a threat to one such as myself.

That such a Master Detective shall one day arise, I regard almost as an inevitability. Indeed, I feel it is likely I have already become aware of his presence, exploring and investigating the outer strands of my web. While I am not entirely certain, it is my belief that the existence of a Mastermind of Crime—though not as yet my actual identity—may already have been deduced by some hidden nemesis. Thus I have taken steps to attempt to identify who among the brightest minds of our time might be disguising himself and hiding amongst my shadows? Who is it that may one day threaten me? Yes, I write "me", for the time for all pretences has now passed.

I have, thus far, considered eighty-seven potential threats to my continued operation as a Criminal Mastermind—people who I reasoned might, under certain circumstances, prove themselves capable of becoming a danger to my anonymity, or indeed to my very existence. I reasoned early on that I could not easily have so many prominent individuals killed, for most are doctors, lawyers, clergymen, scientists, authors, petty nobles and the like. I could not simply have them *all* killed, at least not without causing far too great a public outcry and arousing suspicion and interest where as yet there is none. I therefore began to test each of my suspects to determine which of these eighty-seven might truly become a poisoned thorn in my side. I watched them. I studied them. I devised tests. I set puzzles. Those who failed to solve my riddles, I let go. Like a benevolent fisherman throwing back the small fry, I removed the barbs of my hook from the throats of those of lesser intellect, reasoning that if they failed to solve the problems I had presented them with, they certainly could not succeed in outwitting me in games that were played for higher stakes. I whittled down my eighty-seven to forty-three. I reduced forty-three to seventeen. From seventeen I subtracted a further eleven. At last I had half-a-dozen firm suspects, six Napoleons of Detection who might potentially one day face me in the field. To my great surprise, one was a woman. She, I decided, would be treated as a special case. The other five men I wished to test still further. Each of these five had passed all my earlier trials, so I determined to send each one a puzzle so intricately complex that I could barely solve it myself. Should anyone decrypt this problem, I would know that individual could undoubtedly pose a threat to me. I arranged that the solving of the problem would lead ultimately to the discovery of the bottle containing this letter.

When I began to write, I addressed you, my dear reader, with the phrase "To Whomsoever is reading these words." In truth, as I am writing this I do not know which one of you has solved my most artful puzzle and claimed this letter as his prize. If no one has solved my greatest riddle, then I write these words to no one and I am at no risk at all. If you have opened the bottle and for some reason you have not immediately read these words, then for reasons which will shortly become clear, I know I still am safe. Likewise, if by remote chance, the hiding place of the bottle had been discovered accidentally and its letter has somehow fallen into unintended hands, again I need feel no concern and I am in no danger, as you will realise when you read further. But whoever you are, if you are now reading this, it is only fitting that I explain why I have no fear that you will use my words against me in any court of law.

You may have wondered why I have set down this information in so rambling a manner? Why haven't I yet got to the point? Why do I seem to procrastinate and delay, taking my time in telling you of my plans, drawing out the moment when I will reveal my secrets? Indeed, you may wonder why I have set down any information at all?

Before I answer that, let me offer some further data. I am well known as a mathematician. My training in the sciences is however both wide and deep. I have no small knowledge of chemistry. There exist certain substances which are described as being *pyrophoric*, a term stemming from the Greek πυροφόρος, *pyrophoros*, meaning "fire-bearing." A chemical that is pyrophoric will ignite spontaneously when in air at normal room temperature. I have myself discovered that this reaction can be abated by storing the pyrophoric substance in an inert gas. No doubt others will also soon discover this and publish their findings. No matter. For now, however, I have kept my research and discovery a secret, for I have my own uses for this knowledge. The bottle that contained this letter was filled with such a gas. I trust that you did not imagine the gas was poisonous? I hope I did not give you any undue cause for concern on that account. I can assure you the gas was entirely harmless. Besides which, any poisonous gas would either be so strong as to have killed you instantly when you first opened the bottle or else would be so weak as to be easily dispersed in the air, thus becoming harmless. Now where was I?

It was no especial difficulty for me to impregnate the paper upon which I have written these words with certain pyrophoric chemicals. It was a far greater task to mix them with a selection of other reagents in order to delay such a reaction so that the paper would not burn the moment it was exposed to air. Such chemicals can create quite an unpleasant smell so I took the precaution of disguising them with a liberal application of varied perfumes. By the time you have finished reading these words, the paper upon which they are written will almost certainly have begun to imperceptibly smoulder and then shortly afterwards will burst into flames, so I advise you to continue reading while you still have the opportunity. In case you are wondering, water will not stop the reaction, it may even hasten it. You have no way of preventing this paper from self-immolating within the next few minutes.

You may now see why I feel confident that even though I present you with an explanation as to how I will perpetrate a Perfect Crime, I need have no fear of this evidence being used against me, for within moments it will no longer exist. By explaining all this in writing I am presenting you with a full confession, but one which will shortly disappear before your eyes in an almost proverbial puff of smoke. My crime will have a witness—you yourself shall be that witness—but you will be quite unable to act upon your knowledge. I am *doubly* sure of this.

I posed the question as to why I have written this letter in so protracted and circuitous a fashion. I will now answer that. I did so in order to increase the time it would take you to read my words. I wished to ensure ample time for the chemicals with which I have soaked and coated the paper you are now holding to do their work. I am sure that even if you read extremely quickly, by now their full absorption is utterly inevitable. I ensured that I coated the paper with a sufficient strength even to penetrate through cloth, in the highly unlikely event you are reading this whilst wearing gloves.

As time draws irrevocably on I feel I should however at last make a true confession. I have not been entirely honest with you. Did you expect me to be? Did you think I would play this game by anyone's rules but my own? In tests of logic, one must always consider the possibility that any given statement may be false. Even so, I have not lied to you.

Or have I?

I will admit that I have withheld some information up until this point.

You may have noticed a rather unusual odour emanating from the paper upon which my words are written, an unpleasant, slithy smell not fully hidden by the aromas of exotic scents that I applied to this letter. I told you that this was due to certain chemicals with which I had coated the paper. That was the truth.

I implied that these chemicals were simply to delay the speed at which this letter will begin to combust. That was only partially true. *Some* of the chemicals I used were employed for this purpose. Others, well… There is no polite way of putting this and I'm afraid you may think me rather ill-mannered. Some of the other chemicals were employed solely for the purpose of poisoning you. This letter was thoroughly soaked in a mixture of some of the finest toxins that can be bought (or indeed, stolen), including the atropine-like alkalines found in the pancreatic juices of the lesser-spotted, and thrice-cursed, Ethiopian Tove. One I even isolated myself, from the bile ducts of the little known rodent *Rattus Gigantus Sumatranus*. And another I distilled from the venomous outgrabeations of a pure-bred Mome Rath But I digress, and under the circumstances, that is rather rude and I hope you will forgive me for my lapse in manners.

I have conducted rigorous tests of the poisons that have by now been thoroughly absorbed through your skin and are even at this moment coursing through your veins. I would estimate that at present you have probably already lost most motor-neural functions, that you cannot stand and are effectively suffering a numbing paralysis in all your limbs. No, don't try to get up, you will only fall, and besides which, it is quite pointless. Very soon this paralysis will spread to your heart and your lungs. Your pulse will slow and your breathing will become laboured. The toxins will not as yet have clouded your mind, which, being your greatest attribute, I have generously allowed you to retain as a functioning faculty for as long as possible, as I am sure such an inquiring soul as yourself will be interested to observe all the details of this experience.

I feel that there is little more to write and as you have such a short time left I would not wish to waste it further.

I bid you a fond farewell and hope that, in whatever moments remain to you, you will be assured that I remain your humble and obedient servant,

Prof. Moriarty

It was hard for Alastair to make out the familiar name through the wisps of smoke spiralling up from the paper, which gently dropped from his now nerveless hands and fell onto the pile of letters arranged upon the table, swiftly setting them ablaze. His final thought was that, like the White Rabbit, he would indeed be late—the late Alistair Underland.

Angel by Name
by
Joh\nnes Toivo Svensson

I've never trusted angels. In my line of business, a suspicious nature comes with the territory, but I am especially wary when it comes to angels. Ancient rat instincts warn me against them. Still, when you live on 50 bucks a day plus expenses, a job is a job, which is why I found myself in a questionable neighbourhood—the kind where the shadows might stick to you if you walk down the wrong alley—with an uneasy sensation in the pit of my stomach and a loaded .38 in my pocket. An insistent wind pulled at me, bringing with it the scent of sewage and desperation. I pulled my coat more tightly around me and looked around. It was, nominally, a residential area, cracked brownstones lining the street on both sides broken up by a few restaurants and a nightclub. However, it had fallen on hard times an eternity ago and now everything was covered in a sheen of greed, grease and decay.

The inhabitants seemed to mainly be Skulkers and Ghosts looking through trash for lost treasures, but occasionally a citizen could be spotted, in a hurry to get somewhere, anywhere other than where they were, ignoring the vendors and hustlers stuck to the street-corners. The cobbles themselves had been cannibalised by other more aggressive streets, leaving holes and bare patches where the weeds could find purchase. The nightclub two blocks down loomed over the surrounding houses, promising booze and sex if you'd just come inside and let it devour you. Not the kind of neighbourhood you'd think angels would be associated with, and farther into the city than I usually wanted to go.

My tail touched something sticky and I pulled it off the ground, turning my attention back to the job. The apartment building in front of me was three storeys high, made up of reddish brown bricks, steel and mould. The door to the stairwell was rusted and one of the glass panes was smashed. The call-button hung from a wire and the wall-mounted speaker whiled away the time by crackling quietly to itself. My whiskers twitched as I caught a whiff of musk and dust from inside. After making sure no one was paying attention to me, I reached a paw in through the window to undo the lock, and slipped inside.

The stairwell was full of debris and spider webs. The ground floor apartments were boarded up from the outside with notices proclaiming them to be condemned, though the light and music spilling out through the cracks told me that nobody really cared. The stairs wound their way around a central pillar housing a shiny metal elevator door, above which a display flashed symbols I didn't understand in repeated sequence like a chant. I turned the sour smell of the elevator over in my mouth a few times and decided I'd rather take my chances with the dust and the spiders.

The second floor seemed to be better kept-there was certainly less debris and fewer critters. Of the two doors on the landing, one was marked "Emotional Trauma" in angry letters. The other was crisscrossed in black and yellow police tape, making it my immediate focus. I picked up a fallen nameplate from the floor in front of it, confirming that it bore the right name before I approached the door. The police tape drew tight as I closed in, making a plastic whispering sound, denying me access. I growled at it, showing all my teeth and my investigator's license. The tape hesitated for a moment, before relaxing and allowing me to duck through.

If the stairwell was a mess, the inside of the apartment was a disaster area, a chaotic jumble of broken furniture and interior decorations. Someone had tossed the place and tossed it good. It had more piles of random stuff than a hamster's winter cottage and was a lot less neatly organised. I licked my paws and slicked the fur on my ears down, trying to make sense of my impressions. Judging by the smell, an angel had been here in the last few days, the lingering scent of pigeon feathers and electricity skittering across my tongue. Underneath, there was a low-key note of peanuts and copper that I couldn't identify. There were no sounds in the apartment, if you didn't count sounds from outside—there were no clocks ticking, no taps dripping, nothing at all making a noise.

Looking at the things strewn about the floor, I could surmise that they were probably all objects that had at one time been part of the room's interior in a more orderly manner. This room had been torn apart by someone, probably someone looking for the same thing that I had been hired to retrieve. Judging by the mess, either they hadn't found it or they were enjoying breaking things too much to stop when they had. Hopefully, it was the former. It would be bad for my pay check if I had arrived too late. It also meant that if it was still here, I was not the only one looking for it. Nothing like a little extra pressure.

I poked my nose in through the door on the left and looked around the kitchen. The floor consisted of equal parts cutlery, broken dishes and dry goods. The refrigerator door stood open, wilted produce hanging off the edge of the shelves, the stench of kelp and rotten meat wafting towards me. I'd check in there later. If the thing had been hidden in a cookie jar it would already have been found, and the rest of the place wouldn't be in such a state. It didn't make sense to hide things in kitchens anyway-it's where you look for things. You look for food, you look for cutlery, you look for that old bag of candy that you hid away. A looking-for-things place is a bad hiding-things place.

The door to the living room was lying on the floor in front of the doorway opposite the kitchen and I stepped over it into the room, trying to disturb things as little as possible. The presence of electric pigeon was stronger here, reminiscent of my employer but again with differences that I could not place. There might have been a note of copper to him, but the rest was off. A relative perhaps? A twin?

I made my way into the middle of the room, stopping there to turn in a slow circle, examining everything carefully. The big-screen television was smashed into pieces scattered across the floor, each of the shards of screen showing silent images of different shows. The writing desk had been toppled, spilling papers, ink and pens all over the nearby carpet. Paintings had been ripped off the walls, exposing naked brick. Whoever had been here before me had been thorough, checking for hidden safes in all the same places I would have: behind bookshelves, mirrors and paintings.

They had pulled out drawers and emptied the contents, they had smashed open unlikely looking porcelain pigs and wolves, they had rolled away all carpets from the floor, carelessly throwing them to the sides of the room. All of which told me that if they'd found it, it hadn't been in one of the obvious hiding places.

I tasted the air again. Frustration. Anger. Failure. It was still here somewhere. Well, though time was against me, the only way I was going to do better was to be even more thorough. I started with the carpets, rolling them out, examining the patterns, sniffing and tasting the fringes. Then I moved on to books and ornaments, looking for odd shapes or strange titles. Covers in mauve or puce. I picked up paintings and looked at them, scratched at them, sniffed at them. I did this until I caught an out-of-place scent coming from one of the paintings. The painting was of a closed trapdoor or hatch in a wooden wall, barely seen through deep shadows. There seemed to be some sort of curtain or drapery at the edge of the picture. I sniffed closer, catching the aroma of pine and cloth, not cotton but coarser material. Not curtains, a woven carpet. I carried the painting to the window, but it was still too dark to see the motif properly. I looked through the blinds to make sure no one was watching from the street and then I opened them. Light fell in through the window illuminating the painting, and the whole image brightened as if the sunlight were painted onto the canvas. Yet there was still a shadow covering most of the picture. I moved and the shadow moved, revealing a portion of the image more clearly. The trapdoor was made of wood, covered in green paint that had started to dry and flake. The carpet was a faded blue with stains, it seemed to be mostly rolled up. There were a few glass shards next to it.

I shifted the painting toward the light again to get a better look, but there was something peculiar about how the shadow slid across the surface. I was right up next to the window by now, the large neon sign of a sun on the building across the road should have been illuminating it clearly, but there remained a dark edge right across the middle of the painting. Not a shadow on the painting, but in it. I frowned and held my hand in front of the painting, casting the shadow of my hand over the picture. I could see it across the shadow that was already there, almost the same, but perceptibly different. The shadow of my hand was a thing impressed on the picture from without, the other shadow was part of the image. A painted shadow, but it had moved, I was sure of it.

I stepped away from the light and the painted shadow moved, leaving the image. I stepped back and the paint darkened again. I turned and the dark shape changed into a pronouncedly rat-shaped form wearing the outline of a trench-coat.

I walked a few steps, twitched my nose and sniffed the painting again. None of the odours that should be there were present, but I could smell leather now, leather and rubber. A pair of shoes. I crouched down to the floor, the scent of my own shoes filling my nostrils, identical to what I had detected in the painting. I put the painting on the floor and moved to the side. The shadows were gone now, both real and painted, and the whole of the trapdoor was revealed to me, the painted wood inside the frame very much the same as the floorboards around it. I tilted my head, then pushed the painting into place, to the position where it "fit", where what was in the painting continued outside the frame. I moved my hand over it, ensuring that both shadows, real and painted, matched on the canvas. I nudged it a tiny bit to the right and waved my hand again, noting the smooth transition from frame to painting. Then I reached down and grabbed the metal ring of the trapdoor. It opened with a creaking sound, revealing a ladder that led down into the dark.

I sniffed the air rising from the hole, sensing mostly dry earth, sharp metal tones and paper with a chemical aftertaste, before climbing down into the cellar below. The light falling in through the trapdoor revealed an underground room. It was obviously made for storage, shelves covering the walls, valuables filling the shelves. Against the far wall, half in and out of the light, was a safe, an exclusive letter-and-emotion-based model. I scurried over to it then paused, sniffing at it. I could sense comfort and peanut butter coming from the area just in front of it. Residue from the last time it was opened perhaps. I settled myself cross-legged on the floor, my tail curled up around my leg and onto my lap and I tried to think of where I felt the most comfortable. I filled my mind with the sensations of my favourite hangout: a small alcove in my local pub, where I could be alone with my drink and not think too hard about things. When I felt a smile tug at the corners of my lips I started to try different words. H O M E didn't work. R E L A X didn't either. I shrugged and on impulse I tried S E C R E T, the most common letter-code to a safe I knew, and there was the happy click of a latch releasing. The door swung open revealing a few shelves containing black bags and a small wooden box hung with a padlock. There were carved symbols on the box, feathers and a star.

I reached in and brought it out of the safe. It smelled special. Like honey and gold. I was certain this was what I was looking for.

"Turn around slowly and don't let go of the box." The voice was accompanied by the smell of ozone and feathers, with that tinge of copper I recognised all too well. A bright light filled the room. I growled, but followed instructions.

"Atheriel," I said, addressing the angel holding the shotgun. "I am working for you. There's no need for guns. Just pay me my fee and I'll hand you the box and we can both walk away alive."

The angel shook its head, the light it emitted almost obliterating all the features of its face. "I am sorry. It's nothing personal. You are an excellent sleuth, you succeeded where I failed, but I am afraid I can't risk you telling anyone about this."

Where he failed? So he was the one that had searched the place? Then why had the scent been off?

"Tell them about what?" I asked, stalling for time. The angel towered over me in size, impressive even with his wings folded, and I doubted I could take him in a fight. My gun was a heavy weight in my pocket, but one I had no hope of reaching in time. "I don't even know what this is. You don't want to kill me. I've told people I am working for you. They'll connect the dots if I turn up dead."

"No, I don't think so. You didn't tell anyone. You know how to be discreet—that's why I chose you. Still, you might let something slip by accident, and you know enough that other people can work it out if I let you go. Hand me the box."

I shook my head, whiskers trembling. "If you are going to shoot me, shoot me. Only you won't while I'm holding the box, will you? Whatever is in here, I bet it's fragile enough that it won't survive the fall to the floor."

"Give me the box and I won't shoot you." The angel licked its lips with a long black tongue, razor-sharp teeth showing in its wide smile.

"Swear to it."

The angel's eyes narrowed. "I swear," it said.

I could smell the betrayal from where I stood. I threw the box at him, and ran for the ladder hoping to get around him before he could react. The light from the angel's form flashed brightly and a fearsome angry face was outlined in black, blinding me. I stumbled about, trying to find my way, but found myself bumping into shelves and stumbling over sacks on the floor. I could hear the ladder creaking and smell the angel retreating up it. I followed those sensations, but the trapdoor closed before I could reach it. There was the sound of canvas ripping and the trapdoor was gone, replaced by a simple earth ceiling. I hissed in despair and slid down the ladder and to the floor below, where I lay until my vision fully returned.

It was dark in the room now, the only light coming from the occasional gem sparkling in silence. I tried and failed to find some sort of light to turn on, eventually giving up, trusting to my rodent eyes to adjust to the darkness. I found a door, but it was locked, and too solid for me to break through. I cursed myself for getting involved with angels. I had known the job was at least partially shady, but I hadn't counted on being personally considered a loose end. I dusted myself off and tried to calm down. Then I kicked at a few shelves and tried again. I pulled up a wooden crate filled with papers and sat down on it, resting my head in my hands.

When you thought about it, it didn't really make sense. Oh, the angel turning on me made sense. Atheriel had a respectable, holier-than-thou facade built up and anything that might tarnish that was a danger to it. The scent didn't make sense, though. Like my employer's, yet also *not* like it. The safe didn't make sense either. If you went to all the trouble to have a two-part association lock in the way of even finding your storage room, why would you use the most common letter association code for the safe? Normally, I would have chalked it up to the safe being created that way, but whoever had hidden this room had been devious. They wouldn't settle for a pre-set safe. Sammy on Ratchet Street could get you a good imprintable one for a reasonable exchange and she did good work. Anyone with the collection of rare and strange objects-not to mention cash-I could see in this room had lots to bargain with. If you thought there was a risk that your safe would be found, why not get a good one? If, on the other hand, you didn't think anyone would find the safe, why have one at all?

With my employer trying to kill me, the case was officially over, but I never could stop my brain from working-even when I wanted to-and since I seemed to be stuck in here anyway, I wanted to keep my mind on the here and now. There were two ways this could end and I preferred not to think about either of them. I examined the safe again, it was a pitch-black thing, had been even when there had been light in the room, with metal legs fused into the floor to prevent people from making off with it. I closed the door and examined the dial on the front. The letters were emotionally loaded and their meaning could be sensed even with the lights off. I twirled the tumbler. Then I twirled them the other way and then back again and then the other way. Each time there was a subtle twinge in my hand when I passed the correct letter for the combination I had used. I cleared my throat, nervously. The safe *wanted* me to enter that combination. It encouraged me, with subtle clues that you normally would not consciously notice. I opened the safe and faced the same half-empty shelves.

I closed the door to the safe again, spinning the tumblers shut. I rested my paw on the dial and I could feel what it wanted me to do. Go right, it said to me through tingling sensations in my fingers and a spark from the S told me that *this*, this is the letter to choose. I took a deep breath and tried to ignore what it wanted me to do and reached deeper, tapping into what it didn't want me to do. Left was allowed, Right was encouraged, but right past the S, that elicited a feeling of dread, of having made a mistake. Slowly I rotated the dial further until I reached a letter that my fingers wanted to skip, that absolutely could not be the right one. I stopped there on the I and felt something shift. Right was now encouraged, left would be a mistake. I turned it left.

By going against my instinct I spelled out I P R O M I S E N O T T O S T E A L, feeling the promise fold into effect as soon as the last letter was in place and the door swung open again. There were no shelves in the safe this time, only a jar with the word COOKIES stencilled on the side and a large lid made of cork. I rubbed my paws together to get rid of the tingling feeling of the vow the safe had made me take and lifted the jar. Looking wasn't stealing after all. As long as I put it back I would be ok. I steeled myself and pried open the lid. There was a pleasant bluish light coming from the open jar and I tilted it to look inside, the light warming my face.

As I was alone, there was no one around to hear me exercise my vocabulary of curses.

By the time the door opened, I was thirsty and hungry. I had lost track of how much time had gone by, but it had at least been several days. At first I thought it was Atheriel who had come back, but the outline in the door was different. Even so, the light emanating from it was of the same quality, and the scent of electricity and pigeon was there as well, with that familiar undertone of peanut butter. It *was* an angel, but not the same angel. The other part of the scent I'd caught in the apartment.

This door was in the wall to one side of the room instead of the hatch in the roof—another indication that it wasn't Atheriel. If my former boss had known a different way in, he would never have had to hire me. The new angel looked at me, and then laughed a melodic laugh.

"So, Mr Rat. I take it that you are the one my mate sent to steal from me?"

I found myself taking off my hat and holding it against my chest.

"That's true. But the story I was told was that you had stolen the object in the first place. Then he betrayed me and left me in here to starve." I looked down at my shoes. "I had to drink your wine, by the way." I gestured to the empty bottles lying on the floor. "Sorry about that."

The angel laughed again. "That is quite all right. They were for guests anyway. And did Atheriel get what they were after?"

I looked down again. "I'm afraid I had to give him the box."

It smiled a broad, thin smile. "I see. What is your name?"

I shuffled my feet, feeling like a school boy in the principal's office, small and afraid of being made smaller.

"My given name is Radadan."

"Well then, Radadan the rat. I absolve you of all guilt associated with this. You may go freely about your business, but never show your face to me again."

I bowed and said my thanks, sidling around the edges of the room, stepping cautiously around the angel's form until I had my back to the door. Then I bowed again and slipped up a few steps to the streets in an unfamiliar part of the city beneath a roiling green sky. It was raining outside and I put my hat back on, closing my coat tightly around me. If that was the last time I had dealings with angels I would count my blessings and find that I had at least one.

I looked both ways along the street and picked a direction to walk. I put my paw in my pocket and brought the thing I had been sent to collect out in front of me. The stone was about as large as my fist and slightly translucent, milky shapes swirling around its dark blue depths. Deep inside was the form of a small mostly hairless being glowing softly, curled up into a ball. Somehow the figure's appearance was not coloured by the stone around it, yet still it was very clearly not on the surface. It floated around inside the egg, waiting to be hatched.

It hadn't been stealing to keep it, you can't steal a person, and anyway the angel had absolved me of all guilt. I would not give it to Atheriel of course, because he had betrayed me and also for the same reason that I did not leave it in the safe. I didn't know what they wanted it for, but I doubted it was anything good. Ancient rat instincts tell me to be wary of things larger than me that have sharp pointy teeth. Especially anything that eats its young.

Johannes has been making up stories for almost as long as he has been reading them. His mind is drawn to the odd and strange, and he has a love for things that shake his perceptions of the world. Currently, he is preparing for the inevitable collapse of society by studying software development, which he assumes will be somehow useful in the apocalyptic wasteland.

FROM THE AUTHORS

All of these authors and I would like to thank you for coming along with us while we detected and discovered, searched and sleuthed. We hope you enjoyed the book, and if it was worth your hours of reading, then please spend a moment more and let it be known. All reviews are greatly appreciated, as they not only bring in more readers, but help in allowing all of us to justify the immense amount of time we spend on these endeavors.

--Jessica Augustsson, www.JayHenge.com

44977071R00161

Made in the USA
Middletown, DE
22 June 2017